T·H·E
BERNINI
QUEST

ANN PORT

Ann Port

ISBN: 1466251247
ISBN-13: 9781466251243

Dedication

*This book is dedicated to my husband, Mike; to my
incredible friends who support me, not only in my literary
efforts, but in all aspects of my life; to Cynthia, for instilling
in me a love of art; to Puff, for two great trips to Rome; to
Jarka, guide extraordinaire, for showing me The Eternal
City and introducing me to Bernini, and to my two patient
friend/editors,Louise Turner and Janice Healey.*

CHAPTER ONE

The "1812 Overture" blared from Emma Bradford's bedside table. She rolled over and looked at her boss's face on the lighted cell phone screen. Before answering she glanced at the clock. It was only six a.m.

"My God, doesn't Jack realize I'm not on the breaking news desk this morning?" she grumbled as she answered. "Please tell me there's no damn charity luncheon you want me to cover," she said without her usual cordial greeting.

"Good morning to you too," Jack replied with a little too much sarcasm for the early hour. "Obviously you're sleep deprived, so I'll hang up and call someone who wants to get up and cover the story I had in mind for you. Talk with you later."

Through the fog of sleep, Emma realized her boss was teasing. "Wait," she said sleepily. "I'm an easy mark. Whatever it is, I'll take the job and suffer in silence, though while I listen to Mayor Marino mumble his way through his standard speech, altered to fit the occasion, I'll be dreaming of the morning when I get a call and hear you say you want me to do something worthwhile."

"I apologize for asking you to take on another tedious assignment, Emma, though you won't be listening to our always smiling, less-than-articulate mayor. So are you going to hang up on me in favor of a few more hours of sleep or get up and pack your bags? You can get your beauty rest during the flight."

Emma was suddenly wide awake. She turned on her reading light and swung her legs over the side of the bed. "An out-of-town assignment," she said eagerly. "Where are you sending me?"

"Do you have a pencil and paper handy?"

"My pen's poised."

"You'll leave Logan at two this afternoon on Delta, Flight 30, Seat 2B. After a layover of an hour and twenty minutes at JFK, you'll depart on Alitalia 8189, seat 2A, and arrive in Rome at 7:25 a.m. A driver, who will take you wherever you need to go during your stay, will be waiting outside the baggage claim."

Emma couldn't believe what she was hearing. "Rome? Rome, Italy?" she said eagerly.

"No, Rome, Georgia," Jack jested. "A car will pick you up at your apartment at 11:30."

"I'll be ready," Emma replied, breathlessly. "Oh my God, Rome. Have I told you you're the greatest producer I've ever had?"

"You mean the only producer you've ever had."

Emma laughed. "That too. What's the story? Though I don't care if I'm covering the pope's tea party."

"The pope gives tea parties?" Jack chuckled. "I guess I'll have to find a permanent correspondent to do daily reports from the Vatican. Maybe you could apply for the job while you're over there."

"Come on, Jack. It's too early in the morning for joking."

"You're right." Jack cleared his throat, and Emma could picture him forcing back a smile. "Here's what I know," he said. "I checked my e-mail after we wrapped the eleven o'clock news last night. The powers that be in New York want us to cover the opening of a year-long Bernini exhibition in Rome. I immediately thought of you. If I remember correctly, you majored in art history at Wellesley."

"I did, and I hope this isn't a deal breaker. . . I wasn't a fan of the Baroque, but I admire Bernini. Who wouldn't?"

"Maybe someone who doesn't know who the guy is? Apparently this exhibition's a big deal. So do you want the job?"

"I'm already packing. How long will I be in Rome?"

"Ten days. We'll carry your reports live on the EyeOpener Monday through Friday with special reports on Saturday and Sunday. It's possible you'll have national exposure if your story trumps the one submitted by the WABC reporter from New York, so be creative. The exhibit's jointly sponsored by the Italian government, the Vatican, and some famous museum."

"I'm sure it's the Borghese," Emma said, feeling even more enthusiastic. "From the moment my professor in Art History 101 mentioned the museum, I've wanted to see the collection."

Emma could almost hear Jack's smile "See, I knew you were the right woman for the job," he said.

"Who's my competition?"

"Michael Kelsey, and though this isn't a contest, kick Kelsey's ass. I've heard he is one."

Emma laughed. "Then tell me more about my non-competition."

"Kelsey majored in journalism at Yale, so he's well educated, but why WABC is sending him to cover an art exhibit beats me. He's a Geraldo-wannabe investigative reporter who got his start in sports reporting. No doubt he thinks Bernini's a lineman for the New York Giants, but I've already said too much. You'll have to make up your own mind about Michael."

Jack hesitated for a moment. "What?" Emma said, not sure what her boss wanted to say.

Jack responded guardedly. "Though it's not my usual MO, in this case I'll offer a little fatherly advice. Be careful. Kelsey has a reputation for being reckless. He'll jump into the fray without thinking things through, and he's shot off his mouth a few too many times. I imagine he'll think the assignment's an unpleasant task rather than an opportunity, so he probably won't be pleased about wasting his time in Rome. But whether he wants to cover Bernini or not, he's a competitor. He'll fight you for the story."

"Then I shouldn't tell him he's been given a girlie assignment?"

Jack chuckled. "Not a good idea. According to my sources, Michael gets to Rome on Friday morning. I'm sending you two days earlier so you can get your bearings, and, okay, I admit it, get a jump on the competition."

Emma shook her head and rolled her eyes as she spoke: "Lucky me, I'm trying to outshine an Ivy League jock."

"And I'm going to be sure you do. You said your pen is poised, so take this down. Tomorrow morning at ten, a guide, an art expert named Nicola Adriani, will meet you by the concierge desk in the Excelsior lobby."

"The Excelsior. First a Business Elite seat from New York to Rome and now a five-star hotel. Didn't we just get a memo about cutting back?"

"Apparently not when it comes to this Bernini guy. I have no idea why ABC News or the Vatican thinks this is an important story. The e-mail said to spare no expense, so I reserved a suite. You and your crew will have a sitting room to plan interviews and store the equipment. Helen Taylor will be your production manager and Ron Sullivan your cameraman. They'll arrive early Friday morning."

"They're staying at the Excelsior too?"

"No, they'll be at the Quattro Fontane, a business hotel near the Spanish Steps. They'll meet you in the Excelsior lobby Friday afternoon at three." Jack paused, and Emma heard the sound of shuffling paper before he continued: "I've already made arrangements with hotel security. You'll be able to leave cameras, computers, or whatever, in your room without worrying about someone walking off with them, and you'll have one maid for your entire stay. She'll have the only other key to the suite."

"Thanks for giving me Helen," Emma said enthusiastically. "She's top-notch, though I only know Ron by reputation."

"He's the best. As I told you before, for reasons unbeknownst to me, this exhibition's a big deal to the Vatican and the Italian government, which makes me wonder why ABC didn't send a network star. Anyway, the pressure's on you to do a good job."

"I'll do my best."

"I know you will, and since I'm such a great boss, the station will pay for an extra day of sightseeing at the end of your assignment, but work before play. Tomorrow, your driver will drop you and Nicola off at the Church of Santa Maria della Vittoria, where you'll begin a two-hour, two-mile walking tour which Nicola calls 'Bernini's Rome.' At 12:30 you'll have lunch."

"Sounds like we're on a tight schedule—depart 10:15, lunch 12:30."

"Actually, you are. Under ordinary circumstances it's impossible to get a ticket to the Borghese on short notice, and it's particularly difficult now that the Bernini exhibition is about to begin and there's a renewed interest in the artist. Miraculously, Nicola was able to use her contacts to get you into the museum. You'll have two hours. When you're finished the driver will drop you off at the hotel and come back to pick you up Friday morning at ten for a look at Bernini's works in Saint Peter's."

"Give me a second to finish writing," Emma said.

"Take your time," said Jack. "You're only keeping me from my beauty rest."

Emma laughed. "Of course I am."

"Are you still awake?" Emma said moments later. "Because I have a question."

"I'm here, so ask away."

"I'm landing in Rome early in the morning. Most hotels don't allow check-in until around two. Will I have a problem getting into the suite?"

"By now you must know I think of everything," Jack said, feigning surprise. "Your rooms will be ready when you get to the hotel. My considerable experience with overnight flights is they land at least thirty minutes early, so you'll have time to take a shower and change clothes before your Bernini tour begins. The Excelsior concierge, Walter Ferrari, is the best I've encountered in all my years of travel. Don't hesitate to ask him for anything you need. I'll give him a heads-up call before I go back to the station this afternoon. Do Boston proud, Emma. Kick New York's ass."

"Count on it. I'll start my research right away."

"Ah, I'm glad you mentioned research. Clearly my brain isn't fully engaged at this hour of the morning." He paused, again shuffling pages. "The research staff put together a list of Bernini works they want you to feature in your reports, so you'll be able to narrow your focus. If the Bernini material isn't on your computer by the time you get to Kennedy, give me a call. I'll be sure you have everything before your international flight departs. By now your e-ticket and the Excelsior confirmation number should be on your computer. If for some reason they're not, call me back later, but don't panic too early. I didn't get home until after two and had to set my alarm to call you at this ungodly hour. Let me sleep as long as possible."

"Are you sure you got home at two? It sounds like you worked all night."

Jack chuckled. "Not me. I have a staff that's sleep deprived as well."

"Lucky you. I won't disappoint you. Forget Michael Kelsey. He's toast."

"Call me at the station when you get to Rome. You're six hours ahead of us. That makes it 1:30 a.m. in Boston, so I'll just be ending my day. Good luck, or as they say in Rome, Buona fortuna. I'm going back to bed."

"Sleep well, and thanks again, Jack."

Emma hung up and put her phone back on the table. Excited and eager to begin her Rome adventure, she threw off covers, went to the kitchen, made a pot of coffee, and turned on her laptop. While she watched the coffee drip, she thought about what had brought her to this moment—her first important assignment.

During a senior seminar at Wellesley on television's influence on politics, Emma found her passion. She applied to and was accepted by the prestigious Medill graduate program at Northwestern University, where, in a year and a half, she earned her Master of Science degree in Journalism. Eager to show the world what she could do, she accepted a position at WCVB Boston.

It took only days on the job for Emma to realize that, despite her excellent education, which no doubt helped her get her foot in the door at Channel Five, her assignments were of little consequence. Without complaining, she sweated her way through ribbon cuttings under Boston's hot July sun; attended ground-breakings in forested areas where mosquitoes outnumbered the celebrities fifty to one, and struggled to remain standing when reporting on nor'easters battering Cape Cod. Sure, covering the Bernini exhibition wasn't exactly serious journalism, but it beat listening to Mayor Marino talk about his plans for the new Government Center.

Deciding to shower, dress, and pack before beginning her online Bernini search, Emma took her coffee into the bathroom. As she looked in the mirror, she continued to reflect on her first days at WCVB. It hadn't been an easy beginning. Her coworkers initially misconstrued her shy reserve for aloofness, but as she gradually opened up, got to know people, and began to fit in, she shed the standoffish label. Though she'd proved herself a competent reporter, there were still those who believed she got the job because she looked good on camera. But why wouldn't they think that? She had always felt blessed.

At a petite five-feet, four-inches tall, Emma drove her friends crazy. While they dieted and embarked on a rigid exercise routine to fit into size-six pants, she ate everything she wanted and wore a size four. While they spent hours in the beauty salon having their hair permed or foiled, it took her about fifteen minutes to wash her thick, naturally blond hair in the shower, blow it dry, and style it with just a little hairspray. Except for a hint of blush to enhance her fair complexion and a touch of mascara on her long lashes, she wore very little makeup. Everyone said her eyes were her most striking feature. Azure blue, they reflected her many moods; smiling when she was happy, shooting darts at those who crossed her, and exuding sympathy when compassion was needed.

Appreciating she was on a tight schedule and couldn't afford to spend additional time thinking about what had been, Emma showered and dressed in a pair of grey slacks and a long-sleeved red and white-striped shirt. She took out a red sweater in case the plane was cool, removed her passport from her locked cabinet in the closet, put it in a passport case, and stuck it in her purse. *Wouldn't it be great if I got to the airport without my passport and missed the plane,* she thought as she began to pack.

With no idea what clothes she might need in Rome, she pulled out two suitcases and packed for any event she might be required to cover. When she had to sit on her big suitcase to close the zipper, she realized she was taking too much. *But better too many clothes than not enough*, she thought as she picked up her purse and rolled the bags to the front door.

She ate a cup of yogurt and a piece of wheat toast, printed her e-ticket, and put in with her passport. On a whim, she went on the WABC website, clicked on the list of reporters, and scrolled down to get a look at Michael Kelsey. "What a hunk!" she whispered. She enlarged the thumbnail picture and Michael's face covered the screen. Her smile became a frown. "And he obviously knows it."

She reduced the picture to the bottom of her screen, typed Michael's name on her browser's search line, and scrolled down to a clip of him interviewing MVP Eli Manning after the Giants won the 2008 Super Bowl. Before watching the feed, she opened the Giant's website to look up Manning's personal stats. He was six-feet, four-inches tall and weighed two hundred twenty-five pounds. Knowing that, she could estimate Michael's height and weight as the two men stood side by side. She began to watch the interview.

As soon as the two men appeared on the screen, Emma paused the feed. Michael was almost as tall and, as far as she could tell, as muscular as Eli, though it was hard to be sure since the quarterback was wearing football pads and Michael wore a sport coat. She clicked play and continued to watch. Michael looked to be six-three or four and probably weighed somewhere in the vicinity of two-hundred pounds. He definitely had the body of a quarterback, or maybe a tight end. She paused the interview again and Googled Michael. Sure enough, he'd been a quarterback at Yale.

She brought the WABC thumbnail back to her desktop and zoomed in so once again Michael's face covered the screen. She had no doubt most women would find her competition irresistible. He had a full head of red-gold hair and striking, wide-set green eyes. A few freckles on his nose added to his boyish charm.

Emma reduced the photo again and returned to the video. She concentrated on Michael, eager to learn more about him and become familiar with his style. By the end of the segment, she realized he wasn't a stereotypical sportscaster. He was talented; a rising star with tremendous potential. It wouldn't be easy to upstage him, and it wasn't because he had a handsome face. Exuding wit, charm, and a deep sense of self-confidence, he was the kind of affable, easygoing reporter with an innate ability to draw out the person he was interviewing. She knew he could take care of himself under any circumstance. She wouldn't take him for granted.

Trying to put thoughts of her handsome, talented competition aside, Emma washed her breakfast dishes, put them away, and sat back down at the computer to begin her Bernini research. For the next hour, she downloaded the artist's biography, a list of his works, and information about all his famous sculptures around Rome as well as his creations in Saint Peter's. She saved pertinent files in Word documents and printed color pictures of the pieces in the Borghese and in the spectacular basilica she could hardly wait to see.

When she was finished, she packed her computer and her files in her leather briefcase and looked at her watch. It was 9:30, two hours before the car would arrive. "I need a city guidebook," she said. She put her briefcase with her suitcase and carry-on, went downstairs, and caught a cab to the Prudential Center.

The cab dropped her at the Copley Marriott and she crossed the bridge to the Pru. She quickly located the travel section at Barnes & Noble and, after leafing through several books, chose *Eyewitness Travel: Eyewitness Rome*, because it had the most detailed write-ups as well as colorful maps. In the art section, she selected two books, the lightest she could find; one about the Baroque period and one about Bernini.

Satisfied she had what she needed, Emma caught a cab outside Lord & Taylor department store. She arrived back at her apartment at eleven, stuffed her new books into her briefcase, freshened up, and, growing more excited by the minute, went back downstairs to wait for the car that would take her on what she hoped would be an exciting adventure.

CHAPTER TWO

The town car pulled up to Emma's apartment at 11:30. The driver put her bags in the trunk, and they began the short drive to Logan. With rush hour over and it being not quite lunchtime, there was very little traffic on the usually crowded surface streets and Ted Williams tunnel, and in no time he pulled up outside the Delta terminal.

There was only one person in front of Emma in the Business Elite check-in line, so it took no time for her to check her bag, go through security, and find a comfortable chair in the first-class lounge near gate seventeen. She picked up a cup of coffee and a sweet roll, and to conserve battery power, attached her computer to a nearby plug.

Her itinerary for the ten days in Rome was in her mailbox. Though interviews were still being arranged, she was already scheduled to meet with Donato Martelli, the curator of the Borghese and co-chairman of the Bernini exhibition committee. As an added bonus, she'd have her own personal guide at the Vatican, Monsignor Peiro Scala, a rising star in the church and private secretary to Cardinal Giancomo Amici, the other co-chairman of the exhibition.

Emma had just finished copying files to her hard drive when her flight was announced. She repacked her computer, went to the ladies room, and arrived at the gate just as the woman behind the desk was calling for first-class passengers to board.

There won't be much conversation on this flight, she reflected when she found her seat. Her neighbor was already asleep, his head resting against the window. After hoisting her carry-on into the overhead rack and shoving her briefcase under the seat in front of her, Emma took out her travel guide and a pad of colorful sticky note tabs. As the plane took off, she created a color code. The Bernini fountains and miscellaneous pieces would be tagged with yellow, the important sculptures at the Borghese with red, and the Vatican masterpieces with green. Orange tags would be used to mark the places she wanted to visit during her free time or on the last day of the trip. As soon as they were airborne, Emma began to read and sort Bernini's works into categories. Concentrating on what she was doing, it seemed like no time at all had passed when she felt the pilot begin the descent into New York. As the wheels hit the tarmac, if possible, she was more excited than she'd been when they lifted off in Boston.

After a short walk to the International Terminal, Emma presented her ticket at the Business Elite lounge and again found a place to plug in her computer. When she opened her e-mail, there was the promised list from the research department along with a note explaining that the bolded items were must-covers. Emma read:

THE BORGHESE
1. **Pluto and Proserpina**
2. Aeneas and Anchises
3. **Apollo and Daphne**

4. David
5. Bust of Cardinal Scipione Borghese
6. Truth Unveiled by Time

SAINT PETER'S
1. Piazza, colonnade
2. Constantine's statue
3. Baldachino
4. Saint Longinus
5. Urban VIII's Monument
6. Alexander VII's Monument
7. The Blessed Sacrament Chapel

MISCELLANEOUS
1. Church of Santa Maria della Vittoria—Ecstasy of Saint Theresa
2. Triton Fountain
3. Elephant obelisk in Piazza della Minerva
4. Fontana del Quattro Fiumi

Emma saved the list to her assignment documents so she could refer to it on the plane. Using the remaining blue sticky notes, she marked the must-cover sites in her guidebook. Ten minutes later, she cheerfully boarded her flight to Rome.

She put her carry-on in the overhead compartment and, as she had on the trip from Boston to New York, shoved her briefcase under the seat if front of her. She had just sat down and fastened her seatbelt when the flight attendant arrived with a tray of juices and champagne. Emma knew she should be drinking water, *but why not celebrate with one glass of the bubbly?* she thought. "Champagne please," she said.

For the next fifteen minutes, she sipped champagne and waited for her seatmate to arrive. Just as the door was about to close, an obviously out-of-breath man raced through and stopped beside 2B. Emma looked up to see who would be sitting next to her for the next eight hours. He sat down and held out his hand. "Michael Kelsey," he said.

Emma was stunned. Hadn't Jack said her competition would arrive in Rome on Friday? Michael apparently mistook her surprised look and lack of response for admiration. "You must be a fan who can't believe she's sitting next to me," he said, his green eyes quizzical and smiling.

Emma fumed. For some inexplicable reason, she immediately disliked the man. *What an arrogant jerk,* she thought. "A fan?" She flashed Michael an insincere smile. "Are you some famous person I should recognize? I was thinking you're lucky you didn't miss the flight. Or would they have held the plane?"

If Michael heard Emma's sarcasm, he didn't let on. "To use an appropriate cliché, better late than never," he said grinning. "I'm a WABC investigative reporter."

Emma decided to twist the needle a little more. "Really?" she said, raising an eyebrow. "You mean like Geraldo who investigates for Fox? He's one of my favorites. I don't believe I've seen you on air."

Michael laughed. "You're obviously not from New York *or* a sports fan. If you were, I'm sure you'd recognize me."

Emma couldn't resist another comment. "Maybe not," she said, exuding contempt. "I watch CNN for news, and ESPN and NESN for sports."

Michael shrugged. "Your loss." He was grinning as he sat down and fastened his seatbelt. "Going to Rome for business or pleasure?"

"A little bit of both," Emma said, seething from Michael's last comment. "What about you?"

"I'm on assignment."

"How interesting. What *crucial* story are you covering?"

The flight attendant interrupted the conversation. "May I take your—?"

Emma didn't give her time to say her name. She handed her the empty glass. "Thank you," she said.

"No champagne for me?" Michael asked.

"You boarded late, so I'm afraid you'll have to wait until we take off, Mr. Kelsey."

"Damn New York traffic," Michael said. "I would have been here—"

"Maybe you should have left the station earlier," Emma said coolly. She turned to back to the attendant. "Is it too late for me to use the ladies' room?"

"Not if you hurry."

Emma followed the flight attendant up the aisle, which was clear except for several stragglers who were rushing to get to their seats. Instead of going into the restroom, she joined her in the small galley behind the half-pulled curtain at the front of the plane. "This may sound strange," she said, "but could you do me a favor?"

"If I can I will," the attendant said hesitantly.

"I hope it won't be a problem. I'll be working with Mr. Kelsey in Rome and I'd rather he not know who I am until we're formally introduced. Since the computer has the accurate information, could you possibly pencil in a different name on your manifest? Call me Julia Phillips."

The flight attendant grinned and extended her hand. "I'm Wendy. Nice to meet you, Julia, and just between us, I don't blame you. I rarely talk about passengers, but in this case, I'll make an exception. I've flown with Michael Kelsey before. He's arrogant and demanding. You'd think he's George Stephanopoulos, who, by the way, happens to be very nice, and not a local ABC-wannabe."

Emma laughed. "Exactly my opinion, and I just met the man."

"Then you're clearly a good judge of character. Of course I'll keep your secret, but now you'd better get back to your seat. They're closing the door."

Emma returned to her seat and fastened her seatbelt just as the plane was beginning to push back from the gate. *Damn,* she thought. *With my competition sitting beside me, I can't do any work unless I want him to know who I am and why I'm going to Rome.* She quickly retrieved her briefcase from under the seat and took out *Eyewitness Rome.* When she opened to the history of the Roman Empire, Michael leaned in and looked over her shoulder. "I gather this is your first visit to Rome," he said arrogantly.

"It is, so I have a great deal of reading to do before we land."

"I'm going to be extremely busy, but if I have any spare time, I'd be glad to give you a personal tour of the historic sites."

"Thanks, but I've already hired a knowledgeable guide," Emma said as, unable to mask her irritation, she rapidly turned the pages of the book.

Her disdain fell on deaf ears. "Well, if he or she doesn't show up, call me," Michael said, smiling. "I'm setting up shop at the Excelsior. *La Dolce Vita.* Where are you staying?"

Oh Lord. How am I going to escape this guy? Emma wondered. "Lucky me," she said sarcastically, "I'm booked at the same hotel."

Again Michael failed to note Emma's disdain. "Really," he said. "Since we're sure to run into one another along the way, maybe you should tell me your name."

You have no idea how many times we'll run into each other, and not just at the hotel, Emma reflected. "I'm Julia Phillips," she said.

"Nice to meet you, Julia Phillips."

"Nice to meet you too," Emma said less than enthusiastically.

Michael opened his briefcase and removed his computer. "I have work to do after we take off. Ever heard of an artist named Bernini?"

"I took a couple of art courses in college. Wasn't Bernini was a Baroque sculptor?"

Michael fidgeted. Clearly he didn't want to admit he knew nothing about the artist he was assigned to cover. He continued without answering Emma's question. "I'm reporting on an important art exhibit featuring the guy. If I play my cards right, my reports will get national coverage. All I have to do is beat out some rookie reporter from Boston."

He leaned over as if sharing a secret. "I've never heard of the woman, so besting her should be a walk in the park."

My God, the man's unbelievable, Emma thought. The Manning interview made her think Michael was an intuitive reporter with enormous potential. In only ten minutes, his behavior had negated any positive opinions she'd initially formed. *Jack was right*, she mused. *Michael Kelsey is an overbearing, egotistical, condescending, unmitigated ass.* "I wish you luck," she said without making eye contact.

"Thanks, but in this case I doubt I'll need it." He leaned across Emma and looked out the window. "I wish this damn plane would take off. I need to get to work. Like I said, I have to get the jump on the competition."

Emma kept her eyes buried in her book to hide her grin. "I know exactly what you mean," she said.

In order to avoid more chitchat, she continued to read while the plane raced down the runway and lifted off. When they reached 10,000 feet, Michael removed his briefcase from beneath the seat in front of him and took out his computer. "I can't wait till we have internet service in the air," he said. "I just got the assignment, so I haven't had time to do my research."

You mean it wasn't important enough for you to spend your valuable time finding out about the man you'll be covering, Emma thought. *You were probably out on the town with some honey.* She looked up at Michael. "Won't the lack of advanced notice keep you from staying a step ahead of the *competition*? I think that's how you put it."

"Not really." Michael smirked. "If you recall, I said I'm dealing with a rookie."

"Ah yes, now I remember."

"Since I don't have access to the web, maybe I could take a look at your guidebook when you're finished reading. My boss said Bernini was pretty famous, so there must be a few write-ups about his work."

"There probably are." Emma looked at Michael with obvious disapproval. "You didn't think to buy your own a guidebook when you were told you'd be traveling to Rome?"

Michael winked. "I had other things to do."

"Of course you did." Emma shook her head in disbelief.

Emma continued to read until Wendy arrived with hot towels, signaling the beginning of dinner service. From the minute the ramekin of warm nuts was delivered until she ate the last bite of her hot fudge sundae, Emma could hardly wait for the meal to end. Obviously assuming she'd be fascinated by everything he had to say, her narcissistic seatmate droned on about the famous people and extraordinary events he'd covered during his three-year tenure at WABC.

After the hot fudge sundae bowl was removed, Emma put her guidebook back in her briefcase so Michael wouldn't pick it up while she was away from her seat, stepped over his computer that lay on the floor, and went to the lavatory. "Are you all right, Julia?" Wendy asked as Emma passed the galley.

"Just eager to go to sleep."

"What's the matter? Too much noise?"

Emma laughed. "Much too much; a perpetual cacophony."

"Good luck," Wendy said, as Emma left the lavatory five minutes later and headed to her seat.

Michael was already under a blanket, his seat in a full recline. He moved his footrest so she could get by. "I hate to check out on you," he said as she sat back down, "but I was out late last night and need to be on my game when I meet the blonde bimbo."

Emma turned and stared in astonishment. "Nice way to talk about a colleague, and what makes you think your competition's a blonde?"

"I don't know, but she must be a looker. Most of the women in the business are drop-dead gorgeous. Wonder how they got their foot, or whatever, in the door."

Emma frowned, but Michael rattled on. "Can't get enough of Megyn Kelly on that afternoon Fox show, *America Live*. I remember when she was reporting for WJLA, the ABC affiliate in Washington. She's hot."

"You mean Megyn Kelly the Syracuse graduate and respected litigator?"

Michael looked baffled. "She's the one. How come you know more about her than I do?"

"Because when I watch her, I see beyond the gorgeous face and sexy body and appreciate the work of an educated, talented woman."

Before Michael could respond, Emma lowered her seat to the sleeping position, turned her back, and covered herself with her blanket. "Jerk," she muttered as she closed her eyes.

————

Emma slept soundly until the overhead lights were turned on. When she looked up, Michael was nowhere to be seen. She raised her seat to an upright position and looked toward the front of the plane. There was only one person in line for the lavatory, so she took off her seatbelt and removed the complimentary Business Elite travel bag from the mesh pouch in the seatback in front of her. Still groggy, she padded up the aisle.

When she approached the galley, she heard a familiar laugh. She peeked inside. There was Michael talking *at* Wendy, whose expression said "get me away from this man." Emma gladly came to her rescue, pulling the curtain back and sticking her head inside. "Any chance I could get some coffee?" she asked.

When Michael looked at Emma, Wendy grimaced. "Good morning, *Julia*," she said, emphasizing Emma's codename. "I just made a fresh pot. Cream or sugar?"

"Neither thanks."

"I'll bring it right away."

"Sleep well?" Michael asked.

"I did." Emma turned back to Wendy, who was pouring the hot brew. "How long before we land?"

"About an hour. We'll be serving breakfast in ten or fifteen minutes."

When Emma got back to her seat, Michael was thumbing through the in-flight magazine. "No work to do?" she asked.

"Not without the internet. I'll connect when I get to my room. Speaking of the hotel, you're welcome to share my car. No need for you to take a cab."

Emma turned toward the window and rolled her eyes. "I'm all set," she said, turning back, "but thank you anyway."

Michael persisted. "Did your company arrange a ride?"

Emma's aggravation intensified. "Though you might not believe it, Mr. Kelsey, I'm perfectly capable of making my own transportation arrangements."

Michael seemed genuinely surprised by her hostile tone. "You don't have to be so defensive," he said. "I only meant—"

"I know what you meant," Emma said with exasperation. "Forget it." Michael started to explain, but she stopped him. "I said let it drop."

While Michael ate sausage and eggs, Emma had a cereal, fruit, and yogurt. "On a diet?" he asked.

Usually able to write off anyone who irritated her, Emma had no idea why she was allowing the infuriating pain in the ass get to her. She turned and shot him an incredulous look. "Why, you think I need to lose weight?"

There was something in Emma's tone that wiped the smirk off Michael's face. "I didn't mean—"

"Of course you did." Emma buried her head in the guide-book. Michael evidently picked up on her disdain, because he kept quiet during the rest of the meal.

Wendy had just removed their dishes when the seatbelt sign came on and the pilot announced their approach into Fiumicino Airport. Michael undid his seatbelt, leaned down, and put on his shoes. When he sat up he was grinning. "In case you didn't read it in your guidebook, Fiumicino is also called Leonardo da Vinci," he said.

Emma didn't know if the man was serious or mocking her, but she felt her blood pressure soar. "Thanks," she grumbled. "I might not have figured that out on my own. When you said you'd take me on a personal tour, I realized you've been to Rome before. How many times does one have to visit a city before he or she can be called an expert like you obviously are?"

Michael seemed astonished by Emma's contempt. There was no arrogance in his response. "My best friend lives in Vatican City," he said. "Two months ago he was promoted, or whatever you call it, to monsignor. I spent a week over here with him."

"But you've never reported from Rome."

Emma wasn't sure, but she thought Michael looked sheepish, and he was less boorish when he spoke: "No, but I did come over with a few fraternity brothers after I graduated from Yale. It was one of those 'if it's Tuesday it must be Belgium' trips. You said this is your first time in the city?"

Emma wasn't going to let a few minutes of "Michael the nice guy" change her opinion. "When I graduated from college, I went straight to graduate school," she said.

Emma fully expected Michael to make a sarcastic comment, so she was surprised when he didn't. "You sure I can't give you a ride?" he said politely.

"No, thanks."

"Could I at least show you the way to customs and immigration?"

The offer seemed to be genuine, but Emma still couldn't let go of her hostility. "You don't have to take care of me, Mr. Kelsey," she said. "I'm perfectly capable of reading signs and following directions."

Michael looked at her quizzically. "Have I said or done something to irritate you, Julia?"

My God, is he just now catching on? Emma mused. When she answered, it was like someone else was speaking. "You mean besides being the most arrogant, egotistical, condescending man I've ever met, and to put it in terms you might understand, a bona fide jackass?"

Clearly taken aback by Emma's intense denunciation, Michael winced. "Wow. So much for trying to be friendly. Are you always this uncivil?"

"I guess you bring out the best in me." Emma took a deep breath; she'd already alienated the man. He'd be furious when he found out who she really was, so though she wanted to continue, she backed off.

There was no further conversation during the remainder of the flight. Thankfully it wasn't long before Emma heard the jet's wheels lock into place. She looked at Michael. "I guess we're here," she said. "Good luck with Bernini. Once you figure out who he was, you may learn to appreciate his work."

Michael smirked. "I doubt it, but then, who knows? I suppose anything's possible."

As soon as the wheels hit the tarmac, Michael turned on his cell phone. Apparently he had a few messages, because he listened intently while the plane taxied to Terminal Five. When the seatbelt sign was turned off, he stood up and removed his carry-on from the overhead compartment. "Would you be offended if I offered to help with your suitcase," he said, "or would you like to do it yourself?"

"I'd appreciate the help," Emma replied as nicely as she could. "It's the burgundy bag."

Michael put the suitcase on the floor and extended the handle. "Enjoy your stay in Rome," he said. "Maybe I'll see you around the hotel."

"I'm sure you will." She wondered what Michael would think if he knew she was the rookie blonde bimbo he'd be competing with for the Bernini story.

CHAPTER THREE

M ichael was one of the first to deplane. When Emma arrived at passport control, she spotted him near the front of the Fast Track line. Assuming this was one of the perks for flying Business Elite, she joined the other twenty passengers in that line waiting to be admitted to Italy.

The man in the booth compared Emma's face to the picture in her passport and waved her through. In only minutes, she passed through customs and followed the signs to the baggage carousel. At home, the wait for luggage took almost as long as a flight from Boston to New York, so she was surprised when the bags immediately began to tumble down the ramp. She spotted Michael standing by the carousel and looked the other way. When her bag made its way to where she was standing, he'd already left the building.

To be sure his car had already left the limo area, Emma took her time. She assumed Michael's bosses had arranged an early check-in, and she didn't want to meet him in the Excelsior lobby. *Wouldn't it cause a scene if he discovered I'm not Julia Phillips, but rather Emma Bradford, blonde bimbo personified?* She laughed silently. *What a scene he'd make.*

She retrieved her bag and looked around. A pleasant-looking, olive-skinned man in his late thirties held up a large sign bearing her name in large letters. *God, I hope Michael didn't see that,* she thought. When she was sure her competition wasn't lurking around waiting to see who was meeting the driver, she breathed a sigh of relief and walked forward.

"Ms. Bradford? Buongiorno," the man said when she drew close. "I will be your driver while you're in Rome. My name is Girolamo Basseni. Please call me Giro." He handed her his card. "Mr. Ferrari thought it would be better if you call me directly instead of going through him. You can reach me day or night. I live near the Spanish Steps, so I can be at the Excelsior very quickly."

Thank God I can understand you, Giro, Emma thought as she extended her hand. "Nice to meet you, Giro," she said. "I'll try not to be too demanding during my stay in Rome."

Giro nodded. "One more thing," he said. "I hope my English isn't confusing. I learned in school and have tried to improve for my American clients, especially when I talk about the famous places."

"Your English is excellent, and I love your accent," Emma said. "Perhaps you'll teach me a few Italian words in the upcoming days."

"I'll begin right now," Giro said, smiling. 'Grazie,' which means 'thank you.' But please, if you don't understand, ask me to explain."

"I'll do that," Emma said, thinking she and Giro would be just fine.

Giro took hold of the suitcase handles. "This way to the car," he said.

When they neared a money exchange window, Emma paused. She planned to use her credit card for most of her expenses, but she needed cash for tips. Besides that, stalling would give Michael a head start and, hopefully, keep her from running into him in the limo parking area. She withdrew two-hundred-fifty dollars' worth of euros, and, after lamenting the horrible exchange rate and the weak dollar, said to Giro, "I'm ready."

"There shouldn't be too much traffic on the way to the city," Giro said as he stepped aside so Emma could exit the terminal. "Since I'm not coming back for you and Nicola until ten, you should have plenty of time to unpack before we leave."

"You know Nicola?"

"I've driven for her three or four times. In my opinion she is the best guide in Rome."

Emma smiled. "That's good to know because I need all the help I can get."

As they walked the short distance to the limousine lot, Emma kept her head down. She was sure Michael would recognize her clothes if he spotted her, so she had no idea why she was taking this ludicrous precaution of hiding her face. *Maybe if he sees me and doesn't think I see him, he'll be on his way without saying anything.* She could only hope.

Giro opened the door to a brand-new Mercedes sedan. "Nice car," she said. "It smells new."

"Grazie mille," he said, smiling. "I picked it up yesterday. You are my first passenger."

During the first part of the forty-five-minute drive, there were no traffic issues, but the nearer they got to the city, the heavier the volume of cars on the road. Along the way, Giro pointed out noteworthy sights. Despite his accent, Emma could hear the sarcasm as he showed her the huge cement buildings erected by Mussolini, but when they entered the city, he spoke with pride. "I wish I had time to take you by Rome's historic places, but—"

"I imagine you've been told we're pressed for time. Hopefully you can take me to see the sites I've missed on Saturday when I have free time to explore."

"It will be my pleasure. We will turn onto the Via Veneto in about ten minutes. Between now and then, there's not much for me to talk about." Giro looked in the rearview mirror and smiled.

"In that case, would you mind if I ask you a question?"

"Not at all. I'll answer if I can."

"When I received this assignment, my boss couldn't tell me why Rome and the Vatican are enthusiastically promoting a Bernini exhibition at this particular time. Are we celebrating some sort of anniversary in the artist's life?"

Giro seemed hesitant to respond. The journalist in Emma sensed he wanted to answer her question, but for some reason, he felt uncomfortable. "I'm sorry if I'm putting you on the spot," she said.

"You're not. I have my own ideas, but they are just my opinions."

"Nonetheless, I'd like to hear what you have to say."

"Very well. I do not believe this exhibition is being held just to celebrate Bernini. I mean, he was a great artist who should be honored, as you will see when Nicola shows you his sculptures in Saint Peter's and Rome—"

"Then, in your opinion, what is the reason we're celebrating Bernini?'

Giro was clearly choosing his words carefully. "Let me say, the exhibition was the idea of Cardinal Giancomo Amici, a very important conservative who is against Pope John's liberal agenda."

Suddenly thinking she might have stumbled on the real reason for the extraordinary interest in the exhibition, Emma leaned forward. She knew Giro was uncomfortable, but the reporter in her took over, and she persisted. "Why would that be important?" she asked.

"I really can't say, other than that Bernini created in another time when there was a conflict in the church. Perhaps the cardinal thinks ... oh, I don't know. As I said, I am just guessing."

Sensing that Giro didn't like expressing his opinion to a stranger, Emma backed off. "Thank you for telling me what you think," she said, as she again questioned whether or not there was a secondary, and perhaps more significant, reason for the Bernini exhibition.

"This is the Via Veneto," Giro said when he finally turned onto the fabled thoroughfare that was packed with traffic. "Less than a hundred years ago, it was a quiet road on the outskirts of the city. Back then there no cars or scooters racing around, just carriages and horses. Maybe you know, the street was made famous by the director, Fellini, in the movie *La Dolce Vita*. Today it is still popular because of its location. I tell the people I drive to imagine a triangle with the Excelsior hotel at the top, the Borghese gardens at one of the bottom corners, and the Spanish Steps at the other."

"So the Via Veneto is close to many famous places."

"It's in the middle of four Romes. This part of town is modern Rome, but if you look around you can see remains of Imperial Rome, Renaissance Rome, and Baroque Rome—so four Romes. I hope I can show you what I mean."

"Make it the first item on our must-see Saturday list."

As they inched along the Via Veneto, Emma watched pedestrians dart into the road without warning, taking their lives in their hands as they confronted the miniscule Smart Cars and scooters zooming in and out of the lanes of traffic, overtaking cars on the wrong side, and boldly turning the wrong way onto one-way streets.

"How do you drive in this traffic?" she asked as a particularly aggressive Vespa rider came dangerously close to scraping the car door as he sped by.

Giro laughed. "I'm used to crazy Italian drivers. I think you have crazy Americans in your country, right? Please don't worry. Enjoy the sights!"

Taking her driver's advice, Emma looked out at the many upscale restaurants, posh shops, and inviting sidewalk cafes along the famous roadway. It wasn't long before Giro pulled over on the corner of the Via Veneto and Via Boncompagni. He pointed straight ahead. "There it is," he said with pride.

Emma gazed at the massive, beaux arts building as Giro continued: "The Excelsior opened in 1906, but it was recently restored. There are eight hotels on the Via Veneto, but I think the Excelsior is the most beautiful. As we Italians would say, '*Il pui bella di Roma*': the most beautiful in Rome. When you go home and tell people where you stayed, they will be jealous."

Emma recalled Michael's smug attitude when he told her he was staying at the Excelsior. "I'm sure they will be."

Blaring horns forced Giro to pull away from the curb. Just beyond the corner, he entered a circular driveway and pulled up to the grand entrance to the lobby, where a man dressed in tails and a top hat opened Emma's door. "Buongiorno, Madam. Are you checking in?" he asked.

"I am," Emma said.

"The bellman will meet you at the front desk after you have registered. He will deliver your luggage to your room."

Giro popped the trunk and walked to the back of the car to supervise the luggage extraction. Emma joined him. "Thanks for the enjoyable and informative ride," she said. "I'll see you in a little while."

"I'll be waiting here at ten. *A dopo,* which means 'see you later.'"

"You're a good teacher, Giro." Emma smiled. "A dopo."

As Emma pushed through the revolving doors into the opulent entrance, she glanced toward the reception area and sighed with relief. Michael was nowhere to be seen.

Before approaching the desk, she crossed the marble floor and climbed the few stairs to the lobby entrance. "Oh my!" she whispered as she looked up. Gleaming chandeliers hung from soaring ceilings, and sconces along the walls emitted soft light. The gigantic windows were draped with rich golden fabrics and covered with scalloped-bottom Roman shades. Luxurious Empire furnishings, some chairs straight-backed and upholstered with red and beige stripes and highly polished mahogany veneers, and others in barrel style and upholstered in light gold, were grouped in intimate seating arrangements around gilded, round or octagonal glass-top tables. There were massive arrangements of fresh flowers on corner tables and smaller bouquets scattered throughout the lobby. Despite the grandeur, the room was warm and inviting; *a perfect place to meet friends or to entertain business associates,* Emma mused.

She half expected the receptionist to be snooty. Instead, the girl smiled warmly. "Buongiorno! May I help you?" she asked cheerfully. Emma removed the reservation confirmation from her purse and handed it to her. "Ms. Bradford," she said. *"Benvenuto.* Welcome. We've been expecting you. My name is Maura." She typed Emma's name into the computer. "Your passport, please." Emma handed her the document. "You have a very nice suite on the fourth floor. When we finish here, the bellman will show you the way."

"Thank you." Emma said as she handed Maura the ABC credit card.

"Oh, you also work for ABC television," she said. "You just missed Mr. Kelsey."

"I'm sorry I did," Emma said, though she was really thinking: *You have no idea how glad I really am.* "Is Mr. Kelsey's room on my floor?" she asked.

"No. He's on three. For security purposes, we are prevented from giving out specific room numbers, but you can reach him from any hotel phone. The operator will connect you."

"Grazie," Emma said. *At least I won't meet Michael in the fourth-floor hallway,"* she thought with relief.

Maura pressed a bell, and a bellman appeared. "Suite 4201 please," she said as she handed him the keycard.

The bellman nodded. "Please follow me, Ms. Bradford."

"Arrivederci," said Maura.

"Yes, Arrivederci," Emma said, smiling.

As they passed the concierge desk, Emma paused. The bellman turned to see why she stopped. "Can you tell me if one of the men over there is Mr. Ferrari?" she asked, surveying the men helping hotel guests.

"Certainly. Mr. Ferrari is the man on the phone at the end of the counter."

"Would you mind if I introduced myself before we go upstairs?"

"Not at all. I'll wait in the hallway by the elevator."

Emma went to the desk. While she stood aside, waiting for Mr. Ferrari to finish his conversation, she realized why he was Jack's favorite concierge. Short, probably not much taller than she, he had a full head of gray hair parted down one side. His tanned face was animated as he spoke in rapid Italian, his expressions reflecting what he was hearing on the other end of the line. At once he was quick to grin, and, in an instant, his smile turned upside down into a frown.

When he hung up, Emma approached the desk and extended her hand. "Buongiorno, Mr. Ferrari, I'm Emma Bradford. I believe Jack Burnett told you to expect me."

The concierge grinned and covered Emma's hand with his. He spoke in understandable English with a thick Italian accent. "Buongiorno, Ms. Bradford. Mr. Burnett called me. He said to take good care of you." His eyes twinkled. "Please ask for anything you need. I confirmed with Nicola this morning. She will meet you in the lobby at ten."

Emma looked at her watch. "Then I have forty-five minutes to get settled. Grazie, Mr. Ferrari."

The bellman stood aside while Emma entered one of two small elevators. Between the two of them and her two bags, there was no room for the guests who came up behind them. The bellman waved them away and pushed the button for the fourth floor.

The snail-like elevator finally opened into a large room off which several hallways extended. "Follow me," the bellman said. He led Emma toward a hall to the left. They were nearly as far as they could go when he stopped at an attractive set of double doors. He inserted the keycard into the slot and stepped aside so she could enter first.

Emma looked around. The room was clearly designed to merge modern technology with the soft, elegant ambience of a bygone era. She had no idea how the decorators managed to create the look, but the flat screen television hanging between two oil paintings of the Via Veneto during the street's glory days looked like it had been there forever. Opposite the TV there was a green velvet overstuffed sofa. Two comfortable chairs in matching green with beige and soft red stripes sat on either side, and a cocktail table was centered between them. A round conference table with four straight-back chairs had been placed in a corner by the window to take advantage of the natural light streaming in.

The bellman pointed toward the desk sitting to one side of the TV. "That is your internet connection," he said. He opened a door beside a double closet. "And this is your guest bath. Shall I put your luggage on the racks in the bedroom?"

"Please."

Emma followed the young man into the second room. Velvet-covered chairs and rich damask patterns in the red, green, and beige wallpaper picked up the colors in the sitting room. With wonder, she looked up at the Bohemian chandelier hanging from the high ceiling. Fabric on either side of the huge, Empire-style king-size bed was drawn up in pleats and attached to a mahogany cornice at the ceiling above a matching mahogany headboard. The sides of the fabric matched the comforter as well as the draperies on the double door which led out onto a balcony. There was a marble faux fireplace across from the bed, and, above it, a second mounted flat-screen television. Beside the fireplace an over-stuffed lounge chair sat near a mahogany table covered with magazines.

The bellman put Emma's suitcases on the large bench at the foot of the bed, crossed the room, and opened a door. Emma walked over and peered into a huge, modern bathroom with a large Jacuzzi tub, a separate shower, double sinks built into a marble counter, and a bidet. "The room is perfect," she said as she handed the man ten euros. "Thank you very much."

"Grazie." The bellman grinned, obviously pleased to receive such a generous tip. "The list of services is in the top drawer of your desk. Please let us know if we can be of service. Arrivederci."

"Arrivederci," Emma said as the bellman departed. She locked the door and looked at the clock. *I'd better hurry if I'm going to be in the lobby on time.*

After showering and changing into casual slacks, a Polo shirt, and Nikes, Emma was ready to go downstairs. Instead of waiting for the elevator to make its way to her floor, she took the stairs. At 9:55, she entered the hotel lobby.

Standing by the concierge desk and talking intently with Mr. Ferrari was a tall, slender, olive-complected woman. *That has to be Nicola,* Emma thought as she approached the desk.

"Ah, Ms. Bradford, you are right on time," said Mr. Ferrari. "This is your guide, Nicola Adriani."

Emma extended her hand. "Nice to meet you, Ms. Adriani."

"Nicola, please."

"And please call me Emma."

"Giro is waiting out front," Nicola said. "Shall we get started?"

"As soon as I leave the key at the desk, I'll be ready." Emma paused. "That is, if you think I'm dressed appropriately for the Borghese. I wanted to wear sneakers for our walk, but I don't want to be too informal for the museum."

"You're fine. Your shoulders are covered and you're not wearing shorts, so you can go into the churches. There's no dress code for the Borghese." Nicola turned to the concierge. "We're all set for tomorrow morning?"

"Giro will meet you here at 8:30."

After saying good-bye to Mr. Ferrari and leaving her key at the desk, Emma pushed through the revolving door. Giro was waiting by the Mercedes. "Buongiorno, Giro," Emma said.

"Buongiorno," Giro said, smiling.

Emma slid inside, and Nicola got into the front passenger seat. She looked back at Emma. "I hope you don't mind if I sit up front. It will be easier for me to communicate with Giro."

"Of course I don't mind," Emma said.

Giro looked in his rearview mirror. "I put a bottle of water in your cup holder, Emma. There's a cooler with more in the trunk. It's fall, but it's still warm, so you should have something to drink when you walk."

"Good advice. Grazie molto."

"You're speaking Italian like a native," Nicola teased. "Before we get started, I'd like to tell you about my credentials."

"I'll bet you studied in Scotland," Emma said.

Nicola smiled. "What gave me away?"

"Could it be your excellent English with a slight Scottish accent, which, I might add, makes you the perfect guide for me?"

"Thank you. Yes, I did my undergraduate work at the University of Saint Andrews, Prince William's alma mater, in part, to learn English. After graduating, I spent a year in New York before returning to Rome to earn two advanced degrees in art history, one with an emphasis on ancient Roman history and antiquities and the other in seventeenth century Baroque art."

"I'm certainly in good hands," Emma said. "With all those degrees I'm surprised you don't teach."

"I may someday. Right now I'm working on a book, coincidentally, on Bernini, so showing special visitors around Rome is a temporary job. But enough about me. Our first stop is the Church of Santa Maria della Vittoria, just north of

Termini station. We'll walk to see several of Bernini's works before Giro picks us up at the Piazza Navona at 12:15.

She reached back and handed Emma a thick folder. "Our walk will trace Bernini's influence on the development and appearance of the center of Rome. I thought you might want to take notes, so rather than delay us or frustrate you because you're trying to write down everything I say, I've prepared information about the Baroque period, Bernini, and his sculptures. That way you can listen and not worry about missing anything."

Emma thumbed through the papers. "This looks great. Thank you."

Nicola smiled and continued: "So we don't waste any time talking generally about Bernini or characteristics of Baroque art at our first stop, I'll give you a general overview on the way to the church. Jack told me you majored in art history in college."

"I did. I took courses on Renaissance and Baroque art, but I was obsessed with the Impressionists."

Nicola laughed. "I don't want to sound condescending, but most Americans are."

"From the look on your face and your tone, I'd say you're not partial to Monet and Renoir."

"Quite the contrary. I appreciate Impressionism, though I prefer the Baroque. When you've spent more time in Rome, I believe you will too."

Emma smiled. "You'll have to be very persuasive to win me over."

"I'm up to the challenge," Nicola said, smiling in return. "So I'll begin with preliminary propaganda. I'm sure you realize that to understand the art of a particular period, it has to be viewed in light of what was happening when it was created."

"That much I know."

"Good, they you'll appreciate that Baroque style reflects the life and events taking place in the seventeenth century, which many historians call the first modern age. Throughout the century, human awareness of the world increased."

"I recall there was a flurry of scientific discoveries."

"Which shaped not only the mindset of the time, but also the art. For example, Galileo's investigations of the planets inspired artists to be astronomically accurate in their paintings. In 1543, the Polish astronomer, Copernicus, published his theory that the earth wasn't the center of the universe. In art, this resulted in the rise of pure landscape paintings containing no human figures. What I just told you was an aside of sorts. In the future, I'm not going to talk about things you don't need to know for your reports."

"Though I'd like to hear it all, I suppose that's wise," Emma said.

"More practical than wise. So, keeping with my assignment, most significant for you as you look at Bernini's works are the religious events which occurred during the century. In an effort to stem the spread of Protestantism, the Roman Catholic Church launched the Counter-Reformation movement. The popes and princes of the church promoted emotional, realistic, and dramatic art as a means of spreading the faith."

So that's it, Emma thought. *That was what Giro was trying to say when I asked him why a Bernini exhibition now. The popes during Bernini's era used him to promote the faith. Could Cardinal Amici be doing the same thing? Is he using Bernini to launch his own counter-reformation in response to Pope John's liberal agenda? Could there be another story behind the story?*

"The Catholic elite became highly influential patrons of Baroque artists such as Bernini and his rival, Borromini," Nicola was saying. "Do you remember the characteristics of Baroque art and architecture?"

"Refresh my memory," Emma said, quickly deciding to keep her thoughts to herself.

Nicola nodded. "In general terms, the term 'baroque' means 'elaborate with many details.' Among the papers I gave you is a detailed explanation of Baroque characteristics, so I'll be brief. The first characteristic of Baroque art is a sense of movement. I'll show you what I'm talking about when we get to the Borghese. The second characteristic is intense spirituality—this is particularly evident in depictions of ecstasies, martyrdoms, or miracles. We'll view one of Bernini's most famous works, *The Ecstasy of Saint Theresa,* when we visit the Cornaro Chapel."

"A work on my must-cover list."

"Not surprising. It's an amazing sculpture. The third characteristic of Baroque art is realism and individualism. Baroque artists tried to portray the passions of the soul through the facial features of their subjects. Finally, expect to see great detail in the Baroque sculptures; not only in the faces of the subjects, but in things like the realistic rendering of cloth and extremely lifelike skin textures. I'll explain more when we actually view Bernini's works. Right now we're at our drop-off point, the Church of Santa Maria della Vittoria."

Emma looked out the window at the famous church as Nicola turned toward Giro. "The traffic's heavy," she said. "Please park around the corner so I can spend a little time talking about Bernini before Emma and I get out."

Luckily Giro didn't have to go far. Fifty-feet from the church, a car was pulling out. He quickly backed into the parking place. "We're starting off the day well," Nicola said. "So let's sit for a moment while I give you a quick overview of Bernini's life and career."

"Is the information on the papers you gave me?"

"What I'm going to say and much more, so I'll be brief. Baroque style was born in Rome, and its founding father was Gian Lorenzo Bernini, the preeminent Baroque artist of the seventeenth century. Bernini was born in Naples in 1598, the son of a sculptor-father who began to teach him sculpting techniques at an early age. When Bernini was seven, the family moved to Rome, and by eight the young prodigy was already creating. I know you'll need to be general with your biographical comments, but it's important to note that Bernini's character and methods of work were formed during his childhood. Throughout his life, he was a complicated and enigmatic man, but in terms of his work ethic, there can be no argument. He worked tirelessly, chiseling practically without pause for seven hours through long, hot Roman days. Even his much younger assistants couldn't keep up with the master."

"A point I'll make in my initial presentation."

"Good. Most important, as we look at his sculptures, Bernini was profoundly Christian. He believed God endowed him with unusual gifts. In return, he was driven to use his talents to glorify his maker and share his faith with the world. I suppose you could say that his art was the outward and visible expression of his faith. None of his works were, in his opinion, good enough to repay the debt he owed God. His often-used self-denigrating phrase was: 'At least it's not bad.'"

"That's a great line."

"I agree. In your folder you'll find a detailed summary of the artist's patrons and sponsors, so for our purposes, I'll cover the highlights. At age ten, Bernini produced his first authenticated work: *The Goat Amalthea with the Infant Jupiter and a Faun.* Soon after that, Pope Paul the Fifth became his first patron, but the first high-ranking individual to truly appreciate Bernini's extraordinary talent was Cardinal Scipione Borghese, Pope Paul's powerful nephew, who was also a great patron of the arts. It was Scipione who entrusted Bernini with his first commissioned pieces. We don't have time right now, so I'll tell you more about the cardinal when we're at the Borghese Museum."

"Bernini's bust of Cardinal Borghese is also on my must-cover list."

"As it should be. In light of what I just said, I'm going to skip over the reign of Pope Gregory XV and talk about Maffeo Barberini, who, in 1623, was elected Pope Urban VIII. Urban was a man of spotless virtue with a fiery disposition and a keen understanding. He was religious, and at the same time, he seemed to grasp the importance of the new sciences."

"An ideal pope for the seventeenth century."

"And for Bernini. Urban reigned for nearly twenty-one years, during which time Bernini was the most employed and richly rewarded artist in the world. Under Urban, Bernini began his architectural career, and for the next fifty years, his fingerprints were all over Rome; his vision and genius shaped the city and Saint Peter's forever." Nicola took a deep breath. "So now that you have the basics, shall we begin our walk?"

"Absolutely," Emma said as Giro got out and opened her door.

"Don't forget your water," he said to Emma and turned to Nicola. "I'll see you at the Piazza Navona."

"Grazie, Giro," Emma said as she followed Nicola toward Santa Maria della Vittoria.

CHAPTER FOUR

"If you don't mind, I'd like to ask you a question I asked Giro earlier," Emma said as they approached the church.

"Of course," Nicola said.

"Is there a reason the Vatican is sponsoring and promoting a Bernini exhibition at this point in time?"

"A reason?"

"Yes. Is some sort of anniversary or special event in the artist's life being celebrated?"

Nicola looked puzzled. "Not that I know of. What did Giro say?"

"I don't think I'm betraying him by telling you his thoughts on the matter. He believes Cardinal Amici, the conservative co-chairman of the exhibition, may be trying to launch a counter- reformation of his own against Pope John's liberal policies."

Nicola was clearly surprised. "Through Bernini?" she said.

"Through what Bernini symbolizes. You just told me the church used his art to counter the rise of Protestantism."

"That's true, but as far as I know, the church today isn't in a struggle for survival."

"Though he didn't come out and say it, Giro seems to think it is."

"I was raised Roman Catholic, but I no longer actively practice my faith."

"Then as we Americans say, you're a fallen Catholic," Emma said, smiling.

Nicola laughed. "That's a good way to put it. Unfortunately for you, I'm so fallen that other than what I read in the papers, I can't speak about what's happening in the church. It's possible Giro's right. I might give his theory more credence if the Bernini exhibition was strictly a Vatican-sponsored event, but it's co-sponsored by the city of Rome and the Borghese."

"And the city wouldn't have an agenda," Emma thought out loud. "I'll bet you're thinking I'm a journalist looking for a story within a story."

Nicola smiled. "I don't know—are you?"

"Not anymore. From now on, I'll concentrate on what is and not what might be. Shall we go take a look at Saint Theresa?"

"Absolutely," Nicola said. "Let's appreciate Bernini for what he created and not for what he may or may not represent in current Vatican politics."

Emma nodded. "So talk to me."

"With pleasure. Cardinal Scipione Borghese, Bernini's first patron, commissioned the Church of Santa Maria della Vittoria, which was designed by the early Baroque architect, Carlo Maderno."

Nicola led Emma through the door and up the center aisle to the left of the altar. "I told you art could only be understood in context of the times," she said, "but it also helps to know about the person being portrayed. Saint

Theresa was a Spanish mystic who was born in 1515, during a time of intense religious turmoil. She died in 1582. Among other things during her long life, she authored numerous books, including *Interior Mansions*, where she describes the many different steps one had to take on the path to mystical union with God."

"Was the book Bernini's inspiration for the sculpture?"

"That's what most scholars assume. Theresa's words would have been rated R if your American movie-rating system existed during the Counter-Reformation, not because she lived during prudish time, but as a celibate nun—"

Emma finished the thought: "She wasn't expected to have knowledge of sexual ecstasy. I read that in my guidebook during the flight from Boston to New York."

"Good, then you have a basic understanding. Before we walk up to take a closer look at the sculpture, I want you to see it from this perspective." Nicola pointed to the side of the sculpture as she continued. "Bernini modeled the chapel after a theater. Notice that eight members of the Cornaro family, including the cardinal, are watching the scene playing out on the center stage as it reaches the climax." Nicola grinned. "No pun intended."

"Of course not," Emma said, smiling.

"They witness a great moment of divine ecstasy when the swooning Carmelite nun, experiencing a mystical moment, falls into a trance and abandons herself to the joys of heavenly love. Let's go a little closer."

As Emma walked up the aisle toward the sculpture, she was astonished by the magnificence of the scene. Theresa's robes seemed to be on fire. Golden rays, their source cleverly hidden by the altar, beamed down, illuminating the blissful expression on her face as she slid down from a soft bed of clouds to collapse beneath the looming angel who readied his golden dart to pierce her heart.

"I see what you mean about Baroque artists revealing the passions of the soul through the facial features of their subject Emma said. "Saint Theresa is a perfect example."

"She definitely is. So standing here looking at the sculpture, what's your overall impression?"

Emma gazed at the incredible scene. "I'm amazed that Bernini represents Saint Theresa's mystical experience so sexually, given the sculpture was created for a church. I'm amazed by the erotic passion of her vision implied in her dreamy pose and the rise and fall of the folds in her robe, which, if I recall, is another Baroque characteristic. I'm amazed by the rapturous look on her face."

"And I'm amazed at your insightful comments. Are you sure you need me?"

Emma smiled. "Definitely."

"Good. I would hate to be fired after our first stop. Before we move on, go all the way up to the sculpture and take one more look."

Emma started forward and then quickly turned back. "I can't," she whispered.

"I'm sorry?"

"Suddenly I feel the need to pray. I'll explain later."

Emma bowed her head, walked to the side of the church away from the center aisle, knelt, and buried her head in her hands. "God, I don't mean to sound irreverent, but please don't let Michael Kelsey see me," she prayed silently. "And thank you for giving me enough time to change my clothes so maybe he won't recognize me."

While Michael stared at the statue and talked with a man who, from behind, Emma could see wore a clerical collar, she motioned to Nicola. "Come on," she whispered. "I'll take a closer look at the sculpture when I come back to film."

"Did something happen in the church? Did you see someone you didn't want to see?" Nicola asked, as they hastily left the church and headed toward the Triton Fountain.

Emma inhaled and exhaled deeply. "Since we're spending today and tomorrow together, I suppose you should know about my rival, Michael Kelsey, a reporter with WABC in New York."

Emma told Nicola about the plane ride with her insufferable colleague. When she finished, Nicola grinned. "It seems we're going to have to make sure you're the one who has the most interesting story, though I hope your interest in Mr. Kelsey isn't an overriding concern as you do your Bernini research."

"I assure you, I'm not interested in Michael Kelsey, except perhaps how to avoid him."

"That's good to know, she said, but without much conviction. "So our next stop is another of my favorite Bernini Sculptures." Darting through traffic, they crossed the street to an island in the center of the road. "The inspiration for the fountain was a passage from Ovid's *Metamorphoses,*" Nicola said. "In my humble opinion, the Triton, Bernini's first major assignment from Pope Urban, and, for that matter, his first water fountain, is one of the most beautiful fountains in the city."

Nicola motioned for Emma to move closer and then pointed up at the fountain. "The giant oyster shell that's suspended on the tails of four dolphins holds Triton, the son of Neptune, the Roman god of the sea," she said. "Bernini created Triton as a merman, half man and half fish, with a muscular upper body and a scaly fishtail."

She paused to let Emma soak up the scene. A short time later, Emma nodded and Nicola continued. "Triton's head is thrown back, and he holds a conch to his lips in an effort to quench his thirst from the stream of water bursting from a jet high above him." She pointed at the spewing water and then downward as she spoke: "The water flows down his body before splashing onto the shell on which he's sitting. The excess water then percolates over the edges of the shell and downward into the circular pool which represents the ocean."

"I know I'm overusing the word, but I can't help it," Emma said. "The fountain is amazing."

"I wholeheartedly agree. There's one interesting bit of trivia you might want to share with your viewers if you need filler. The fountain was once used as a municipal mortuary. A town crier would walk around and ask the people to come and identify the unidentified bodies which had been left there."

"Keep feeding me tidbits, would you? They have audience appeal. Maybe they'll help me best Michael."

"Michael again?"

"Sorry. I can't seem to think of anything except making my reports better than his. I realize how childish I sound."

"Are you sure that's all it is?"

"Positive. Believe me, this is not an example of 'The lady doth protest too much, methinks.'"

Nicola nodded. "Ah, you quote *Hamlet*. Then you must know Queen Gertrude isn't using 'protest' as an objection or denial. The principal meaning of the word in Shakespeare's day was 'vow' or 'declare solemnly.'"

"Then I solemnly declare I'm only interested in professionally besting Michael Kelsey."

"As I said before, that's good to know."

After a few brief stops, including the façade of the Palazzo Barberini, they passed the Pantheon. "Are we going in?" Emma asked.

"Saturday. We need more than fifteen minutes to see the building. We're headed to Piazza della Minerva to see the Elephant Obelisk, which the Italians affectionately call 'Bernini's chick.'"

Emma raised an eyebrow. "Really?" she said. "I didn't come across a reference to a 'Bernini's chick' in my guidebook."

"Ah, then you do need me. Pope Alexander the Seventh wished to erect an ancient Egyptian obelisk in the piazza and commissioned Bernini to create something to support the pillar. If that information isn't in your guidebook, you can read more about it in the papers I gave you. Sufficed to say, the finished product is typical of Bernini's inexhaustible imagination."

"It's darling," was Emma's immediate reaction when they rounded the corner and she saw the enchanting baby elephant carrying the obelisk on its back.

"Most would agree with you, though at the time, Father Domenico Paglia didn't think the sculpture was so cute."

Again Emma looked at Nicola curiously. "Why's that?"

"One of the most interesting features of this elephant is its smile. To find out why it's smiling, you have to go around to the animal's rear." Emma hesitated. "Go ahead," Nicola said.

When Emma reached the back of the sculpture, she laughed. The elephant's muscles were tensed and its tail was shifted to the left. "Did Bernini intentionally sculpt the animal to look like it's, for want of a better word, defecating?"

"He did."

"I'd love to use that in my report if I can figure out a way to make it G-rated. What was Bernini's motive?"

"He was making a political statement. If you can use that angle, I'm sure you can make your report acceptable. Father Paglia was a Dominican friar who was also one of Bernini's principal adversaries. The positioning of the elephant's rear to face the friar's office was the artist's final salute, his last word on the disagreement."

"The audience will love the story," Emma said. "Besides being different and amusing, the placement of the elephant illustrates Bernini's sense of humor."

"I think that's an appropriate approach."

"Good," so tell me more."

"There's nothing more to say that's not in your guidebook, so let's move on to the Piazza Navona, one of my favorite sites in Rome."

"A place I'm dying to see."

Retracing their steps back along the Corso del Rinascimento, they turned onto the Via del Salvatore and approached Piazza Navona. "Before we see the fountain up close, we'll pause for a minute so you can soak in the atmosphere," Nicola said.

Emma looked out at the square lined with luxurious cafes, Baroque palaces, and three lavish fountains. "I know we're pressed for time, but could you tell me a little bit about the history of the piazza?" she said.

Nicola checked her watch. "I guess we can spare a little time. The square was originally an amphitheater built by Nero. In 86 AD, the Emperor Domitian turned it into *Circus Agonalis*, a stadium for athletic contests and chariot races, thus its oval shape which you still see today. It was huge, with space for more than thirty-thousand spectators."

"Was the square called Piazza Navona back then?"

"No. The name Navona is actually a medieval corruption of the Latin word for gymnastic contest, 'agon', which also explains why Borromini's great Baroque church behind Bernini's fountain is called Saint Agnese in Agone. The name morphed into 'in agone' to 'navone' and eventually to 'navona. In the fifteenth century the ramshackle huts which had begun to spring up around the edges of the square gradually disappeared, and the first *palazzo* were constructed." Nicola hesitated before continuing. "Even though you won't be able to use the information in your Bernini presentation, how about yet another tidbit?"

"Of course," Emma said, "keep them coming."

"From about 1650, the piazza was flooded every Saturday and Sunday in August. It was used for staging mock sea battles and aquatic games. Up until a century ago, the area was still covered with water on August weekends. Drivers of the ornate carriages of Roman nobles and prelates would circle the water, giving their rich and powerful masters a cool respite from the heat when they were unable to get away to their country villas."

"Interesting."

"I wish I had time to tell you more—"

"But we're on a tight schedule."

Nicola sighed. "I'm afraid so. As you can see from out here, Navona Square is one of Rome's liveliest piazzas. Over the years I've learned that, no matter when I show up, if I stop and listen, I hear life all around me."

"Would you mind elaborating so I can plagiarize?"

"Not at all. Though in a different way, the piazza is beautiful and lively every moment of the day: in the early morning when there are a few joggers who dodge the street sweepers swooshing by; at noon when it's filled with people eating in the cafés or enjoying lunch on the edge of the fountains; in the evening when the buildings that line the edge are bathed in the golden glow of sunset; at night when it's packed with revelers and lovers strolling hand in hand. I could spend twelve to eighteen hours here and never get tired of people watching."

"I wish I had the time."

"But since you don't, if you really want to appreciate the beauty of the piazza without the hustle and bustle, its best to visit early in the morning."

"If just for a short time, could we come back here after we visit the Pantheon on Saturday?"

"We'll definitely make time. I'd like for you to see the Fountain of the Moor as well as the Neptune. Today we'll concentrate on Bernini's masterpiece, *the Fontana del Quattro Fiumi—*"

"The Fountain of the Four Rivers."

"Yes, it's a classic example of Baroque architecture. Inaugurated in 1652, it was Bernini's first design for Pope Innocent." Nicola paused. "Tidbit alert, and this is something you might actually be able to use."

"Do I need to take notes?"

"I think you'll remember this one. The fountain was so expensive that a bread tax was imposed on the people in order to cover the cost."

"Really? It must have been important to Innocent if he risked incurring the people's wrath."

"It was. Remember, we're dealing with the Counter-Reformation. Some art historians believe Innocent's purpose for commissioning the fountain was to proclaim the influence of the church and the papacy on all four continents."

"Is that true?"

Nicola shrugged. "Possibly, but whatever the pope's purpose, Bernini's fountain is a masterpiece of rearing sea horses, sea serpents, and muscle-bound river gods topped by an obelisk brought to Rome by Emperor Maxentius for his circus in the early fourth century. It's actually a theater in the round. There's something happening on all sides. Why don't we walk around it to see the show, so to speak, from all perspectives?"

Emma nodded and followed Nicola as she continued to talk: "The semi-prostrate marble giants are arranged on a rock at the center of carved grottoes decorated with flowers, exotic plants, and animals. The demi-gods are meant to personify the four continents known at the time."

"Which supports the theory about why Innocent commissioned the fountain."

"Exactly. The Danube is a symbol of Europe, the bearded Ganges represents Asia, and the Rio della Plata, portrayed here as black man, denotes the riches of the Americas. See the coins on the ledge?"

Emma looked closely and nodded.

"The fourth figure, the Nile god, symbolizing Africa, is presented with a shrouded head because the source of the Nile was unknown when Bernini submitted his design."

Emma continued to study the fountain. "Did Bernini design all four figures?" she asked.

"No, each one was created by one of his contemporaries. Their names are in the folder, though I doubt you'll have time to talk about them with everything else you have to say. For example, you might want to mention the animals. There are seven of them in the fountain: a horse, a sea monster, a serpent, a dolphin, a crocodile, a lion, and a dragon."

Emma looked closely at the animals positioned near Africa. "What's this supposed to be?" she asked, pointing.

Nicola laughed. "I hope my answer doesn't ruin your opinion of Bernini. The master's assistants did most of the work on the fountain, but Bernini himself carved that particular animal, and it's certainly not one of his triumphs. It's supposed to be a crocodile."

"Really?"

"Really. Bernini had never seen any of these exotic animals in person, so he sculpted them from bad sketches drawn by others."

Emma looked back at the so-called crocodile. "You're right," she said. "It's not one of his best creations."

"Ah, now I know you have an appreciation of great and not so great art."

"I wouldn't go that far," Emma said.

"I disagree," Nicola said, smiling, "but back to the fountain. Remember when we first talked about Bernini, I mentioned his religious fervor?" Emma nodded. "Though not apparent at first glance, probably because you're looking at the monstrous figures, this fountain contains a religious message." Nicola pointed upward.

"Is that a dove on the top of the obelisk?"

"It is. The dove, which denotes the Holy Spirit, was also Pope Innocent's symbol. The image appears in several places on the fountain, and because of its prominence, some believe the *Fontana del Quattro Fiumi* was meant to be a religious metaphor. The doves are supposed to be reminders of the pope's role as the earthly interpreter of divine will."

Emma opened her mouth to respond, but quickly changed her mind.

"You were going to tell me you don't think Michael will have that information," Nicola said.

Emma grimaced. "Though I hate to admit it, I was."

"Apparently Mr. Kelsey occupies your thoughts whatever we're talking about."

Emma shook her head. "It may sound that way, but he really doesn't."

"Perhaps not, but in your mind you've created a rivalry. Because you have and because it's an interesting story, I'll tell you about the legendary rivalry between Bernini and

Borromini. In part, the competition came about because the two great artists were so different. Bernini was the polished and refined associate of princes and popes, while Borromini was an introverted, quick-tempered, melancholic man who often defied the established rules of architecture. While Bernini's architecture was generally inspiring and uplifting, Borromini's, though sometimes joyous, could also be depressing and grim. One of Borromini's critics described his work as 'the embodiment of the soul's tormented passage through its earthly existence,' and that may be true. While Bernini lived a long life, Borromini committed suicide at age sixty-eight, possibly as a result of nervous disorders and depression."

"I can only imagine how difficult it would be for Borromini to witness Bernini's successes," Emma said.

"I'm sure it was. Though I could cite numerous other examples of the rivalry, the conflict between the two men is best illustrated here in the Piazza Navona. It began when Borromini accused Bernini of stealing the commission for the *Fontana del Quattro Fiumi* by presenting Pope Innocent with a silver model of the design."

"Did that actually happen?"

"I don't know, but Bernini got the job. The pope made a memorable comment about the commission. He said: 'It will be necessary to employ Bernini in spite of those who do not wish it, for he who desires not to use Bernini's designs, must take care not to see them.'"

"Quite a compliment," Emma said, "but before you tell me more about the Bernini/Borromini rivalry, I'd like to comment on what you said before. Michael and I aren't competing for a story. We're working independently. Thus, we're not rivals."

"Aren't you?" Nicola said, her tone exuding doubt.

When Emma started to defend herself, Nicola held up her hand. "Why don't we try to forget Michael Kelsey and enjoy Bernini's fountain."

"Fine with me," Emma said. "I know I sound ridiculous, so no more mention of Michael. Tell me how the Bernini/ Borromini rivalry is perpetuated in the Piazza Navona."

Nicola smiled. "Very well: First, by the position of the river gods on the side of the fountain facing the church. Take a look and tell me what you immediately notice."

Emma studied the figures. "Their backs are turned toward the church."

"Exactly. Some say in contempt. Notice the Rio Della Plata's hand is raised."

"I see. Is there a reason why?"

"Many who espouse the rivalry theory say the river god is trying to ward off the church's imminent collapse. Others say he's cringing and his arm is raised in a pleading gesture as if he were saying: 'Please don't make me look at this horrible church.'"

"Is he really doing either?"

"You'll have to decide for yourself. The shrouded head of the Nile also perpetuates the rivalry. I told you the Nile god's head is veiled because the source of the river was unknown at the time, but people came to believe the god's face was covered so he didn't have to look at the church."

"Another audience grabber."

"If I were watching, I would like to hear about the myths as well as the facts and decide for myself whether to believe them or not."

"Something I could ask the audience to do."

Nicola nodded. "Yes, and while we're discussing the rivalry, here's one more thing for you to consider: look at the façade of the church. Borromini's daring design covered the entrance of an older, conventional, and uninteresting church which was badly in need of refurbishing. I told you he often ignored the accepted rules of architecture."

"You're talking about the concave façade."

"That and much more. Many believe Bernini was expressing his contempt for the unconventional design when he created the fountain."

"Interesting."

"There's more."

Emma nodded. "Go on."

"Look at the statue of Saint Agnes at the base of the right belfry." Nicola pointed upward. "Note that Borromini positioned her looking away from the fountain, perhaps, as the legend says, in disdain. To further the belief she's sending a message to his rival, Borromini placed Agnes' hand on her breast in righteous indignation as if to say, 'How dare you put that monstrosity in front of me?' Or perhaps as others believe, 'Rio della Plata, put your arm down; there's no way this church will fall. It's constructed too well."

"Is there any truth to the legends?" Emma asked.

"The fountain was completed in 1651 and the church in 1657, so obviously the stories of the symbolic placements and expressions of the river gods can't be true. As for Saint

Agnes, you'll have to make up your own mind about whether or not Borromini is sending Bernini a message."

"A teaser for me and my audience."

"If you'd like, this evening I'll type a list of interesting facts and legends and give it to you in the morning."

"Fantastic!"

"Good. As we cross the piazza turn and look at the fountain from afar."

Near the north entrance to the piazza, Emma paused to look back at the Four Rivers as well as the nearby Neptune Fountain. After a few minutes, Nicola took her elbow. "I hate to hurry you, but if we're not at the Borghese on time, we won't be allowed in, and it's important for you to see Bernini's sculptures before you report on them. Also, I promised Jack I'd take you to his favorite restaurant."

"I'm starving." Emma sighed. "It's been a long time since I ate breakfast on the plane," *with the ass Michael Kelsey,* she thought, but she didn't say anything.

Nicola looked across the street. "There's Giro," she said as she looked both ways and headed out into traffic. "It's time for lunch."

CHAPTER FIVE

During the drive to lunch, Emma and Nicola discussed themes Emma might use for her shoot. By the time Giro turned onto Via Monza and pulled up in front of a sign pointing up the street to La Grotta Azzurra di Sandro, Emma was comfortable with her plans for a segment on Bernini's fountains, though she still wasn't sure how she'd make her discussion of Theresa's ecstasy G-rated.

"This is it," Nicola said. "Jack's favorite happens to be my mother-in-law's preferred place to eat out, and that's saying something. She's a fantastic cook and except for eating here, she likes to prepare her own meals at home."

Emma invited Giro to join them, but he declined, saying he had calls to make. "I'll find a parking place nearby," he said to Nicola. "Call me when you're ready to go."

"I will," Nicola said. She turned to Emma. "Shall we go?"

"I'm with you."

"I hope you don't mind, but I've taken the liberty of ordering," Nicola said as they approached the restaurant door. "The menu is quite extensive, and, in my opinion, you should have a little taste of everything."

Nicola wasn't kidding. After a glass of complimentary champagne, the food came, and came, and came. Emma wondered if the waiter would ever stop putting plates of antipasti on the table. First came squid prepared in three ways: as a salad, lightly breaded, and broiled. Next, the waiter delivered a large plate containing mussels, shrimp, and anchovies. The final antipasti platter held salmon on toast points and oysters on the half shell. "I'm stuffed," Emma said when the waiter cleared away the plates from the first course, "and I'm an eater."

"But we've only begun." Nicola inclined her head in the direction of the kitchen. Coming out the door was a waiter bringing the main course. In front of each woman he placed plate containing a piece of white fish, several langoustines, and a gigantic prawn.

"Are you serious?" Emma groaned as the man refilled their champagne flutes. "I'll need a nap if I keep eating and drinking like this."

"Trust me," Nicola said. "The meal is very light."

"Maybe it would be if we hadn't already eaten so much. Now I see why Jack's such a fan of this restaurant." She tasted the white fish. "Mmmmmmmm," she said. "You're right. It is light and it's delicious."

Emma was amazed when, not long after food arrived, she looked down at her nearly empty plate. "To quote one of our American comedians, 'I can't believe I ate the whole thing,'" she said as she leaned back and took a deep breath.

Nicola laughed. "I didn't order dessert, but if you're interested, the restaurant serves delicious sweets."

"Thanks," Emma said, patting her stomach, "but I couldn't eat another bite, and this time I mean it."

Nicola took out her wallet, but before she could remove any euros, Emma handed the waiter her company credit card. "This is on Jack," she said.

Nicola reluctantly put her wallet away. "Thank you, Jack."

"He says 'you're welcome.' I can't wait to send him an e-mail. He'll be green with envy when I tell him what I ate."

While Emma settled the bill, Nicola called Giro. He was waiting in front of the restaurant when the women emerged. "Did you finish your business?" Emma asked.

"I did. How was lunch?"

"Delicious. I ate so much I may skip the Borghese and take a nap in the back seat."

Giro chuckled as Emma slid into the backseat.

Ten minutes later they pulled up to the curb beside of the villa. Giro jumped out and opened Emma's door. "I'll be back to pick you up at four," he said.

"Very good," Nicola said. She turned to Emma, who had just stepped out of the Mercedes. "We're approaching from side of the villa. It's impossible to tell now, but before the latest restoration, the façade had fallen into great disrepair. What you're seeing now is the original creamy marble color and paler background tones. The pillars have also been refurbished to their previous shade of ivory, which resembles travertine."

"Travertine?"

"A light-colored limestone used in early Roman construction. Once you know what it is, you'll recognize it all over Rome. I should have told you when we were at the *Fontana del Quattro Fiumi*. The rock in the center of the fountain is made of travertine. Anyway, the villa's original double staircase was altered to a pyramid shape in the eighteenth century. It too has been reconstructed and is topped by ancient vases containing cornucopias, though they are copies of the originals."

"Are the originals in the villa?"

"Unfortunately, no. They should be, but they're on display in the Louvre."

"And you hate it."

Nicola frowned. "Of course I do. As much, I imagine, as the Greeks hate that the Elgin Marbles are in the British Museum, but that's a story for another time."

Nicola presented her credentials at the desk and was given the tickets to enter at two o'clock. She turned to Emma. "You'll have to check your purse before we go in."

"After I do, I'd like to buy a guidebook. I may want to take a few notes as you talk."

"Good idea. I'll wait for you here."

Ten minutes later, guidebook in hand, Emma met Nicola near the door. "We have about five minutes before we can enter," Nicola said. "While we're waiting, I'll tell you about the museum collection. The original sculptures and paintings in the gallery belonged to Cardinal Scipione Borghese. As a patron of the arts, he was drawn to Renaissance works and contemporary pieces which he felt might generate a new golden age. He also promoted new sculptures, especially marble groups by new artists."

"Bernini."

"Among others."

Nicola's spiel was cut short by a man standing at the door to the first salon, who announced in English: "Those of you with tickets for two o'clock may enter." He repeated the announcement in Italian.

Nicola and Emma moved with a small crowd to the entrance. They presented their tickets and were admitted to the first room.

"I hate to ignore the fabulous pieces on display, beginning with the one over there of Pauline Bonaparte," Nicola said, "but to see and understand Bernini's sculptures we're going to have to leave some pieces as well as the rest of the museum for another day."

"But not Saturday."

"Not unless your station can pull strings to get us back in. I doubt I could do it twice."

"Nor would I ask you to."

"Whew, Nicola said. "For a minute I was worried. At least you'll be back to film."

"But only what we're seeing today."

"Then let's take a look at the statues. When we're finished, I'll give you a few minutes of free time. As we walk toward *Apollo and Daphne*, how about a little background?"

"Excellent," Emma said as she opened her guidebook and took out her pen.

"No need to take notes. The information, in much greater detail, is in your packet."

Emma nodded and closed the book as Nicola began to talk: "Between 1618 and 1625, Bernini produced a group of sculptures based on myths from the *Metamorphoses* and the Bible for Cardinal Borghese. Most critics, and I concur, believe they're the some of the finest sculptures he produced. Shall we start with my personal favorite of all Bernini's works?"

"Absolutely." They walked into the next room. "Amazing!" Emma exclaimed as they paused before a massive sculpture containing two entwined figures.

"This sculpture, which tells the final part of the myth of Apollo and Daphne, is a perfect example of what I mean about Bernini's ability to create movement in marble. Take a closer look. It depicts Daphne as she tries to escape from the pursuing Apollo—"

"And is being turned into a laurel tree."

"You're familiar with the story. I'm impressed. As far as the sculpture is concerned, you have to go all the way around to see Daphne's transformation. Go ahead. As you walk, look at your guidebook and take notes if you want." Nicola looked at her watch. "We're still on schedule."

"It's amazing how Bernini captures the exact moment when the nymph's toes take root," Emma said ten minutes later when she was back with Nicola in front of the statue. "You can almost see her fingers and hair sprout leaves. I'm going to use my favorite word again—"

"The sculpture is amazing," Nicola teased.

"It is."

"Do you have any questions?"

"Not at the moment. Show me more, though I'm not sure any of the other sculptures in the museum could come close to this one."

"Besides *Daphne and Apollo*, tell me what's on your must-cover list."

"*Pluto and Proserpina, David,* and the *Bust of Cardinal Borghese.*"

"Then let's move on to *Pluto and Proserpina.* Again, I'll talk while we walk. The sculpture depicts Pluto, the powerful god of the underworld, abducting Proserpina, the daughter of Ceres, who is the Roman goddess of harvest and fertility. Interceding with Jupiter, Ceres obtains permission for her daughter to return to earth for half the year—"

"And every spring the earth welcomes her home with a carpet of flowers."

"Again, I'm impressed. You obviously studied Roman mythology."

"In elementary school and a bit little in college art classes."

"Then I won't bother repeating the stories. I'll concentrate on the art. In *Pluto and Proserpina*, Bernini creates remarkable energy. If you use that line in your presentation when you come back to film the Borghese segment, you may want to have your cameraman walk around the statue with you to film all elements of the story as it unfolds."

"So, like in *Apollo and Daphne*, Bernini shows the elements of the story in a single piece."

"He does. Walk around and talk a look."

While Nicola waited, Emma spent ten more minutes studying the magnificent sculpture. "I'll try a new word to show my appreciation," she said as she returned to the place where she began. "The statue is incredible."

"I agree. Shall we move on to *David*?

"Okay, but after seeing this sculpture and *Apollo and Daphne*, I'm at a loss. How can I make my viewers see what I'm seeing and feel what I'm feeling?"

"I'm not sure you'll be able to, though I can hear the admiration for Bernini's works in your voice. Hopefully your viewers will hear it too."

"I'll have to make sure they do."

"I've said Bernini's work extends beyond the sculpture itself," Nicola said as they walked toward *David*. "In this magnificent piece, Bernini shows the young shepherd in the process of slinging a stone at the imaginary Goliath, who occupies a place behind the observer of the sculpture."

"He's out of sight, but the viewer, knowing the story, realizes he's there."

"Exactly. Cardinal Scipione gave Bernini the commission for the sculpture when the artist was only twenty-four years old. He completed the work in seven months."

"Really," Emma said. "It's amazing someone so young could be so skilled."

"It truly is. So once again, let me set the scene." This time instead of waiting for Emma to see the sculpture on her own, Nicola joined her, repeating the biblical story of David as they walked around the statue.

"It's magnificent," Emma said when they arrived back at their starting point.

"Not amazing?"

Emma smiled. "That too."

"Would you like another tidbit?"

"Need you ask?"

"David's face is a Bernini self-portrait executed with Cardinal Borghese's assistance. The cardinal held a mirror to enable Bernini to complete his work." Nicola held up her hand. "Don't say it."

"Say what?" Emma said, feigning ignorance.

"Now what could I be thinking?" Nicola didn't wait for Emma to respond. "Shall we take a look at Cardinal Borghese's bust?" she said, walking forward. "It's another excellent example of Bernini extending the sculpture beyond the medium. After we're finished, you'll have about a half-hour of free time. Go back and take notes about the statues we just saw, take a quick peek at the sculptures we skipped, or go upstairs and see the museum's fabulous painting collection, which includes some of Bernini's works. It's up to you, but first the bust. You can read a detailed account of the sculpture among the papers in your folder, but I do want to point out that, in the bust, Bernini captures his patron turning to address an unknown person."

"As in the statue of David, a subject beyond the sculpture itself."

"Yes, you're an excellent student."

"Who is eager to hear more from her amazing teacher."

Nicola smiled and took a bow. "There's a second, identical version of the sculpture here in the museum. When he finished the first, Bernini discovered a small defect in the marble in the cardinal's forehead. In order to satisfy his patron, in just fifteen days, he made the second from a perfect piece of marble."

"Another tidbit."

"I'll add it to the tidbit list tonight. So go see the museum. I'll meet you back at the bookstore at four."

Emma spent her free time taking a closer look at the sculptures they'd just discussed. Standing in front of each piece, she read the blurb in the guidebook and jotted down her own thoughts as well as some of the interesting points Nicola had made. By four, she knew what she wanted to tell her viewers, though she still had no idea how to convey her feelings.

"This is an incredible place," Emma said as she and Nicola left the building and walked by the formal gardens on the way to the car. "I wish I had more time to explore."

"Next time you're in Rome—"

"The Borghese will be at the top of my list."

Definitely pleased, Nicola nodded. Because her home was nearby, she said good-bye at the car, telling Emma she'd see her at the concierge desk at 8:30 in the morning.

When Giro dropped Emma at her hotel, repeating what Nicola said about seeing her tomorrow, she was almost afraid to go in. Would Michael Kelsey be in the lobby? Would he see her? *I dodged him once today, I can do it again. I'm too tired to worry about Michael or anything else,* she mused as she pushed through the revolving door. Once again, she was relieved when Michael was nowhere to be seen.

Mr. Ferrari was busy with another guest, but he saw her out of the corner of his eye, smiled, and waved. Emma picked up her keycard at the desk and, too tired to walk up the stairs, took the elevator to the fourth floor.

Entering her room, she immediately kicked off her shoes. *Oh God, I was supposed to call Jack when I got here,* she thought as she opened her e-mail. It was 10:15 in the morning in Boston, and she didn't want to awaken her boss, so she e-mailed him saying she'd arrived safely and telling him about the day with Nicola, including the great lunch.

Not wanting to disturb Mr. Ferrari, she called the Doney, the hotel restaurant, and made a reservation for eight o'clock. She arranged for a 7:15 wake-up call so she could get ready for dinner and then plopped down on the bed for a much-needed nap.

———

When the phone rang, Emma was sound asleep. She picked up the receiver, and knowing the call would be a recording, set it back down. For a short time she thought about skipping dinner and going back to sleep, but realizing she had to get herself acclimated to Rome time, she dragged herself off the bed, took a shower, and dressed in one of the three dresses she'd brought with her.

She took the elevator to the lobby and rounded the corner to the Doney. The room was about half full, and the maître d' led her to a table by the window overlooking the Via Veneto. "Is this satisfactory, or would you prefer to dine outside?" he asked.

"This table's perfect," Emma said, smiling.

"Your waiter will be right over, but before he comes, may I suggest a bottle of wine?"

Emma wasn't sure she'd make it through dinner if she drank. *But why not*, she thought. *I'm in Rome. I should enjoy myself.* "That would be wonderful," she said. "Is there something you recommend? I prefer white."

"Then I suggest Blange Cerreto. It's a crisp Italian wine which goes well with fish if that's what you're considering for dinner. We serve a light Mediterranean cuisine at the

Doney which features several unique fish specialties which your waiter will tell you about."

"The Blange Cerreto sounds perfect."

The maître d' returned with the bottle and a glass as the waiter served a small complimentary appetizer. "It's smoked fish, endive, and carrot," he said as he handed her a menu.

Emma tasted the fish. "Delicious," she said.

"I'll give you a few minutes to enjoy your wine before I take your order."

"Grazie," Emma said.

She sipped the wine while she watched the people pass by the window. Deep in her own reverie, thinking about the day she'd spent with Nicola and how she'd present the information to her audience, she heard a deep, familiar voice. "Julia Phillips. It's interesting I should meet you here at the Doney, especially since you're not registered at the hotel."

Emma turned and looked up to see Michael, who was clearly annoyed. "You checked at the desk?" she asked.

"Of course I did." He glared. "After our pleasant plane ride, I thought you might like to have dinner with me."

"Why?" Emma said in disbelief. "Because you're so famous and it would be an honor for me to be seen with you? You're incorrigible."

Michael snickered. "But you have to admit I'm loveable. So, Julia Phillips, who are you? You're obviously not who you said you were."

Emma hesitated. *What the hell,* she thought. She frowned as she spoke. "I'm the rookie blonde bimbo you're going to outdo so easily."

Michael was clearly surprised. When he spoke, his voice exuded hostility. "You deceitful—"

"I may be deceitful, but I'm not an over-proud, arrogant, self-centered, wannabe-Geraldo reporter who thinks he's God's gift to women, or, for that matter, the TV audience in general."

Michael was obviously startled by Emma's bitter indictment. He scowled and raised his voice. "And that's your opinion of me?" he said, looking astonished.

"How could it be anything else? Weren't you the one who suffered under the illusion that I, like all women, would bow down and kiss your feet? You haughtily told me how proud and excited I should be to have a seat on the plane next to you? Believe me, I was anything but happy, especially when I had to listen to your braggadocio every minute I was awake. You're an ass and you can kiss mine."

"I love you too," Michael growled.

Emma couldn't believe what she'd said or why she continued to allow Michael Kelsey get to her. Her eyes followed him as he smirked, turned, and stomped out of the dining room.

It wasn't long before the maître d', who obviously observed the entire encounter, came to the table. "Is everything all right?" he asked tentatively.

Emma sighed. "It is. I apologize for making a scene."

"You didn't, but you're obviously upset."

"More surprised than upset, but I'll be fine. If you'll send the waiter over, I'd like to order. I'm tired after a long trip and an even longer day. I need a good night's sleep."

The waiter recommended a starter of pasta with fresh sausage and fennel seed. Emma ordered that and his other suggestion, grilled fillet of amberjack, a wild Mediterranean sea bass, prepared with capers, lemon, and marjoram served on a bed of spinach—a house specialty.

Probably because he felt sorry for her, the maître d' brought Emma a small dish of lemon mousse with a pistachio sauce. "Grazie molto," she said, "A perfect ending to a perfect meal, *and it would have been had Michael decided to eat elsewhere and not seen me in the restaurant.*

After charging the meal to her room, Emma went back into the lobby and took the elevator to the fourth floor. When she got to her room, the light on the telephone by her bed was blinking. She picked up the receiver and pushed the voicemail button. "You have one message," the computerized voice announced.

In seconds she heard Michael's voice. "There's no way you're going to beat this pompous ass," he said hostilely. "I'm going to kick yours."

"We'll see about that," Emma told the recording defiantly, "but not tonight." She sighed and got ready for bed, though she wondered if Michael Kelsey would haunt her dreams.

CHAPTER SIX

Light was peeking through a crack in the drapes when Emma opened her eyes. "My God, what time is it?" she mumbled as she rolled over and looked at the clock. She sighed. It was only seven; thirty minutes before her scheduled wakeup call.

She got up, stumbled to the bathroom, and stared in the mirror. "I look like I've been on an all-night bender," she groaned as she turned on the shower.

The pulsating water beating on her from four nozzle levels helped to wash away the grogginess. She dressed in a pair of navy blue slacks and a tailored blouse and left her room to go downstairs for breakfast.

The restaurant was set for a buffet. A long table covered with chafing dishes over Bunsen burners sat along the back wall of the room, and large, round tables filled the center. As a different maître d' from the night before led her to a table, Emma glanced at the pastries, fruits, juices, cereals, and assorted breads waiting to tempt her.

She waved aside the menu, telling the waiter she'd have the buffet. "Coffee and orange juice?" he asked.

"Both, thanks."

"Regular or decaf?"

"Something that will help me get rid of my lingering jet lag."

As she waited for the coffee to arrive, Emma looked around the room. "Oh my God!" she whispered. *The ass is standing at the omelet station.*

She considered leaving before Michael saw her, but she abruptly thought better of it. *Why should I let the jerk drive me out of here? I'm staying at the hotel, and I'm not the one who was childish enough to leave an angry message.*

She watched Michael take his omelet to a table close to the pastries and then stood up. *There's no way in hell he won't see me, so why wait?* she thought. She deliberately walked alongside Michael's table. "Good morning, Mr. Kelsey," she said, smiling defiantly.

When Michael looked up to see who was speaking, Emma wondered if he was shocked to see her in the restaurant or surprised she had the nerve to speak to him. "Morning," he said gruffly.

Even knowing it would be wise to move on without saying anything else, Emma couldn't help herself. "I hope you slept well," she said sarcastically. "I certainly did."

"I slept very well, thanks," he said without making eye contact.

"I'm sure you did. Enjoy your breakfast. You're going to need all the sustenance you can get if you plan to kick my ass." She turned her back and headed toward the hot food tables, leaving Michael with his mouth open.

She filled her plate with scrambled eggs, bacon, and a small scoop of potatoes. Knowing Michael was watching, she walked back to the center tables containing the cold selections, once again deliberately passing close to where he was sitting. *Chalk one up for me,* she mused as she put a pastry and several slices of cantaloupe on her plate, and, head held high, returned to her own table.

She was finishing her second cup of coffee when she sensed someone standing by her table. Thinking it was the waiter coming to give her a refill, she looked up. It was Michael. This time he didn't seem angry, but self-conscious and ill at ease.

As she waited for him to speak first, Emma held her breath. She had no idea what the man wanted, and she definitely didn't need another unpleasant encounter. "Emma. May I call you that?" he said amiably. Not waiting for her to answer one way or another, he continued: "There's no excuse for my rude and boorish behavior on the plane, and I sincerely apologize for acting so atrociously when I saw you having dinner in here last night."

Though there was tension in his voice, Emma heard no sarcasm, so she softened slightly. "I can't condone your behavior, but I can certainly understand why you'd be furious with me," she said. "No one likes to be deceived."

She wasn't sure, but she thought she saw Michael's eyes flash. He paused for a moment and took a deep breath as if marshaling his thoughts. "I suppose that's true," he said calmly. "More particularly, I'd like to say I'm sorry for the rude message I left on your phone. It was childish. I've never been so unprofessional. I have no idea why I lashed out at you. I regret my behavior and, I repeat, I'm sorry."

Emma's smile was heartfelt. "Apology accepted," she said, "and while we're at it, I'm sorry I provoked you and called you those less than flattering names. Like you, lashing out isn't my usual MO."

"Maybe it's time for us to make peace." He smiled and extended his hand. "I'm Michael Kelsey, and you are?"

Emma hesitated. "Emma Bradford." She grasped his hand. "Nice to meet you, Michael Kelsey." Emma couldn't tell if Michael was going to continue or not. She felt a little better about him, but she wasn't at a point where she wanted him to sit down and talk.

Apparently Michael felt the same way. "So, Emma Bradford," he said with a smile, "have a good day. I'm sure you have a lot to do. I believe you told me you were out to best some cocky reporter who's been assigned to the same story you're covering."

Emma smiled. "I am, though the reporter you're referring to isn't *quite* as horrible as I first thought he was."

"Good to know. Maybe I'll see you later."

"Possibly. If not, have a good day."

When Michael left the dining room, Emma leaned back in the chair. "What just happened?" she wondered aloud. "Did I just spend two minutes feeling good about Michael Kelsey?" *Who the hell is this guy? Is he the jerk I met on the plane ride, the ass who left me the message last night, or the nice guy who just walked away from my table?* "I guess only time will tell," she whispered.

Emma finished a third cup of coffee before going upstairs to her room. With a short time to spare, she turned on her computer. There was an e-mail from Jack complaining that she was in Rome while he was stuck in Boston covering Mayor Marino. She e-mailed him about Nicola and where she was with the story. She followed that e-mail with a quick note to her parents, and then she freshened up and went to meet Nicola for a second day of touring.

When she reached the bottom of the stairs near the concierge desk, Nicola was talking with Mr. Ferrari. "Are you ready to go?" she asked. "Giro's waiting."

"I am," Emma said. "Buongiorno. How are you this morning, Mr. Ferrari?"

The concierge's eyes sparkled. "Molto bene, grazie."

Emma smiled. "I hope your day continues to go well."

"Enjoy your tour of Saint Peter's," said the concierge. "You have a very good guide."

"I'm sure I will. Thank you."

As they walked toward the car, Nicola handed Emma several sheets of paper stapled together. "The tidbits I promised to provide," she said. "I had fun preparing the list."

"And I'm sure I'll enjoy reading and incorporating what you wrote into the reports."

Giro was holding the door. "Buongiorno, Emma," he said cheerily.

"Buongiorno. It's a beautiful day," said Emma.

"It is. The sun is warm, but not too hot, and there's a nice breeze." He turned to Nicola. "Are we still going to the Vatican?"

"We are." As before, Nicola got into the front passenger seat. "And, Giro," she said, "please approach the basilica from the Via della Conciliazione."

As Giro pulled away from the hotel, Nicola looked back at Emma. "While we drive I'm going to try to give you information about Vatican City and Saint Peter's, but only what you'll be able to use in your reports."

"So we can concentrate on Bernini when we get to the basilica."

"That's right. Everything I'm telling you is in my notes." Nicola paused, took a small breath, and began: "In the first century, Vatican City was an empty hill on the west side of the Tiber opposite the city of Rome. Between AD 14 and AD 33, Agrippina the Elder, the first Emperor Augustus' granddaughter, drained the low hill and surrounding areas so she'd have a place for her gardens. Later in the first century, Caligula began to construct a circus on the site, though it wasn't finished until after his death. That task was left to his son, Agrippina's tyrannical and extravagant grandson, Nero. If we had time I could go on for hours about Nero's rule; maybe while we're driving on Saturday."

"I'd like that. So let me understand. The area which is now Vatican City wasn't always associated with the church?"

"No, but like before, since you won't have time to include ancient history in your reports, I'll concentrate on Bernini and his association with Saint Peter's, but first I want to give you a few essential facts about Vatican City. It's a landlocked, sovereign city-state; a walled enclave of about a hundred acres within the city of Rome. The territory includes Saint Peter's square, distinguished from the territory of Italy by a white line along the limit of the square just outside the ellipse formed by Bernini's colonnade."

"Though I have a general idea, would you succinctly define ellipse and colonnade?" Emma asked. "I may want to use the terms in my presentation from the square and I want to be accurate."

"Certainly," Nicola said. "Simply put, an ellipse is a stretched circle with slightly longer, flatter sides. A colonnade is a row of columns supporting a roof which creates an arcade, or covered walkway."

"Thanks."

"You're welcome. Moving on, Vatican City has a population of around nine hundred, so it's the smallest state in the world both in terms of population and area."

Giro turned onto the Via della Conciliazione. "We're now on the grand approach which runs from the Tiber River to Saint Peter's," he said.

"I have goose bumps just thinking of where I am," said Emma.

"You're not the first of my clients to say that," Nicola said. "This avenue was constructed by Benito Mussolini after he signed the Lateran Treaty, which recognized the Vatican State as sovereign territory. You should know that Vatican City is an absolute theocracy. It's ruled by the Bishop of Rome, who is chosen for life by a conclave of cardinals. The bishop, aka the pope, has a secular title: Sovereign of the State of Vatican City. This is different from his religious authority over the Holy See, the central governing body of the Roman Catholic Church."

"Then the Vatican and the Holy See aren't one in the same?" Emma said.

"No, they're two separate entities. The term 'Holy See,' in Latin, '*Sancta Sedes*,' refers to the pope's spiritual and pastoral power. In essence, it's the central government of the church which allows the Vatican to make treaties and send or receive diplomatic representatives. The highest state functionaries of Holy See are the clergymen of the Catholic Church."

"It sounds complicated."

"It really isn't. All you have to remember is there are really two states within one and the pope heads both—the secular and the religious."

Nicola turned to Giro. "Would you park for a few minutes before driving up to the barricade to let us out? I'd like to give Emma a few facts about Saint Peter's before we begin our tour."

"Certainly."

Giro found a parking place in front of a souvenir shop near the end of Via della Conciliazione and backed in as Nicola continued: "The current Saint Peter's, which was begun in 1506, replaced an earlier church of the same name. It was begun by Constantine in AD 323, but not completed until after his death. Over the years, many prominent artists and architects, including Bramante, Raphael, Michelangelo, and Maderno, have modified and changed the shape of the basilica. It was Maderno who designed the palatial façade with a balcony above the central door where the pope delivers his blessing. This became a problem for Bernini. Shall we get out and go see what I'm talking about?"

"Absolutely," Emma said as Giro got out and opened her door.

"When should I come back for you?" he asked Nicola.

"I made 1:30 lunch reservations, so how about one? That should give us plenty of time to get to the Travestere, even if we encounter traffic." She looked at Emma. "What time do you need to be back to the Excelsior?"

"I'm meeting my producer and cameraman in the lobby at three."

"Then we'll enjoy a leisurely lunch. While we're eating I'll answer any questions you may have after our morning tour." She turned to Giro. "We'll see you at one, Giro."

They walked to the wrought-iron portable fence separating Rome and Vatican City. "I can't believe I'm standing outside Saint Peter's Square," Emma said as she looked toward the façade. "On television I've watched so much history play out here over the years: Easter and Christmas blessings, papal elections when the cameras focus on the white smoke coming from the Sistine chapel, and massive funerals like the one held for Pope John Paul the Twenty-third."

"I confess I'm still moved every time I come here," Nicola said, "but I guarantee, what you're feeling now will pale in comparison to what you experience when you go inside the basilica for the first time."

Emma breathed in the scene in front of her. Even at the relatively early hour, the piazza was a beehive of activity. Excited tourists, trying not to trip over one another as they looked upward instead of straight ahead, followed guides brandishing closed, mostly red, umbrellas high above their heads. Awestruck nuns in traditional habits ambled slowly as they marveled at the grandeur of the piazza and the basilica looming above it, while priests in cassocks, rushing to work, all but ignored the magnificent scene.

"Okay," Emma said after several minutes, "I'm ready, though I could stand here and people-watch for hours."

"I'm sorry we don't have the time. If we're going to fit a month's worth of viewing into one day—"

"We have to keep moving."

"Yes, but because the square was Bernini's design, we should spend a little more time out here before going inside. The square as you see it now was built between 1656 and 1667. See the Egyptian obelisk in the middle?"

"It's pretty hard to miss," Emma said, her eyes focused on the giant obelisk. "Don't you find it ironic that a pagan monument graces the greatest Christian square in the world?"

"That same thought often crosses my mind. But what was once pagan is now dedicated to the Holy Cross and has become a symbol of humanity reaching out to Christ. Since you won't be able to say much about the obelisk in your report, I won't talk about it and the other notable places in the piazza until Saturday."

"I already wonder if we'll be able to visit every place I want to see in one day," Emma said.

Nicola shook her head. "Probably not. You'll have to start making a list of things you want to see next time you're in Rome."

"I'll do that. So tell me about Bernini and Saint Peter's Square."

"With pleasure. Bernini conceived the piazza as an enormous six-hundred-fifty-foot oval encircled by two colonnades consisting of a hundred-eighty-four Doric columns and eighty-eight pillars of travertine marble arranged in four rows and topped by an entablature with one-hundred forty saints."

"Entablature?"

"A structure that lies between the columns and the roof. Bernini referred to the colonnades as the 'motherly arms of the Church.' They had three symbolic purposes. They were meant to embrace Catholics and reinforce their belief, plead with heretics to reunite with the church, and show agnostics the true faith. You said you watched Easter services on television."

"For as long as I can remember."

"Then you know the pope blesses the crowd in the square from the Benediction Loggia above the central entrance to the basilica. It's also here where the words '*Habemus Papam*,' are spoken to announce a new pope and where he gives the *Urbi et Orbi* blessing to the city and the world; thus the problem Maderno created. Bernini had to design a piazza where the events taking place on the Loggia could be seen by everyone gathered below. But there was another ceremony he had to take into consideration: a papal blessing given to pilgrims from the window of the pope's private apartments, up there at the right end of the third floor of the Apostolic Palace."

"Those are the pope's apartments?" Emma asked, her voice exuding excitement.

"They are. I'll come back to them in a moment. First let me finish with the piazza. Besides the two issues I just mentioned, Bernini faced a third problem. In keeping with its prominence among the churches of the Catholic world, the basilica required a grand approach with covered areas for processions and protection against the sun and rain for pedestrians and coaches. Taking all this into consideration, in March 1657, he presented his design. Shall I elaborate?"

"Personally, I'd like to hear everything, but in terms of my needs for the Bernini segments, I don't think so. I'll probably stop with the number of columns and the saints perched on top."

Nicola smiled. "I like the perched line. Do you have what you need here?"

"I'm sure I do," said Emma.

"Then because you're interested, I'll return to the pope's apartments. The pope occupies two floors." She pointed to the top of the building. "On the upper floor, the third when you're looking up from here, he resides with his two private secretaries and a few servants. On the floor below he receives visitors in several opulent reception rooms."

"The third floor windows are open," Emma said excitedly. "Do you think the pontiff will be at the opening of the exhibition tomorrow?"

"I don't know for sure. The Vatican newspaper, *L'Osservatore Romano*, reports he's been suffering from a virulent flu bug, but despite his illness, he insisted on coming to Rome. I imagine you'll see him from the one of those windows, and, if he's feeling better, at the reception. Will you be attending?"

"I'll know later today when I meet with my producer. I certainly hope so."

"Maybe you and Michael can attend together," Nicola teased.

Emma frowned. "I'm sure he'd love to take me."

They stood in the security line for about five minutes. When they got to the checkpoint, Emma took off her fanny pack and put it on the belt. "You can wear it into the church," Nicola said, "but I won't be able to take my backpack with me. There's a check room right below the stairs, so we'll stop there for a minute before climbing up to the portico."

When Emma finished using the nearby restroom, Nicola was waiting at the base of the stairs. "Before we go inside, let's take a look at Bernini's statue of Constantine in the right portico," she said. "Bernini was given the Constantine commission by Pope Innocent X in 1654, but the statue wasn't completed until 1670, during the reign of Pope Clement X. It's considered to be one of Bernini's masterpieces."

Emma glanced at the list of Bernini's works the station had provided. "The sculpture isn't on my must-cover list," she said. "Is it worth mentioning in one of my segments?"

"In my opinion, yes, if for no other reason than as a further example of the theme we discussed at the Borghese— the movement in Bernini's sculptures." They stopped about ten feet from the statue." I'm going to describe the sculpture. As I do, I'd like for you to note the words I emphasize."

"I'm listening," Emma said.

"Good. Bernini has seized the moment when Constantine was struck by the vision of the labarum in the sky."

"Labarum?"

"A military banner carried out in front of Roman emperors. Constantine's labarum contained Christian symbols which proclaimed his conversion. So, in the sculpture, the emperor sits astride a *galloping*, or some say, *rearing*, horse. Bernini has carved an expression of disbelief on the Emperor's face as with *outstretched* arm he *gazes* toward the heavens. He is *startled* by the apparition of the cross appearing above him and the Greek words saying: 'In this sign you shall conquer.'

"The startled look, another example of Baroque artists attempting to create realistic facial expressions," Emma said.

Nicola nodded. "Behind the group is a large marble drapery which imitates fringed damask interwoven with gold. It *flutters* in a mystical wind *blowing in* from the west, which symbolizes divine inspiration. The drapery emphasizes the movement of the horse and, at the same time, acts as a sort of background. Speaking of the horse, take a closer look. There's an incredible sense of tension expressed in the animal's *protruding* eyes, the swollen muscles of its legs, and the veins of its belly."

"Galloping, rearing, gazes, startled, flutters, blowing, charging, protruding. I hear and see the extraordinary amount of movement in the sculpture," Emma said, appreciation on her face and in her voice. "I'll definitely fit Constantine into my report, perhaps when I enter the basilica to talk about what Bernini created inside."

Nicola nodded. "Are you ready to go in?"

"Ready and excited."

Emma gasped when entered the immense basilica. "Oh my God. It's unbelievable," she said with awe. "The people up near the main altar look like dwarfs."

"Before I begin the Bernini tour, I'm going to give you a half-hour to walk around on your own. Take a look at the Pieta, the chapels, the monuments. Like millions of pilgrims before you, rub Saint Peter's foot. Do anything you want. I suggest you take a look at the middle altar in the gallery of the left transept. It's the spot where Saint Peter died in Nero's circus, but I'll stop talking. If I mention everything

I want you to see in this incredible place, we'd still be here tomorrow morning and you wouldn't have begun your thirty minute tour. So enjoy your free time, short though it is. From here on, it's only Bernini."

CHAPTER SEVEN

"There aren't words to describe what I think," Emma said when she rejoined Nicola. "Fabulous is an adjective that comes to mind, though it can't come near to what I'm feeling."

"At lunch you can tell me about everything you saw. Now we're going to take a look at Bernini's fabulous bronze baldachino. Before I tell you about it, I want to stress yet again: I'm only providing information you might be able to use in your report."

"I wish we had time for you to show me everything."

"So do I, but unfortunately, we don't. First a little background about the baldachino. Urban the Seventh wanted a monumental structure to mark the location of Saint Peter's tomb. In 1606, Paul the Fifth had placed a nine-meter-high wooden canopy over the altar, which, in Urban's mind, was unsuitable for the grandiosity of the basilica. In 1624, with no economic restrictions, he commissioned Bernini to build an inspiring structure worthy of its location and function. The result of the collaboration between the two men was arguably the most important bronze structure in Roman Baroque art and architecture. The baldachino occupied a good part of Bernini's time from 1626 to 1633. From the beginning, the enormous undertaking was plagued with problems which would have intimidated a lesser man."

"Bernini did all of this by himself?"

"No. He collaborated with other artists and architects, including Borromini and Maderno."

Emma tilted her head. "Bernini actually worked with Borromini?"

"He did," Nicola said, smiling, "which shows feuds can be suspended and competitors can work together."

"If you're talking about Michael and me, perish the thought."

"Whatever you say," Nicola said. "So, back to Bernini's creation. Here's a line you might use in your presentation: 'arguably, the baldachino is a perfect illustration of the enormous change from the simplicity of early Christian architecture to the flamboyance of the Baroque.'"

"It's incredible." Emma shook her head. "Amazing, incredible, I'm beginning to sound like a broken record.

"Not at all," Nicola said. "I could talk about the baldachino for hours, but staying on topic, tell me where you see movement in the structure."

Emma walked up to the altar and looked more closely. "There's movement in the spiral fluting of the columns and in the canopy, which, it seems, is supposed to imitate cloth."

"Good—what else?"

"In the draping decorated with chains of flowers hanging in loops. They appear to be fluttering in the breeze."

"Excellent. It won't be long before you don't need me anymore. Take a closer look before we move on to the main altar."

"I'll need at least a dozen thirty-minute segments to report adequately," Emma said when she arrived back at her starting point.

"Then let me make your job more difficult and give you even more to think about. Above the main altar is another of Bernini's masterpieces—his splendid, gilt-bronze *Cathedra di San Pietro*, or Saint Peter's Throne. This was the last of the large monuments the great artist designed for the basilica."

"The Alpha and the Omega," Emma said, a pensive look on her face.

"Exactly. The altar completes the forty years Bernini spent decorating the interior of Saint Peter's. When he finished the cathedra, his son, Domenico, wrote poignantly, 'he created the beginning and the end of that great Basilica,' referring of course to the portico and this altar at the westernmost end of the basilica. So your Alpha and Omega comment is almost a quote."

"I have goose bumps."

"Believe it or not, so do I, and I've been here hundreds of times. This is the final collaboration between Bernini and his great patron, Alexander the Seventh. It's clear Bernini always intended the Cathedra Petri to be glimpsed through and framed by the baldachino. The long approach up the nave was to be made all the more exciting by the partial vision. The visitor finally moving from behind the baldachino is finally treated to a burst of glory. See the wooden and ivory chair?"

Emma looked closely and pointed. "Up there."

"Yes. For centuries, the faithful believed it belonged to Saint Peter. It turned out this was another legend. Using modern techniques, archaeologists now date the chair from around the ninth century, but whether Saint Peter sat on it or not, it symbolizes the power of the pope and the continuity of the teachings of the church."

"Once again, amazing!" Emma exclaimed. "How will I be able to find appropriate words to express my admiration for the cathedra and for the rest of Bernini's sculptures?"

"The audience will understand. Your admiration shows on your face."

"I hope you're right."

"Right about what?" Emma heard a deep, growling voice behind her. "Fancy meeting you here. Sightseeing, or are you working?"

"Michael Kelsey, I might ask you the same thing," Emma said irritably.

"Working, of course. I just left the Alexander Monument."

"You're seeing Saint Peter's on your own?"

"No way. Apparently you aren't either."

"I'm sorry." Emma turned to Nicola. "Michael Kelsey, this is my guide, Doctor Nicola Adriani. Nicola has two advanced degrees in art history."

Michael extended his hand and snickered. "Really? A doctor. I'm impressed. Nice to meet you, *Doctor* Nicola. I hope you're not giving Emma too much interesting information. In case she hasn't told you, I'm her competition."

Nicola smiled. "I think she mentioned your rivalry once or twice."

"I'll bet she didn't use flattering words."

Nicola started to respond, but Michael cut her off. "Only kidding," he said, grinning.

There was no time for further comment. Coming from the direction of Alexander's tomb, a handsome priest approached the group. *Another hunk off limits because of the stupid celibacy rules,* Emma thought.

"This is my *expert* guide, Monsignor Steven Laurent. Emma, I told you I came to Rome to see him get his current gig."

He turned toward the priest, who rolled his eyes. "Steven, this is the infamous Emma and her Vatican guide, *Doctor* Nicola Adriani."

When he obnoxiously stressed the word "doctor," Emma grimaced. *The ass is back,* she thought.

Steven extended his hand, and his eyes smiled when he spoke. "It's so nice to meet you, Emma. Michael told me all about you." He then shook hands with Nicola. "Doctor Adriani."

"Nice to meet you, Monsignor. Please call me Nicola. Mr. Kelsey's putting too much emphasis on my education."

"Steven, please. I don't stand on formalities when I'm talking with friends."

Emma laughed. "If Michael's told you about me, I'm surprised you think I'm a friend."

Steven looked puzzled. "Am I missing something?"

"Forget it," Michael said crossly. He turned to Emma. "Steven's my Bernini source, and, believe me, he's great."

"I'm afraid my old friend exaggerates my knowledge of Bernini, and, frankly, I can't imagine why he'd feel the need," Steven said.

Emma looked at the handsome priest. He was slender with a square jaw, expressive, large brown eyes, and a thick mop of unruly, dark-brown hair.

Seemingly recognizing Emma's thoughts, Steven brushed his hair from his face. "I'm sure after flying all the way from New York to Rome with Michael, you know to take what he says with a grain of salt."

Emma grinned. "That's an understatement. Michael said you've known each other for a long time."

"Sometimes I think it's been too long. We went to elementary school and high school together."

"And nursery school," Michael added.

"Our mothers were best friends before we were born," said Steven. "After high school I was blessed to attend Notre Dame while Michael went off to some insignificant college. I can't seem to recall the name." He paused. "Ah yes, now I remember. It's a little place called Yale. Despite my friend's inferior education, I chose to keep him around. I rarely tease him about the sad fact he wasn't accepted by my Alma Mater."

"Or rather opted to turn down their generous scholarship offer to go Ivy League," Michael said flippantly.

"Emma, are you going to believe a priest, a representative of God on earth, or this brute?"

Emma laughed. "Do you need to ask?"

Steven continued: "Over the years we've managed to remain close, though sometimes I wonder why I put up with my friend here. I guess it's because every once in a while he surprises me. Recently, he was kind enough to join me and my family in Rome when I became a monsignor."

"And now you're helping him beat me." Noticing Steven's quizzical look, she said: "Michael didn't tell you that he and I are bitter rivals."

"Quite the contrary. He said he watched several of your reports, and admires your skills and ability to connect with the audience."

Really?" Emma said dubiously. "I can't—"

"Weren't you going to show me the baldachino, or whatever it's called?" Michael said quickly, turning to Steven. "I'm sure we're keeping our friends here from continuing with their tour."

"Anytime you're ready." Steven turned to Emma: "Would you like to join Michael and me for dinner tonight? I'm taking our friend to one of my favorite restaurants."

Emma fought to keep from laughing when she saw the stunned look on Michael's face. At first she was going to refuse the invitation, but seeing Michael look so uncomfortable, she reconsidered. "How nice of you to ask, Steven," she said. "I have a three o'clock meeting with my producer and cameraman, but we should be finished in an hour or so. I imagine they'll want to head out and take some preliminary shots. They won't need me, so I'd love to join you."

"You don't have to spend the evening preparing?" Michael smiled, but his eyes weren't smiling. He wasn't asking—he was pleading with her to tell him she needed to stay in and work.

At that point, even if she needed to write copy, Emma was going to dinner, if only to watch Michael squirm. If she had to, she'd stay up all night to be ready. "No," she said. "Thanks to *Doctor* Nicola, I have everything I need for all seven broadcasts."

Steven seemed to be enjoying the repartee between Michael and his competition. "So, my friend, why don't you bring Emma to the restaurant with you?" he said. "I'll meet you both at Dal Bolognese at eight. After we leave here, I'll call and change the reservation." He winked conspiratorially at Emma. "The place is crowded, but I eat there twice a week. We won't have a problem."

"You eat out that often?" Emma asked.

Steven chuckled. "Emma, I'm not a cloistered monk, nor am I poor."

"You can say that again," Michael said sarcastically.

Steven shot him a look and turned back to Emma. "I often say Mass at Santa Maria del Popolo, and since the restaurant is in the Piazza del Popolo, it's a convenient place to stop in for a bite afterwards. Dal Bolognese is one of Rome's in-places for writers and artists. Knowing what I do about you, I have no doubt you'll enjoy it."

"One of the 'in-places' you frequent," Michael teased. "Monsignor or not, you haven't changed a bit. Eating well is one of your sins."

Steven laughed. "But certainly not yours, my friend."

"I look forward to joining you and hearing more about your friendship, or whatever it is you two share," Emma said. "I'm fascinated." She turned to Michael. "See you later?"

Michael grimaced. "I suppose I'll meet you in the lobby at 7:30."

"Now that your plans are made, shall we take a look at the monument to Alexander the Seventh?" Nicola asked Emma. "Nice to meet you, Monsignor; Michael."

Michael nodded. "Bye *Doctor* Nicola. Have a good day."

"Oh we will," Emma said with a snide smile.

"Your Michael Kelsey is worried you'll have the better report," Nicola said once Michael and Steven were out of ear-shot. "He seems brash and blustery, but, in my opinion, he's not as awful as you make him out to be. Clearly he hasn't poisoned the monsignor's mind against you."

"That may be true, but you have to admit, he was acting like a jerk when he kept calling you doctor over and over. He was a lot better than he was on the plane coming over here, though not as pleasant as he was when he stopped by my table at breakfast this morning. I'll be interested to see which Michael shows up for dinner tonight." She laughed. "I love how uncomfortable he was when Steven asked me to join them."

"You'll have to tell me all about it when we meet on Saturday, but now, back to work if you want to have the best Bernini report. It's obvious Michael has a knowledge-able guide."

Emma laughed. "But so do I, *Doctor* Nicola."

"In that case, I'll try to live up to your expectations. This is the second monumental papal tomb Bernini cre-ated in Saint Peter's," she explained as they approached the Alexander Monument. "It was commissioned by the Pope Alexander during the final years of his papacy and completed in 1678, the year after the pope died. Bernini was eighty when he created the design, so because of his advanced age, he supervised the sculptors who translated his drawings onto marble, though it's said he himself put the finishing touches on the pope's face."

"Another legend?"

"It's supposed to be true. The finished product epitomizes Baroque style as well as the art of funeral monuments in general. Did I mention that Alexander's reign encompassed the golden age of the Roman Baroque? During the twelve years he was pope, it reached its pinnacle and heard its swan song."

"Another good line," Emma said.

"Hopefully you can use this too: Bernini's monument perfectly portrays Fabio Chigi, who became Pope Alexander. At the time of his election, which incidentally took eighty days, he was fifty-six years old. As in the case of the sculpture of Saint Theresa, the revelation of the passions of the soul through the realistic sculpting of facial features can be seen in the rendering of the pope. Alexander was a delicate patrician with a narrow, finely-chiseled face and a high forehead. From his expression, it is clear he was penitent and devout, ever mindful of this transitory life, but above all, he was an intellectual who was determined to advance the cause of learning. Another tidbit?"

"Need you ask?"

"The pope kept his coffin in his bedroom and a skull carved by Bernini on his writing table."

"Why would he do that?"

"Because he felt he would be a better pope if he thought about death and realized he was mortal."

Emma shook her head. "Lord, how will I fit everything I want to say into the allotted time? The schedule says I'm to report on both the Alexander and Urban monuments in one segment, so, though it kills me to ask, please give me just the basics."

"I'll try, but considering this is my favorite Bernini sculpture in Saint Peter's, it won't be easy. In Alexander's face and position in the sculpture, Bernini created a sense of spiritual humility. Follow with your eyes as I talk. The kneeling pope, carved in white marble, his hands clasped before him, is perched high up on a pedestal. Note he looks up as if concentrating on heavenly things. The monument is topped by four statues, the virtues which distinguished the pope's life. They are Justice, Prudence, Charity and Truth. In this tomb, Truth, who also symbolizes religion, has a sorrowful expression. Look at her foot to see why."

Emma moved closer. "It's placed on a globe."

"But not just anywhere; on England, symbolizing the pope's futile attempts to quell the rise of Anglicanism."

"The Counter-Reformation."

"Exactly. Like before, I'll give you a few minutes to take a closer look."

Emma walked up to the monument. As she looked at Truth, she again thought of the question she'd asked both Giro and Nicola. *Why Bernini? Why now? As Truth's foot is placed on England, is Cardinal Amici symbolically putting his foot on Pope John's liberal ideas and policies, policies the cardinal feels will damage the church?* she wondered. *Is this a significant story behind the story?* With nothing to substantiate her theory, Emma again decided to keep her thoughts to herself.

"Amazing," Emma said when she rejoined Nicola. "The monument perfectly exemplifies the four characteristics of Baroque art I'll be covering in the series."

"I feel that Alexander's monument is one of the greatest accomplishments of the Baroque age. Shall we take a look at, to use your favorite word, another 'amazing' achievement?"

They made their way through the crowds toward Urban's monument. When she saw Michael and Steven by the baldachino, Emma looked the other way rather than acknowledging them. *Two conversations with Michael Kelsey in one day is enough,* she mused. All of a sudden she wondered if she'd made a mistake by agreeing to go to dinner with him and his friend.

Nicola's voice brought Emma back to the moment at hand. "So, like we did, or started to do before you had a sudden need to pray in the Cornaro Chapel, let's stand here for a moment before we go up to take a closer look."

Emma grimaced as Nicola smiled knowingly and continued: "Urban gave Bernini the commission for the tomb in 1627, but it wasn't completed until 1647, three years after the pope's death. What Bernini created is truly a masterpiece of sepulchral art. Note the incredible energy in the beautiful female allegories—Justice to the right and Charity on the left. And look at the stateliness of the bronze statue of Pope Urban dressed in a rich ceremonial cape. Wearing the papal triple tiara, a symbol of his office, Urban is a truly awe-inspiring, majestic figure."

"In contrast to the humble, spiritual, Alexander."

"Yes, as he did in Alexander, Bernini sculpted Urban's personality. Do you see the movement in the monument?"

"In Urban's gesture."

"And in the female statues as well. Look at Charity. Holding a child in her arms, she leans lazily against the sarcophagus as she mournfully gazes down at another child who points toward the dead pope. Justice holds a sword and scale. Like her counterpoint, her eyes are also sad as she looks up toward the heavens to seek comfort from God."

"The figure of Death is remarkable," Emma said.

"Death depicts Bernini's theme. Her head and face, partly concealed by a cap, she appears at Urban's feet in the form of a winged skeleton rising from the sarcophagus. In her hand she holds a scroll of parchment on which she writes the name and title of the deceased pontiff, and on the edges of other sheets are the first letters of the names of popes who preceded Urban in death. For example, 'P' stands for Paul the Fifth Borghese."

"Don't you find it ironic that Bernini placed the skeleton among beautiful figures?"

"An intentional irony. His message is that death comes to all humans including the beautiful, the powerful, and the holy."

"The ultimate irony," Emma said pensively.

Nicola looked at her watch. "I planned to spend a few minutes in the Chapel of the Blessed Sacrament, but I'm afraid we don't have time. You need to see Saint Longinus before we leave the basilica. So, a little general information about the piers while we walk?"

"Absolutely."

"In architecture, a pier is an upright support for a super-structure. In the case of Saint Peter's, surrounding the balda-chino are four great piers which support the gigantic dome. Each of the piers contains a large niche holding a colossal statue of a saint representing one of Saint Peter's four major relics: Saint Helena, the True Cross; Saint Veronica, the veil used to wipe Christ's face on the way to Calvary; Saint Andrew's head, and the Holy Lance of—"

"Saint Longinus," Emma said, "but I'm afraid that's all I know. I was going to read about Longinus on the plane—"

"But Michael was sitting beside you."

"I'm afraid so. I couldn't show any more than a touristy interest in what I planned to see in in Rome."

"Then I'll tell you about Longinus, the soldier who pierced Christ's side with a lance from which, according to the gospels, blood and water flowed. In his design, Bernini recreated the intensely dramatic moment when the soldier-saint acknowledges Christ to be the Son of God. Note his face is vibrant and full of devotion. In his right hand he brandishes the spear he used to pierce Jesus' side, while with his left he indicates reverent amazement at what he has done. Now you tell me, as you did at Urban's monument, how does Bernini convey movement in Longinus?"

Emma looked closely. "Through the saint's spread arms—"

"Which, at the time, was a pose unprecedented in statuary. What else?"

"Through the cascades of his drapery and Longinus' disheveled locks."

"Good job. You're ready."

"If I am, it's because of you. The guidebooks don't provide the information you've given me. Grazie molto."

"Prego," Nicola said, clearly pleased by the compliment. "To supplement what I've said, you'll find a complete list of Bernini's works in the back of your guidebook, though I think you have more than enough for your segments."

They walked through the portico, descended the stairs, retrieved Nicola's backpack, and stopped at the kiosk. Emma chose two books; one was about the art and history of the Vatican, and the other, *A Guide to Saint Peter's Basilica.*

"There's Giro," Nicola said as they entered the square. "Are you hungry?"

"Would it bother you too much if we don't go to lunch today?" Emma said contritely.

"Really." Nicola looked surprised. "You're not hungry?"

"Actually I am, but my mind is overflowing with ideas. Under the circumstances, I'd like to go back to the hotel, order room service, and spend some quiet time organizing my thoughts before Helen and Ron arrive."

"There's been a change of plans," Nicola said to Giro as they neared the car. "Emma has a great deal of work to do, so we're skipping lunch."

"Then I'm taking you to the Excelsior?" Giro said to Nicola.

"You are."

Thinking about how to present all the information Nicola had provided, Emma said very little during the ride to the hotel. "Thank you both so much, or should I say grazie mille?" she said to Nicola when Giro pulled into the circular drive. "It's been a wonderful two days."

"Prego," Nicola said as she got out of the car.

Emma handed her an envelope. "If my shows are successful, it will be because of you and the incredible information you've given me."

"As well as your ability to absorb the information I've provided."

Emma reached out and gave her guide a hug. "I'll be in touch about Saturday."

"E-mail or call, whichever's easier. My phone is always on. My number and e-mail address are on the card I gave you yesterday morning. Here's another in case you mislaid the first."

Emma took the card and turned to Giro. "I don't know what time we'll need you tomorrow morning. My guess is Helen and Ron will want to get an early start."

"Call me when you know. You also have my card. Remember, I live close by."

"Near the Spanish Steps, on one of the points of the triangle."

Giro beamed. "That's right."

Emma thanked her guide and driver, said good-bye, and went to prepare for her meeting.

CHAPTER EIGHT

When she got to her suite, Emma changed into sweats and perused the room service menu. While waiting for her linguine with clams and dried tuna eggs to arrive, she checked her e-mails. Jack's message said she was invited to the kick-off reception; Helen would have the information and credentials.

She had just finished responding when the room service waiter arrived. As she ate the scrumptious lunch, Emma looked through the pages of Nicola's notes. After calling downstairs to say the lunch table was in the hallway ready for pickup, she opened the files she'd downloaded before leaving Boston on Wednesday morning. When she looked up a biography of Bernini in one of the books she purchased at Barnes & Noble, a quote by his son jumped out at her. She began her spiel with the words Nicola used when she first talked about Bernini on the way to Santa Maria della Vittoria, and ended with the line from the book:

One of his eleven children, his sculptor son, Domenico, summed up his father well when he said: Aspro di natura, fisso nell'operazione, ardent nell'ira, which is translated as: 'Stern by nature, rock steady in work, warm in anger.' Bernini's biography is rich in anecdotes and legends, some of which I'll share with you over the next week as I report from Rome.

She made a note to ask Giro for help with her Italian pronunciation and began to work on a tentative schedule for the week ahead. Her producer and cameraman would have the final say about her script and where to shoot, but, knowing Helen, Emma was sure her input would be important.

As she typed, Emma made a marginal note to stress the movement in Bernini's sculptures: his ability to expand the works beyond the medium itself, his realistic portrayal of facial features, and his use of symbolism and irony to underscore his theme. After several revisions, she e-mailed Jack: *Realizing I haven't met with Helen yet, here's what I'm thinking in terms of how the segments will run, though I have no idea how long it will take us to film each part. Of course I'm open to revisions and suggestions.*

1. Saturday—Introduction and Bernini a brief bio
2. Sunday—Borghese—Brief blurb about the Cardinal's role in beginning Bernini's career; *Apollo and Daphne*, *Pluto and Proserpina*
3. Monday—Borghese, The *Bust of Cardinal Scipione* , *David*
4. Tuesday—Outside Saint Peter's—the square, portico, and possibly, Constantine
5. Wednesday—Baldachino, High Altar
6. Thursday— Longinus, monuments of Urban and Alexander
7. Friday—Triton fountain, Fountain of Four Rivers, Bernini's Chic
8. Saturday—Ecstasy of Saint Theresa and wrap up

By 2:45, Emma had finished her preliminary planning. She changed back into the slacks and blouse she'd worn that morning and took the stairs down to meet Helen and Ron.

Mr. Ferrari, who was on the phone when she reached his desk, smiled and pointed toward the lobby. Emma gave him a thumbs-up and went into the elegant room. Ron and Helen, their gear all around them, took up an entire grouping of chairs to the right of the entrance. They stood as Emma approached. "You look rested and ready to go," Helen said as she extended her hand.

Emma took it, appreciating her producer's firm grip. From the first time she worked with Helen, she'd admired her professionalism and skill. Feisty and often outspoken, the producer was meticulous and thorough to a fault. Word around the station was nothing escaped her eye, and if you crossed her, you'd better watch out. She could be tough, even ruthless at times.

Though she wasn't sure, Emma figured Helen had to be in her early forties. Slender, she had short brown hair with just a hint of auburn, a full mouth, and a long, slender neck. High cheekbones set off her expressive, dark-brown eyes. Emma had never seen her producer without her trademark, a cardigan tied around her waist. She often wondered why Helen wore the sweater, but thought it would be rude to ask.

"Were you able to take a nap after your long flight?" Emma asked.

"I did," Ron said. "Helen had to work."

"I'm Emma Bradford." She extended her hand to the cameraman.

Helen frowned. "I apologize. I assumed you knew each other."

Ron shook Emma's hand. "Emma and I have been on the same shoot, but we were never formally introduced. It's nice to meet you."

"You too," Emma said as she studied Ron. He was a pleasant-looking, middle-aged man with hazel eyes, light-brown hair receding at the corners, and an expansive smile. He was hardly obese, but he obviously liked his food. He wore a wedding ring which looked tight, so Emma figured he was suffering from middle-age spread.

I'm pleased to be working with both of you," Emma said. "When Jack gave me the assignment, I was thrilled to be doing something besides listening to Mayor Marino, but I want to tell you, after spending time with Nicola, my guide for the two days I've been in Rome, I've become a Bernini enthusiast. I'm thrilled to be reporting on the artist's life and work. Whether you're an aficionado of the Baroque or not, the man was a genius."

"Your enthusiasm will play well for the camera," Helen said, "but I'm puzzled. When I hear you talk, it sounds as if you've only recently become familiar with Bernini's sculptures. Jack told me you majored in art history at Wellesley."

"I did, but I wasn't particularly interested in Bernini or Baroque art until yesterday morning. Now I can't seem to get enough of either."

"I don't know much about Bernini, but I agree with Helen," Ron said. "Your enthusiasm will light up the screen."

"I hope so."

"Shall we set up shop?" Helen asked. "Jack said we'll be able to store everything in your sitting room."

"That's the plan. Let me help." Emma picked up two large canvas bags.

"Thanks," Ron said. "It'll be great to park the stuff in one place."

They were approaching the elevator when Emma heard a deep, baritone voice coming from the direction of the entrance. "Did you get everything you needed at Saint Peter's?" Michael bellowed.

She turned toward the door and grimaced. "I did. You're back early, so apparently you think you know it all."

Michael walked toward the trio. "That's not necessarily true." He smiled at Helen. "So Emma is joined by Boston's best. Hi, Helen; Ron."

"Good to see you, Michael," Helen said. "Jack told me you're our WABC competition."

Good to see you? You can't really mean that, Emma thought as she watched Helen and Michael shake hands.

"You two know each other?" she asked, surprised by the warmth of their greeting.

Michael grinned. "We've crossed paths a few times." He picked up the bags Emma had put back on the floor. "Let me help you get this heavy equipment upstairs."

"Thanks ..." Ron began.

"No thanks," Emma said as she attempted to take one of the bags from Michael.

Michael wouldn't let go. "Why, so you can loudly proclaim that chivalry's dead and I'm a jerk? I couldn't allow a statement like to ruin my otherwise squeaky-clean reputation. Shall we go?"

Apparently Helen and Ron saw nothing objectionable in Michael's actions. "Thanks, man," Ron said.

Emma's jaw tightened. *God, I hate the macho-man crap,* she thought. *"Thanks, man." How disgusting.* "I'm not going to fit in this tiny elevator with all of you plus the equipment," she said snippily. "I'll meet you by the elevator on the fourth floor."

"Doesn't look like I'll make it either," Michael said cheerfully. "I'll take the stairs with you, Emma."

Emma glared. *He's trying to irritate me and get me to embarrass myself in front of Helen and Ron.* She persisted with a silent curse and replied: "Or you could wait for the other elevator."

Michael flashed his white teeth. "What, and miss spending a little more time with my favorite rival? I'll happily lug heavy bags for that privilege."

A deep frown revealed Emma's displeasure. "I'm sure you would," she grumbled.

Taking two at a time, she raced up the stairs. Beating Michael up by thirty seconds, she waited for him in the hall, her hands on her hips.

Michael was out of breath when he got to the fourth floor. "You obviously need to work out more often," she said as Ron and Helen came off the elevator. "Not in top football shape anymore, huh?"

Michael's smile was for show. He was clearly annoyed and embarrassed. "It's called jet lag," he declared a little too brashly. "My body hasn't adjusted to Rome time."

"That's odd." Emma said. "It only took one good night's sleep for me to adapt—the first night I arrived, the same evening I found a rude message on my voicemail when I returned from dinner."

"Is anybody going to tell me what's going on here?" Helen asked impatiently. "Clearly you two aren't friendly rivals."

"Oh, but we are," said Michael. "After you finish with your meeting, Emma and I are going to have dinner with a good friend of mine." He turned and looked Emma, his eyes glinting mischievously. "You're looking forward to a pleasant evening with Steven and me, aren't you?"

"Absolutely! I can't wait," Emma said, smiling insincerely. "Helen, shall we put away the equipment and start planning? I have so many great ideas. I skipped lunch to put my thoughts on paper." She turned to Michael. "Did you skip lunch too?"

Michael showed contrived astonishment. "Heavens no," he said. "Remember, my guide, Monsignor Laurent, is a gourmet. How could I ask him to miss a meal? And anyway, I'm ready to go tomorrow."

Clearly uncomfortable, Helen changed the subject. "Who's your production manager?" she asked as they walked toward Emma's room.

"David Shaffer. Know him?"

"I do. He's good."

"He is. Bill's my cameraman."

"Bill Stevens?" Ron said.

"The one and only."

"We've known each other for years. You have a great crew."

"Thanks," Michael said, "but so does Emma."

Emma was amazed when Helen smiled shyly. *He has her hoodwinked,* she reflected, and she wondered how far she could go to change her producer's mind. She didn't want to begin their meeting with a bitch session about Michael Kelsey. *I'll take the high road and not bad-mouth Michael,* she decided as they reached her door. She inserted and removed her card, went into the suite, and held the door for the three lugging the equipment.

Michael put the bags down and looked around. "A suite," he said, "and I thought ABC was on a money-saving kick."

Emma thought she heard resentment in his tone. "Really? I had no idea that was the case," she said with contrived amazement. "Are you saying a reporter of your prominence on a week-long assignment doesn't have a suite? I'd think your station would want you to be as comfortable as possible."

"Thanks for helping with the bags," Helen said, her annoyance evident. "Unfortunately, we're pressed for time. Vezio, our driver, is picking Ron and me up at 4:30 so we can take our preliminary shots. So, though I'd love to hear you and Emma continue with your less-than-pleasant banter, we're going to have to say good-bye, Michael. We'll see you at the reception tomorrow."

Michael seemed disappointed. "Sure thing," he said. "Good luck with your meeting." As he put his hand on the doorknob he turned back and grinned. "I'll see you in the lobby at 7:30, Emma."

"I'll be there with bells on," Emma said irritably.

"What the hell's going on between you two?" Helen asked as Michael spun around and slammed the door behind him. "Are you here to report on Bernini or to beat Michael Kelsey for national recognition? Because if it's the latter, you're not going to be showing your appreciation for Bernini, you'll be announcing your dislike for a fellow reporter. It's likely he'll be shooting where we are, so you'll have to ignore him."

"You're right," Emma said sheepishly. "It's really nothing. Michael and I were seatmates on the flight from New York to Rome. We didn't hit it off."

"It's more than that, though I'm not sure what it is. I'm telling you, Emma. Let it go. You're here to do a job. Do it and forget about Michael Kelsey."

"I apologize," Emma said. "I'll be the consummate professional from now on."

"Good to hear," Helen said gruffly. "I hate to begin our relationship this way, but it's part of my job to see that you do well, and if you're harboring hostility … Well, you understand."

"I do, and I've been appropriately chastised."

Helen softened. "Then let's set up and see what you've come up with after your day and a half of touring. Here's a list of interviews I've already arranged as well as a few which are pending."

Emma perused the paper. "This looks great."

During the next fifteen minutes, Ron unloaded his equipment while Helen unpacked her briefcase and spread her folders on the table by the window. Emma took out her notes and looked them over while they waited for Ron to join them. "Would you like for me to order something from room service?" she said as they gathered at the table.

"I'm fine," Helen said. "Ron?"

"I just ate lunch, so I'm all set."

"So what are you thinking?" Helen asked. "Let me see what you have."

"I didn't bring a printer, so why don't I send my ideas to your computers so you won't have to take notes?"

"Good idea," Ron said as he sat down at the table and opened his laptop.

Because they were using wireless connections, it took several minutes for Emma's e-mail to get to Ron and Helen's computers. "Here it is now," Helen said. "You have it, Ron?"

"It's showing up as we speak."

"Give me a little time to read your suggestions," Helen said as she concentrated on her screen.

While her producer perused the notes, Emma held her breath. *God, let her approve. I need something to get me back on her good list after making a fool of myself with Michael,* she thought.

When Helen looked up, Emma knew she was pleased. She took three sheets out of a file. "Look at my plans. Except for a couple of changes, which I'll explain shortly, they're very close to yours."

Emma examined Helen's agenda. "I like your idea of putting *The Ecstasy of Saint Theresa* first and moving everything back a day. It really doesn't fit in after the fountains. Before we go into the church, I'll talk about Baroque art in general and stress the themes I plan to emphasize in Bernini's works."

"I'm glad we're on the same page." Helen smiled. "I would have listened to your arguments about why we should finish with Saint Theresa, but I think wrapping up outside with the fountains would work better."

"I couldn't agree more."

"You've mentioned themes. Care to share?" Helen said.

"Of course. Bernini's sculptures are full of movement."

Ron looked confused. "Movement in marble?"

Helen laughed. "Stick to your camera work, Ron." She turned to Emma. "I know what you mean. What else do you plan to stress?"

"Bernini's ability to expand the sculpture beyond the medium itself."

Once again Ron looked perplexed. "I'm not even going to ask," he said.

"Maybe that's a good idea," Emma teased. "I'm also going to talk about Bernini's use of symbolism and irony as a means of conveying the message of the Counter-Reformation, as well as the intense spirituality and great detail we'll see in the faces of his subjects and the rendering of their garments."

Helen glanced at her notes again. "It seems like you have a lot of information to cram into seven short segments."

Emma frowned. "That's the problem. I can't decide where to cut. Everything I know about the pieces Nicola showed me is pertinent, and one detail leads to another."

"You'll figure it out. So here's how I envision our shooting schedule. I've made special arrangements in the museum and the Cornaro Chapel. That's why the changes. Hopefully we'll be able to shoot everything at the Borghese in one day. Same goes for the fountains. It's difficult for me to judge without seeing everything first. I'll have a better idea after Ron and I do our scouting and preliminary shots later today. And we'll be shooting out of order. For example, we'll be in the Borghese early Sunday morning and will film Saint Theresa when we're through, though the shows will air in reverse. So here it is:

1. Saturday: Introduction and a brief Bernini bio; Shots from Saint Peter's and the opening reception; Interviews with Vatican bigwigs; Characteristics of Baroque art and Bernini's themes; *Ecstasy of Saint Theresa.*

2. Sunday: Interview with curator of Borghese, *Bust of Cardinal Scipione;* Cardinal's role in Bernini's career; *Apollo and Daphne; Pluto and Proserpina, David, Saint Theresa.*

3. Monday—Saint Peter's Square, Portico, Constantine's statue.

4. Tuesday—Baldachino; Cathedra.

5. Wednesday— Urban and Alexander Monuments; Longinus.

6. Thursday—Triton, Four Rivers, Elephant Obelisk.

7. Friday—anything we've missed.

"Sounds great," Emma said.

"I'm glad you approve. I know it's early, but we've been given special permission to shoot at the Borghese beginning at 6:30 a.m. The curator, Donato Martelli, will talk with you about the museum's role in the exhibit." Helen handed Emma a sheet of paper. "I didn't want you to spend time Googling Mr. Martelli, so I had research find out what they could. The first group of tourists will be admitted at 8:30. Is it possible to report on four sculptures in two hours?"

"Absolutely. I'll work on the copy tonight. You said we're doing Saint Theresa the same day?"

"Right. Ron and I will film in the church after the five o'clock mass this evening when there aren't so many tourists milling around. This afternoon while Ron was napping, I arranged for the church to be closed to the public for thirty minutes after the nine o'clock Mass tomorrow morning. Since there's an eleven o'clock service, we'll have the place all to ourselves from ten to 10:30. Will that give you enough time to report on Saint Theresa?"

"It should."

"Good. Now back to tomorrow and our first shoot in Saint Peter's Square. I'm hoping we can wrap up that segment in ten to fifteen minutes. How long it takes will depend, in part, on the crowd. We don't want the ever-present wavers behind us. You'll meet with Cardinal Giancomo Amici at eleven."

"You're kidding," Emma said enthusiastically. "You've exceeded my expectation if you've managed to arrange a meeting with the cardinal himself?"

Helen smiled proudly. "It pays to stay awake and work the phones. Cardinal Amici has been one of the driving forces behind the exhibition, and he'll take part in the opening ceremonies in Saint Peter's Square. When you leave him, you'll be accompanied by Piero Scala, his private secretary, to a predetermined position with a good view of the pope's windows. The ceremony will kick off at 12:30 with a papal blessing. When the pope is finished, you'll do about a one-minute follow-up. You've heard this before. We're on a tight schedule, so you'll have to get the cardinal's story in less than an hour."

"You've done an incredible job, Helen," Emma said.

"Thank you. Following the blessing, there's the reception. I'm hoping to arrange a meeting with the *pope's* private secretary, Monsignor Masella Cipriano."

"Nicola told me the pope has two private secretaries," Emma said.

Helen looked at her notes. "My information says he has only one, but I'll do some checking."

Ron took out a legal pad. "So tell me what shots you might want me to get, ones we can use while you're talking."

"You have the list of sculptures I plan to cover in the Borghese," Emma said. She picked up her notes and scanned the pages. "Let's see. In case we have time, you might want to shoot *The Goat Amalthea with the Infant Jupiter and a Faun.* I didn't see the sculpture, but it was Bernini's first authenticated work. It's noteworthy because he sculpted the piece when he was only ten years old."

"Didn't you say we have access to the inside of the Borghese this evening?" Ron asked Helen.

"We have an hour beginning at 8:35."

"I'll film your goat statue," Ron said. "We'll show it during your introduction tomorrow so the audience will see what you're talking about and you won't have to use program time to report on a less significant sculpture, at least in terms of our report."

"Good idea," Helen and Emma said in unison.

"What else?" Ron asked.

"Everything else is on the list," Emma said. "I don't know what you'll want to shoot before I actually do the report from the location. We'll need outside shots of the Borghese and Santa Maria della Vittoria, and I want a shot of the Piazza Santa Maria Sopra Minerva."

"Will do. Anything else?"

"Piazza Navona," Emma said. "Ron, I know it's asking a lot, but could you get footage early in the morning, before the crowds arrive? If you find a street sweeper, take a picture of him." Ron looked perplexed. "All will become clear," she said as she continued to peruse her notes. "We definitely need a picture of the façade of the church of Saint Agnes in Agony. It's the building behind the Four Rivers Fountain. Please take a close-up of the sculpture of Saint Agnes near the left belfry. I think it's on the left. Anyway, you'll see it."

Helen rifled through her papers. "Did Bernini carve Saint Agnes?" she asked. "I don't see the statue on our list."

"No," Emma said, "but the rivalry between Bernini and Borromini is legendary. I plan to talk about it when we're at the fountain, though I won't have time to share all the tidbits Nicola gave me." She turned to Ron. "Get some footage of the river god facing the church, the one carved with his hand extended toward the façade. At the moment, I can't remember which one it is. And please take a close-up of the shrouded face of the Nile. I have an interesting tidbit about him."

"You've done an excellent job of preparing," Helen said.

"Thanks, but a great deal of credit goes to Nicola. She's a walking guidebook. Jack proved to be a genius by bringing me in two days early and putting me in her capable hands."

"Shall we agree not to heap too much praise on Jack?" Helen moaned. "I'm not sure I can stand all that ego."

"My lips are sealed," Emma said, smiling.

"Good. I assume you want us to look for movement in all the statues and fountains." She looked at Ron. "And I don't mean the flowing water."

Ron frowned. "Give me a little credit, will you? And I don't need to be reminded of what I said."

"Of course you do," said Helen. "It keeps you in line."

Her mind racing, Emma didn't give Ron time to reply. "In the Borghese, I'd like for you to film the sculptures from all sides. In other words, shoot while you walk around *Apollo and Daphne*, *Pluto and Proserpina*, and *David*. Incredibly, Bernini tells a different story from every angle."

Ron continued to take notes. "Will do."

"One more thing. In Santa Maria della Vittoria, I'd like a broad shot of the Cornaro Chapel. Bernini created *The Ecstasy of Saint Theresa* as if it's an act in a play. You'll see what I mean when you get there."

"It sounds like we have lots to do, Ron," Helen said. "And Emma, let me say once more: I'm impressed with your organization. I'd like to see your copy prior to the shoot, not to critique what you've written, but to be sure we don't go over the time we've been allotted. Incidentally, I'm sorry you had to do so much of your own research, but I thought, by having you decide what you want to say, we'd have better and more personal reports."

"No need to apologize. I'm actually enjoying the process. To date when I've reported, I've been required to read what someone else wrote."

"Now you'll have ownership in what you report. I want you to know I'll be calling Jack to see if he'll extend the allotted time for each broadcast to seven minutes rather than five."

"Really?"

"Yes. As I said before, you have a lot of interesting things to say."

"I do. I'll get to work as soon as you leave. When you get back to your hotel after shooting, you'll have an e-mail with the copy for tomorrow's report, questions I've prepared for the cardinal, and what I plan to say about *The Ecstasy of Saint Theresa.* I'll e-mail the Borghese report to you later tonight. It will take me until Sunday evening to write reports for the three days we'll be spending at Saint Peter's."

"Excellent," Helen said.

"If we stay on schedule, I'll have some of Friday and all day Saturday to see Rome, unless you think it's unethical for me to stay here on ABC's dime after I've completed my assignment."

Helen smiled. "You don't know if you'll be finished. A lot can happen in two days. Who knows, you might discover a good follow-up story for a Sunday broadcast."

"I'll keep my eyes and ears open in case I find something worthy of airtime," Emma said as she again wondered about Cardinal Amici's possible ulterior motive for the exhibition.

Helen handed Emma her card. "I have your cell phone number. This is mine. Call me anytime. We'll be out until at least ten tonight, so if you think of anything you need for tomorrow or Sunday, let us know."

"What are the plans for tomorrow morning?"

"We have our own driver, Vezio Sabatini. We'll likely be out and about before you get up. Let's plan to meet at the end of the Via della Conciliazione, just outside Saint Peter's Square, at nine. We'll have a truck from Orbit, our European affiliate, at our disposal for the entire shoot. After you're finished in makeup, we'll go over any changes I've made to your copy, confirm our schedule for the next few days, and film your introduction before you meet with the cardinal."

"I'll show you the shots I've taken of the square and the pope's windows," Ron said, handing her his card. "If you need anything else, tell me then or text me anytime. There's plenty of time for us to do the editing before the first broadcast airs."

"You'll be using the Orbit News truck for editing?"

"And for everything else we need," said Ron. "We're meeting our crew at the Borghese at five. We'll take our outside shots while it's still daylight, and they'll cart us all over Rome before we go back to the Borghese for the inside shots."

"Will you need any of the gear?" Emma asked. "If so, I can get you a key to the room."

"I'm not sure, but it might be a good idea if we have access just in case," Ron said. "I promise to call before we barge in."

"No problem. I should have had two cards made when I checked in. I'll go down with you when we're finished here."

"Great," said Helen. "So, Emma, after your introduction in front of Saint Peter's, we'll film the first part of your meeting with Cardinal Amici before you meet privately for forty-five minutes. You'll probably want to quote him in your other reports, so be sure to take a recorder with you."

"The cardinal knows we'll be taping?"

"I told Monsignor Scala. While you're with the cardinal, we'll shoot the reception rooms before the crowd arrives and look for the most advantageous place for you to stand. Next, we'll film the papal blessing. There's a special section reserved for the press."

"Should I be there?"

"Yes. Monsignor Scala will escort you back so you don't have to fight your way through the crowds in the square."

"Do you want me to prepare copy for the pope's blessing?"

"Research did it for you." Helen handed Emma a paper with a short paragraph. "We don't have much time to spend on the pontiff, and, as in the case of Mr. Martelli, I didn't want you to spend your valuable time Googling him."

"One more reason I'm rested and Helen's exhausted," Ron said grinning.

"I've told you many times before, Ron—there's no rest for the weary. After the pope's blessing, we'll film the reception. Again, Monsignor Scala will help us avoid the crowds when we leave the square. I haven't decided how we're going to wrap up the video portion of the report, but you'll give your tease about Saint Theresa at the end of your presentation." Helen looked at Ron, who shrugged. "Anyway, we'll figure it all out, so don't worry about it."

"I'm sure you will," Emma said. "What you've already planned sounds great. Jack said you're the best. He was right."

"He exaggerates," Helen said reticently. "So if we're through here—"

"Let's get the duplicate keycard?"

Fifteen minutes later, card in hand, Helen started toward the revolving door to the street. "Good, Vezio's here," she said as she looked out front. "We'll leave you to your Cardinal Amici research, and, Emma, I don't want my star reporter in jail instead of Saint Peter's tomorrow morning."

"I don't understand."

"Please don't kill Michael Kelsey at dinner tonight."

Emma laughed. "I'll try to refrain, though it won't be easy."

Helen grinned as she and Ron went out to meet the car.

CHAPTER NINE

E mma went back to her room and changed into sweats. Before Googling Cardinal Giancomo Amici, she checked the notes Nicola had provided and wrote the rough draft for her report in front of Saint Peter's, ending with the four characteristics of Baroque sculpture. She saved the information and copied what she'd written onto her travel memory stick. *I'll work on it again when I'm finished with the cardinal copy,* she thought as she typed the cardinal's name onto her Google search line and began to cut and paste facts into a document she would later supplement with information from other sources.

From the first sentence she read, Emma was fascinated by the powerful, seventy-one-year-old prince of the church. *If I were a Catholic, I'm sure I'd know a great deal about him,* she contemplated as she pulled up article after article, some praising, others criticizing the man who had become a rallying point for conservatives. In spite of Vatican traditions, he had publically criticized his colleague, complaining how the young, inexperienced Cardinal della Chesia, who became Pope John the Fourteenth, would negatively influence the policies of the church for decades.

Curious to see what the new pope looked like, Emma reduced the article she was perusing, Googled John XIV, and enlarged the thumbnail picture. His beliefs and policies notwithstanding, the pontiff looked too young to be the leader of the Roman Catholic Church. Emma was used to seeing old men who, she figured, were elected so they couldn't impose their views on the church over a long period of time. The pope was tall, slender, and obviously fit. "I'll bet he works out as much as he prays," she said, wondering if she was being sacrilegious.

She read more about the pontiff. He'd shocked the Catholic world when two weeks after his election he called for abolishing the rule of celibacy and ordaining women and gays. *Wow, he's a liberal's liberal,* she reflected. *No wonder he's so controversial.*

Emma brought the article about Cardinal Amici back to the desktop. "My God! How could these two men possibly work together?" she muttered as she continued to read. "There's extraordinary antipathy between them."

She continued to scroll through the information. In the six months since the pope's election, the cardinal had become an outspoken advocate for the old ways prior to Vatican II. Emma read a particularly acerbic comment he had made in an interview in the *New York Times.* "The papacy isn't a popularity contest. It's about protecting the customs, rituals, and institutions of the church. To my dying breath, I vow to see they're preserved."

That's a declaration of open warfare if I've ever seen one, Emma thought.

In order to understand what went on in the Second Vatican Council, Emma typed "Vatican II" on the search line. She was immediately struck by the first name she read on the page. Pope John the Thirteenth had been one of four popes who took part in the council. *So taking the name 'John XIV' was a symbolic gesture,* she mused. *The new pontiff is telling the world he's going to continue to modernize the church.*

Near the bottom of the article, she stopped skimming and looked closely at the objections of conservatives like Cardinal Amici to the Vatican II directives. He and other traditionalist Catholics believed Vatican II and subsequent interpretations of its documents moved the church away from several important principles of the historic Roman Catholic faith. She read:

> *In contrast to many Catholics' claims that it marked the beginning of a "new springtime" for the Church, the Council was a major cause of the decline in vocations, the erosion of Catholic belief, and the loss of influence of the Church in the Western world. It changed the focus of the Church from seeking the salvation of souls to improving mankind's earthly situation.*

Emma was surprised when she scrolled to the end of the article. It was written by none other than the cardinal himself.

She felt she understood the conflict as she brought the cardinal's page back to the screen and enlarged his thumbnail picture. He was a striking man who oozed elegance and distinction. His full head of gray hair caused his biretta to perch unusually high off his wide forehead. At first glance, he reminded her of the late Ted Kennedy, though his face was slimmer and more sharply chiseled. He had an aquiline nose and wide-set green eyes topped by thick, curved, grey eyebrows.

Emma was immediately struck by the man's powerful gaze. There was something profoundly inexplicable about him. Was it intelligence? Ambition? Cleverness? She didn't know, but whatever it was, the combination spelled one thing—power. "Cardinal Amici would be a powerful adversary," she whispered. "I wouldn't want to be the one who's challenging him."

During the next fifteen minutes, Emma worked on a blurb about the cardinal and made a list of questions to ask during their five-minute filmed interview, most dealing with Bernini, the cardinal's role in planning the exhibition, and his favorite Bernini sculpture. She wondered if she should raise the question of an underlying purpose for the exhibition. *Of course I shouldn't*, she thought. *I just said I'd hate to be on the man's bad side. So why ask a question which could cause antipathy?*

She read over the questions, cutting out a few she felt could be offensive, including one which dealt with his relationship with the pope. *I wonder what I'll find to talk about during the thirty minutes or so we'll be meeting without a camera rolling.* She shrugged. "Oh well," she said aloud. "I'll figure it out as I go along."

She looked at the clock. It was already six. *Why the hell did I accept Steven's invitation?* she asked herself. *I'd be better off staying in and working.* She considered calling Michael to cancel. *On second thought,* she mused, *how could I possibly miss a chance to make the great Michael Kelsey feel awkward?*

More than once over the next forty-five minutes, Emma said a silent prayer of thanks to Nicola. The notes she'd given her before they began their walking tour of Bernini's Rome were excellent. From them, she wrote her copy for *The Ecstasy of Saint Theresa* as well as the introduction to the Borghese and blurbs about all the statues, including the bust of Cardinal Scipione.

"If Helen approves, and I think she will, I won't have any more copy to write until we're ready to report from Saint Peter's Square," she said. "One more time: grazie molto or mille, whichever it is, Nicola. I'll drink a silent toast to you at dinner tonight. And speaking of dinner ..."

Emma quickly e-mailed her copy to both Helen and Ron. She took out Giro's card and called him to let him know the plans and then took a shower.

The hot water beating up and down her body was refreshing, and she lingered. When she got out, it was seven. She dried her hair, put on her makeup, perhaps a little more to emphasize her eyes than she usually wore, and went to her closet to figure out what to wear. Her first choice was a black dress which showed off her figure. "Who am I trying to impress?" she said as she hung the dress back in the closet. "Steven said the restaurant's casual." She took out a pair of black slacks and a brick-red blouse. "This is better."

She slipped into heels which accentuated her long, shapely legs, took her passport, credit cards, and money out of her fanny pack and put them into a black evening bag. In case the evening was chilly, she removed a black blazer from the closet as well. "Too businesslike," she said. She put it back and chose a black cashmere cardigan instead. She looked in the mirror. "As Bernini would say, 'at least it's not bad.' Michael Kelsey, here I come." She turned off the lights and left the room.

The man's incredibly handsome, Emma reflected when she reached the bottom of the stairs and saw Michael standing by the concierge desk. He was dressed in gray slacks, a light blue button-down, an open-collared shirt, and a navy blue blazer, all of which emphasized his muscular physique. She shook her head. *He'd be perfect if he'd only keep his mouth shut,* she thought as a smile crossed her face.

"I don't believe it; a woman who's on time," Michael said as she approached.

Emma's smile suddenly disappeared, and Michael looked at her curiously. "Did I say something offensive?" he asked. "A minute ago you were smiling and now—"

"Nothing I didn't expect," Emma said crossly. "Let's just say you made me look like a smart woman." Not waiting for Michael to comment, she continued: "As soon as I drop off my key, I'll be ready to go."

When they pushed through the revolving door, a black Mercedes was waiting. "Nice car," Emma said as the driver held the door for her."

"Only the best when you work for WABC New York," Michael boasted. "This is my personal driver, Lucio Pietro. Lucio, this is Ms. Bradford. She's a colleague from Boston."

Emma quickly appraised Michael's driver. Short and fair for an Italian, he had a full head of light brown hair and hazel eyes. He wore a wedding ring and Emma though: *His wife's obviously an excellent cook, because Lucio enjoys his food.*

"I've heard a great deal about you, Ms. Bradford," Lucio said in excellent, almost accent-free English.

Emma slid into the backseat. "Emma, please," she said.

"Emma it is," Lucio responded, smiling as he shut the car door.

Michael was obviously surprised. "How would you know anything about Emma?" he asked.

"My good friend Giro has the pleasure of driving Emma and her guide, Nicola, around Rome." He addressed Emma. "He speaks highly of you."

Emma wasn't sure, but she thought Michael looked disappointed when he heard Lucio say something positive about her. "We're going to the Dal Bolognese restaurant in Piazza del Popolo," he said to Giro. "There's no need for you to wait. Monsignor Laurent will drive us back to the hotel."

Lucio frowned, and Emma knew he was aware of Michael's displeasure. "Very good, Mr. Kelsey," he said, his tone lacking the affability he'd just exhibited.

"All set for tomorrow's opening?" Michael asked Emma when they had settled back for the ride.

"I am. What about you?"

"I'm ready to go. We're shooting from the obelisk in Saint Peter's at nine."

Emma had no intention of giving away any of her plans, so she didn't respond.

"Where are you setting up?" Michael asked.

"You know, I'm not sure," Emma said. "That's up to Helen. I expect I'll have an e-mail from her when I get back to the hotel."

As they rode along, the silence was deafening. Once again, Michael tried to make conversation. "Will you be attending the reception following the pope's blessing?" he asked.

Emma managed a smile, though she was irked, and she knew her annoyance was obvious when she spoke: "Of course I'm going," she grumbled. "Do you really think Boston's such a minor market I wouldn't be included, while you, by virtue of the fact you're a famous and much-admired New York reporter, would be asked to attend?"

"I didn't mean—"

Emma turned her body away from Michael and looked out the window. "Forget it," she said sharply. "Why don't we sit back and try to enjoy the ride. I'm looking forward to a pleasant evening with Steven."

Emma couldn't believe how nasty she sounded. It wasn't like her. Every time she opened her mouth, she was acting like a bona fide bitch. Why was she letting this arrogant jerk push her buttons? She thought about Helen's warning. *If we don't get to the restaurant very soon, I may murder the man and dump his body in the Tiber.* She chuckled.

Michael scowled. "Is something funny?"

"Only to me."

"Care to share?"

"Not really." She spoke to Lucio. "How far to the restaurant?"

"Not that far in terms of distance, but unfortunately we have to drive." Lucio glanced over his shoulder. "Would you like to hear something about where we're going?" he asked Emma.

"Of course I would. Thanks for asking." She studied Michael's face. *He's not happy,* she thought. *Good!*

"We'll be entering the Piazza del Popolo through a famous gate off the Via Flaminiam, an ancient road built in 220 BC to connect Rome to the Adriatic coast."

Michael rudely interrupted. "I don't think Emma needs or wants to hear you talk about ancient history all the way to the restaurant."

Emma turned and glared at Michael. "That's not true." She reached forward and tapped Lucio on the shoulder. "I'd love to hear more of what you have to say, Lucio. I enjoyed the information Nicola provided about Rome."

Lucio waited for Michael to respond. "Oh, all right," he finally said, though grudgingly.

Emma could see Lucio's grin in the rearview mirror. She noticed he didn't include Michael when he spoke. "So, Emma," he said, "the Piazza del Popolo is a huge, cobbled oval standing at the top of a triangle of roads known as the Trident. It forms a grand entrance to the heart of Rome. Do you plan to visit Santa Maria del Popolo?"

"I hope to," Emma said. "Now it seems I'm going to have at least a day and a half to explore Rome with Nicola rather than the one I originally thought I'd have on Saturday."

"You're that far along with plans for your reports?" Michael said skeptically.

Emma grinned, but she didn't respond.

Lucio smiled again. "Shall I continue?" he asked.

"Please do," Emma said. "Michael's lucky to have a driver who can tell him about what he's seeing."

"I'm afraid Mr. Kelsey isn't interested in what I have to say."

Again Emma didn't give Michael time to comment. "Well, I certainly am," she said.

"Then I'll continue. I highly recommend a visit to the church. It contains *Daniel and the Lion*, a decoration by Bernini."

"Bernini?" Emma heard surprise in Michael's voice.

"Yes, sir," Lucio answered. "And that's not Bernini's only connection to the square and Santa Maria del Popolo. In 1655, Pope Alexander the Seventh asked the artist to update the Renaissance church to a more modern Baroque style. After Bernini finished his work, it became a favorite burial site for the rich of the city."

"I'll have to put the church on my must-see list," Emma said. "Grazie mille, Lucio."

"Prego," Lucio said. "There are a few other famous places in the square associated with Bernini. There's the sixteenth century Porta Del Popolo. In the seventeenth century, Pope Alexander VII commissioned Bernini to decorate the inner face of the Porta."

"The guy's everywhere," Michael groaned.

"Of course he is," Emma said. "I thought you'd know about everything he created. Could it be that you and Steven are having too much fun?"

"So, Lucio, how do you know all this stuff?" Michael asked, ignoring Emma's comment. "You could have told me a lot while we were driving from place to place. Why didn't you?"

"Because you never asked," Lucio said, a matter-of-factly. "I thought you wanted me to keep quiet and remember my place."

"I never—"

"I'm sure Mr. Kelsey made you think he already knows it all," Emma said disparagingly, "but I'm also curious. How is it you're so knowledgeable? And you speak English like a native speaker."

"Thank you for the compliments," Lucio said. Emma could see him smile in the rearview mirror. "My mother was American, so I was bilingual from the day I could speak. As for my knowledge, I have a doctorate in Roman history. I'm currently teaching two seminars at Rome University—one on ancient Roman history and the other on Roman culture from the time of Imperial Rome to the beginning of World War I. I drive to supplement my income. At one time, I planned to become a priest. I entered the seminary, but I met my wife to be, fell in love, and, five children later, find myself a happy professor. As the church sees it, to be a priest is to give up one's manhood. I was forced to make a choice. I chose to be a man."

Emma was amazed by Lucio's hostile tone. She wanted to probe for more information, but lost her chance when Michael said: "You never mentioned that."

"Again, you didn't seem interested," Lucio said coolly.

Luckily they pulled up in front of Dal Bolognese, because, clearly, Michael didn't have a response to his driver's reproof. "Here we are," Lucio said. "You don't want me to come back for you?"

"No thank you," Michael answered. Emma wasn't sure, but she thought she detected a new element of respect in his response.

"Buona notte," Emma said. "I hope to see you again, Lucio. You've made the drive to the restaurant a fascinating and enjoyable experience."

Lucio grinned. "Grazie," he said. "You've been a wonderful passenger."

Boy, that's a slam on Michael, Emma mused as she got out of the car.

Steven was waiting by the bar when they entered the restaurant. Pointing to his watch, he rose to greet them. "You're late," he said. "That's not like you, Michael. If anything, you're usually early, especially if there's food involved."

Michael frowned. "Your guest wanted my driver to show her around the piazza."

Steven took Emma's hand. "I'm glad I'm dining with at least one person who's interested in seeing the sights. Good for you, Emma. I hope you took advantage of Lucio's knowledge."

"You know Lucio?" Michael asked, looking surprised.

"Not before he started driving you. We've had a few chances to talk while we we've waited for you to finish your business. He's a learned man who would have been a great priest."

"Another strike for celibacy," Emma teased.

Steven looked at her quizzically. "Another strike?"

"The fact you're off the market tells me it's a rotten rule."

Steven laughed. "I believe that's a compliment, so I'll say thank you."

Emma wasn't finished. "I'm curious," she said with a twinkle in her eye. "Why are so many priests as handsome as Hollywood leading men with incredible sexual magnetism to boot? Do all of you take up celibacy as a safe harbor from the opposite sex?"

Steven laughed. "You are direct, aren't you, Ms. Bradford."

"When you two finish your love fest, I'd like to sit down," Michael said impatiently. "She's just trying to throw you off balance, Steven."

Steven ignored his friend. "This way, Emma." He took her arm. "I hope you don't mind, but I took it upon myself to order two of the house special starters—*miso di pasta,* which is four pastas on one plate, each with a different and delicious sauce, and my favorite, thin slices of Parma ham and melon."

"I can't wait to try them."

"Did you order a bottle of wine?" Michael asked as Steven seated Emma.

"Not yet," Steven said. "I thought it would be polite to wait and see whether Emma prefers red or white?"

Michael grimaced as Emma answered: "White," she said. "I had a bottle of Cerritos Blange last night. I was enjoying it until I was rudely interrupted. After that, I didn't enjoy much of anything."

"Then we'll order a bottle of your new favorite and a bottle of red for my friend here, even though I imagine he was the one who did the rude interrupting."

"How could you possibly know that?" Emma teased.

Steven laughed. "A lucky guess on my part."

"Boy this is going to be a wonderful dinner," Michael said sarcastically. "Why don't we call it the 'beat up on Michael fest'?"

"Sounds good to me," Emma said.

"Isn't it time you two relaxed and let bygones be bygones?" Steven asked, looking at Michael. "No one's beating up on you, and to be frank, my friend, you're being a real jerk."

"My sentiments exactly," Emma said. "You can't know how many times I've thought the same thing over the past couple of days."

Steven wasn't letting Emma off the hook. "And you, my new friend, are for some unknown reason egging him on. If I wanted to eat in a hostile environment, I could dine with a bunch of priests who are arguing Vatican politics."

"Point made," said Emma. "Shall we agree to a truce, Michael? At least for tonight."

Michael smiled sheepishly. "I suppose I've been duly rebuked. Okay, I can stop being as jerk as you've both called me, for one night." He paused. "Is that doubt I see in your eyes, Emma?"

"Not at all," Emma said, "but time will tell."

The evening was enjoyable and the food exceptional. Emma couldn't believe she ate all of her lasagna verde and tagliatelle alla Bolognese. "I'd lick the plate if I could," she said, leaning back when the waiter came to take away her empty dish.

For dessert they ordered the dolce della mamma, a concoction of gelato, zabaglione, and chocolate sauce. Never one for sweets, Emma tasted everything and let the men eat the rest.

To Emma's surprise, the truce held. During the meal, she laughed often as she listened to Steven and Michael share stories of growing up together. While they talked about their experiences, Michael relaxed, dropped the swagger, forgot he was a reporter competing for a story, and acted like a pleasant, affable human being. Though most of the conversation was about them, the men made a successful attempt to include Emma, asking questions about her life, her family, and her interests.

The good guy finally showed up, Emma mused as Michael signed the credit card receipt. *If only he could be this way all the time, I might actually like him.*

The conversation continued during the drive back to the hotel. Emma let Michael sit up front with Steven. As she watched the two men interact, she wished she had a best friend, someone who had traveled the road of life with her.

"I'll see you at the reception tomorrow," Steven said to Emma as he helped her out of the back seat.

"I look forward to it." She leaned in and kissed him on the cheek. "It's been a wonderful evening."

"I hope we didn't bore you with all our talk of the past," he said.

"Quite the opposite."

"Then shall we plan to get together again later this week?"

"I'd love it," Emma said. Michael didn't respond.

Strangely, getting out of the car transformed Michael. Once again he became the cocky, obnoxious reporter she detested. "If you two will stop fawning all over each other, we can say good night," he said crossly. "I have work to do before I go to bed."

"Really?" Emma said with renewed animosity. "Since I'm already prepared for tomorrow morning's shoot, I'll be able to get my beauty rest." She paused. "But then you don't need to do that, do you, Michael? You're beautiful enough."

Steven laughed and shook his head. "Good night, you two," he said. "Maybe you can call another truce before tomorrow. I certainly hope so. Neither of you knows what you're missing."

Michael looked puzzled. "Fat chance," he said quickly.

Emma knew what Steven meant and quickly rejected the idea. "Night, Steven, and thanks." She turned and waved as she pushed through the revolving door.

Michael waited while Emma picked up her key. They rode the elevator in silence. "Bye," Emma said when Michael got off at the third floor.

"Yeah," Michael said sourly. "See you tomorrow."

"You certainly will." Emma pushed the button and the door closed.

CHAPTER TEN

Emma's six o'clock wake-up call jolted her out of a sound sleep. She showered, dressed in a black pantsuit, and because blue was a color the camera liked, chose an eggshell blue silk blouse which accentuated her blue eyes.

Instead of working while she ate, she relaxed and thought about Michael Kelsey. Who exactly was the man? The fact that he could be rude and obnoxious was a given, but why? *Is he trying to keep others at arm's length? Does he have to believe he's the best?*

By the time she finished eating, Emma had more questions than answers. "I may never know what makes the man tick," she said as she pushed the table into the hall, "but then why should I care? Hopefully I'll never see him again after we leave Rome."

Mr. Ferrari wasn't behind the concierge desk when the elevator reached the lobby. She left a note asking him to phone Nicola to see if she would be available for more touring on Friday afternoon as well as Saturday, and then she went to meet the car.

"I hear you met a friend of mine last evening," Giro said when she settled back for the ride to Saint Peter's.

"I did. I gather Lucio isn't happy about driving my rival, Michael Kelsey, around Rome."

Giro laughed. "No comment, but I will say, Lucio is jealous of me."

"A confirmation and a compliment," Emma said as Giro pulled out onto the Via Veneto. "Before we start to talk and I forget, I'm going to read a sentence in Italian. I need help with my pronunciation."

Emma read the line she planned to use to introduce Bernini to her audience. Giro made a few corrections and she read it again.

"Perfect," Giro said. "You sound like an Italian."

"I don't think so, but I'll practice just before we get to the square."

Like the first time she'd seen Saint Peter's from the Via della Conciliazione, Emma had goose bumps when she saw the dome of the basilica rising to the heavens. "Do you ever get tired of this?" she asked.

"Never. Every time I see Saint Peter's my beliefs are renewed."

"Would you mind pulling over?" Emma said. "Before I get out I'd like to ask you a couple of personal questions. Feel free not to answer. I don't want you to be uncomfortable."

Giro pulled up by the Orbit truck and turned off the car. He looked back at Emma. "What do you want to know?" he asked. From his tone and the unease evident on his face, Emma realized he was uneasy as he waited for her to begin the conversation.

"While I was doing my research for today's shoot, I Googled Cardinal Amici. I wanted to find out everything I could about him before our meeting later this morning. I also Googled Pope John. Am I wrong in thinking the two men have all but declared open warfare?"

Giro still looked and sounded anxious as he answered: "They have, but Google won't say how nasty the fight has become."

"I know about the ideological differences—a young, liberal pope versus an old, conservative cardinal—"

"Who broke an unwritten rule of the church: be quiet and don't say anything bad about Holy Father." He paused and Emma waited until he was ready to continue. "May if I give you some advice, Emma?" he said hesitantly.

"Of course," Emma answered.

"Always remember; when you're in Vatican City, keep your thoughts to yourself, and never write anything down."

Emma leaned forward. "You're kidding," she said. "Is it really that bad?"

Giro nodded yes. "That's what I've heard from my friends who know."

"Frankly, I'm surprised. Nicola told me Vatican City is an autocratic theocracy, but I didn't realize freedom of thought is discouraged."

"That's what makes the conflict between Pope John and Cardinal Amici so bad. In the old days, people who disagreed with the pope kept quiet, or maybe they talked about problems and complained to others in secret. Now the argument is in the newspaper and on television every day."

"Because Cardinal Amici passionately disagrees with the pope?"

"Yes. He says it's his God-given duty to keep the church from changing. He wants to preserve the old beliefs and values."

"So what about you and others your age? I may have misinterpreted your reaction when I mentioned Cardinal Amici, but my guess is you weigh in on the liberal side of the argument."

"Probably, like most Italians, I fall in-between the pope and the cardinal."

"Care to elaborate?"

Giro sighed deeply. "I'll try."

Once again Emma realized she was pushing the man to do exactly what he'd just told her not to do; voice his opinion about Vatican politics. Still, she couldn't give up. "So what do you think?" she asked.

Giro began tentatively: "I believe the Catholic Church needs to be more modern. If it doesn't change, we will lose more members and priests. We have had a celibacy problem in my family. I have an uncle who became a priest. He fell in love with a nun. To marry, they had to give up their vocations. Why couldn't they continue to serve the church and be married at the same time? And look at Lucio—"

"He told us he left the seminary because he fell in love. He said to be a Catholic priest is to deny one's manhood, or something to that effect."

"That's true. Like my uncle, why can't Lucio have a life in the church and a wife and children? Everyone knows celibacy was not an order from God. It was something adopted by a group of fat old men who worried about power, influence, and who would inherit their land."

"You're preaching to the choir," Emma said pensively.

Giro looked puzzled. "Sorry," Emma said. "That's an American expression for 'I agree; you don't have to convince me.'"

"I understand. I also believe women should be priests. Who said that only men can preach the word of God? I can't believe Jesus would forbid a woman from celebrating Mass."

Emma shook her head in agreement. "So far we're on the same page," she said. "I'm an Episcopalian, and we ordain women. I admit, at first it was hard for many to accept, but now it seems natural to see a woman standing at the altar. I hear what you're saying and not saying, if that makes sense."

"I guess it does," Giro said, smiling.

"What about the ordination of gay men?" Emma asked, realizing again she was pushing the envelope.

Giro hesitated and she waited. "This isn't easy for me to talk about," he finally said, "maybe because I'm confused. I think people have the right to have a relationship with anyone, unless they're committing adultery, which, I feel is an unforgivable sin. I guess I believe marriage should be between a man and woman, but I understand a man could love a man and a woman a woman. Oh I don't know," he grumbled, clearly frustrated. "I suppose I am undecided on this issue."

"If you had to choose between Pope John and Cardinal Amici, which one would you support?"

Again Giro waited before responding. "I really don't know," he said pensively. "Probably the pope, but I don't think we can make all those changes so fast without causing problems for Catholics like me." He paused again, and

Emma let him gather his thoughts. He inhaled deeply before continuing. "I know what I just said, but I also think going back to the time before Vatican II would be bad for Catholics. I suppose I would like a pope who would take his time and not force us to change."

"Well said. Thank you for being so open with me," Emma said. "One more question. Do you think most Italian Catholics share your feelings and opinions?"

"I can only talk about what my friends think. They do. I know many older people support the cardinal and want things to stay like they are, and there are younger men and women who think it would be great if the pope made the changes he has been talking about without waiting."

"Do you see a possible remedy, a way for the two sides to come together?"

"Not unless either the cardinal or the pope changes his mind, or if the pope dies and the conclave chooses someone who will listen to both sides, but since Pope John is only forty-seven years old, he will probably live for a long time."

"What if Cardinal Amici dies? I believe he's seventy-one."

"His secretary, Piero Scala, will carry on for the conservative side. He leads a group of young priests who support the cardinal."

So the conflict would continue," Emma said pensively.

"I guess it would."

"You've clarified the issue for me," Emma said. "Thanks for being so open."

"Please don't quote me," Giro joked, but Emma knew he was being serious.

"I promise to keep your confidence to the death," she said. "A good reporter never reveals her sources."

Giro laughed. "Very good. Call me when you want to go back to the hotel, I'll drive right over."

"You're not staying for the ceremonies?"

"I don't like crowds, so I'll watch on television, but I would like to see your report."

"If you'd like, I'll make it a point to get a DVD of the entire week."

Giro nodded. "Grazie," he said. "Want to check your Italian pronunciation one more time?"

"Absolutely."

"Excellent," Giro said when Emma finished the phrase. "A dopo."

"You will," Emma said.

Giro let her out and Emma waved as he pulled away. She crossed into Vatican territory and entered the truck to see Helen intently looking at computer screens on the wall. The producer glanced up momentarily. "There's a makeup woman waiting for you in the back," she said. "Ron's standing in the square with the camera angled toward the pope's apartments. He's sending me the preliminary feed right now."

"That's exactly the place I would have chosen."

"Other than early morning tourists, the crowds haven't started to come to the square, so I'd like to shoot as soon as you're out of makeup. Are you ready with the copy?"

"I am." Emma said. Absorbed with what she was doing, Helen nodded in response.

It only took ten minutes for Emma to be camera-ready. She paused at Helen's monitor. "I'm heading out to meet Ron now," she said.

"Good. Hopefully we'll be able to do this in one or two takes. When we're finished, you can help with the editing. I'd like to be sure we've included what you want us to show while you're speaking."

"Thanks, Helen."

The producer still didn't look up. "You're welcome," she said nonchalantly.

When Emma left the truck, a van was pulling up. *God, I hope Michael's not editing from the same truck we're using,* she mused as she waited to see who emerged from the sliding door. *I couldn't stand to be in such close quarters with him for any length of time.*

Her worst fears were realized when a man holding a camera exited the truck. Emma figured she was looking at Bill Stevens. Tall and thin with slightly sunken cheeks, a mop of grey hair, and wearing black-rimmed glasses, the cameraman had on a brown patterned sport coat with a wrinkled open-collar shirt and brown loafers. *He looks more like a college professor about to give a lecture than a man who's going to shoot a TV program,* Emma though as she looked at Michael trailing closely behind. Eager to avoid having a conversation with her nemesis she'd left at the hotel the night before, she looked away and went to meet Ron.

Her effort to get away from Michael was unsuccessful. He headed towards her. *He could have avoided this encounter,* she thought irritably as he arrived where she and Ron were standing.

"I'm not interrupting your work, am I?" he asked haughtily.

"Of course you are," Emma said huffily.

"Not that you need advice from me, but are you sure a shot from the area of the obelisk wouldn't be a better choice?"

"My God!" Emma exclaimed. "You're the most unbelievable know-it-all I've ever met." She turned to look at Bill. "I'm Emma Bradford," she said, extending her hand.

Bill shook hands. "It's very nice to meet you, Emma."

"I was sure you'd met our great Boston reporter before," Michael said, his voice dripping with sarcasm.

Emma was sure Michael hadn't seen the disapproving look Bill exchanged with Ron. "We're set to go, Emma," Ron said. He turned to Michael "It's too bad I didn't have your recommendations before I started setting up, Michael. I'm sure our segment would be better if we heeded your advice."

Ron's disdain went right over Michael's head. "Yeah, sure," he said and looked at Emma. "Good luck."

Emma struggled to keep her response as calm and reasonable as possible. "Thanks," she said warily. She considered adding "you too," but thought better of it.

"Like you said, the man's unbelievable," Ron said when Michael and Bill were out of earshot. "I wanted to blast him, but—"

"Why get into a pissing contest with a skunk?"

Ron laughed. "Exactly! If you're ready, let's do this."

Emma ran through her spiel so Helen could make changes before they did the actual report. Her only suggestion was to ask Ron to move slightly to the right. "You're cutting off part of the pope's window," she said into Ron's earpiece. "Have her stand back about two feet."

Ron relayed the message. "She wants you to move back."

"Here?"

"Looks good. Shall we do our first take?"

"Anytime you're ready." Emma took a deep breath and began her introduction. She covered the upcoming exhibit opening, talked about Bernini, and gave an overview of what her viewers could expect in the days ahead.

"Great," Ron said when she finished. "I don't think we'll need a second take, but we'll see what Helen has to say. Good Italian pronunciation."

Emma smiled. "Thank Giro. He coached me during our drive over here."

Five minutes later, Helen spoke to Ron in his earpiece. "She says it's a wrap," he said. Emma laughed. "What's so funny?" he asked.

"I don't know. The phrase 'it's a wrap' makes me think of old movies."

"You must have heard your producer use the term before."

"I suppose I have, but it wasn't particularly funny until now."

As she and Ron turned to walk back to the truck, Emma looked at the obelisk where Michael was animatedly doing his report. "I'll bet he looks great on camera," she said.

"You'll be able to see for yourself. The feed will come into the truck."

"Will Michael know I'm watching him?"

"Does it make a difference if he does?"

"Not at all."

"Good, because it's possible his producer, David Shaffer, will tell him."

"So Michael will be able to watch my report?"

"Unless you tell Helen you don't want him to, though I can't imagine what you'd say to convince her to keep your report under wraps without sounding unprofessional and, in a word, idiotic."

"It would sound ridiculous, wouldn't it?"

Ron shook his head. "Duh!"

Helen was smiling when Emma reached her monitor. "Do this well every time we shoot, and you'll have all day Friday to enjoy Rome. You looked great. Want to take a look?"

"I do. Thanks."

"Obviously Ron has some editing to do before you see what your audience will. Ron, tell Emma what you're thinking while she watches this part of the show."

Ron moved closer to the monitor. "Most of the report will feature you speaking. I plan to show a photo of Bernini when you first introduce him. When you mention his fingerprints being all over Rome, I'm going to do a quick montage of the Borghese, his chick or whatever you called it, the Four Rivers Fountain and the Triton, and finish up with a wide-angle shot of Saint Peter's Square. I took footage of each one after our meeting yesterday."

"Sounds great," Emma said. "To use your words, 'what else?'"

"When you get to the part about the faun statue, I'll show it briefly. It didn't do much for me, so I'm glad it's not a part of the program."

"Then I shouldn't waste my time taking a look?"

"Not in my opinion, but this is from the guy who thought you were talking about marble actually moving when you talked about movement in a statue."

"Good point," Emma said, grinning.

For the next half-hour, Ron edited while Emma and Helen watched over his shoulder. "So let's look at what we have," he said. "Hopefully this will be it."

They watched the screen. "You did a great job," Emma said when the segment ended. "I wouldn't change a thing."

"Neither would I," the irritating, intrusive baritone voice said from behind Emma.

She turned and gave Michael a scathing look. "I didn't hear you sneak up on us," she said, startled as much as she was angry.

"Why would I have to sneak? We're sharing the same truck. I have every reason to be in here. Since David's working in the back, I have to walk by you to get to him. Why so sensitive? Can't you accept a sincere compliment when it's given? I said I wouldn't change a thing in your report. I meant it."

"Thanks," Emma said tentatively. "I thought you were Michael being Michael. Frankly, I never know which one of you will show up, so I'm on guard all the time."

She expected an arrogant retort, but it didn't come. Instead, Michael smiled.

"I'd better get to work on my report," he said, though with none of the bluster and conceit he usually displayed.

"Good luck," Emma responded, and oddly, she meant it.

Emma had no idea what to think. Who was this new Michael? Or was this Michael always lurking in the background? Was she dealing with Dr. Jekyll and Mr. Hyde? She had no idea, but she wasn't going to try and find out. *I'm not stupid enough to push my luck,* she thought. *I'll enjoy this Michael until the ass emerges again, as I'm sure he will.*

At 10:40, Michael was still concentrating on the monitor in front of him. "Shall we go see Monsignor Scala?" Helen asked Emma. "We're supposed to meet him beside the fountain on the right in five minutes. I don't think it's a good idea to keep Cardinal Amici waiting."

"God no!" Emma exclaimed as she thought about the imposing man who had stared back at her from the computer screen. "I have my recorder right here."

Ron picked up the camera. "I'm ready too."

"Then let's go meet the lion in his den." Emma wasn't sure if Helen knew how appropriate her choice of words happened to be.

Five minutes later, a priest approached the fountain. As he came closer, Emma appraised Piero Scala. He wasn't at all what she anticipated him to be, though when she thought about it, she wasn't sure what she'd expected. Serious was the word Emma initially chose to describe the young priest, or maybe solemn. When he reached the trio waiting for him, his expression was strained, and he looked somber. "Father Scala?" Helen asked, extending her hand.

"I'm afraid not," the young monsignor said solemnly. "I'm Monsignor Angelo Paterni, Cardinal Amici's new secretary."

Emma was surprised "New secretary?" she asked. "What happened to Monsignor Scala?"

Monsignor Paterni paused before answering. His face showed great anxiety, and the whites of his blue-grey eyes were red. He'd obviously been crying. "Piero died last night," he said somberly.

Emma was stunned. She thought of the conversation she had with Giro during the ride over. "Last night?" she said incredulously. "Had he been ill?"

"No." The monsignor took a deep breath through his nose and exhaled through his mouth. "That's the mystery. There's no apparent cause of death. The cardinal's doctors assume Piero had a heart attack, but he was a young man and very fit."

Emma didn't know what to say. It wasn't every day a man you were scheduled to meet dropped dead, especially one so young. She considered her next question might be too much, but decided to ask it anyway. "Will there be an autopsy to determine cause of death?"

Angelo seemed surprised by the question. "The cardinal asked for one," he said hesitantly, "but his request was denied."

Emma knew she was pushing, but her instincts told her there was a story here, so she continued to prod. "Wouldn't everyone want to know how Monsignor Scala died?"

She quickly realized she wasn't going to get an answer from Angelo Paterni. He shrugged and shot her a "don't-go-there" look, so she backed off.

"Cardinal Amici will conduct Piero's funeral Monday morning at San Pietro in Vincoli, the church where Piero worshipped as a child," he said.

"Monday? So soon?" Emma said, looking at Angelo skeptically. "Is that common practice in Rome?"

Once again, the monsignor looked uncomfortable. "It's the family's decision," he replied. "They're being guided by Cardinal Amici."

"I see," Emma said, but she really didn't.

"I assume our appointment with Cardinal Amici will be postponed," said Helen.

"No. That's what I came to tell you. Despite his over-whelming sorrow, the cardinal knows Piero is with God. He will keep his appointment. He asked me to tell you he has been working on the Bernini exhibit for over a year and cannot let his personal grief keep him from continuing with his scheduled activities. He knows you understand why he will be limiting the entire conversation to fifteen minutes, rather than the five while you were filming, followed by a private discussion."

"We appreciate Cardinal Amici's willingness to meet us during such a difficult time for him," Helen said.

"Then if you'll follow me, I'll take you to the cardinal's office."

The monsignor flashed his ID badge to the brightly dressed guards at a large doorway, and they were admitted to the area beyond Bernini's columns. They walked by the Court of San Damasco. "This way," he said as they climbed the stairs to the second floor of the Medieval Palace.

Two security guards in dark uniforms stood outside the cardinal's door. "I have a question," Emma said when the two men stood aside so Angelo and his guests could enter.

"Is it business as usual around here, or is the cardinal being protected because his secretary died?"

Angelo hesitated. "The building is always under surveillance," he whispered, "but the Swiss Guard rarely protects the individual offices."

"These men are members of the Swiss Guard?" Emma asked.

For the first time, a smile curled the edges of Angelo's lips. "They don't always wear the traditional costumes," he said. "They have their ceremonial role, but they regularly shed their stripes for plain clothes and join members of the Vatican police in guarding the Holy Father."

"But they're guarding a cardinal, not the pope."

"Ms. Bradford, I have no idea why this particular arm of the Vatican security forces is protecting Cardinal Amici," Angelo said with apparent frustration. "I am not privy to security arrangements. If you will follow me, the cardinal is waiting."

He led Emma, Helen, and Ron through a room containing a desk and a gathering of chairs in front of a large sofa. "This is the antechamber where Pietro usually worked," he said. "Now it will serve as my office."

"Were you and Monsignor Scala friends?" Emma asked.

"We went to seminary together. I will certainly miss him."

"But you're not interested in finding out why he died?" Emma quickly realized she'd pushed too hard as Angelo's eyes flashed.

"It is not my decision to make, Ms. Bradford."

"I apologize for my insensitivity," Emma said.

Angelo nodded and knocked on an ancient door. "Enter," Emma heard from behind the barrier. Angelo pushed open the door.

Dressed in full vestments of scarlet silk, the cardinal was sitting behind his desk. He rose as Angelo introduced Emma, Helen, and Ron. It was evident the grieving man was making a concerted effort to be hospitable, but his smile was forced, his grief apparent, his eyes forlorn. When he spoke, his deep voice was shaky. He spoke in excellent, formal English with only a trace of accent. "I rarely dress in all this finery," he said. "It is unclear if I will have time to change between our meeting and the opening ceremonies. You may not be aware, but the plans have changed. I will be standing by the pope on the Benediction Loggia."

"He won't be blessing the crowd and opening the exhibition from his window in the Apostolic Palace?" Helen asked.

"No. My office would have notified you earlier, but I was just informed by Masella Cipriano, the pope's secretary. Our appearance together is to be a show of unification during these difficult times."

And you're not too happy about it, Emma reflected. "I'm sorry for your loss," she said.

"Piero was a fine young man with a bright future. He will be missed by all who knew him."

"I'm sure he will be," Emma said.

Cardinal Amici motioned to a chair opposite his desk, and Emma sat down. "While your producer and cameraman set up for the interview, tell me about yourself," he said as he settled back in his chair.

Taking a deep breath, Emma presented a brief biography.

"And this is your first visit to Rome?" the cardinal asked.

"It is, but certainly not my last. I love the city and hope to see much more of it before I return home a week from tomorrow."

"Your enthusiasm is evident. What have you seen so far?"

"I've been concentrating on Bernini. A fabulous guide has been showing me his works."

"And you appreciate my favorite artist?"

"I do. In only days, realizing it's difficult to compare schools of art and artists, Bernini has become my favorite artist too."

"Have you always admired the Baroque?"

"I confess, not before I arrived in Rome, but I'm a fan now."

A faint smile came to the cardinal's lips. Emma studied his face. There was something profoundly inexplicable about him. She quickly realized she was sitting in front of an intelligent, clever, and powerful man. When she first saw his picture, she realized this wasn't a man to trifle with. After meeting the cardinal in person, she knew her first impression had been accurate.

"We're ready to begin, Eminence," Helen said.

"Where would you like for me to stand?" the cardinal asked.

"You can stay where you are. Emma, if you'll move your chair near the corner of the cardinal's desk, we'll make this an informal discussion."

After thanking the cardinal for his time, Emma asked the question she had asked Giro and Nicola: "Eminence, why is the Vatican joining with the city of Rome to showcase Bernini? Is 2011 a milestone in the artist's life?"

The cardinal nodded. "There need be no particular reason to celebrate the life of, arguably, the greatest artist of the Baroque period. Bernini was a promoter of the True Faith. The world today is in conflict both socially and politically. What better time to celebrate the life of a man who, through his art, attempted to bring stability to religion?"

He's confirming what I've though all along; this is going to be a politically charged interview, Emma thought. She considered changing her questions, but she had no idea what else to ask. Though she didn't want to be a part of a religious debate, she had to stay on task. *There's no doubt the cardinal's using my question about the exhibition to express his political position.* "What's your role in promoting the exhibit?" she asked.

The cardinal smiled slyly, telling Emma with his expression that he knew she was aware of his ulterior motive. "For the past year I have been working closely with Donato Martelli, the curator of the Borghese Museum," he said. "From the beginning, our goal has been to introduce Bernini to the world, through both his architectural achievements and his sculptures here in the Vatican and throughout Rome. My focus has been here at Saint Peter's and in other churches."

"In other words, you're promoting Bernini's religious works."

The cardinal nodded. "I am. Donato has concentrated on the more secular pieces, including those on display in the Borghese and the fountains which decorate the piazzas of Rome."

"What would you like to see come out of the renewed interest in Bernini?" Emma asked, though she was nervous about the answer she expected to get.

The cardinal smiled broadly as he began to answer: "Bernini sculpted during the Counter-Reformation, a time when the church was struggling against the spread of Protestantism. Through his religious art, he hoped to renew religious fervor and return those who were straying and embracing unorthodox and unconventional opinions back to the fold. In many ways, the church today finds itself up against similar challenges."

Emma knew the cardinal was referring to the pope's liberal beliefs. "And you believe an understanding of the messages in Bernini's art will bring about renewed faith."

"It is my hope," the cardinal said, a faraway look in his eyes.

They're never going to show this interview, Emma thought. *It's far too political and controversial. I'm sure they don't want the Bernini exhibit to turn into a platform for two differing points of view.* In an effort to make the interview more acceptable, she changed the subject. "Do you have a favorite sculpture, Eminence? One you would want all visitors to Rome to see?"

When the cardinal answered, Emma knew he was determined to make his point. "My favorite is Bernini's Monument to Alexander the Seventh in Saint Peter's."

Damn, Emma thought, angry with herself for falling into the cardinal's trap. *Why didn't I see that coming? There's no way I can avoid asking a follow-up question.* "Could you tell the audience why you've chosen this particular piece?" she asked, though she knew the answer.

The cardinal's expression said "gotcha." "Of course," he said. "Alexander was a pope faced with the spread of Protestantism, particularly in England when King Henry the Eighth defied Rome and was eventually excommunicated for ignoring church teachings in order to fulfill his own personal desires." The cardinal smiled. "And my pun is intended."

"I thought it was," Emma said, smiling in return.

"In Alexander's Monument, Bernini shrewdly shows the church's reaction to heresy. He created an allegorical figure of Truth. Her foot is placed on a globe, but not randomly. The great artist portrayed her stomping on England, symbolically crushing those who opposed the teachings of the church."

Emma was stunned. Cardinal Amici was in effect declaring war on the pope and using her interview to do so. He was threatening the Holy Father, promising the church would stomp out the pontiff's efforts to make significant changes.

Helen came to her rescue. "Time's almost up," she said. "One more question, Emma."

Emma nodded. "Cardinal Amici, what events have you planned for the rest of the year?"

Realizing he'd made his point, the cardinal continued less controversially. "Throughout the year, we will have special exhibitions. For example, next week there will be a celebration in Piazza Navona near the *Fontana del Quattro Fiumi*. Next month we will feature *Apollo and Daphne* at the Borghese."

"It sounds like a fabulous exhibition," Emma said. "I'm sure it will be a wonderful year as you showcase Bernini and the Baroque."

"I hope you will come back to Rome a year from now for the closing of the exhibition," the cardinal said.

"I'll try." Emma smiled and stood up. The cardinal also stood and extended his hand. When Emma took it, she didn't feel flesh. There was a piece of paper in his palm.

The cardinal nodded and Emma took the paper. "I hope to see you again very soon, Ms. Bradford." His request sounded more like a plea than an invitation.

"It would be my pleasure," Emma responded. "Thanks for giving me your time, especially in light of the death of your secretary. May I express the condolences of the entire ABC Network as well as my own?"

The cardinal grimaced. "Thank you," he said, a sad and distant look in his eyes.

Angelo ushered her, Helen, and Ron out of the room and back toward the square. He said good-bye, promising to return and take them to the reception at 12:45. They arranged to meet at the same place where they'd left the square to go to the Medieval Palace.

"What the hell was that?" Helen asked when Angelo was out of earshot. "Cardinal Amici turned everything you asked into a promotion of his own political agenda. We can't use anything he said unless it's the last sentence about upcoming events, but we can't run a one-sentence interview."

"Thank God we're not airing the meeting," Emma said. "To say the least, I was uncomfortable."

"With good reason. We'll talk about it later. We're going to have to find a few minutes of filler. We'll see if the pope's secretary, Monsignor Cipriano, will let us film your interview."

"Let's hope he will."

While Ron and Helen scurried to find a new location to film the papal blessing, Emma lagged behind. She opened the note clasped tightly in her hand. It contained four startling sentences.

Piero's death is my fault.

I'm being guarded, not protected.

My life is in danger.

God help me!

"Oh my God," Emma said under her breath. "This is the real story, not the Bernini exhibition."

CHAPTER ELEVEN

As she followed Helen and Ron to the obelisk, Emma struggled to compose herself. Over the years she'd been teased for wearing her heart on her sleeve, but now she was apprehensive and couldn't let anyone know, was what she was thinking. "You all right?" Ron asked. "You look upset."

"I'm fine," she said brusquely. She looked at Helen. "What do you want me to do? Obviously the circumstances have changed, and what I planned to say won't work."

"Do what you're trained to do: report. This is breaking news, so treat it as you would any major story that's constantly changing."

Ron still seemed concerned about the change in Emma's demeanor." I don't mean to pry," he said, "but something's obviously bothering you."

"I told you there's nothing wrong," Emma said a little too sharply. "I get like this before a shoot. I guess it's because I'm a perfectionist. Where are we filming?"

"It appears the Vatican can work miracles. They've managed to part the sea of humanity and block off a part of the square below the balcony. See the spot?"

Relaxing a little, Emma smiled at the cameraman's biblical reference and looked toward the façade of the basilica. "Just beyond the obelisk?"

"It looks like a few of the news crews just realized there's been a location change, so if we hurry, we'll be able to secure a place where we can get both you and the balcony in the picture. We'll do the intro with you standing in the fore-ground and the empty balcony behind you. When the pope emerges to give his blessing, I'll pan upward and film him. When he goes back inside I'll come back to you for a closing statement."

"There's been another sudden and, I might add, atypi-cal modification to the original plan for the papal blessing," Emma said. "From what I've read, everything the Vatican does is flawlessly scripted down to the second. The pope's handlers, for want of a better word, rarely make any last-minute alterations to the schedule. This time they've made two."

"How will the new plans impact us?" Helen asked.

"If we were merely covering a blessing, we wouldn't be affected at all. But this isn't about the opening of the Bernini exhibition anymore. It's about church politics. The balcony has suddenly become a stage for what may be an Academy Award-winning performance. Cardinal Amici will be appearing with the pope."

"I have no idea what you're talking about or where either man stands would be important," Helen said.

"There's no time to explain, but what you shoot will be critical when I report the new story."

"New story?" Ron looked confused.

"Later. Right now I need for you to get shots of the pope and cardinal standing side by side. When they first come out and throughout the pope's blessing and the cardinal's speech, film only them and no one else, okay?"

"Got it."

"Good. During the first part of the ceremony, don't bother with anyone else in the papal party. Your screen should be filled with the cardinal and the pope. I want to be able to interpret their body language, to see how they interact with one other, and I won't be able to see anything definitive from this distance. When I look at the images you've captured, I should be able to learn a great deal about what they're feeling and thinking. When both men have finished speaking and pause to wave to the crowd, please zoom in on each separately. I need close-ups of both men's faces."

"What if they don't pause?" Ron asked.

"I'm sure they will. As I said, this appearance is political, and the pope will want to milk it for all it's worth."

"If the two men stand close together, I'll be fine, but taking their faces up close won't be easy from way down here. I'll put on the best long-distance lens I have."

"Good. Do the best you can. If you can get a clear shot, their facial expressions will tell me a great deal."

Helen seemed confused. "Body language? Facial expressions? Is there something going on I don't know about?"

"Yes, but now's not the time and nor is it the place for me to tell you what it is. If what I suspect is true, I won't have much leisure time to tour Rome. Please trust me on this one, Helen. You'll know everything very soon."

"Ron will get the shots you need," Helen said. "What else can we do to help?"

Emma continued to speak to Ron. "Besides taking close-ups of the pope and Cardinal Amici, I need for you to get a clear picture of the entire group amassed on the Benediction Loggia."

"That's the balcony."

"Yes. Do it before the two important men arrive if possible. First pan up and down the line, taking a close-up of every face, the bigwigs in the front row and, if you can get clear shots, the not-so-important people standing behind them. I have to be able to identify every one of them. And please take the group as a whole. Zoom in as close as you can as long as you don't cut anyone off. It's possible there's a veiled political message in the way each person is positioned on the loggia."

"You think the scene will be orchestrated?"

"My guess is yes."

"I'll do the best I can. You're asking me to do a lot in a short time."

"Get what you can," Emma said brusquely.

"I said I'd do what I could." Ron's response to her snappish reply left no doubt he wasn't used to being ordered around by a reporter.

Emma took a deep breath. When she spoke her voice was softer. "I'm sorry, Ron. I'm sure you can see how nervous I am, but that's no excuse for bad manners."

"It's okay. I'm being too sensitive, and we're both under a great deal of pressure. Apology accepted. Anything else?"

"As a matter of fact, there is."

Ron bowed. "Your wish is my command."

"Thank you. There's not much time for me to finish telling you what I need. After you're through filming my spiel, before the guests come in and the pope and cardinal are in position behind the microphone, please take pictures of everyone standing in the square watching us—those inside the barriers and those standing outside."

"That's easy."

"Good. Keep shooting. If anyone approaches me, film the encounter. Please, Ron, whether it seems significant or not, keep the camera rolling until I ask you to stop. Will you do that?"

Ron looked at Helen for approval. "Do what she asks, Ron," she said.

"I can handle it, but as I said, I'm not sure if I'll be able to accomplish everything you're asking. It really depends on how long the ceremony lasts."

"I know," said Emma. "Whatever you get will be fine."

"Can I do anything for you?" Helen asked.

"As a matter of fact, yes, and your assignment is crucial. I need a translator. The cardinal is going to say a few words, and I'm sure he'll speak in Italian. I want someone to tell me everything he's saying—literally every word. I know there's not much time before the ceremony begins, but I see a sea of white collars in the square. Among them there must be at least one priest who speaks both Italian and English and who would be willing to translate for me. And please tell me you have a digital recorder with you."

"Always. Why?"

"If you are able to find our translator, stick the recorder in his face. I can't miss a word."

"Like Ron, I'll do my best. In all this craziness, have you given any thought to what you're going to say?"

"None whatsoever, but whatever I say, don't stop because you think I'm off topic."

"Will do. I take it this shoot isn't about the pope blessing the Bernini exhibition anymore."

"It is, but from a different perspective. Bernini is going to be the means of making a political statement, though as I said earlier, at this point I'm not sure who's going to be the Academy Award winner for the best actor in a drama." Ron was clearly puzzled. "You may not understand now, but I promise, you will," Emma said.

"I'm off to find a priest," said Helen.

"Good luck. If I can't have an instantaneous translation, I'm in trouble."

"Consider it done."

While Helen disappeared in the crowd and Ron took preliminary shots so he'd have a better idea of camera angles and distances, Emma jotted down a few notes. She hadn't made much progress when, minutes later, Helen returned. A middle-aged man, rail-thin and slightly balding walked behind her.

"Mission accomplished," she said proudly. "Next time give me a difficult assignment. This is Father Paul, and coincidentally, he was standing just outside the barrier waiting to watch you report. Father Paul, meet Emma Bradford. I told her you'd translate Cardinal Amici's speech for her."

Father Paul was clearly surprised. "Ms. Taylor said you needed a translator, but she didn't say it would be the cardinal's speech I'd be translating. But sure, I'll help you out, Ms. Bradford."

"Emma, please. You're an American, Father."

"Chicago born and raised."

Ron interrupted the conversation. "The guests are gathered on the balcony," he said. "I have some pretty good close-ups. Helen said the word in her earpiece is that the pope and cardinal are due to come out in five minutes. You ready?"

"As ready as I'll ever be," Emma said. "As soon as I'm finished, shoot the crowd out here."

"Will do, but first let's shoot the intro. If we have to do it again, we'll film again after the ceremony is over."

Emma stood with the loggia behind her. "Give me the signal when you're ready."

Ron focused in on Emma's face. Seconds later, camera rolling, he pointed to her. Emma nodded and began:

This is Emma Bradford, reporting from below the Benedictine Loggia in front of Saint Peter's Basilica, where, in just a moment, we're about to witness an historic event. Pope John XIV will offer a papal blessing to officially open the Bernini exhibition. This is a scheduled appearance, and, on the surface, appears to be nothing out of the ordinary, though I'm told it's highly unusual for the Vatican to make changes to the pope's agenda at the last minute. The original plan was for the pontiff to bless the crowd from the third-floor window of the Apostolic Palace, where he gives his Sunday blessings to the pilgrims gathered in the square. However, in this instance, it is not where the pope is standing, which makes this a newsworthy event. It's about who will stand beside him on the balcony. My sources tell me Cardinal Giancomo Amici will appear at the pope's right hand. Could this remarkable pairing signal a thaw in the bitter feud between these two men? If so, it would truly be a momentous occurrence. Why? Because from the day the forty-seven-year-old, extremely liberal pope was elected, ultra-conservative Cardinal Amici has been an outspoken critic of the pontiff's proposed reforms, which include such radical changes such as the ordination of women and gays and the elimination of the rule of celibacy, thereby allowing priests to marry.

This dispute between the two powerful members of the church hierarchy is unlike any seen before. That's because the bad blood which exists between the pontiff and the cardinal is aired daily in the media. Though the pope himself has said very little publically, Cardinal Amici hasn't minced words when it comes to his opposition to the pope's efforts to modernize the church.

In a strange turn of events, the cardinal's secretary, Piero Scala, was found dead in his apartment early this morning. The pope's personal physician issued a statement saying the forty-one-year-old man passed away due to a massive heart attack, though friends and associates paint a picture of an individual who was extremely fit with no prior history of heart problems. At this point, my sources tell me the doctor's finding is definitive and no autopsy will be performed.

More in a moment. The pontiff's party is gathered on the loggia. And yes, both Cardinal Amici and the pope are moving to the microphone. Let's pause so we can listen to what is being said.

"My God!" Helen whispered as she moved closer to Father Paul, her recorder extended toward his mouth.

Emma shrugged and turned to Ron. "Get all of this," she mouthed. Ron nodded and started to film.

Though she'd never seen the pope in person, Emma had seen him on television. She was standing quite a distance away, but it was obvious he was tired and weak. He definitely wasn't the dynamic force he'd been before his illness. His voice was shallow when, in both Italian and English, he launched the Bernini exhibition. He gave his blessing for a successful venture and looked at the cardinal who, eyes down and shoulders slumped, stood at his side. The pontiff spoke in Italian, and Father Paul translated in Emma's ear.

> *I would like to take this opportunity to thank my friend and brother in Christ, Cardinal Amici, who, over the past year, has been the driving force behind this exhibition. On this auspicious occasion, His Eminence has graciously consented to say a few words.*

Aware of the drama playing out above them, the crowd stood silently as the pope stepped aside and allowed Cardinal Amici to take center stage. A strange uneasiness came over Emma. She was watching history being made, and she wasn't sure what was going to occur. As the cardinal moved slowly to the microphone, thoughts of his stealthily delivered note flashed through Emma's mind.

Cardinal Amici was noticeably nervous. *He's not only nervous, he's scared,* she observed. *Friend and brother in Christ, my foot. More like enemy and thorn in my side, and the guards standing behind him are the proof.* Helen stuck the recorder close to Father Paul, and Emma leaned in to listen as the cardinal began to speak.

Your Holiness; brothers and sisters in Christ. Today we begin a year of celebration. We honor one of Rome's greatest artists, Gian Lorenzo Bernini, a man who, through his work, glorified our Savior and advanced the work of the church in a world mired in the throes of regional heresies and filled with individuals who fought to change church doctrine to fit their particular needs with total disregard for the implications of their actions.

The cardinal paused and looked directly at the pope. Emma tapped Ron on the shoulder. "Move in on the pontiff's face," she said, loud enough for the camera to pick up her words.

While Ron took the shot and Helen taped Father Paul's translation of the cardinal's speech, Emma continued to talk, not for the broadcast, but in order to record her thoughts about what was going on. In short, choppy, unpolished sentences, she described the pope's reactions. "The pontiff is visibly upset. My guess is he had advanced knowledge of what the cardinal planned to say and realizes he's no longer sticking to his carefully scripted speech. Cardinal Amici is using Bernini's art to criticize the pontiff for his radical reform policies. Even from this distance I can see the cardinal glaring at the pope."

"I'm zooming in," Ron mouthed.

Emma nodded and continued: "If I'm able to see how disturbed the pope is from down here on the square, the cardinal must know he's facing reprisals for his disobedience. However, the pontiff's obvious displeasure doesn't seem to be a deterrent. Cardinal Amici is standing straighter. He's no longer hunched over as he was when he walked onto the loggia, and he's showing none of the timidity he displayed when he began his speech. His voice is strong and decisive. I'm going to listen." She turned to Father Paul and whispered, "Please translate word for word."

"I'll do my best," the priest said, as Emma listened.

Today I join with Pope John to reconfirm our belief in the True Faith and honor the message Bernini put forth in all his magnificent sculptures. On this spot at this moment in time, I vow to work until my dying day to see the values and traditions so aptly personified by Bernini during the Counter-Reformation of the seventeenth century are maintained and strengthened during these equally troubling times. I dedicate this exhibition to the faithful everywhere, asking God to bless my beloved secretary, Monsignor Piero Scala, who died before he could see the fruits of his tireless work. May God bless you all in the name of the Father, the Son, and the Holy Spirit."

The cardinal made the sign of the cross over the crowd, crossed himself, and stepped away from the microphone.

Emma turned to Helen. "Did you hear what he said and see what he did? This is unbelievable."

"I'm not sure I understand what you mean," Helen said. "Did the cardinal say something you didn't expect to hear?"

"Actually, he did. He made a profound statement, but what he didn't say was even more shocking. He was frightened and nervous at first, but he pulled himself together and defied the pope in front of the world. This was not about Bernini. He was talking about what's going in the church today."

Helen frowned. "I'm afraid you've lost me."

"Without saying the words, he let Catholics know he will fight to prevent the pope from making major changes in doctrine and practices, even if it costs him his life. It's as if he's daring Pope John to have him eliminated, and, by mentioning his dead secretary, he's as much as accusing the pontiff of having Piero killed as a warning to him and his fellow conservatives. Then he blessed the crowd. I'm not sure, but that seems highly inappropriate considering the pope just gave his blessing. I'll have to do some research, but my gut tells me Pope John won't be too pleased to be upstaged."

"You're sure that's the message the cardinal's delivering? If it is, it's mind-boggling and could be a huge story."

"I'm sure, though I have no idea how I'm going to prove what I know."

In a flash Emma, realized she'd been talking in front of Father Paul. She turned to face him. "Father, you must be privy to Vatican politics. Doesn't the cardinal's clear defiance of the pope surprise you?"

Emma could see that Father Paul's smile was forced. "Frankly, Ms. Bradford," he said, "I didn't see anything unusual in Cardinal Amici's words. Everyone knows he advocates returning to pre-Vatican II practices."

"True, but it can't be wise to express an opposing view; at least not publically and when he's standing at the pope's side."

"Perhaps in the past, Ms. Bradford, but we live in a modern world. Freedom of speech is encouraged in the Holy See."

That's a bunch of bunk, Emma thought as she recalled Giro's warning. She wasn't sure which side the priest was on in the debate, so she decided not to pressure him any further.

"Thanks for your help, Father. Are you a tourist like I am, or do you work here in the Vatican?"

Father Paul answered, but he was more reserved than he'd been when they first met. "I'll be working in the Vatican archives for at least the next two years. I'm a linguist. Along with several other priests, my assignment is to translate ancient as well as a few more recent documents. Computer experts will then transfer the translated text to computer files which will be made available to scholars. I'm currently working on key documents written during the seventeenth-century Counter-Reformation."

Emma was astonished. Father Paul had heard every word she'd said about Bernini and the cardinal's use of Baroque art to promote his agenda. Was the priest giving her a message by telling her what he was doing? Had it been the pope or cardinal who gave him the assignment?

"What a coincidence," she said nonchalantly. "Your work is taking place during the year the Vatican's celebrating Bernini, a great Counter-Reformationist." She paused. "It is a coincidence, isn't it, Father? You aren't doing this for political purposes to give the church conservatives a basis for stalling the pontiff's proposed reforms."

She waited for the priest to continue, but instead of speaking, he stared at her defiantly. *You are,* Emma decided as she saw the priest's hostile body language. "But of course you're not," she said sarcastically. "Again, thank you for helping with the translation."

Helen stared at Emma, obviously amazed by what was going on and unsure where her reporter was going with Father Paul. She was surprised when Emma didn't press the priest for more information. "Yes. Thank you, Father," she said.

"Could we have your full name?" Emma asked. "I'd like to express my gratitude on air and mention I was assisted by a fellow American."

"Father Paul will do," the priest said.

"Thanks, Father Paul," Ron said. "Emma, before we head to the reception, I'll leave this disk with the guys in the truck so they can get to work." He turned and headed toward the trailer with Helen following close behind him.

As Emma turned to follow them, the priest grabbed her arm. He was no longer the smiling, affable man from Chicago who was doing her a favor by translating the cardinal's message. A scowl had replaced his grin. "For your own good, leave it alone, Ms. Bradford," he admonished. "What is or isn't going on here isn't your concern. It's a non-story. Don't report on what you think you know."

"Are you the spokesman for the Catholic Church, Father?" Emma said.

Father Paul's gaze bored into her. "For your own sake, remember what I've said, Ms. Bradford."

Suddenly, Emma put her arm around the priest, and, catching him off guard, turned him toward the truck. "Ron!" she shouted. Hearing his name, the cameraman abruptly spun around. "Please take close-ups of our excellent translator," Emma called, "and Helen, snap a picture of him on your cell. Come on, Father Paul. Smile for the cameras. Are you getting the shot, Ron?"

It was obvious the cameraman had no idea what was happening, but he followed Emma's orders and pointed the camera towards her. "I am," he called out.

"Good." Emma's eyes met Father Paul's. "Thanks for everything, Father. You were a huge help. I'll give you credit when I report on the events of the past few days and for whatever stories I uncover in the future."

The priest's eyes narrowed. "I strongly suggest you heed what I said." He smiled, waved at Ron, turned abruptly, and disappeared into the crowd.

It was clear Helen was confused. "I want to know what the hell just happened," she said insistently when Emma walked up.

"And I'm eager to tell you, but not now. Here comes Monsignor Patini. Ron, there's no time to go to the truck. Keep shooting. I want pictures of everyone who speaks to the cardinal at the reception and everyone in the vicinity. I know I'm barking orders, Helen, but this is huge."

Angelo had a smile on his face as he approached. "Are you ready to go to the reception?" he asked. "Cardinal Amici is eager to say hello." He leaned toward Emma. "His Eminence would like a word with you in private after the reception. When I ask you to come with me, please do so immediately."

Remembering Father Paul's warning, Emma hesitated. *To hell with Father Paul,* she thought. *I'm running with the story.* "I look forward to meeting with the cardinal again, Monsignor," she answered.

Helen and Ron followed behind Emma and Angelo. When Emma looked around, Helen nodded. *Good, she told Ron to take pictures,* Emma thought with relief.

"Remembering we need additional footage for tonight's show, I've just arranged an interview with the pope's private secretary," Helen said with they got to the door.

Emma saw Angelo wince. "Really? When?" she asked Helen.

"In ten minutes. Ron's going to set up now. I'm afraid you'll have figure out what you're going to say as we shoot."

"No problem. I'm on it."

As they entered the Sala della Guardia Palatina, Angelo took Emma's arm. "Be careful," he said, concern on his face.

Once again, Emma was taken aback. "I've heard those exact words more than once today. Do you think I have reason to be worried, Father?"

She saw apprehension in Angelo's eyes, but he didn't answer the question. "Take care of yourself. That is all I have to say."

"Of course I will," Emma said quietly and firmly.

She looked around the opulent room resplendent with huge Gobelins tapestries hanging on the wall, priceless art of the Old Masters and large pieces of gilt furniture. Cardinal Amici was nowhere to be seen, and she didn't have time to ask Angelo where he was. Ron, who had set on the other side of the room, was motioning for her to join him. He nodded to Helen, who went to find the pope's secretary. Moments later, she returned with a pleasant-looking priest with dark hair and chocolate-colored eyes. "Emma, this is Monsignor Masella Cipriano," she said.

Emma quickly appraised Pope John's secretary. There was something deeply mysterious about him. In an instant she discerned intellect, drive, energy, and, above all, ambition.

She was clearly dealing with a powerful man who was used to getting his way. In his gaze, Monsignor Cipriano showed none of the strain which had been apparent on Angelo's face. "Ms. Bradford," he said. "Welcome to Vatican City."

"It's nice to meet you, Monsignor," Emma said guardedly. "Realizing you're a very busy man, I want to thank you for speaking with us."

"You are very welcome," Masella said. "I must apologize for what must be a short interview. Being Pope John's representative at the reception ... well, I'm sure you understand."

"Of course I do. Shall we begin so you can return to your duties?" Emma smiled at Ron. "I believe we're ready," she said.

Ron signaled he was ready to film, and Emma began to talk. "This is Emma Bradford reporting again from Rome. We're at the kick-off reception for the Bernini exhibition. With me is Monsignor Masella Cipriano, Pope John's private secretary." She turned to the priest. "Monsignor, thank you for giving us a few minutes of your time on this busy day."

"It is a pleasure to be with you, Ms. Bradford."

"I'm sorry His Holiness can't be with us. I understand he's been ill."

Emma could tell the monsignor was surprised by the direction the interview was taking. His eyes said "this isn't the topic I planned to discuss." "His Holiness has been suffering from a virulent case of influenza," he said, facing her instead of the camera. "Thanks be to God, he is feeling stronger every day."

"We're glad to hear that," Emma said. "And speaking of illness, what can you tell me about the death of Cardinal

Amici's secretary, Piero Scala? I understand his sudden passing last night was a shock to most who knew him."

A dark cloud passed across Masella's face. "It certainly was," he said quietly. "Monsignor Scala was a personal friend. For the past year, we have worked together on the Bernini exhibition. I know he would want me to tell you about the events which will take place in the months to come."

"I'm sure our audience wants to hear about what they'll see if they come to Rome, but first, I'd like to ask one more question."

Emma saw a warning look in the monsignor's eyes, but she pushed ahead anyway. "Is there a reason why a standard autopsy won't be performed on Monsignor Scala? I was told he's to be buried before a definitive cause of death has been established."

The monsignor's eyes spit fire, and he took a deep breath. Emma realized he was making a concerted effort to remain calm. "The choice not to conduct an autopsy was made solely by Piero's mother and father," he said. "Qualified medical examiners informed them their son died of a heart attack. They chose to accept their professional judgment, which is what we all should do; let the matter drop and allow our brother in Christ to rest in peace."

"But—"

"But as devastated as we all are by Monsignor Scala's death, you are here to talk about the Bernini exhibition. His Holiness is most impressed by the job Cardinal Amici and his co-chairman, Donato Martelli, the curator of the Borghese Museum, have done arranging this exciting year-long celebration. Each month there will be special events to honor the great sculptor. On behalf of Pope John, I extend an invitation to your audience." He smiled, and, for the first time, looked directly at the camera. "Join us in Rome as we celebrate Bernini. Now, if you will excuse me, Ms. Bradford, I have guests to greet."

"Of course," Emma said. "Thank you for your time, Monsignor."

Masella turned off his forced smile at the exact moment Ron stopped filming. "Had I known your intent, I would have never agreed to this interview," he said angrily. "I assumed you wanted to talk about Bernini."

"I apologize if I asked a question that upset you," Emma said. "I wasn't aware a discussion of the pope's flu bug or the death of a Vatican priest was off limits."

"You are in Rome to report on Bernini," Masella said firmly. "Please do that and nothing more, Ms. Bradford."

"I'm afraid it won't be possible to do what you ask, Monsignor," Emma said defiantly, "but now that the camera's no longer rolling, perhaps you could answer two more questions."

Masella was clearly annoyed. "What is it?" he said huffily.

"First, from everything I've heard, popes have two private secretaries, yet Pope John has only one. Why is that?"

Masella scowled. "However many secretaries a pontiff choses to have is not a written rule. I suppose His Holiness feels I am able to handle the work. And your other question, Ms. Bradford? I believe you said you have two."

"I do," said Emma. "Why the sudden thaw in relations between the pope and Cardinal Amici? Everyone who reads a paper or watches television realizes there's little hope for an ideological compromise."

The monsignor smiled, but his eyes were cold. "As I said, Ms. Bradford, enjoy the Bernini exhibition. If there is anything else I can tell you in that regard, please do not hesitate to contact me." He turned and stomped away.

Helen left her position beside Ron and approached Emma. "I'm not sure what it is, but I'm positive you're onto something," she said. "Monsignor Cipriano doesn't want you to keep investigating. You realize you're challenging a powerful man."

"Please don't tell me to back off or be careful," Emma said. "It seems like everyone I've seen today has advised or warned me either verbally or with his body language."

"Quite the contrary," said Helen. "We're definitely going to pursue your story."

Emma sighed. "I was hoping you'd say that. Thanks for trusting my instincts."

"Ron and I are going to the truck to separate out the Bernini segment. We'll put all your Vatican interviews and the footage Ron shot in Saint Peter's Square on a separate disk. But first tell me everything you know or suspect."

"Gladly, but not now." Emma looked to her right. "Here comes Angelo. On the way to the reception, he said the cardinal wants to meet with me privately. Before I forget, please print your cell phone pictures of Father Paul. He may be more than an American priest who happens to be working in the Vatican archives."

Helen grinned. "That was an interesting move. We have it on tape. I can see the headlines now: 'ABC reporter manhandles Catholic priest.'"

"If our Father Paul is a priest. I'll join you in a little while. First I need to see the cardinal."

Helen held out her recorder. "See if you can tape the interview."

"There's no way," Emma said resolutely. "I won't even ask for permission. Cardinal Amici doesn't know me. It was coincidence I happened on the scene during a critical time in his conflict with the pope. Trust me, he would never allow me to record our conversation and risk having the recorder fall into the wrong hands."

Angelo stood aside while Ron and Helen finished their conversation. When they were through, he approached Emma. "Cardinal Amici will see you in his office now, Ms. Bradford," he said. "Follow me, please."

From time to time, Angelo looked around apprehensively as he led Emma through several buildings and courtyards. When they reached the cardinal's office, one of the two men standing at the door stepped directly in front Emma, preventing her from entering. "The cardinal is not well," he said sternly. "The activities of the day were too much for him, and he is resting. Please phone for another appointment, Ms. Bradford."

A sick feeling came over Emma as she recalled the cardinal's note—*I'm being guarded.* "You know my name?" she responded, trying to maintain her cool. "How could that be?"

"We keep track of all the cardinal's appointments," the man said.

"George Orwell would love this," Emma said snidely. "Is it normal practice for Big Brother to be watching the prelates of the church?"

The burly guard smiled, though he obviously wasn't pleased. "Monsignor Patini will show you out, Ms. Bradford," he said. "Have a nice day." His body language said "don't mess with me."

"Would you like to go back to the reception?" Angelo asked.

Helen looked at her watch. "I haven't scheduled anymore interviews," she said. "Emma?"

"Frankly I've had enough for today."

Emma knew better than to argue. "Thank you," she said. "I'll make another appointment with Cardinal Amici."

"I'll walk you to your truck to be sure you get there safely," Angelo said when they reached the open piazza.

Emma raised an eyebrow. "Safely?" she said. "That's an interesting choice of words. You know, Monsignor, with a couple of word changes, one of Shakespeare's most famous lines could describe the state of affairs in Vatican City. In *Hamlet*, Marcellus, one of the guards on duty when the ghost of King Hamlet appears early in the play, says: 'Something's rotten in the state of Denmark.' He means there are strange and evil events occurring. If he were in Rome today, Marcellus might say: 'Something's rotten in the Holy See.' I can't tell you how many times I've been warned to concentrate on Bernini and forget everything else, and now you're telling me I need an escort so I won't be harmed while I walk across Saint Peter's Square to the Orbit News truck?"

"Perhaps there wouldn't be a reason for worry if you would take everyone's advice. Report on Bernini and leave it at that, Ms. Bradford."

"As I told Monsignor Cipriano, I'm afraid that's not possible. Do you have any idea why Cardinal Amici wanted to see me this afternoon?"

"I believe he intended to ask you to come to Piero's funeral tomorrow and hoped you would bring your cameraman with you."

"I can do that."

Before speaking again, Angelo looked around. Satisfied there was no one within earshot, he whispered, "You obviously know the cardinal is being guarded. The Vatican police outside his door are not there for his protection. He is, in effect, a prisoner in his rooms."

For a moment, Emma considered telling Angelo about the cardinal's note, but she quickly decided the information would be best kept to herself. "I figured that," she said. "Under the circumstances, will he be allowed to officiate at Monsignor Scala's funeral?"

"As far as I know. It would look bad if he was prevented from saying Mass, and the Vatican is all about presenting a united front to the world."

"Ironic in light of what just happened on the loggia," Emma said. She didn't give Angelo time to respond. "Would they dare use the same excuse the guards gave me? And who are 'they'? Did the pope post the guards outside his door?"

"I have no idea."

"I apologize if I'm being rude, but I think you do. You don't want to confirm my suspicions. Do you have your boss's private e-mail address? I'd like to write to him."

Angelo was clearly uncomfortable. "The cardinal's computer was confiscated just before his appearance with the pope," he said.

"So he's completely cut off from the outside world?"

"It appears so, but—"

Emma interrupted: "I realize I'm rudely changing the subject, but did the cardinal appoint you to this position, Father?"

"I was Piero's assistant, so it was natural for me to step into his place."

"Of course it was," she said, perhaps a little too sarcastically "I'm sorry if I sounded accusatory. It wasn't my intention, but I'm having trouble understanding. I'm going to ask you a question."

"I'll try to answer."

"Is there any chance Cardinal Amici has anything to do with the pope's so-called flu?"

"Of course not," Angelo said quickly and adamantly. "Why would you think such a thing?"

"Because I've been told the only way the conservatives can possibly stop the pope from enacting the changes he proposes is to elect a new pope and—"

"Ms. Bradford. I hope you're not thinking Cardinal Amici would do anything to harm the pope. If you are, I suggest you keep your thoughts to yourself. Piero died of natural causes, and the pope has the flu, nothing more. Now that you're safely at the truck, I'll say good afternoon."

"Thanks for all you've done to help us with the shoot," Emma said. "Please give the cardinal my regards, and tell him I'm sorry we were unable to meet this afternoon."

"When I see him, I will. I'm sure he is equally disappointed." Angelo turned and walked rapidly back across the square.

Ron and Helen were working when Emma entered the truck. "I've finished today's broadcast," Ron said, "and I've finished the other task. Here's the disk of your interview with the cardinal, the translation of his speech from the balcony, your encounter with Father Paul, and your interview with Monsignor Cipriano."

"Are you going to use any of this in the Bernini broadcast?" Emma asked.

"No," said Helen. "We've added the pope's blessing and the lines from the cardinal's spiel which refer to the exhibit, but nothing more."

"Good. I want everyone to think I'm backing off." She handed the disk back to Ron. "Would you make several copies for me?"

"You think someone might try to steal the original?"

"I'm not sure, but after everything I've seen and heard today, I wouldn't be surprised."

"I want a complete rundown before I show you the footage," Helen said, "and while I'm thinking about it, here are the pictures I took of Father Paul." She handed the photos to Emma.

"Thanks. I think I have a way to find out who this man is. He's probably a priest, but I also think he's involved in whatever's going on."

"Want to tell us what you're thinking?"

"I do, but not in here. Why don't we take a walk before I watch the show?"

"Good idea. It's rather crowded in the truck. Come on, Ron."

As they left the trailer and walked toward the obelisk, the square had emptied out, and only the usual tourists were milling around. "Before I tell you everything, I want to warn you," Emma said. "By revealing what I know, and asking you to be a part of the investigation, I could be putting you in danger, so it's up to you."

"It's too late now," Ron said. "We're already involved, and from what I've seen, there's no way you'll be able to report on this story by yourself."

"Then here's what I've discovered so far." For the next fifteen minutes, Emma told Helen and Ron everything that had occurred throughout the day, beginning with Giro's portentous advice and ending with Angelo's final warning to keep her thoughts to herself, "which brings the experience full circle," she said.

"One man may have died because of this conflict. Are you sure you want to keep investigating?" Helen asked. "As I said a while ago, these are powerful men with weighty causes. They'll stop at nothing to have their way."

"Helen, I'm a journalist. This is what I've always wanted to do. I didn't sign on to report on Mayor Marino and Junior League luncheons. That said, it's your call. As Ron said, I can't do this alone."

"It seems you know what you're doing, so we'll pursue the story. I wanted to be sure you're going into this with your eyes wide open."

"I am. Thank you, Helen."

"Not so fast. I have one condition, and I don't think you're going to like it."

"You're making me nervous."

"I want you to ask Michael Kelsey for help."

"Excuse me?" Emma said in disbelief.

"Emma, he's a good guy and a great reporter. It's a shame you two got off on the wrong foot. Yes, he can be a blowhard, and he may seem slightly egotistical."

"Slightly?"

Helen laughed. "Okay, extremely egotistical, but once you get to know him, he's a loyal friend and a great reporter. I know you're concerned he'll steal your story. I guarantee he won't even try. If you're going to solve this mystery, if there's a mystery to be solved, you'll need to have a man with you, and please don't say anything about women being able to do anything men can."

"Even if it's true?"

"Nine out of ten times you'd be right, but if you had a man with you, especially a jock like Michael, whoever wants to stop you, or worse, might think twice. I see that 'you've-got-to-be-kidding' look, but you know I'm right. Do you think Father Paul would have confronted you if Michael was standing by your side? You were a woman alone." She laughed. "Though when he did, I'm sure he had no idea you were going to accost him."

"It was a split-second decision. I didn't plan to grab him and swing him around."

"I know. I may be risking bodily harm by insisting, but I won't agree to pursue the story if you don't tell Michael everything."

"After all you've seen, do you really believe Michael and I can work together?"

"You're both professionals, Emma. Give Michael a chance. If you do, Ron and I will sign on and ask Bill and David to work with us. A team of six can get more done than one person, so if you believe in your story—"

"Alright, I'll talk with Michael. If he responds positively, I'll bring him on board, but it's going to kill me."

"But you know it's the right thing to do."

"What about the Bernini reports?"

"We go ahead as planned, so let's go take a look at tonight's show so you can make any last-minute changes before we send it to Boston. When we're finished, you can talk with Michael."

"I hope you're right about the guy."

"You asked me to trust you. It's your turn to trust me."

"I suppose I have no choice," Emma said crankily.

"That's right, you don't. So shall we go back at the truck and take a look at the segment. Perhaps you'll have an opportunity to speak with Michael."

"Maybe I will," Emma said sourly as she followed Helen and Ron back across the square.

Emma watched the show on the monitor at Helen's station. "Seven minutes and not five," she said, her mood suddenly improving. "You called Boston?"

"I did. I told them your reports exceeded my wildest expectations; that what you have to report is worthy of additional time. Before you thank me, I told them we'd have a wrap-up special on the weekend."

"Really. On Bernini?"

"If that's all we have. I'm thinking we may have something extraordinary for the feature."

"If we can figure everything out by then."

"We have the week. If we're not quite there, I'll extend our stay."

"Do we show Michael what we have?"

"Not in the trailer."

Ron handed Emma a DVD. "When did you do this?" she asked.

"When you were watching the show." He handed a copy to Helen. "Here's one for you, and I'll keep another with me."

"I see Michael in the back of the truck," Helen said. "Why don't you go back and make nice while we send the segment to Boston. Set up a time to meet and talk."

Emma rolled her eyes and sighed. "If I must."

"That's my condition. If we don't talk before then, I'll see you at the Borghese at 6:30 tomorrow morning."

"If I survive this ordeal." Emma rolled her eyes.

"I'm sure you'll be fine." Helen grinned.

Emma walked back to where Michael was working. "How's the segment look?" she asked nicely, dreading his response. Would the Michael that Helen talked about show up, or would Michael, the ass, answer?

"Pretty good, though I'm surprised you're interested. Since you are, care to take a look?"

"I'd love to," Emma responded, wondering if she was showing a little too much enthusiasm.

If she was, Michael didn't seem to notice. He started the segment at the beginning. Emma watched the five-minute presentation he'd shot outside Saint Peter's Square. "Great show," she said, meaning the compliment.

"But not as good as yours. I'm hoping you won't be angry, but I watched your show while you were in the square with Ron and Helen. It's really great, Emma."

"Thanks." Emma turned to leave, sighed, and turned back. "Michael, I may have a lead on an incredible story. Helen wants me to tell you what I know and see if you're willing to help me out."

Emma didn't have to wait for an answer. He stood. "Of course," he said. "Tell me what I can do."

"I can't tell you here. I'll let Giro know I'm ready to go and meet you back at the hotel."

"Why don't you call Giro and tell him you don't need the car? Lucio's here. You can ride with me. When we get back, let's have a drink at the sidewalk café outside the Doney. You can tell me everything while we relax."

"If I can relax. I don't want to talk about the story in front Lucio, or anyone else for that matter."

While Emma called Giro, Michael turned to Bill. "You guys okay without me," he asked.

"We are. We'll see you at the Borghese in the morning."

"I'll be there."

"Ready?" Michael said as Emma hung up.

"I am," *but for what?* Emma wondered.

CHAPTER TWELVE

Neither Michael nor Emma said much during the drive back to the hotel. Though the nice guy had shown up, Emma wondered how long before the jerk reemerged.

"Do you need to go up to your room before we have that drink?" Michael asked when Giro dropped then at the hotel entrance.

"Actually, I do. I feel grubby after filming all day. It may be fall, but the sun's summertime hot. Would you mind if we postpone our conversation? I'd like to take a quick shower and change into more comfortable clothes."

"Not at all. I'd like to shed this suit. I'll walk you to your door, go to my room, and come back to get you."

"You don't need to escort me."

"I know, but humor me. How long do you need?"

"About a half-hour?"

"Thirty minutes it is."

Emma laughed. "What? No comments about a woman who's able to get ready so quickly?"

"No way. My bad-boy behavior's a thing of the past." Michael paused. "Do I see doubt in your eyes?"

"Forgive me if I'm skeptical. For the moment I'll just say thank God for small miracles and leave it at that. Let me get my keycard." She went to the desk while Michael waited by the elevator.

"Do you always leave your key at the desk when you're away from the hotel?" Michael asked when they were on their way to the fourth floor.

"I do. My station manager arranged for additional security so Ron and Helen could leave the cameras and computers in the room. Besides the two of them, the maid has the only other access. When I leave my key at the desk, security knows I'm away. They can monitor the hallway to be sure no unauthorized person tries to get in. Under the circumstances, I'm thankful Jack took extraordinary precautions."

"Are you worried about the computers or your own safety?"

"Until this morning, the equipment, but, truthfully, now I'm not sure how to answer your question. I'll tell you why after you buy me a drink."

"I'm buying?"

For a moment Emma thought the ass was back, but she saw the twinkle in Michael's eye. "If you want me to think you've changed, you will."

Michael laughed. "In that case, I'll buy as many drinks as you want."

"One will be sufficient. Any more and I'll be lying on the floor, which would be interesting footage if you had a camera. I've just been filmed manhandling a priest, so why not passed out drunk?"

"You manhandled a priest?"

"No comment. I'll see you in a while." Emma went into her room, leaving Michael standing at the door.

Before showering, she checked her e-mail. Jack had forwarded a copy of Helen's praiseful note as well as his congratulations for a job well done. She read a missive from her mom. Not wanting her to worry, she sat at the desk and typed a short response telling her how busy she was and how much she was enjoying Rome. After promising to call soon, she turned off the computer and took her shower.

The water was invigorating and, once again, she lingered longer than she originally planned. After she toweled off, she had only ten minutes before Michael was supposed to pick her up. "There's no way in hell I'm going to be late and not hear about it," she said, so she hurriedly dressed, put on a daub of makeup, and raced to the door.

Michael was walking toward her when she stepped outside. "Great timing," she said.

"I'm impressed." He quickly rephrased. "What I meant to say was I knew you'd be ready and waiting for me."

"You mean you hoped I wouldn't be so you could give me a load of crap."

"Would I do that?"

"If I recall, it's your MO."

"I can see you're enjoying yourself, but, Ms. Bradford, you're referring to the old Michael. You're having drinks with the new and improved model."

"That's a relief, because I'm going to take a chance that the man I glimpse from time to time is the real Michael Kelsey."

As they entered the elevator, Michael suddenly became serious. "I assure you, he is, Emma. No more acts. Trust me."

Emma hesitated. "I'm trying to, though truthfully, I'm only doing so because Helen insists on it. She won't run with the story unless you're on board. I know I'm onto something big, but I've been warned to leave it alone so many times today, I don't know what to do. You meant it when you said 'trust me'?"

"Without a doubt."

"Then ply me with liquor and I'll tell you everything, though for the moment, what I'm going to say is for your ears only."

"You have a deal, and as far as the liquor part goes, I wish I'd known ordering a few drinks on the plane—"

"Are you sure you want to go there?"

"Maybe not," Michael said, grinning.

When they were comfortably seated at a table away from other customers and the drinks had been served, Emma began: "Bernini's not the story," she said, "though he's play-ing a role in what's currently occurring in the Vatican."

Michael leaned forward. "That doesn't make sense. A dead artist is playing a role?"

"I didn't say it well. What I mean is the message Bernini conveyed through his art is being used by conservatives to keep the pope from imposing significant changes in church doctrine."

"How's that possible?"

While she sipped her martini and nibbled on cheese and crackers, Emma told Michael everything she knew for sure as well as what she believed was happening. She was surprised more than once during the conversation. Michael showed incredible insight and a deep understanding of the seven-teenth-century Counter-Reformation as well as the conflict between the liberals and conservatives currently occurring in the Holy See. At one point, she stopped talking about the events of the day and asked: "How is it you're so up-to-date on what's going on?"

Michael's response was reassuring. When he began to talk, he wasn't showing off or bragging about how much he knew; he was explaining. *Maybe Helen was right,* Emma pondered as she listened to his answer.

"I'm Catholic," he began, "so even if my best friend weren't a priest, I'd be aware of the controversy between the various factions in the Vatican. Secondly, I may come across as a jerk, or as you called me, 'a Geraldo-wannabe,' but I assure you, I do my homework. Why ruin my reputation by letting you or anyone else know how much time I put into background research for my shoots? You snore."

"Excuse me!"

"Not loudly, and it's really kind of cute. While you were sleeping, I was cramming. I didn't just miss the plane because I left the station late and encountered heavy traffic. I spent too much time at the bookstore looking through books about Bernini. I confess, when I was given the assignment, I thought the guy played third base for the Yankees."

Emma laughed. "You really bought books?"

"I did, and I downloaded everything I could find on the Web, but you're sworn to secrecy."

"My lips are sealed, but have you ever considered that the intelligent, conscientious reporter who's talking with me right now would be respected by his bosses and peers and be assigned more significant stories? He's much more believable than the jerk who sat with me on the plane. I certainly like him better, and while I'm on the topic, I apologize for the name-calling." Emma paused. "And I don't snore."

Michael laughed. "All right, it was my imagination, but with regard to your so-called name-calling, believe me, I deserved your contempt. I have no idea why I kept on making a fool of myself. Maybe I'll figure it out before we leave for home."

"Shall we both forget what happened?"

Michael nodded. "I hope you can."

Instead of responding, Emma pulled out a picture of Father Paul and handed it to Michael. "Any idea how we can find out who this is?"

"Why? Do you think he's important?"

"I don't know."

Emma told him about Father Paul's translation of the cardinal's speech and the events that followed. "Do you trust Steven?" she asked. "I mean, I know you trust him, but enough to involve him in our investigation of Vatican politics?"

"I'd trust him with my life."

"Though it may sound overly dramatic, it may come to that if we pursue this story. Bottom line, I believe someone in the liberal faction killed Monsignor Piero Scala, Cardinal Amici's private secretary, and it's possible that members of the conservative bloc are responsible for Pope John's flu bug."

"Let me get this straight." Michael leaned in and whispered: "You think the liberals killed Piero Scala and the pope is being poisoned by the conservatives."

"Is the idea really that farfetched? I know Piero didn't have a heart attack. Maybe his death was a warning?"

"A warning?"

"A message to the cardinal to stop."

"Stop what? Poisoning the pope? How could Cardinal Amici or his representative get through the cadre of doctors and administer the poison? If you meant get the cardinal to stop speaking out, wouldn't Piero's death have the opposite effect? Emma, all you have is conjecture. You have nothing concrete on which to base your theory."

"I know the cardinal was frightened when he appeared with Pope John on the loggia today."

"How can you know that? You were standing below him. Unless you had a pair of high-powered binoculars, there was no way you'd be able to see his facial expressions or read his body language."

"I have proof on the DVD, which you'll soon see, but I didn't need the video to know. Look at this." Emma took a piece of paper out of her purse. "When the cardinal said good-bye after our interview, he left this note in my hand."

Michael's eyes widened as he read. "He really believes his life is in danger?" he said. "You talked with him. Was he agitated? Was he acting rationally?"

"I'd say he was morose, but why wouldn't he be? He lost his trusted secretary and friend. Otherwise he was perfectly rational. As for the part about the guards, trust me, it's true. I had a personal encounter with the brutes."

"When?"

"During the reception. Cardinal Amici instructed his new secretary, Angelo Patini, to bring me to his apartments. And while I'm thinking about it, the cardinal was supposed to be at the reception. Why was he a no-show? Don't you find it strange? He's a co-chair of the event. He'd be expected to attend."

"Considering his position, I suppose so," Michael said pensively, "but tell me more about your encounter with the cardinal's guards."

"When we got to the office, two burly men prevented me from going inside. Thinking we could communicate electronically, I asked Angelo for the cardinal's e-mail address. He told me the cardinal's computer has been confiscated."

"You're kidding."

"I'm deadly serious."

Michael shook his head. "If you don't mind, let's not use words referring to death or dying." He took out a small pad from his pocket. "Okay, let's write down what we know."

"Are you sure that's a good idea? Giro told me in Vatican City no one dares express an opinion inconsistent with the official position. He also warned me never to write anything down."

"We're not in Vatican City, we're in Rome, and this is for our personal use, to organize our thoughts. I don't know about you, but I've always found it easier to figure things out when I put my ideas on paper."

"I'm a visual learner too. All right, but guard the list with your life."

"There you go again. Didn't I ask you to skip the grim reaper references?" He put up his hand as Emma started to comment. "Just kidding. Talk to me."

"Let's see; to date this is what we know for sure or surmise: First, we know the pope has been ill. It could be the flu or perhaps drugs which cause flu-like symptoms. He was obviously weak and not himself when he appeared on the loggia today."

"What makes you think so?"

"I watched him closely and have pictures to confirm what I saw. Ron put all pertinent interviews on the disk along with close-ups of the group amassed on the loggia, front and back rows, as well as the pope and the cardinal standing side by side during both of their presentations."

"Really. Why'd you think to do that?"

"I had the cardinal's note, remember? I wanted to see if there was any merit in what he was telling me, so I told Ron what to shoot. I haven't seen the footage yet. Maybe we can both take a look at it after we're finished here."

"Good idea. Do you have a DVD player in your room?"

"I think I saw one in the sitting room."

"Then let's keep writing down our thoughts. When we've finished our drink we'll go upstairs. While you're setting up the DVD, I'll call Steven. How about asking him to join us for dinner?"

"Fine, if you really think we should involve him. I'd hate for him to meet the same fate as Monsignor Scala."

"He won't."

"What makes you so sure?"

"Steven's not a political creature, and he's definitely not ambitious, so he wouldn't be a threat to either side. He's really apolitical. He became a priest to serve God in a practical way. When we were going to dinner last night, I alluded to his wealth. He's rolling in family money and uses much of the interest he receives from his fortune to support the works of the church. He assumes he was elevated to monsignor because of his charitable deeds. Maybe it's because I've known him all my life, but I've never pictured Steven as a pious priest. He's essentially a philanthropist, a businessman and problem solver disguised in priest's robes."

"Couldn't he have found a way to contribute without taking Holy Orders?"

"Apparently not, though he never really explained his choice to me. So what else?"

"Second, Piero Scala's dead. The cardinal says he was murdered, but there won't be an autopsy to confirm his assertion one way or the other. The party line is the family is listening to the cardinal's recommendation and refusing the examination."

"But we know the cardinal asked for an autopsy."

"Exactly. Think they're putting him in the ground so quickly to keep his mom and dad from changing their mind?"

"More of your conspiracy theory?"

"Possibly, but for some reason Cardinal Amici wants me to attend the funeral and bring Ron and his camera along."

"Are you going?"

"I plan to." She hesitated for a moment. "Will you join me?"

"Try and keep me away. I'll ask Bill to come along. He and Ron can divide the filming duties."

"Good, because I already know what I want them to shoot."

"Tell me later so we won't have to waste time making plans in the morning, and while I'm thinking about it, remind me to call David and change tomorrow's filming time from eight to seven so we'll have plenty of time to finish before the funeral begins."

"I'll try to remember, but at this point my mind's cluttered."

"Then let's unclutter it a little more. What else?"

"Where was I?" Emma looked at her notes. "Okay, number three: I believe Masella Cipriano, Pope John's private secretary, knows what's going on. He may actually be involved."

Michael raised an eyebrow. "Once again, you know this how?"

"His demeanor when I interviewed him. Granted, he had no idea I was going to blindside him with questions about Piero Scala's death as well as a few other controversial issues."

"You did that?"

"As I said, I'll show you the DVD when we get upstairs. When I was on the tour of Saint Peter's with Nicola, I was excited to see the windows of the pope's apartments were open. I asked her to tell me about the pope's rooms in the Apostolic Palace. She said the pope lives on the third floor with his two secretaries and a few servants. I asked Masella why he was Pope John's only private secretary."

"You're kidding?"

"I'm not."

"Why would you ask that, and what did he say?"

"I asked because I believe Masella is key to whatever's going on in Vatican politics. His answer provided further proof. He became agitated and told me the number of secretaries a pope employs isn't set in stone; that he can handle the job."

"But you think there's another reason."

"I do, call it woman's intuition. . ." Emma paused and smiled. "On second thought that wouldn't be a wise thing for you to say. I may be way off base, but I think Masella wants exclusive access to the pontiff; access that would be shared if there were a second secretary."

Michael finished writing. "Okay, I can buy that. What else?"

"Number four: Angelo, the cardinal's new secretary, is also involved, or he knows more than he's willing to share. I can't put my finger on it, but something's not right. He was rude when I asked him if the cardinal was the one who appointed him to take Piero's place."

"Why wouldn't he be testy? You were more or less accusing him of being involved in something shady."

"That was my intention. Is it too farfetched to think he's a mole?"

Michael laughed. "You've been watching too many spy movies."

"I don't like spy movies. I prefer old musicals, but the fact that I've seen *The Sound of Music* twenty-five times isn't important right now."

"Maybe not now, but you can be sure we'll talk about it on the way back to New York." Michael didn't wait for Emma to respond. "Tell me more."

"Number five: My interview with the cardinal was political from the first moments. It was evident he hadn't invited me to interview him about Bernini, the subject we were scheduled to discuss."

"I know I'm playing the devil's advocate, but that's not surprising. The cardinal feels strongly about the pope's proposed changes. It would be natural for him to want to share his beliefs and opinions with a reporter, especially if he thinks his secretary's death has something to do with internal politics."

"Even when he agreed the topic of conversation was the Bernini exhibition, a project he's been planning for over a year?"

"Absolutely. In his mind, he's involved in a second Counter-Reformation. The only difference is this time a groundswell of Protestant belief isn't the problem. He's dealing with a force from within in the person of a liberal pope." Emma nodded almost imperceptibly as Michael continued: "I can see you're skeptical."

"I'm not sure it's skepticism. It's hard for me to wrap my head around what appears to be happening. We're not living in the Middle Ages, a time when popes and cardinals resorted to murder to promote their own agendas."

"I know, Emma, but this isn't a minor philosophical disagreement, a topic for church elders to discuss behind closed doors. The pope made it clear that he plans to change the face of the Catholic Church forever. He's going beyond what those taking part in Vatican II ever thought of doing, which many Catholics, myself included, would welcome. If it's going to survive, the church must adapt to modern times."

"I agree, but be honest. How passionate are you about the proposed changes?"

"I'm not passionate about them at all, but then Steven calls me a 'fallen Catholic.'" Emma laughed. "Did I say something amusing?" Michael asked.

"Not really, it's just that Nicola and I recently had a conversation about fallen Catholics. Go on, I'm sorry I interrupted."

"No problem. Let's see. Where was I when I was rudely interrupted?"

"Michael—"

"Ah yes, now I remember." Michael was suddenly serious again. "There are many Catholics who are adamantly for or against change. I imagine passions are intense in Vatican City. The question is, how far would either side go to insure their plans to bring about change or prevent change from being implemented?"

"Probably not as far as murder or poisoning."

"Maybe not, but then again—"

"Your gut tells you it's possible."

"Exactly."

The waiter came back to the table, interrupting the conversation. "Would you like another drink?" he asked.

Michael turned to Emma. "I'm all set," she said. "Why don't we go upstairs, take a look at your interviews, and call Steven and David?"

"That works for me."

Michael settled the bill, and rather than going back through the dining room, they walked to the front door of the hotel. "Before we go in, would you mind if we go across the street to the ATM?" Emma pointed. "There's one over there on the corner. I tipped Nicola with most of the money I got at the airport when I was stalling."

"Stalling?"

"Yes. I confess I didn't want to see the obnoxious man I sat with on the plane, so I thought I'd kill time until I was sure he was out of the parking lot."

"He must have been insufferable if you felt you had to go that far to avoid him."

"Oh, he was. I hope I never see him again."

"I'm sure you won't. Rome's a big city. I imagine he disappeared into the crowds and is gone forever."

As they crossed Via Veneto and neared the hotel entrance, Emma gasped and grabbed Michael's arm. He turned and saw the concern on her face. "Tell me what's the matter," he urged.

"Angelo Patini is sitting in the backseat of that car."

"What car? Where?"

Emma nodded in the direction of the limos parked on the other side of the circle. "The black one over there."

Michael looked at the car. "You're right," he said. "Why would he be here?"

"I have no idea."

"Then let's ask him. Come on."

Michael didn't give Emma time to protest. They walked directly to the car, and Michael tapped on the window. "Monsignor Patini," he said when the window opened, "we haven't been introduced. I'm Michael Kelsey, Ms. Bradford's ABC colleague. What brings you here to the Excelsior?"

Angelo was clearly startled. "I want to speak with Ms. Bradford."

"You couldn't talk with her on the phone?"

"I thought, I mean I decided that speaking with her in person might be better," he stuttered.

"Better for whom?" Michael said, frowning.

"Would you care to join us in the lobby, Monsignor?" Emma said, not waiting for Angelo to answer Michael's question. "It would be more comfortable for all of us."

"Of course," Angelo said, but Emma could see he was fidgeting nervously.

Michael opened the back door. Angelo got out of the car and followed him and Emma into the foyer and up into the lobby. When all three of them were seated, Emma and Michael on a couch and Angelo opposite them in a straight-back chair, Angelo seemed reluctant to begin the conversation.

"Please don't hold back on account of me," Michael said. "Ms. Bradford and I are covering the Bernini exhibition together."

Angelo's eyes widened. "Since when?" he asked. "Ms. Bradford didn't say anything to me about having a partner."

"I'm not exactly her partner. I became involved when I realized there's more to what's going on in Vatican City than the opening of an art exhibit. That's true, isn't it, Father?"

"Actually it's not," Angelo said, "but that is not why I'm here, Mr. Kelsey. I came to say that Cardinal Amici feels an American reporter attending a private funeral would be intrusive."

Michael raised an eyebrow. "A private funeral? I saw the announcement on the English version of the morning news, so I know that friends were invited to attend. Does that suggest a private funeral?"

"Perhaps not, but the invitation excludes members of the media."

"So no one from the Italian press will be there?" Emma asked. From the look on Angelo's face, she knew she'd scored a point.

"I suppose there will be a few reporters in attendance," Angelo said tentatively.

Michael smirked. "Then expect us to cover the funeral for ABC."

"Then you should know Cardinal Amici will not be speaking with you. He made it clear. He will grant no interviews."

"Then his nap must have brought about a change of heart," Emma said. "Didn't you say he planned to ask me to attend the funeral? I think he expected we'd have a chance to talk and perhaps find a way to work together to solve the mystery of Monsignor Scala's murder."

Angelo frowned. "We are sure that no murder occurred, and the cardinal withdrew his invitation out of respect for the Piero family."

"I'm sure that's it," Emma said, "but my interest is piqued, so I'll be attending despite the cardinal's change of heart." She stood up. "So we'll see you in the morning, Monsignor. If you'll excuse us, Michael and I have work to do. We want to review the footage from all my interviews today as well as the event which took place on the Benedictine Loggia."

"You recorded everything?"

"Of course. I'm a reporter, remember?"

"Nice to meet you, Monsignor," Michael said. "See you tomorrow."

Angelo nodded. "It seems you will." He looked at Emma. "Please remember what I and others told you today."

"Of course I'll remember, but not for the reason you're suggesting."

"Then good luck. I'm afraid you may need it."

"I'm not sure what the last part of your statement means, but thanks for the good wishes," said Emma. "Come on, Michael. Bye, Monsignor."

"God, you've got balls," Michael said when they got to the elevator.

"Put your arm around me, would you?" Emma said, and Michael grinned. "Not for that reason. Hold me up. My knees are weak."

"I have that effect on you?"

"No, Angelo Patini does."

"You did a great job, Emma," Michael said seriously, "though your candor may have made an enemy of Cardinal Amici's secretary. At the very least, he's nervous."

"I know, but I couldn't sit there and listen to all that bull."

"If it's any consolation, I'm now totally on board. You definitely have a story."

"We do. It's about time we worked together."

"We will, but you'll do all the reporting."

Emma stood back and looked at Michael curiously. "Really?" she said skeptically. "You don't want credit?"

"Absolutely not. So shall we take a look at what's on the disk?"

"I'm feeling stronger every minute." Emma said as she pushed the button for the fourth floor.

CHAPTER THIRTEEN

While Emma put the disk in the DVD player attached to the TV in her sitting room, Michael phoned Steven. Though she couldn't hear what was being said on the other end, more than once she heard Michael say: "I'll tell you later."

"I knew the man wasn't cut out to be a priest," Michael said as he hung up. "He should have been a detective. I don't think he's been this energized since our senior year in high school, when we won the state football championship."

"Think he'll still be excited when he finds out we're investigating what's happening in the Vatican?"

"Probably more so."

"Before I push the play button, call David. I'm not sure how much longer I can remember to remind you."

"I'm on it!" Michael pushed a button on his cell.

Emma excused herself and went to the powder room. When she returned to the sitting room, Michael was just hanging up. "Was David okay with the time change?" she asked.

"He wasn't particularly happy about having to get up an hour earlier, but he came around when I told him why we had to film two Bernini segments in one day."

"You didn't tell him everything."

"Only that we have a funeral to film on Monday and we're doing some preliminary investigating which could lead to a big story. I'll fill him and Bill in on the details at the Borghese in the morning. Let's not waste time. Shall we take a look at what Ron put on the disk?"

Pausing and rewinding often, they watched Emma's interviews, the ceremony on the Benedictine Loggia which included her running commentary about the cardinal and pope, and her assault on Father Paul. "I guess I'm lucky," Michael said when they finished a second viewing.

"Lucky?"

"That you didn't attack me in the airplane like you did that poor priest."

Emma grinned. "You were dangerously close to feeling my wrath. So what do you think? Do you agree there's more to this story than meets the eye?"

"I definitely do."

"Good." Emma looked at her watch. "We have a couple of hours before Steven arrives, and I really have to work on my Saint Peter's Square presentation."

"You're that far along?" Michael groaned. "I haven't even started the Borghese copy."

"How can I possibly sit here and do nothing to help a fellow reporter who continues to spin such a sad tale? Your stellar reputation would definitely be ruined if you appear bleary-eyed on camera, though I'm sure that's happened more than once in the past."

Michael feigned annoyance, though the twinkle in his eye gave him away. "If so, it was only because I stayed up late preparing. I'm the consummate professional, and, frankly, I'm offended by what you're insinuating."

"Of course you are." Emma grinned, stood up, walked to the desk, picked up the papers Nicola had given her, and handed them to him. "Consider this my way of making amends for hurting your feelings and an effort on my part to save your reputation."

Michael looked puzzled. "What's all this?"

"It's a thank you for believing in my story. Do you have photos of the Bernini sculptures in the Borghese?"

"I told you I almost missed the plane so I could buy my picture book."

"That's right, you did, and though I'm inclined to make a comment about jocks and books with pictures, in the spirit of our renewed cooperation and to keep from wounding your fragile ego yet again, I'll refrain."

"As if you hadn't already made your point." He took the folder. "How would you like to take this new spirit of team-work to the next level?"

Emma looked at him suspiciously. "What does that mean?"

"Though I could come up with a suggestive response, it means why don't we join forces? Do we really need to conduct two interviews with the curator? Why don't we report jointly and air the shows as planned in Boston and New York? If we end up on *Good Morning America* or *ABC World News*, we'll both be in the spotlight. The best part is if we're a team, we'll cut our individual workloads in half and be able to concentrate on the real story."

"You really want to do this?"

"Absolutely."

"But being a reporter in the New York market, you definitely have the edge when it comes to receiving national coverage."

"I may have thought so before, but not after I watched your show. You're good, so call it an act of self-preservation. Plus, you understand art, and however much I study, I can't speak authoritatively on the subject. I'll look like a lost jock who's pretending to be cultured." He opened her folder and read. "For example, I'm reading about movement in *Apollo and Daphne.* I can tell you everything you want to know about movement on the New York Giant scrimmage line, but how the hell does a marble sculpture move?"

"Funny, Ron asked me the same thing," Emma said, smiling.

"Thank God I'm not the only one without a clue. See how much I need you?"

"And I'll be there for you. How could I live with myself if I were singlehandedly responsible for damaging your spotless reputation?"

"Pretty easily, I imagine. No more about the reputation, please."

"I can't help myself. You're so easy."

"Keep that in mind," Michael teased, "but seriously, are you on board with the idea? There's no chance you'll change your mind?"

Emma nodded. "None whatsoever if we can convince David and Helen."

"That shouldn't be a problem. I'll talk with them while you work on your Saint Peter's report, and here's where the teamwork comes in. I've finished my factual, and, honestly, very boring, version based on Steven's lecture. I confess I tuned him out more than once as he droned on about Bernini's art. In the spirit of our newfound cooperation, when I get back downstairs, I'll e-mail my copy to you. Maybe you could use some of what I wrote and add enough of your own material to put a little pizzazz in the program."

"I will, but what about who says what? Do you want to get together and script the show?"

"You decide. Do whatever makes the report flow smoothly. I trust you'll give us equal screen time."

"I'll give it my best shot. You said most of what you wrote is factual, so I'll add the tidbits Nicola gave me, but first the Borghese. I'll go back through that presentation between now and dinner."

"Then I'll head downstairs and make the calls."

"You really don't think David and Helen will nix the idea?"

"I hope not. We have one thing going for us. Our stations weren't competing—you and I were the ones fighting for the spotlight. My guess is our working together will make the story more significant and help the ratings in both venues, so why wouldn't our bosses go for it?"

"You make a good point."

"Let's find out if I can sell it. If we're given the go-ahead, I'll ask David to call Donato Martelli. We can interview him together at 6:30."

"I imagine he'll appreciate the extra half-hour he was giving you. He's going to have his hands full with the official opening of Bernini in the Borghese. I have all the notes necessary to prepare for Saint Theresa. I'll script that show too. And speaking of scripting, how do you want this to go? Do you want our presentation to be folksy, a discussion-type format with us chatting about the sculptures?"

"Is that what you want?"

"Not really, but we're partners, remember?"

Michael grinned. "I like that. Thanks for consulting me, partner. I really prefer a more formal approach. We're not sitting on the *Good Morning America* set yet."

"No, but we may be after we break the Vatican story."

"Wouldn't that be nice."

"It would be, but back to the Borghese. My first thought is to give you the intro and let you lead the audience into the museum while you talk about the villa."

"That works for me."

"Good. We're going to have to make the intro short or we won't fit everything we want into one report, so I divided the Borghese into a couple of days." She paused. "Maybe it would be easier if you look at the schedule Helen and I came up with." She went over to her desk, picked up the schedule sheet, and handed it to Michael.

"This looks fantastic," he said as he scanned the plan, "but I can't see how are you're going to cover everything in five minutes."

"I forgot to mention. Helen arranged for seven-minute segments. Will David be able to get the extra time?"

"I have no idea, but it could be a deal breaker. New York rarely changes the time they've allotted for this type of feature."

"Maybe they'll relent when they realize we're doing important investigatory work."

"An angle I'll have David pursue."

"So please go make those calls and see if we can work together."

"I'm going, but before I do, will you tell me what you're looking for at the funeral? I'd like to give Bill a heads-up so he and Ron can get together and firm up their plans."

"I'd like for Bill to keep his camera on the cardinal and those serving Mass with him while Ron films the crowd. We need to know who's there, both in the seats and standing around. I want to know if the cardinal's still being guarded, and if he's refusing interviews, not because he chooses to remain silent, but because he's being prevented from speaking. I want Ron to zoom in on the members of the clergy in attendance."

"Why?"

"Because of the information we got from looking at the body language and facial expressions of the people on the loggia when the pope and Cardinal Amici opened the exhibition. For example, we realized the pontiff was weak due to his recent illness. We saw the cardinal was hunched, tense, and obviously frightened when he walked out with Pope John, but as he began to speak, he became defiant and resolute. He glared at the pontiff as if to say 'There's no way I'm going to let you get away with making the changes you want to make.' And then there were the clues in Masella's facial expressions and body language when I asked him the tough questions. He was angry with me and definitely on the defensive."

"And hiding something."

"That's what I think. I'm hoping we'll gain similar insight by watching the behavior of the congregation at the funeral. I want to know whose face reveals fear. Who's expressing defiance? Who's the enforcer? Is the cardinal fearful like he was before he spoke to the crowd in Saint Peter's Square, or is he determined like he was when he left the loggia? The camera will tell us everything. Do you think Bill will be offended if I give him a list of specific shots I want?"

"Not at all."

"And I owe you an apology."

"For what?"

"For not asking you to contribute your ideas. Have I left anything out?"

"Emma, as I've said several times, this is your story, and you're obviously on top of it. I can't think of anything to add at this point."

"But you will make suggestions."

"Absolutely. Now I'll finally get out of here and make those calls. I should have an answer in a half-hour or so. That should give Helen and David sufficient time to phone the stations and get back to me."

"But you think we've got a good chance?"

"My guess is yes. I'll call you as soon as I get the final word."

"Then I'll start going through the tidbits. If we get the thumbs down, I'll still share them with you, and regardless of what happens, you can give me the, and I quote, 'boring copy' you've completed. Instead of e-mailing your report, bring your Saint Peter's copy with you. The less time we have to spend on Bernini, the more time we'll have to investigate. Call me as soon as you know something."

"Will do."

When Michael closed the door behind him, Emma picked up the tidbit list and lay down on the bed to plan where each bit of information would best fit into the reports.

In what seemed like only seconds, the telephone on the bed table jolted her into consciousness. "Hello," she answered groggily.

"Did I wake you up?" Michael asked.

"Apparently so. Trying to work while lying down was my first mistake. What's the verdict?"

"'We're all set. I figured it would be an easy sell, but I didn't think it would be this simple. David and Helen were on board immediately. Apparently my station manager was excited, because he gave me the extra time without a fight. He must smell higher ratings."

"Helen and David didn't tell them *what* we're investigating."

"They said they only gave the stations a tease, saying that we'll be the lead story on every program."

"Let's hope we are. Now I'm going to get to work on the script for Saint Theresa, but this time at my desk in the sitting room. I'll see you at 7:45."

"Make it 7:30. I spoke with Steven while I was waiting to hear back from David. Angelo had no trouble finding out where you were staying, so it's possible others know as well. You made it clear you're hell-bent on pursuing this story even though he insisted you leave it alone, and if I recall, you didn't back off when the pope's secretary—what's his name?"

"Masella Cipriano."

"Right, when he and your mysterious Father Paul told you to leave it alone. Steven feels he can find out more if we work independently."

"He's probably right. So what's the plan?"

"He'll meet us at eight. I almost forgot to tell you. He wants you to send him a picture of Father Paul. He'll try to figure out who he is and if he's a priest."

"Give me his e-mail address, and I'll do it right away."

"He'd rather you send the photo to his Blackberry. Got a pen?"

"I do, but why doesn't he want me to use the computer? The picture will be larger and clearer."

"Because his laptop is hooked up to the Vatican network."

"And he doesn't know who might have access to the e-mails he receives."

"Exactly. So for now, we'll communicate with him on his Blackberry." Michael gave Emma the number. "I'll be at your door at 7:30."

"I'll be waiting. Before you hang up, is your e-mail address kelsey@wabc.com?"

"It is."

"Then, since I don't have a printer, I'll e-mail tomorrow's script to you when I'm finished."

"I'll bring a hard copy when I come to get you, and speaking of picking you up, wait for me in your room, not in the hall."

"You're worried?"

"Just cautious."

For the next hour and a half, Emma scripted the copy for the Saint Theresa and Borghese reports. Before getting dressed, she attached the files to an e-mail and sent copies to Helen and Bill.

Michael arrived at precisely 7:30. When Emma looked through the peephole, he waved. "Right on time," she said when she opened the door.

"You look fantastic."

"You didn't tell me where we're going and I had no idea what to wear. I hope elegant-casual will work."

"I have no idea what elegant-casual looks like, but if that black dress you're wearing is an example, I wholeheartedly approve."

"Thanks," Emma said, hoping against hope she hadn't blushed.

"Here's my Saint Peter's copy," he said, handing Emma a file. "Use it if you want. I won't be upset if you toss it all out."

"Good to know," Emma said, smiling.

"Steven said L'Altra Mastai is close to the Piazza Navona and isn't a place frequented by people from the Vatican. Shall we go?"

Lucio was waiting when they exited the hotel. "Buona sera!" he said as he held the door open for Emma.

"Buona sera," Emma replied as she slid into the backseat.

Before getting in, Michael stood outside and talked with Lucio. "What was that about?" Emma asked when he moved in behind her.

"Maybe nothing. We'll see."

It wasn't long after they left the Excelsior entrance when Lucio glanced back at Michael. "You were right," he said. "We are being followed."

"Followed by whom?" Emma asked anxiously, "And what made you think we would be?"

"Just a hunch, and to answer your first question, I have no idea who's back there."

"What are we going to do?" she asked nervously. "We can't let anyone know we're meeting Steven."

Michael took out his cell. "Steven, are you on your way yet? You are? We're being followed. No." He listened intently. "Good idea. You'll make the arrangements before we get there? Okay. We'll see you when we do."

After he hung up, Michael tapped Lucio on the shoulder. "This is going to sound like a scenario right out of a James Bond movie, but I want you to drop us off in front of Café Bernini at 44 Piazza Navona."

"I know the place," Lucio said.

"Good. Once we're out of the car, drive away. Hopefully whoever's behind us will think we've gone inside to have a leisurely dinner. In actuality, we'll only have a drink at the bar. Give us twenty minutes and meet us around back. The owner of the restaurant will let us out through the kitchen door. When you're sure no one is following, you can drop us at L'Altra Mastai and come back for us at 10:30."

"Steven's not driving us back?" Emma asked.

"Not this time. If our shadows realize we've left the café, they may head over and wait for us outside the Excelsior. We don't want them to see us with Steven."

When they pull up in front of Café Bernini, Lucio jumped out to open Emma's door. "I'll be behind the restaurant in twenty minutes," he said as he extended his hand to help her out.

"Do you see the car that was following us?" Michael asked.

"When I slowed down, it did too. It's parked about a half-block back."

"Then let's do as we planned. Be sure you aren't being followed when you come back."

"I'll be careful," said Lucio.

"Don't you find it ironic that Steven sent us to the Bernini Café?" Emma said as they entered the small restaurant.

"Ironic?"

"Yes, we're in the Bernini Café, and it's decorated in the Baroque style."

Michael shook his head and frowned. "Don't tell me I'm going to be subjected to an art lesson," he groaned.

"Subjected to?"

"I didn't mean that, partner. I meant let's have a drink and, for a little while, try to forget Bernini and the Baroque."

Emma grinned. "That may be difficult to do in the Baroque Bernini Café."

"Are you Father Steven's American friends?" A smiling man in a grey suit asked as they approached the front of the bar. "My name is Danio."

"What gave us away?" Michael joked.

"The lady is blond and you have red hair, so I guessed you weren't Italian. We don't have many Americans in here at night, though quite a few come in for lunch. The monsignor said you came in for a drink. Maybe you'll come back and enjoy a meal with us before you leave Rome."

"I hope we'll have time," Emma said.

Danio pointed to a table near the back of the bar. "Would you like to sit there?" he asked.

"We would, thank you," Michael said.

Emma ordered a glass of white wine and Michael a beer. Minutes later, the waiter returned with the drinks and what he called the café's 'most famous appetizer,' raw shrimp marinated in ginger and lime. She saw Danio watching from the side of the bar and sampled the hors d'oeuvre. It wasn't great, but she smiled and gave him an enthusiastic thumbs-up.

"I don't think this place will be on my must-return list," she whispered. "It's okay, but I can't imagine it would be on Steven's favorite-restaurants list."

"It was probably a convenient choice because it's close to L'Altra Mastai."

While they sipped their drinks and nibbled at the appetizer, Emma explained the rivalry between Bernini and Borromini and told Michael how Nicola had compared her and Michael's rivalry to that of the great artists.

"I hope Bernini and Borromini made peace like we did," Michael said.

"I don't know if they made peace, as you put it, but I know they worked together on Saint Peter's baldachino."

"Really?" Michael looked surprised. "Steven didn't tell me that."

"I'm full of fascinating tidbits. Another reason you need me."

When Emma finished her wine, Michael motioned Danio to the table. "I'm afraid we have to leave," he said. "If you'll bring the check—"

"The drinks and the shrimp are on the house," Danio said. "Please tell Monsignor Steven I said hello." He led them through a bustling kitchen to the back door, which opened onto a small alley where Lucio was waiting. He said good-bye and returned to the restaurant.

"Did anyone follow you?" Michael asked as Lucio pulled away from the café.

"Not that I could see. Whoever was behind us on the way over is probably waiting for you to come out through the front door."

During the five-minute drive, Michael kept looking out the back window. Lucio was right. No one was following.

"I'll be back at 10:30," Lucio said as he pulled up in front of L'Altra Mastai. "If you're not ready to go, I'll wait."

"Thanks," Michael said. "I'll call if our plans change."

As soon as they entered the restaurant, Steven got up from the bar and walked over to greet them. "It's about time you two got here," he said.

"We were stuck at the Bernini café," said Michael. He looked around. "This place is more your style."

"Is it my fault you had to ditch your tail? And the Café Bernini's not so bad. Good to see you, Emma. Since you've consented to spend time with my obnoxious friend, May I assume you've formed a temporary truce?"

"I guess you could call it that. We decided to join forces to pursue the Vatican story."

Steven cocked his head. "Really? Bless you both." He chuckled as he made the sign of the cross. "So what's my assignment?"

"Your assignment?" Michael said. "You think Emma and I are going to let you help?"

"Of course you are. Whatever you're planning, you'll never succeed without me. I'll tell you why once we're at the table."

Michael smirked. "I can't wait to hear why you think you're so indispensible."

"All in good time. Right now I'm hungry, probably because you're so late."

"For good reason. We—"

"Truce, gentlemen," Emma said. She smiled at Steven. "This is a lovely restaurant."

"Much better than the Bernini Café," Michael said snidely.

"Ignore him," Emma said.

"I've been doing that for years, but it never seems to work. He just keeps on making stupid remarks. So, Emma, I was about to say, this restaurant serves great Mediterranean cuisine."

Not long after the maître d' seated them, a crisply dressed waiter arrived with menus. As he reached out to give Emma hers, Steven waved him away. "May I suggest the sea bass with tomatoes and olives? It's the house specialty."

"It works for me," said Emma.

Michael frowned. "Since I obviously don't have a choice, I guess you can make it three."

While they sipped wine and shared Steven's favorite first course, delicious broccoli ravioli with truffle sauce, Emma and Michael told the priest what they knew and what they suspected was going on in the Vatican. Throughout the conversation, Steven's facial expressions reflected his surprise, but he didn't interrupt.

When they finished the story, Steven took a sheet of paper out of his pocket. "This is what I found out about your Father Paul," he said. "He is a priest. It looks like he's a conservative, though he attended several seminars with Masella, which could indicate he's a liberal."

Emma reflected for a moment. "Or maybe he's spying on the liberals for the cardinal and the conservative faction."

Steven laughed. "He wouldn't have to sit through boring seminars to get information. The Vatican's a political beehive. You wouldn't believe the amount of buzzing."

"Any link between Father Paul and Monsignor Scala?" Michael asked.

"Not that I can tell, though the cardinal's office was apparently responsible for Father Paul's current assignment in the archives."

"So you think he just happened to be standing around and available to translate?" said Emma.

"Possibly. He's an American, and you report for an American network."

"Then why warn me not to pursue the story?"

"I have no idea. Father Paul may be involved in what's happening in the Holy See, or he may have been warning a fellow American to be careful. The Vatican's not a place to be snooping around, especially with so much at stake right now. Did you bring the cardinal's note?"

"I did." Emma removed the paper from her purse and handed it to Steven.

Steven read the cardinal's message. When he looked up, he showed marked concern. "The man's obviously frightened."

"No doubt," said Michael. "Wait until you view the footage Ron took of the scene on the loggia. You'll see how scared he is."

"I definitely want to take a look, but not at the Excelsior. If I'm going to nose around, we shouldn't be seen together."

"You're sure you want to get mixed up in this?" Emma asked. "I'd hate to think you could meet the same fate as Monsignor Scala."

"I'm definitely in, and don't worry about me. Michael will tell you, I'm perfectly capable of taking care of myself."

Michael nodded. "That's an understatement, as I've discovered many times.

Emma smiled at Steven. "When this is over, I want you to tell me all about your childhood escapades."

"I'm sure our friend will pay big money to silence me." Steven laughed. "Maybe I should be worrying about the hit man he'll hire instead of one employed by the Vatican."

"At this moment, hit man may have been a poor choice of terms, my friend," Michael said.

"Let's say it doesn't do much to allay my fears," Emma joked.

Throughout the delicious meal, Emma had only an occasional glimpse of the Michael and Steven who had been with her the night before. Though there were a few laughs, for the most part, they were serious and thoughtful as they made tentative plans and discussed possible strategies they might employ while pursuing the story. Emma was relieved that the decent and kind Michael and not the all-knowing jerk had joined them. As the evening progressed she liked him more and more.

While they enjoyed a decadent chocolate dessert, they decided on the assignments for Piero Scala's funeral. Because he knew the deceased monsignor, Steven didn't think his presence at the ceremony would be suspect. He agreed to watch the clergy in attendance to see if he could determine who was attending and if he had a legitimate reason to be there. In the meantime, he would use his sources to see what he could find out about the pope's health and the cardinal's confinement.

"I love these political intrigues," he said when the plans were finalized. "If necessary, we'll continue to communicate using text messages, but don't send me an e-mail. My preference is we talk in person. If someone decided I was asking too many questions and took my Blackberry—"

"They'd do that?" Emma asked with disbelief.

"Count on it. This is high-stakes poker, Emma."

"Do you think we should get together tomorrow night?" Steven asked as Michael settled the bill.

"Not unless we have to," Michael said. "I don't know if we can fool the people following us two nights in a row. My guess is next time they'll have someone go in and watch us from inside the restaurant. They can't be too pleased about the hours they wasted sitting outside the Café Bernini only to go in and discover we'd left."

"All right, but if the need should arise, I have an idea, though, Emma, you'll have to convert to Catholicism. Come to Mass at San Clemente. I'll be celebrating tomorrow evening at six."

"I'd love to convert, but only to see the church," Emma said. "Why don't we skip Mass and meet you in the temple before you vest? I doubt we'd be followed into such a small space."

"You're right. Anyone following you would be easily detected in the small passageways and tiny rooms."

Michael was clearly frustrated. "Could you two please tell me what the hell you're talking about?" he said.

"San Clemente, my uneducated and uncultured friend, is a church built upon an older church built upon an ancient pagan temple," said Steven. "You can literally see the many levels of Rome in one location."

"I can't wait," Michael said sarcastically.

"Let's hope you won't be forced to become a bona fide tourist," Emma said. "Why would you want to see the ancient Roman sites?"

Steven grinned. "Chalk one up for Emma."

Though they were fairly sure no one knew where they were, they decided to leave the restaurant separately. Emma and Michael lingered until Steven had time to drive away before meeting Lucio for the short ride back to the hotel.

During the drive, Emma nodded off. She awakened with a start when Lucio pulled up in front of the hotel. "Any sign of someone waiting for us to arrive?" she asked, suddenly wide awake.

"Not that I can see, but there are so many cars parked out here, it would be hard to tell." Lucio turned to Michael. "Shall I pick you up in the morning?"

"I'll hitch a ride with Emma, but I would like to have you around in case we have to split up. I don't think Vezio's car will hold me if he has to take the crew and the cameras. We'll meet in the parking lot a little after six."

"I'm afraid there isn't a parking lot at the villa," Lucio said. "Giro will likely drop you at the side entrance by the formal garden. I'll be there too."

"Grazie, Lucio," Emma said.

"Prego," Lucio said. "A domani."

CHAPTER FOURTEEN

There were dozens of people milling around the lobby, but as far as Emma could tell, not one of them was wearing a clerical collar. She quickly retrieved her keycard from the woman on duty at the desk and headed to the elevators with Michael. They were alone in the elevator for the ride to the fourth floor and didn't see a soul as they walked down the hallway toward Emma's room.

"If you don't mind, I'd like to take a quick look around before I go downstairs," Michael said as Emma inserted her card in the slot.

"Sure, if you really think it's necessary."

"I don't know how necessary it is, but I'll sleep better knowing you're safely inside."

"Who's going to search your room to be sure you're okay?"

Michael grinned. "Not to worry. I'm a big strong jock, remember?"

"Of course you are." Emma rolled her eyes. "I forgot."

Michael checked the closets and bathrooms. "Everything's fine in here," he said, "but I don't want you to open the door for anyone."

"Who would be coming to see me at this hour? I'm sure Helen and Ron have everything they need for tomorrow's shoot."

"All the same, if anyone knocks, call me. I'll be sleeping in my clothes."

Emma laughed. "Isn't that a bit much?"

"Probably, but humor me. Remember, we have a sick pope, a frightened cardinal, a dead monsignor who happened to be the frightened cardinal's secretary, a reporter who told the world she's going to pursue the story, and a group of unknowns following the outspoken reporter and her new partner to a restaurant. Forgive me if I'm slightly paranoid."

"Point made. Feel free to leave your shoes on as well."

Michael chuckled. "Good idea. Call if you need me. Are you going straight to bed?"

"I have a few things to do first, but I won't be up for long. I'll see you—"

"Don't say downstairs."

"You didn't let me finish. I'll see you at my door in the morning at 5:55."

"You're a fast learner. Sleep well."

"You too. And, Michael—thanks."

"No thanks necessary. Now put the security lock on the door. I'm not leaving until I hear it click into place."

Emma locked the door, changed into her pajamas, and sat down at the desk. "I won't be able to do this for long," she said as she took out the Saint Theresa script to do some last-minute fine tuning. Too tired to focus, she gave up and went to bed.

She was just drifting off when she heard a faint knock on the sitting room door. Suddenly wide awake and wondering if she'd been dreaming, she lay quietly and listened. There was another faint tap. "Oh my God," she whispered as she threw back the covers. *Someone's out there, but who is it? I'm sure Michael would call before coming back up.*

Moments later, there was a third knock. This time the rapping sound was followed by the swish of a keycard being inserted in the slot and quickly removed.

Is it possible for someone with a master keycard open a security lock? she wondered. "God, I hope not," she whispered.

Terrified, she picked up the phone on the bedside table and punched in Michael's room number. "Please come," she whispered as soon as he answered. "Someone's trying to get in."

"Don't open the door. I'm on my way." The line went dead.

Emma sat on the side of the bed and hugged a pillow to her chest. She listened to the silence in the hall, waiting and hoping whoever was out there would think she was out and go away. *But that won't happen,* she mused. *The security lock's on, so whoever's trying to get in has to know I'm in the room.*

It wasn't long before Emma heard a louder and more insistent knock. Seconds later, the keycard was inserted and removed again. Shaking and weak-kneed, she stood up and inched her way toward the door separating the bedroom from the sitting room. *Hurry, Michael,* she silently implored.

Time passed slowly until she heard a loud knock and a deep familiar voice. "Emma, open up. It's Michael."

She stumbled across the room, took off the security lock, and pulled open the door. Michael, out of breath and obviously upset, barged into the room brandishing an umbrella. "I never thought I'd be so happy to see you," she cried as she fell into his arms.

Michael held her tightly. "Everything's fine now. Calm down."

Feeling stronger, Emma loosened her grip. Despite her anxiety, she started laughing.

Michael looked at her curiously. "What could possibly be amusing at a time like this?" he asked.

"You. You look so damn silly brandishing that umbrella."

Michael blushed, which intensified Emma's delight. "I had to be ready for anything," he said sheepishly, "and the umbrella was the only weapon I could find on short notice."

Emma looked down. "And look at your feet. Didn't you promise to sleep in your shoes?"

"At the time I was gushing with bravado. I didn't think I'd have to rush up here and save you. I guess we both underestimated these people."

When she spoke, Emma was no longer joking. "Who are they, Michael?" she asked. "And why are they coming after me?"

"I have no idea who they are, but it's obvious they're trying to discourage you from continuing with your investigation, and it seems they mean business."

"Did you see anyone out in the hall?"

"No, but I came up the stairs closest to my room on the other side of the building. Whoever it was probably went down the stairs near your suite. All I saw was a woman at the far end of the hall. When she turned to look back, I could see she was carrying towels."

"Towels? At this hour?"

"Strange, isn't it?" Michael walked across to the desk and pushed the housekeeping button. Obviously unhappy with the answers he got from whoever was on duty, he hung up, dialed the operator, and asked to speak with the night manager. After a short conversation, he put the receiver back and motioned for Emma to sit by him on the couch.

"You found out something?"

"I did. Apparently a woman saying she was you called the front desk from a hotel phone."

"Not from a specific room?"

"No. She said she'd just come in and needed fresh towels. The desk clerk knew you'd picked up your key, so she saw nothing unusual in the request."

"So there was someone watching us either in the lobby or out front when we drove up."

"That appears to be the case. The receptionist said housekeeping was short staffed at night, so there would be a wait before the towels could be delivered. Saying she needed them right away, the woman, supposedly you, said she'd send a friend down to pick them up at the front desk."

"Did she?"

"A woman came down in the elevator and asked for towels shortly thereafter."

"Can the receptionist describe her?"

"I don't know. She left for the night and isn't due back until three tomorrow."

"That's convenient. You said you saw a woman in the hallway. Did you see a man?"

"No, but he may have turned the corner by then, or, as I said, maybe he went down a different way." Michael thought for a moment. "Now that I think about it, I did get a whiff of stale cigarettes."

"But this is a non-smoking floor."

"I know. That's why the smell caught my attention at the time." Michael took out his phone.

"Who are you calling?"

"Humor me, will you?"

Michael didn't even say hello, but it was apparent Steven was on the other end of the line as Michael related the recent events. "Do you know anyone in the Vatican police force who's trustworthy?" he asked. He listened and then responded: "Then bring Sante with you to the funeral. Right. No uniform. Super. She's okay, but I'm staying on the sofa bed in her sitting room tonight. I'll talk with you in the morning."

"You don't have to stay here," Emma said as Michael hung up. "I doubt whoever was at the door will come back."

"I know you manhandled Father Paul, but he's a little guy," Michael jested. "I won't be quite so easy to take down. I'm staying. You can close your bedroom door and sleep well because I'll be out here."

Emma opened her mouth to protest, but seeing Michael's determined stare, she decided not to argue. "Alright, I'm forced to admit I'll feel more comfortable knowing you're around."

"Smart answer."

"I take it Sante's a policeman?"

"And apparently a person Steven feels he can trust. He'll bring him to the funeral. In the meantime, get used to being joined to me at the hip."

"My first inclination is to argue—"

"But you're thinking better of it."

"How much does Steven plan to tell Sante?"

"I don't know, but I'm sure he'll be cautious." Michael walked over to the door and flipped the security lock. "You look exhausted. Please go to bed."

"Can I get you some blankets before I go?"

"I imagine there'll be something I can use in here." He opened the closet door and pulled out two pillows and a comforter. "See?"

"Will you try to get some sleep? Remember, this partnership began because I didn't want you looking bleary-eyed on camera. Now, ironically, I'm the one causing the problem."

Michael laughed. "Believe me—I'd rather look like a zombie because I'm watching out for you than from reading about Bernini's sculptures in the Borghese. I'll go to bed as soon as I call hotel security. I want to know who swiped that card. You told me only Helen and one maid have duplicates. We know the maid wouldn't be cleaning during the night. Obviously someone else has a key and could have gotten in if you hadn't flipped the security lock. I want definitive answers when we get back here tomorrow after the shoot. And speaking of tomorrow, how about breakfast at 5:30? We might not have much time to eat once we leave here in the morning. I can leave the card on the doorknob."

"Order strong coffee. I'm not sure I'll be able to sleep. I'll probably need something to get me going."

At the bedroom door, Emma turned back. "Thanks for staying, Michael."

"You're welcome. I'll knock on your door at five. That should give us enough time to eat, get ready, and meet Giro at six."

"A half-hour is more than enough time. I'll see you in a few hours."

———

It seemed like Emma had just closed her eyes when she heard a knock on her bedroom door. Startled at first, she came out of her sleep-induced grogginess and realized it was Michael. "I'll be out in twenty minutes," she called.

"Take your time."

She took a quick shower and dressed in brown slacks and a brown-and-red striped blouse. She removed a red linen blazer from the closet and went to join Michael in the sitting room. When he stood up to greet her, she was surprised to see him dressed in gray trousers, a blue button-down shirt, and a red tie. A navy blue blazer hung on the back of a desk chair. "When did you go back to your room?"

"About four. I was gone ten minutes tops. I figured whoever tried to get in earlier had given up for the night, so I raced down the stairs and grabbed my clothes and notes."

"So you took a chance with my life?"

Michael looked flustered. "I really didn't," he said contritely. "I called security right after you went to bed, asked them to monitor the hall and stairwells which lead to this floor, told them to call me on my cell if they saw anything unusual going on, and—"

"I'm teasing, Michael."

"Whew, you had me worried for a minute. I'd never—"

"I know."

"Good. Anyway, my short excursion confirmed that security's on the job. The night chief called me on my cell to say he saw me leave shortly after I left your room. For a minute I considered turning back in case someone else knew I left you alone and tried again, this time succeeding because the security lock hadn't been engaged."

"You can't possibly think someone at the Excelsior's taking orders from Cardinal Amici or the pope?"

"Probably not, but why take a chance? Someone told Angelo where to find you, and we have no idea who followed us to the Café Bernini. Then there's the attempted break-in—"

"I can't imagine someone at the hotel—"

"Let's not speculate."

"Not an easy task for me, but I'll try. You look like you're ready to go."

"I will be as soon as breakfast—"

The minute Emma said the word, there was a knock on the door. Michael peeked out before taking off the security lock.

The waiter pushed a table set for two into the room and started to remove the lids from the plates. "We'll take care of that," Michael said as he handed the young man five euros.

"Grazie molto," the waiter said. "Please call room service when you have finished."

"We'll leave the table in the hall by six," Michael said.

As the waiter left, Emma took off one of the lids. "Omelets. My favorite," she said as she poured coffee for her and Michael. "I'm glad you thought to order breakfast."

"Another advantage of having a man for a partner—I'm always thinking about food. Shall we make this a working breakfast and go through the Borghese script while we're eating?"

"Sure."

During breakfast they read and reread the copy, made a few changes, and, when they had finished the last bite of their omelets, decided they were ready to shoot.

"We have a little while before Giro gets here," Michael said. "I suggest we stop at the desk on the way out and change the keycard code for your room. I also think we should hang the 'Do not Disturb' sign on the door and ask the maid to skip the room today. If need be, we can call for extra towels this evening."

"You don't think we're being overly paranoid?"

"Would you have thought that a few hours ago? No, until we have definitive answers, it's better to err on the side of caution. In fact, we're not going to stop with the sign on the door. We're going to be sure no one but Helen and the head of hotel security has access to the room. The maid will have to clean while we're here."

"Isn't that a little much?"

"Maybe, but humor me."

There was no one in the lobby when they arrived downstairs. The man at the desk gave Emma two new keycards, and left messages for housekeeping and security making it clear that no one was to enter the room during the day.

The car was outside when they got to the front of the hotel a little after six. "Sorry we're late," Michael said as Giro opened Emma's door. "You know women. It takes a while to put on all that face stuff."

Which Michael is speaking now?" Emma said, frowning.

"The one you've come to know and love?"

During the ride Emma and Michael reviewed their notes. When they pulled up behind Lucio's car at the side of the museum, Lucio got out and opened Emma's door. "David and Bill are set up in front of the gates of the formal garden," he said.

"Thanks, Lucio," said Emma. "I see them up ahead on the walkway."

"Morning," David said as Emma and Michael approached. He held out his hand. "We haven't been formally introduced, Ms. Bradford," he said. "I'm David Shaffer."

Emma shook the producer's hand. "It's nice to meet you David, especially since it seems we're now a team, and please call me Emma."

Emma immediately felt comfortable with Michael's producer. Each time she'd seen him in the days before, he'd been bent over a computer screen or walking to and from the truck with Michael and Bill. Of medium height and build, David was muscular and obviously fit. *I bet I'd see him in the hotel gym if I went down to work-out some morning,* Emma thought. In his mid-fifties, he sported a mustache and goatee, *perhaps,* Emma thought, *to compensate for his receding hairline.* His dark brown eyes were accented by bushy dark eyebrows.

"Helen and Ron are with the curator," David said, interrupting Emma's musings. "You guys all set?"

"We are," Michael said. "I'll be doing the intro from out here while Emma goes in to prep the curator." He looked at Emma. "I should be finished in ten minutes."

"I don't know where Mr. Martelli will want to do the interview, so—"

"Don't worry, I'll find you."

As Emma headed for the museum entrance, she looked back. Michael was doing his presentation about the Villa Borghese. He was standing by the wrought-iron gate in front of the formal garden and, she assumed, talking about the history of the house, the restoration project, the gardens, and the winery, ending, as they'd decided, with an invitation for the audience to join him and Emma for a look at Bernini's spectacular sculptures inside the museum.

Donato Martelli was standing with Emma when Michael entered the foyer. "Where's Bill?" Emma asked.

"He and David are out taking shots of the house and grounds to correspond with what I reported.

"Good. As you can see, we're setting up in front of Bernini's *Truth Unveiled by Time*."

"Was that a sculpture on your list?" Michael asked. "I don't think it was on mine."

"Nor mine, but Mr. Martelli feels it's a piece which merits mention. Ron's confident we'll be able to use at least some of the footage during the broadcast."

"I hope you will," Martelli said. He shook hands with Michael. "Nice to meet you, Mr. Kelsey. Thank you for publicizing the Borghese portion of the exhibition."

"Our pleasure," Michael said.

Emma turned to Ron. "We have a lot to cover in a short time, so we'd better get started."

"Whenever you're ready, Mr. Martelli," Ron said. "Talk and we'll edit later."

"Thank you," Martelli said.

I'd like to welcome our American audience to the Borghese Museum. We're standing before Bernini's Truth Unveiled by Time.

Emma signaled for Ron to stop shooting. "Would you take footage of the sculpture?" she asked. She smiled at Martelli. "I'm sorry to stop you in mid-sentence, Mr. Martelli, but I'm afraid our tight schedule won't allow us time to get back here before the museum opens, and I'd like pictures of the statue without crowds swarming around."

Ron turned the camera back to Emma. "Got it," he said.

"Great. Okay, Mr. Martelli," Emma said. "Again, I apologize for interrupting."

Martelli nodded. "Shall I continue where I left off?"

"Yes, please."

Bernini began to design Truth *in 1645, following Pope Urban's death. By 1652, the statue was complete. In 1665, Bernini again expressed his intent to add the figure of Time to the group, though as you can see, he never did. The powerful personification is unquestionably Bernini's most personal statue. It reflects his belief that truth will always persevere.*

Emma thought about what Martelli said and the figure of Truth in the Alexander monument. *I know what Truth meant to Bernini,* she thought, *but I'd have a hard time defining truth today.*

"Thank you for sharing the information with us, Mr. Martelli," she said. She signaled Ron to turn off the camera. "Frankly, I'm surprised this sculpture wasn't on our list of works to film. We'll air your words in the first part of our broadcast."

"Would you like to continue our interview here in the foyer or go elsewhere?" Michael asked. "Our next segment is about the bust of Cardinal Scipione."

"Why don't we set up in there?" Emma said.

Ron positioned Michael and the curator beside the bust. "Mr. Martelli, you can begin anytime. Just talk. Again, we'll edit later."

Emma interrupted. "Michael, did you talk about the cardinal when you were filming outside?"

"No. I planned to do the bio before I described the bust, but I think our audience would rather hear what Mr. Martelli has to say. He's the expert."

"You don't mind?" Emma asked, surprised that Michael would be so generous with his air time.

"Not at all. Please continue, Mr. Martelli."

"I'd be glad to." Martelli began to talk:

Cardinal Scipione Borghese was born in Rome, the son of Francisco Caffarelli and Ortensia Borghese. When Francisco ran into financial difficulties, Scipione's uncle, Camillo Borghese, paid for his education. In 1605, when Camillo became Pope Paul V, he made his nephew a cardinal and gave him the right to use the Borghese name and coat of arms. Cardinal-nephew Scipione enjoyed enormous power as the pope's secretary and effective head of the Vatican government. During this time, on his own, and on the pope's behalf, he amassed an enormous fortune, which he used to assemble one of the largest and most impressive art collections in Europe. Between 1618 and

1624, Bernini worked almost exclusively for Scipione, creating sculptures which epitomized Baroque art. Cardinal Borghese's patronage did a great deal to establish Bernini as the leading Italian sculptor and architect of the seventeenth century.

Michael signaled Ron to stop filming. "I prepared a presentation about the bust," he said, but why don't you continue, Mr. Martelli."

Martelli nodded as Michael took the microphone and Ron began filming again. "We're standing beside the bust of Cardinal Scipione Borghese, Bernini's first patron. Mr. Martelli, will you tell our audience about the sculpture?"

Martelli put his hand on the pedestal holding the bust.

Many of the most powerful figures in Rome and Europe, popes, generals, rulers, and cardinals, commissioned Bernini to create their likenesses. In this bust, Bernini shows Cardinal Borghese caught in a moment in time—engaged in an action with a nameless, unseen individual. We, the viewer, have no idea who the person is. The action remains forever open and incomplete and calls out for our active participation. As in many of his famous works, in this bust, Bernini creates a little drama—a story which involves the sculpture and viewer, assigning each his role to play.

Emma signaled Ron to turn the camera toward her. "You mentioned the unseen man who converses with the cardinal," she said to Martelli. "This extraordinary ability to extend the sculpture beyond its physical boundaries is a feature of many Bernini works."

Martelli's smile indicated his appreciation of Emma's insight. "You are correct, Ms. Bradford. I imagine you and Mr. Kelsey will be discussing this and other aspects of Bernini's genius as you continue to report on the other sculptures on display here in the Borghese."

"We certainly will," Emma said.

"Mr. Martelli, thank you for giving us a few minutes of your time on this busy and exciting day for you, the Borghese Museum, and the city of Rome," said Michael.

Martelli's handshake was firm. "It is my pleasure to talk with two such knowledgeable reporters. Enjoy the exhibit."

"Knowledgeable I'm not," Michael said when the curator scurried away to complete last-minute preparations for the opening.

"Martelli thought so."

"You mean he realized you knew what you were talking about. Thanks for making me look good."

"I didn't have to. You did beautifully." Emma looked at her watch. "The report took more time than we've allotted, so I'd better get to *Apollo and Daphne*."

"Mind if I watch? I might learn something."

"By all means, join me. When I'm finished, you could be a genuine art lover and proficient art critic."

"You never know." Michael grinned. "As I said before, anything's possible."

"How shall we do this?" Emma asked Ron as they walked through the museum. "Do you want me to stand beside the statue?"

"I thought I'd film as you approach the sculpture. Think you can walk and talk at the same time?"

"If you mean do I need notes, the answer is no. After listening to Nicola and going through the book I bought in the Borghese bookstore, I could talk about *Apollo and Daphne* for hours. On the way I'll recap the two themes Michael and I will be emphasizing and then talk about the sculpture itself."

"Watch me when you get close. When I have the entire statue framed in my lens, I'm going to signal for you to stop."

The camera followed Emma as she talked. She'd just finished what she wanted to say when Ron gave her the stop sign. "Great," he said. "Do your general intro right here. What's your strategy after that?"

"I'll talk about how Bernini captures various aspects of a story in a single statue."

"You're going to walk around it to do this?"

"That's what I planned."

"I won't be able to film you and what you're talking about at the same time. I'll need to concentrate on the statue."

"That's fine. Apollo and Daphne are the stars of this segment."

"All right, let's do this." Ron turned on the camera and signaled for Emma to begin.

Emma took a deep breath and started her spiel.

Apollo and Daphne *is arguably the loveliest statue Bernini created for Cardinal Borghese. His inspiration for the sculpture was the* Metamorphoses *by the ancient Roman poet Ovid. Bernini depicts the aggressive Roman sun god reaching out to grab the nymph, Daphne, at the exact moment when her father, Jupiter, changes her into a laurel tree to keep her from being scorched by the god's touch. Bark covers most of Daphne's body, but according to Ovid, Apollo can still feel her heart beating beneath it. Understood within its original intellectual context, this group represents frustrated desire and enduring despair brought about by love.*

During the final part of the presentation, Ron walked around the statue to capture the visuals that corresponded with what Emma was saying.

"Good job, Emma," Michael said when Ron shut off the camera. "*David*'s next on the list, but wouldn't you rather talk about *Pluto and Proserpina* while you're on a roll?"

"Either way is fine with me."

"Then go ahead. I'm sure I'll benefit from seeing your next presentation. Would you believe I finally get it? I understand how marble can move."

Emma laughed. "Is that so? You asked me if there's hope for you. I think there might be. Are you ready to do the report on *David*?"

"I think so, but I'm not sure I'll be able to do it in one take."

"I'll bet lunch you will."

"You're on. Either way I win, and ABC pays."

Emma skimmed through her notes while Ron planned his shots of the statue. "We'll follow the same plan we had for *Apollo and Daphne*," he said. "While you give the introduction, I'll take pictures of you and the sculpture from back here. When you're finished, I'll shoot the statue from the different angles while you're talking about the different stories it tells." He paused and adjusted his camera. "Whenever you're ready," he said.

Emma nodded and began.

I'm standing by the remarkable marble sculpture of Pluto and Proserpina, *created by Bernini between 1621 and 1622.*

She told the myth of Pluto and Proserpina, gave Ron an almost imperceptible nod, and paused long enough for him to zoom in on Pluto's hand. While Ron focused on the pressure of Pluto's fingers on Proserpina's thigh, Emma made a circular motion with her hand. Ron nodded, zoomed out and began to circle the statue as she spoke about how Bernini incorporated the different aspects of the myth in a single statue.

"Fantastic," Michael said when Emma finished her concluding comments.

"Ready to do the *David* segment?" Ron asked. "We only have twenty minutes before the museum opens to the public."

"As ready as I'll ever be," Michael said. He turned to Emma. "Mind if I add a few thoughts of my own to your perfectly scripted piece?"

"Not at all. I'm excited to see what our jock turned art critic has come up with."

Ron positioned Michael to the right of the statue and pointed. After giving the four-line introduction Emma had prepared, Michael began to add his own thoughts to the script.

When Emma talked about Apollo and Daphne, *she explained that Bernini's works often suggest events occurring outside the sculpture. With* David, *Bernini moved away from the mythological themes to the biblical, but the same concept applies. Bernini's* David *is a man of action caught up in a world-changing event.*

Emma nodded her approval as Michael continued.

Bernini's inspiration came from the Old Testament First Book of Samuel. Let me set the scene. The Israelites are at war with the Philistines, whose giant warrior, Goliath, has challenged any of the Israeli soldiers to settle the conflict by single combat. Though Goliath is not physically present, he is definitely a part of Bernini's sculpture, as are the mysterious man with whom Cardinal Borghese was conversing, and Jupiter, who answered his daughter's cries for help in Apollo and Daphne *and also responded to a devastated mother's pleas in* Pluto and Proserpina.

Emma was both surprised and impressed. Without a script to guide him, Michael was tying the theme to all of Bernini's works in the Borghese. She listened with rapt attention as he wove a tale like a man telling a story to a child.

Bernini captures the moment when the young shepherd, David, has just accepted Goliath's challenge and is about to try and slay the approaching Philistine with a single stone. As he moves through space and runs quickly toward the battle line, David's torso twists and strains, not only physically but psychologically as well. All the tension which has been building up inside him is evident in his face as he slings the stone and strikes Goliath in the forehead, causing the giant to fall face down on the ground.

Most visitors to the museum are unaware that David's face is actually a Bernini self-portrait, which was executed with Cardinal Borghese's assistance. The cardinal volunteered to hold a mirror up to enable the young artist to complete his work.

Michael paused. "Great job," Emma said. "You do the wrap-up."

So that's it from the Borghese. Join Emma and me tomorrow when we report from the Cornaro Chapel in the Church of Santa Maria della Victoria. This is Michael Kelsey signing off from Rome.

"Fantastic," Emma said. "Listening to your report, I would have figured you for a knowledgeable art enthusiast and not a jock who's pretending to understand a sculpture. I'm definitely buying your lunch."

"You really liked it?" Michael asked like a child seeking approval.

"Absolutely. You were great. I love the information you added about the physical and psychological strain in David's body."

"I read the line in your notes, but it didn't make sense to me until I heard you report on *Pluto and Proserpina*. I made a last-minute decision to add the information."

"It fit and made your account even more interesting."

"We're off to set up at Santa Maria della Vittoria," Helen said. "Are you two coming?"

"In a few minutes," Emma said. "There's a cafeteria on the lower floor. I'd like to grab a cup of coffee."

"Sounds good to me too," Michael said. "We haven't reviewed the Saint Theresa segment. I'd like to do a few run-throughs."

"Then we'll tell Giro and Lucio you'll be out in—"

"Thirty minutes," Michael said.

Helen looked back. "Be at Santa Maria della Vittoria by 9:30 so we can start shooting as soon as the crowd clears out."

"My art critic friend and I will be on time," Emma said. As Helen and Ron left the museum, she and Michael headed to the cafeteria.

CHAPTER FIFTEEN

After a cup of coffee and a ten-minute rehearsal, Emma and Michael headed for the car. Lucio and Giro were standing on the curb talking. "You know this is silly," Michael said as he approached the two men. "Emma and I will be shooting at the same location, so there's no need for two drivers. Lucio, why don't you take the rest of the day off?"

"Are you sure you won't need me," Lucio said. "I do have a few things I need to do."

"Giro will take us where we need to go," Emma said.

"If you're sure—"

"Go," Michael insisted. "I'll call if I need you."

As Lucio went to his car, Giro opened the door for Emma and Michael. "Are we still going to Santa Maria della Vittoria?" he asked.

"We are," Emma replied. She turned to Michael. "I saw you and Steven at the Cornaro Chapel the first day we were in Rome."

"Really? I didn't see you."

Emma laughed. "That's because I was praying." She told the story of how she refused Nicola's suggestion that she approach the sculpture, and, instead, walked over, knelt by the side aisle, and prayed.

Michael grimaced. "Prayed I wouldn't see you. Was I really that bad?"

"That and more. Shall I elaborate?"

"We're here, so there's no time," Giro said, "which is probably good for you, Michael." When he pulled up to the front of the church, Mass was over and the congregants were exiting through the main door.

When they went inside, Helen and David were talking with Bill. "Where's Ron?" Emma asked.

"Vezio took him back to the truck so he could edit the Borghese footage," Helen said.

"I'm afraid we're short on time," said David. "Who's doing the intro?"

Michael held up his hand. "That would be me. I'm ready as soon as Bill says the word."

"Word," Bill said. Michael went to where he was pointing, nodded and began:

Art can only be understood in the context of the times in which it was created, so if we're to understand Bernini's sculpture of The Ecstasy of Saint Theresa, *we must know about the saint herself. Theresa was a prominent Spanish mystic and Carmelite nun who lived during a period of intense religious turmoil in Europe. Less than twenty years before she was born, Columbus opened the Western Hemisphere to European colonization. Two years after her birth, Luther launched the Protestant Reformation.*

Like teenagers throughout the ages, Theresa rebelled against the strict rules in her home. When she was sixteen, her father, believing she was out of control, sent her to the Carmelite convent outside Avila. At first she hated living the cloistered life, but as her love of God intensified, she accepted her situation.

Soon after taking her vows, Sister Theresa became seriously ill with malaria. For four days, she failed to respond to medical treatment, and when she awoke she was never truly healthy again. For a while her physical state became a reason not to pray. When she began to seek God's help again, his presence often overwhelmed her senses, and she began to have mystical experiences. She began to write books in which she analyzed these raptures. In one of these books, entitled Interior Mansions, *she describes the steps an individual must take on the path to a mystical union with God. Many art critics see her words as Bernini's inspiration as he designed and created The Ecstasy of Saint Theresa.*

"Excellent," Emma said. "I love the way you weave a story. You did it when you talked about David and now again with Saint Theresa." She paused. "Have I told you I'm glad we're partners and not competitors?"

"I don't think you mentioned it," Michael said self-consciously, "but thanks. You ready to do your thing?"

"I am."

"Anytime," Bill said.

Emma nodded, took a deep breath, and when she saw the red light, began:

Thanks for introducing us to Saint Theresa, Michael.

She turned toward the sculpture.

If a work of art can awaken feelings of passionate adoration and belief in a higher reality, the primary objective of Baroque artists, then Bernini more than achieved his purpose in the Cornaro Chapel; here we find one of the finest examples of mature Roman High Baroque ever produced. At the Borghese, you heard Mr. Martelli say Bernini created little dramas. That's true here in the chapel which Bernini modeled after a theater. Eight members of the Cornaro family, including the cardinal, watch the scene playing out below them on the center stage.

Emma watched Bill move the camera away from her to take pictures of what she was describing. She nodded her approval and continued:

The spectators are observers of a magnificent moment of divine love when the swooning Carmelite nun, her quivering robes seemingly on fire, experiences the mystical moment, goes into a trance, and abandons herself to the joys of heavenly love as an imposing angel towering above her readies his golden dart to pierce her heart.

Realizing Emma was close to the end of her presentation, Bill zoomed out to include her and the statue in the frame. Emma paused, waiting for his signal to continue. Seconds later, Bill nodded and she began her closing.

In Saint Theresa, *Bernini created a mystical expression of the intensity of the experience on the saint's face never before attempted by any artist.*

"You two make a fantastic team," Helen said after Emma concluded and Bill turned off the camera. "I can't believe we've done every one of these reports without retakes. What are your plans for the afternoon?"

"Unless you need us, we'll go back to the hotel and script the Triton and Four Rivers Fountain," Michael said.

"We're way ahead of schedule," David said. "Take the rest of today off. Do some sightseeing."

"Or investigating," said Emma.

"Please be careful," David said. "I'm not sure what you're looking into, but I'm sure a lot of people want you to stop."

"That's an understatement," Michael said. "Believe me—we'll heed your warnings."

"I hope so. What time's the funeral?"

"It starts at ten. Have you and Ron discussed how you're going to split the filming?"

"We'll do it now. What time do you want us at the church?"

"Plan to be there at nine so you can take pictures of the guests as they arrive. Piero Scala was an important man, so there could be a large crowd. Michael and I will be there by 9:30. I doubt we'll be able to speak with the cardinal before the service begins, but I'd like to see who accompanies him into the church. More specifically, I want to know if he's being restricted in any way."

"I'm sure Steven and his friend Sante will be able to identify the people around him," Michael said.

"Who's Steven?" Bill asked.

"A childhood friend turned priest."

"He's helping with the investigation?"

"We didn't feel it would be wise to involve him," Emma said. "He thinks he's identifying guests at the funeral for a news broadcast."

"Your secret's safe with us," said David. "We'll be set up and ready to go both inside and out front of the church by nine. If you think of anything else you want us to film, call my cell." He turned to Michael. "You have the number."

"And, Emma, you have mine," Helen said. "If I need you, I'll leave a message on your hotel voicemail."

Emma thought for a moment before responding. "You know, I'd rather not use the hotel phone."

"Surely you're not worried about a security issue at the Excelsior," Helen said.

Emma glanced at Michael, who nodded his assent. "There may be a problem." She told the crew about the visit from Angelo, having to use clandestine measures to evade the people following them to dinner, and the effort of an unknown person to get into her suite during the night.

David was clearly concerned as he spoke to Michael. "So you're going to stay in Emma's sitting room again tonight?"

"Tonight and every night until we figure all this out."

"Why would you think someone from the hotel is involved?" David asked.

Emma answered: "For one thing, it's not hotel policy to give out room numbers. I learned that when I first arrived and wanted to know where Michael was staying."

"So you could avoid me," Michael teased.

Emma nodded. "You got that right." She turned back to David. "Yet despite this precaution, someone found out where I'm staying and told Angelo. Then the same person or group was waiting for Michael and me to leave for dinner and followed us."

"And," Michael added, "a woman accompanied by a mysterious man knew her room number and somehow had access to a keycard. If Emma hadn't flipped the security lock, he or she might have gained access to her room."

"Are you sure you should be pursuing this story?" Bill said.

"Would Geraldo pack up and go home?" Emma said.

"My partner's insinuating I'm a Geraldo-wannabe," said Michael. "At least I think that was the term her station manager used to describe me."

"I hate to say it, but I thought the same thing about you before this trip," David said. "At first I wasn't too keen on working with you, but after watching you here in Rome, I've changed my mind. You're a great reporter."

"I appreciate the vote of confidence," Michael said, seemingly eager to change the subject. "To answer your question, Emma and I are going to pursue this story vigorously. We'll be meeting with hotel security as soon as we get back to the Excelsior. I made it clear we're to be told who has a keycard for Emma's room and what the hallway and stairwell cameras showed during the night."

"I hope you'll be able to get some definitive answers," Helen said. "David and I will be at the truck with Ron and Bill until about two. After that, I'll be in my room if you should need me."

"So will I," David said. He suddenly looked flustered. "I mean I'll be in my room, not Helen's, and I'll have my cell phone with me." He took a deep breath. "Bill and I are staying close by at the Inn at the Spanish Steps on Via del Condotti." He took a paper out of his wallet and handed it to Michael. "In case I'm out of cell range, here's my card. I've written the hotel number on the back."

"Unless something unexpected happens, we'll be working in Emma's sitting room," Michael said.

———

"Will you need me later today?" Giro asked when he pulled up in front of the hotel.

"Possibly," Emma said, "but I hate to ask you to stay at home if it turns out we don't."

"I'm available twenty-four hours, so call me at home or on my cell. I can be here in ten minutes."

"Thanks," Michael said. "I'm not sure what our dinner plans will entail or if we'll be meeting a friend. We'll let you know."

Emma picked up her keycard at the front desk and joined Michael in the office to speak with Gusto Baldi, the head of hotel security. The short, balding man reported there was no evidence that anyone other than Emma, Helen, and the maid, Dina Sandri, had a keycard to Emma's room.

"I personally did a background check on Dina," Gusto said, a little too defensively, Emma thought.

"Nothing jumped out at you about her or her family?" Michael asked.

"Her two brothers are priests, but that would work in her favor."

"Really?" Emma tried to hide her surprise. "Is Dina married?"

"I believe she's engaged to her brother Mario's best friend."

"What's her other brother's name?" Michael said

Gusto opened his desk drawer and took out a folder. "Coreno Sandri. Why do you ask?"

"No reason. Anything else you can tell us?"

Gusto looked through the file. "Dina's uncle is also a priest. He and Mario work in Vatican City. Coreno is currently assigned to Santa Croce in Florence, but I have no idea what Dina or any of her family would have to do with a reporter who came to Rome to report on the Bernini exhibition. That is why you're here, isn't it, Ms. Bradford?"

Emma wondered at the security agent's almost accusatory tone. "It is, and that's why all of this seems so strange," she said. "Why would anyone want to get into my room?"

"Perhaps it was a case of being at the right door on the wrong floor."

"Forgive me if I'm skeptical," Emma said. "After the keycard didn't work the first time, wouldn't the person trying to get in look at the room number, and, if it's not the right one, leave? And what about the towels? Have you talked with the receptionist on duty?"

"I have. The woman who picked up the towels was of average height with brown hair. Beyond that, she had no distinguishing characteristics. The man who was with her was tall and thin, but she never saw his face."

"And the hallway cameras? What did you learn from them?" Michael asked.

"The woman with the towels walked to your room and knocked several times. She was the one who inserted the keycard. She kept her head down, so we never saw her face."

"She had to know about the camera outside the room," Emma said.

"Possibly, but as I said, I think this was a case of a maid going to a wrong room."

"What about the man who was with our towel carrier at the desk?" Michael asked. "Do we have a description of him?"

"He was never visible on the hall cameras, but the receptionist says he got on the elevator with the woman."

"And the stairwell?"

Emma could see Gusto was becoming increasingly uneasy with each question. "The camera in the stairwell near Ms. Bradford's room was not working," he said nervously.

"Great," Michael said crossly.

"I apologize," Gusto said. "I assure you all cameras are now working perfectly."

"Too little too late," said Michael. "Any chance the camera in that particular stairwell was deliberately turned off?"

"I can't imagine anyone in the security department would purposely leave the stairwells uncovered, but I'll do some checking."

"Did the unidentified man wear a clerical collar?" Emma asked.

"It's impossible to know. The cameras show us nothing, and the receptionist couldn't tell."

"You'll let us know if you discover anything new," Michael said as they got up to leave.

"Of course." Gusto turned to Emma. "I guarantee this will not happen again, Ms. Bradford."

"I certainly hope not," Emma said. "Like Mr. Kelsey, I want to be informed of anything you discover."

"Of course."

As Emma and Michael walked toward the elevator, a concierge beckoned her to the desk. "I have a message for you, Ms. Bradford." He handed Emma an envelope.

"Who left the message?" Michael asked when the elevator doors closed.

Emma opened the envelope and took out a note. "It's from Angelo Patini. He wants to talk with me after the funeral. I wonder why."

"Who knows? Maybe Steven will have an idea."

Instead of going directly to Emma's room, they stopped on the third floor. Michael picked up toiletries, sweats for sleeping, and a pair of jeans.

"It looks like you're moving in," Emma said when he hung his clothes in her sitting-room closet.

"I am. Like it or not, you're stuck with me until we figure out what's going on? Hungry?"

"I am. Shall we order room service?"

"Sure. While you're looking at the menu, I'll call Steven and see what he knows about Angelo, the Sandri brothers, and their uncle."

While Michael and Steven talked, Emma changed into jeans and a sweatshirt. He'd just hung up when she returned to the sitting room. "What did Steven say?" she asked.

"Before I tell you, let's order. I'm starving. Know what you want?"

"The artichokes, langoustine, and basil tempura. What about you?"

"Nothing beats a good old American hamburger."

Emma laughed. "Except you're in Rome. I seriously doubt the chef's a gourmet fast food cook."

Michael glanced at the menu. "I'll take my chances with the burger. It beats veal escalope with ham sage on spicy turnip tops."

"That remains to be seen. So tell me what you learned from Steven."

"For one thing, he doesn't know the Sandri brothers or their uncle."

"But he's going to see what he can find out?"

"He is. As far as Angelo goes, Steven has no idea why the cardinal's secretary wants to see you. As far as he knows, everything is status quo at the Vatican."

"Which may or may not be good."

When the food arrived, as Emma predicted, Michael's hamburger was charred and tough. "It has no taste," he said after taking his first bite.

"I'll refrain from saying I told you so."

"I appreciate your restraint." He held out a greasy, limp French fry. "Care for one of these?"

Emma laughed. "No thanks. I'm happy eating my delicious meal."

"Think we ought to get some work done?" she asked after Michael rolled the table containing her empty plate and his half-eaten meal into the hall. "I'd like to finish scripting the first report from Saint Peter's in case we need the time to work on the real story. Why don't you cover the outside? I'll do the portico and Constantine's statue." She took out

Nicola's notes. "Shall we do a run-through and fine-tune as we go along?"

"Sure. I'll start with a few words about Bernini and Saint Peter's. Here's what I have about the square. I confess I used your notes. Nicola's more interesting than Steven, but please don't tell him."

Emma grinned. "I won't if you cooperate. Your intro, please."

Michael repeated Nicola's spiel about the square. "Any suggestions?" he asked.

"Since you asked, yes. Are you sure your ego can take the criticism?"

"The old Michael might feel threatened, but the new and improved model can take anything you throw at him. So what?"

"Too many facts and figures. Leave out the words 'Doric,' 'travertine marble,' and 'entablature.' They're not words the viewing audience is likely to understand, and you don't have time to explain."

"You're right. If they're like me, a column's a column, and what the hell's an entablature?"

"Just tell them one-hundred-forty saints are perched on the roof. When you're finished, take the audience up the stairs. I'll take over in the portico. I'll use the same technique Nicola used when she talked about the movement in the Constantine statue. Want to hear what I have so far?"

"Absolutely."

The two ends of the portico open toward two vestibules, uniting it with the corridors of the colonnade.

"Too technical. Why not say, 'on the right'?"

"Good idea. How's this?"

On the right side of the portico is the equestrian statue of Constantine. Pope Innocent the Tenth gave Bernini the commission for the sculpture in 1654, but it wasn't completed until 1670, under the patronage of Pope Clement the Tenth. Constantine is considered by many to be one of Bernini's masterpieces.

"Cut out the names of the popes. It's too much, and anyway, who cares?"

Emma repeated what Nicola told her about the statue, emphasizing the action verbs.

"Excellent. I can hear the movement, and I'm not looking at the statue," Michael said.

"I have a few things to add to make it flow better, and I haven't done the wrap-up."

"You have lots of time. Shall we script the inside the basilica or stop for the day?"

Before Emma had a chance to answer, Michael's phone rang. "Hi, Steven," she heard him say. Suddenly his expression was serious. "Sure. We'll be there. I'll call you back with details. Later."

"What was that all about?" Emma asked.

"Steven wants to see us at San Clemente before the Mass, and we can't let anyone follow us." He paused. "How are we going to accomplish that?"

Emma thought for a minute. "I might know a way." She took her cell out of her purse.

CHAPTER SIXTEEN

While Michael listened, Emma called Giro. "We'll take a cab to the Quattro Fontaine and meet you at 2:30," he heard her say. "Does that give you enough time to walk over? Great. Take the back alleys if possible. See you then."

"I got the gist of what you and Giro decided," Michael said. "What's next?"

"I'm calling Helen." Emma took out her producer's card and punched in the number. "Trust me, this will work."

When Helen answered, Emma explained her plan. "So meet us in front of hotel at 2:40," she said. "Make a big deal of our arrival. After we take the elevator up to your floor, Michael and I will take the back stairs down to meet Giro behind the hotel. We'll walk with him through the back streets to his place near the Spanish Steps and drive to San Clemente. No, we're leaving early so if we can't ditch our shadows we'll seem like two people visiting one of Rome's historic sites. Okay, see you in a while."

"Good plan, except for one thing," Michael said. "What if Giro's being watched?"

"He probably is, but if you and I are with Helen at the Quattro Fontane, my guess the person or persons watching him will drive over to the hotel. If they realize we've out-smarted them and go back to Giro's house, he'll be gone. Now my third call."

Emma took out Nicola's card and punched in her number. While the two women talked, she watched Michael's face. Clearly he was impatiently waiting to see if the last part of their plan would fall into place. She smiled, giving him the answer he wanted. "Great," she said. "We'll see you on the lower level at three. Thanks for agreeing to meet us on such short notice."

———

At 2:30, Emma dropped her key at the desk. "We're off to a production meeting," she said loudly.

"Not that anyone cares," Michael muttered as they pushed through the revolving door.

"As you said several times, humor me, will you?"

"Hotel Quattro Fontane," Michael said equally as loud as the doorman in his top hat and tails summoned a cab. "See, I'm on board with the plan," he whispered as Emma slid into the backseat.

Helen was waiting to greet them when they pulled up in front of the hotel. "I'm sorry to spoil your afternoon," she said so everyone in the vicinity would hear. "Ron and I need to rework a couple of scenes we shot this morning and want your input."

"How long will it take?" Michael said petulantly. "You gave us the afternoon off. Emma and I planned to see the Coliseum and the Forum."

Helen looked at her watch. "We'll probably be at it for a couple of hours. I'm afraid you'll have to put off your sightseeing until tomorrow."

Pretending to be irritated, Michael and Emma followed Helen into the lobby.

"Good acting job, both of you," Emma said as they took the elevator to the second floor.

Seeing no one in the halls, Helen led Emma and Michael to the stairwell at the end of the hallway. "What's your plan after you leave here?" she asked.

"We'll meet Giro, walk to his house, and drive to San Clemente to meet Nicola." Emma said.

"What about later? Are you coming back here?"

Emma hesitated. "I hadn't thought that far ahead. We may have to do this again, so when we're finished, we want it to look like we've been inside all the time. We'll have Giro drop us a few blocks away. I'll call and you can open the back door. We'll go out the front and catch a cab back to the Excelsior."

"Any idea what time you'll be here?"

"Around 5:30. Sorry we can't be more specific."

"No problem. Call when you're close."

Giro was waiting in the alley behind the hotel. "I didn't see anyone following me," he said, "but my apartment was definitely being watched. About the time you left the Excelsior in a cab, a black car parked in front of the next building drove away. I couldn't see who was inside, but I think there were two people in the front seat."

Fortunately, no one was in the vicinity of Giro's apartment when they arrived, and with no one to elude, he dropped them at San Clemente a little before three. "What time should I pick you up?" he asked as he opened Emma's door.

"No need for you to come back," Emma said. "We'll take a cab back to the Spanish Steps and walk to the street behind the hotel."

"I don't understand what's going on, but if you change your mind and need the car, just call. I'll be standing by."

Without stopping at either of the two upper levels of the church, they descended to the lowest level where Nicola was waiting. *Thank God for Nicola,* Emma thought. *I don't know how I'd succeed without her.* She waved as they approached her smiling guide.

"It seems you two called a truce," Nicola said when she saw Emma and Michael together. "You look friendly."

"Would you believe we are?" Emma said.

"How did that happen?"

"No doubt it was my irresistible charm." Michael chuckled.

"You mean it was because I knew so much more about Bernini than you did and you needed me." Emma turned to Nicola. "Thanks to you," she said, verbalizing her recent thoughts.

"She's right," Michael said, "so impress me, Ms. Adriani."

"Nicola, please."

"Nicola it is."

"We only have an hour and a half. Will we be able to see everything?" Emma asked.

"Yes, if we get started right now. Let me tell you a few general things as we walk. San Clemente is not one but three churches constructed one above the other on top of the remains of earlier Roman dwellings. So a visit to the church is more like a journey backwards in time. We're going to travel across the centuries where history merges with legend."

"A time machine," Michael said.

"I know you're joking, but in a sense you're right," said Nicola.

For the next hour, they explored the lower level of San Clemente, hearing about Nero's fire, the early Christians who met clandestinely in the long-destroyed villa, and the worshippers of the god Mithras who held their ritual banquet in a well-preserved cave-like room.

'We didn't see anyone who looked out of place in the lower level," Michael whispered to Emma as they went up to the second level of the church.

"Maybe we really did fool our shadows," she said.

"Let's hope so."

"Why don't we assume we did, relax, and enjoy what Nicola has to say?"

"It's a deal."

"We're entering the fourth-century church," Nicola was saying. "Let's walk over and take a look at the frescos. They take us back in time to the church's first-century origins. Saint Clement was the third successor of Saint Peter. According to legend, sometime between 98 and 117, he was banished to the Crimean mines by the Emperor Trajan. There he converted so many soldiers and fellow prisoners that the Romans tied an anchor to his neck and threw him into the Black Sea. Legend says he was rescued by angels and taken to an underwater tomb where he was revealed to believers once every year by a miraculous ebbing of the tides."

"Interesting," Michael said, and from the look on his face, Emma could tell he was sincere.

"There's a humorous fresco in the nave," Nicola said. "Care to take a look?"

"Of course," Emma and Michael said in unison.

Nicola led them across the room and paused in front of a fresco that, to Emma, didn't seem as special as the ones they'd previously seen. "Why's this particular fresco special?" she asked.

"Because it gives us a look at what was funny to the fourth century Romans. The fresco tells the story of a jealous husband who's complaining that his wife is spending too much time at Pope Clements' masses."

"I don't see the humor," Michael said.

"Let me explain. "As you can see, the man is making a fool of himself by mistaking a bulky column for the saintly pope. He blurts out a surprising expletive; *Fili dele pute.*"

"I still don't get it."

"It's not about what the man says. You can probably translate the phrase on your own. What's important is this is the earliest known writing in the Italian language."

"Ah! Now I understand."

For twenty-five minutes, they examined the ancient frescos as Nicola talked. "I wish we had more time to spend down here," Michael said when she finished her spiel. "Emma told me you're taking her around Rome on Friday afternoon and Saturday. Mind if I join you?"

"It's up to Emma. She's my boss."

"I've made an art critic of our jock," Emma said. "Maybe you can do your magic and make him an authority on Roman antiquities?"

As they climbed toward the upper church, Steven was descending. He saw them and turned toward the wall so Nicola wouldn't recognize him. When they were beyond him, Michael turned to Steven and mouthed: "Back in a minute."

"We don't have much time left for sightseeing today," Emma said when they reached the upper level. "We'll take a quick look around and catch a cab back to the hotel."

"Giro's not picking you up?"

"We gave him the afternoon off," Michael said.

As Nicola turned to leave, Emma called her back. "Do you know Giro well?" she asked.

"Not really, though he has driven for me several times over the past year or so."

"Then this wasn't the first time you've worked with him?"

Nicola seemed puzzled. "No," she said. "Why do you ask?"

"Just wondering. He seems like a great guy."

"He is. He knows as much about the ancient sites as I do. If he didn't like to drive, he would make a great guide."

"Thanks," Emma said. "Have a good day and thanks for the tour."

"What was that all about?" Michael asked when Nicola was out of earshot.

"I want to know when Giro started driving."

"You're thinking he might be a plant who's driving you around on someone's orders?"

"I'll admit it crossed my mind."

"You realize that's impossible. When Giro got the assignment, you had no idea you'd be doing anything besides covering the Bernini exhibition. You're over-thinking, Emma."

"I suppose you're right, but we have so many questions and so few answers."

"Maybe Steven can help in that regard."

When they were sure Nicola had left the church, they walked back through the fourth-century basilica and down to the lowest level. "I don't have a lot of time, so I'll get right to the point," Steven said after a quick hello. "I've found out three things: First, the pope has had a sudden and serious recurrence of the flu, and his doctors can't explain why he isn't responding to the medications they've pre-scribed. Secondly, your Father Paul is no longer working on the Counter-Reformation project in the Vatican archives. I don't know what he's doing now, but I have people looking into it."

"What else?" Michael said.

"Angelo's no longer Cardinal Amici's secretary. No one I've spoken with knows why he was replaced."

"You have people looking into this too?"

"As we speak."

"What about the Sandri brothers and their uncle?" Michael asked.

Steven shook his head. "I'm good, but I'm not that good. You just gave me the assignment."

Out of the side of her eye, Emma saw a man standing near the entrance to the lower level. "I think we're being watched," she whispered.

"We are." Steven motioned the man over to them. "This and the instructions I'm about to give you are the primary reasons I needed to see you in person. Emma and Michael, this is my friend Sante. He's a member of the Vatican police force."

"Nice to meet you, Sante." Emma studied the policeman. In his early thirties, he was about six-feet with a slim, though muscular, build. His brown eyes were deep-set above high cheekbones. *He's all business,* was Emma's first impression, *even when he smiles.*

Michael extended his hand. "Thanks for your help, Sante."

"You're welcome, Mr. Kelsey," Sante said, shaking Michael's hand.

"Michael, please."

"And call me Emma."

Sante will be keeping his eye on you at the funeral tomorrow," Steven said. "The cardinal will be celebrating Mass. I'm sure he'll be included in the receiving line. Try to speak with him. Arrange another interview. Speak loudly so everyone in the vicinity will hear what you're saying. Tell him you'll meet him at the obelisk in Saint Peter's square at five. All the time you're talking, keep the camera rolling, not only to film the two of you planning the interview, but also to see if anyone tries to prevent him from keeping the appointment. My guess is his handlers will say he'll be tired or hasn't been feeling well. Head them off before they have the opportunity to stop him from making the appointment. Loudly, even obnoxiously if need be, tell him if he's not feeling well, you'll come to him."

"I'll say our audience demands a follow up," Emma said.

"Good idea. Now I've got to get out of here. I have a meeting with the resident priest before I vest. Do you want Sante to follow you back to the hotel?"

"We're all set," said Emma.

"Then I'll talk with you later tonight." Steven hugged Emma and shook hands with Michael.

"Good job," Michael said.

"Thanks, but I want to warn you one more time—this is serious business. One person lost his life, another lost his job, a cardinal is being held captive in his rooms, and a pope is critically ill."

"We're not giving up on the story," Michael said. "At the moment, you're the one I'm concerned about."

"Don't worry about me. I'm being very discreet."

"I hope so. Now go say Mass and, while you're at it, say a prayer for me."

Steven grinned. "I know being here in a church is a first for you in quite a while."

"You're wrong," Michael said smugly. "I was in Saint Peter's day before yesterday."

"Of course you were. You know what I mean." He turned and walked away without further comment.

Sante said goodbye and followed Steven up the stairs. Several minutes later, Michael and Emma followed. They exited the church and flagged down a passing cab. "The Spanish Steps," Michael said, as they slid into the backseat.

Neither Michael nor Emma said anything during the ride. While Michael paid the driver, she called Helen. "We'll meet you at the back door in ten minutes," she said. "Anything unusual happening? Good."

When they knocked on the door, Helen answered, carrying an ice bucket. "Nice cover," Michael said.

Helen grinned. "I thought so."

They took the stairs to the second floor. Before Emma and Michael entered the hallway, Helen peered out. "The coast is clear. I don't suppose you want to come to my room and tell me what's going on."

"No time this afternoon," said Michael. "We've likely been here long enough to arouse suspicion, so it's time to go back to the Excelsior. We'll fill you in tomorrow."

"I'll hold you to it. So you know, Ron sent the Borghese and Saint Theresa segments to New York and Boston. The shows were well received."

"And why wouldn't they be?" Michael teased.

"Pay no attention to the Michael who just answered," Emma said.

"Who?" Helen said, smiling.

Emma laughed and Michael frowned. They took the elevator to the lobby, pushed through the front door, and hailed another cab.

CHAPTER SEVENTEEN

When the cab pulled up in front of the Excelsior, the ever-present shadows were parked just beyond the exit. "Enough of this crap," Michael growled. He shoved the money for the fare toward at cabbie.

"Stay here," he shouted back at Emma as he began to jog toward the curb. As he approached, the driver in the idling car stomped on the gas and, nearly knocking over a passing scooter, merged into the Via Veneto traffic.

"Gallant, but foolish behavior," Emma said when Michael arrived back at the hotel steps. "You're the one who keeps saying we're dealing with dangerous people, yet you throw caution to the wind. What if the goon had pulled out a gun and shot you?"

"But he didn't."

"Not this time. Could you stop and think before you single-handedly try to take out bad guys?" She paused. "So, during your fool-hearted stunt, did you recognize anyone?"

"No, but my gallant act, as you so aptly put it, provided significant information. The car had a Vatican license plate."

"Which we figured—"

"And our stalkers are amateurs."

"What makes you think so?"

"In my vast experience with spies and murderers, the getaway car doesn't have license plates. Don't you watch CSI and

NCIS? No respectable criminal would give the good guys an opportunity to run their plates."

"Of course they wouldn't," Emma teased. "Don't you love how our TV shows teach the average person so much about crime?"

Without giving Michael time to respond, she pushed through the revolving door, leaving him standing on the curb.

While Emma picked up her keycard, Michael checked with security. "Gusto had no idea who could have had your card," he said when he met her at the elevator.

"So nothing's new."

"I don't know if it's new, but Dina called in sick today, or rather her brother phoned the housekeeping manager to say she's not feeling well and staying home."

"In my book, that says it all. Dina's responsible for my keycard falling into the wrong hands."

"Emma, you're jumping to conclusions. The woman really could be sick."

"It's possible, but I don't think it's a coincidence." She pushed the buttons for the third floor as well as the fourth.

"I don't have reason to stop by my room," Michael said when he saw two buttons light up. "I have everything I need in yours."

"I know, but I need for you to get off at your floor."

Realizing she was being rude, Emma backed off. "You know how much I appreciate you looking out for me, Michael, but I'd like to spend some time alone. I have personal e-mails to answer, and I haven't talked to my parents in days. They're used to hearing from me regularly, and I want them to know I'm fine. Despite the frown that's creeping across your face, I imagine you could use a little alone time."

"But—"

"No buts, please. The people who were waiting for us to come back sped away. It's broad daylight, and the halls and stairwells are being monitored. I'll flip the security lock as soon as I get inside, and I promise not to open the door for anyone."

Michael looked glum. "Okay, but you're going to let me come up for dinner—"

"Actually, I'm not."

"Emma—"

"I don't think I can stand to watch you eat another over-cooked hamburger and, frankly, I'm sick of being locked away because we're worried someone's following us, or worse. I'm in Rome, and I'm going out for dinner. If you'd like to join me, great, but if you prefer to stay in, I'm still going. No room service tonight. When I get to my room I'm calling the concierge for a restaurant recommendation. I'd like an out-of-the-way place which serves authentic Italian food."

"It seems you've left me no choice."

"Actually I have. You can either go with me or wave as I drive away. I'll call you when I know where and when I'm going. You can make your decision then. If you decide to go, I'll let you come upstairs to pick me up."

"Well, I guess that's something."

When they got to the third floor, Emma kissed Michael on the cheek. "I'll call you in a little while."

She sighed as she walked down the empty fourth-floor hall. She was enjoying being with Michael, but it was great to be alone for a change. She inserted her keycard, opened the door, and engaged the security lock. Her first inclination was to change clothes before calling the concierge, but realizing Michael would worry if he didn't hear from her in a timely manner, she threw her purse on the desk and picked up the phone.

Ten minutes later, the concierge called her back and she had a plan. She dialed Michael's room. "You're sure I can't dissuade you," he began.

"Hello to you too. The answer to your question is no. I'm going to the Antico Arco on Piazzale Aurelio at eight. If you'd like to accompany me, be at my door by 7:25."

"I assume you made a reservation for two."

"I did, but I can change it to one if you'd rather not go."

"Will there be anything I can eat?"

"You mean anything you want to eat. The concierge said the restaurant serves creative Italian cuisine. His exact words were: 'The food is like my Italian grandmother would make, using recipes Nonno wouldn't try.'"

"Terrific," Michael said sarcastically. "I guess I have no choice but to suffer through."

"I thought you might see it my way. 7:25 on the dot. See you then." Emma hung up before Michael could protest.

Emma responded to several e-mails, one from her parents and a congratulatory note from Jack, who raved about the shows and expressed his surprise she was working congenially with the Geraldo-wannabe. Glad to be by herself after two days of rushing around, she sat on the couch, put her feet on the coffee table, and thumbed through the hotel magazine before taking a leisurely shower and dressing for dinner.

At 7:25, Michael knocked. Emma peered through the peephole and opened the door. "Right on time," she said.

"What choice did I have? I was afraid you'd leave without me."

"You know I would have."

"Then I'm glad I didn't put you to the test. You look great. I like this elegant-casual dress better than the one you wore last night. Blue's your color."

"Are you sure you're not a fashion reporter?" Emma teased.

"Not yet, but you're making me an art expert. You never know what might come next."

"No, you never do," Emma said pensively. Anyway, back at you. You look great too. I like your brown sport coat and yellow and brown tie."

They took the elevator down and pushed through the revolving doors. "Taxi," Michael said. The doorman walked to the curb and whistled.

"Antico Arco please," Emma instructed when they pulled out onto the Via Veneto.

Though he and Emma assumed they were being tailed, Michael didn't see one of the familiar black cars following behind the cab. "Maybe you scared them off with your gallant attack," Emma said as he turned around for the fifth or sixth time.

"I doubt it, but if they are back there, they're not being quite so obvious. I'm not sure which is better—the enemy you can see or the one you can't. So, tell me where you're dragging me."

"Dragging you? You made the choice to go with me. I would have happily gone alone."

"Happily? That's insulting. So?"

"Sisto, the concierge who made the reservation, said Antico Arco means 'old arch.' The restaurant was named after a nearby medieval gate, the Arco di San Pancrazio, on the Gianicolo Hill."

"Is that one of the famous Seven Hills of Rome?"

Emma raised an eyebrow. "You know about them?"

"I confess, I saw the movie."

"I never figured you for a man who sees chick flicks, especially one starring Mario Lanza."

"I was cultivating my feminine side."

"Sure you were." Emma laughed. "Have I mentioned you're incorrigible?"

"But you love me anyway."

"Don't push it. As for the hill, I didn't see the movie, so you'd be the expert."

The cabbie interrupted. "It's not one of the seven," he said. "They are the Quirinal, Viminal, Capitoline, Palatine, Esquiline, Caelian, and Aventine."

"Thanks for the information," Emma said. "You seem to know a lot about Rome. My guide said the Trastevere area where we're having dinner is special, and it was the first place the concierge thought of when I asked him to recommend a restaurant for dinner tonight."

The cabbie responded in broken though understandable English. "It is. Lots of people I drive say the clubs are hot."

Emma turned to Michael. "See, I'm bringing you to a hot spot. That should appeal to a man like you."

"A man like me?"

"No comment." She spoke again to the cabbie. "What can you tell us about the Antico Arco? The concierge at the hotel says it's a great restaurant."

"Everyone I pick up there say they like the food."

"Sisto said the same thing." Emma turned to Michael. "He told me to ask the sommelier—I think he said his name is Massimo—for a wine recommendation. They're friends, which is how we were able to get a table on short notice."

Michael paid the fare and generously tipped the driver. Before going into the restaurant, Emma leaned toward the driver's open window. "Grazie molto."

"Prego," the driver said, smiling. "Buona notte."

Michael held the door as Emma entered the small, intimate restaurant decorated in white, cream, and dark chocolate tones. They'd just sat down at a table near the back of the room when the sommelier appeared. "Buona sera. I am Massimo," he said. "You're the reporters from ABC. My friend Sisto said to take good care of you. Do you like red wine?"

"Whatever the lady wants is fine with me," Michael said. "I'm no connoisseur of fine wine. Emma?"

"I prefer white, but I enjoy a good red from time to time. We'll happily be guided by your expertise, Massimo. Sisto says you're the best."

"My friend exaggerates," Massimo said shyly. "If you would like to try a different Italian red, I recommend Avignonesi Cortona Merlot Desiderio, a medium-bodied wine with aromas of blackberry and a hint of black olives. It leaves a smoky berry aftertaste that, I think, complements the food here at Antico Arco."

Michael made a face. "Black olives and blackberries in wine?"

Emma laughed. "Forgive my gauche friend, Massimo. We'll try the Merlot."

"Very good." Massimo looked at Michael. "I don't think you would know about the olives if I hadn't mentioned them."

"Bring it on." Michael opened the menu and frowned.

"What, no hamburger and fries?" Emma teased.

"No, but not to worry. I can't wait to try a truffle and rabbit-meat salad and fried zucchini blossoms."

"Zucchini blossoms are delicious. I'll order them and you'll see. You opened your mind to art. Now open it to something other than hamburgers."

"I eat lots of things besides hamburgers, but they're not on the menu. What's an Italian restaurant without lasagna, chicken parm, or spaghetti with meatballs?"

"An Italian Italian restaurant."

Emma ordered the fried zucchini blossoms as an appetizer, and for dinner, duck breast in wine sauce with stewed cannellini beans. Michael was still scanning the menu offerings when the waiter asked, "And you, sir?"

"I'll have guinea fowl and grilled vegetables."

"A good choice." The waiter took the menus and left the table.

"Guinea fowl's as close to chicken as I could come," Michael whispered.

Massimo brought the wine and started to pour a taste into Michael's glass. He waved him away. "Let Ms. Bradford taste the olives and blackberries. I'm too *gauche* to judge what is or isn't good."

Massimo nodded and poured for Emma. She took a sip and held the wine in her mouth for a moment before swallowing. "It's delicious," she said. "Michael, I promise, you won't know you're drinking black olives."

"Shall I pour a glass for you, sir?"

"Sure. Like the lady said, I'm opening my mind to all sorts of new things." Michael's smile gave him away, and Massimo, who had seemed concerned about his recommendation, grinned and poured. Michael took a drink. He paused before commenting. "Not bad," he muttered, "but I think it tastes more like green olives than the black ones."

Emma shook her head. "We're not giving up on him yet, Massimo. The wine is delicious."

The sommelier left the table, and Michael leaned toward Emma. "I didn't see a car following the cab," he whispered. "Nor has anyone suspicious come into the restaurant since we arrived."

"Maybe we should take cabs all the time instead of riding with Gino and Lucio," Emma said, "but for the next couple of hours, I don't care who's following us, who's responsible for Piero's death, who's being guarded, who's ill and why—"

"I get the point."

"Good. Now tell me about you. I want to understand how the unmitigated ass I met on the airplane can turn out to be such a great guy."

Two hours later, Emma finally felt she was getting to know the real Michael Kelsey. "We would have saved so much time if you'd shown me the man I'm sitting with at Antico when we first met," she said as she sipped her coffee. "He's a pleasure to be around."

"Maybe you'll like him even more when you hear him admit he liked the zucchini blossoms and the wannabe-chicken."

"I certainly like that he can acknowledge he was wrong."

Michael frowned. "Enough of the sentimental crap for now. I'm tired, and you haven't had much sleep either."

"I'm exhausted."

"Then let's get out of here."

"Could you write down the name of the wine for me?" Emma asked when Massimo came over to say good-bye.

"Of course." He pulled out a pad of paper. "I'm not sure you can find this vintage in the United States, but there is an excellent wine shop around the corner from the Excelsior on Via Lombardia. You can get it there and they will ship it home for you. Tell them I sent you. I sometimes go there to buy special wines."

"I will," Emma said. "Grazie mille."

The maître d called a cab. During the ride to the hotel, Emma closed her eyes. Michael let her sleep. When they got to the hotel he woke her up and accompanied her to the desk. "Anything messages for us," he asked the receptionist as Emma picked up her keycard.

"Not for you, Mr. Kelsey, but there is a note for Ms. Bradford." She removed an envelope from beneath the desk and handed it to Emma.

Emma's throat tightened as she removed the folded paper. "What is it?" Michael asked, concern showing on his face and in his voice.

She read the note and sighed. "Thank God it's nothing. Gusto wants us to know he hasn't seen anything unusual in the hallways near my room or in the stairwells leading to the fourth floor. The cameras are working, and the man on duty will be monitoring the area throughout the night, so—"

"Don't even think about it. Alone time before dinner was one thing. Leaving you without protection all night long is something else. I'm staying on the sofa in your sitting room. If you say no, I'll park myself in the hall outside your door. I mean it. I need my rest, so do this for the great guy who joined you for dinner."

"How could I refuse those pleading eyes?"

"I've often been told I should have been an actor."

"If we blow this assignment, maybe you could start a new career. Are we stopping by your room first?"

"No need. I left my sweats in your sitting-room closet. I'll pick up my suit for the funeral in the morning."

"Nothing seems to be out of order," Emma said after they looked around the suite. "Are you sure—"

"Absolutely. Breakfast in the morning? How about another omelet?"

"No thanks."

"Then what?"

"Nothing up here. We don't have to leave until nine." She paused. "Have you called Lucio?"

"Before I picked you up for dinner. I gather you want to have breakfast at the Doney."

"I do. I told you earlier, I'm sick of room service. It's fine if we have to be out of here first thing, but tomorrow we have the luxury of sleeping in."

"Think 7:30 is too early? That should give us plenty of time to enjoy breakfast and come back up to finish getting ready for the funeral."

"If I'm not up, wake me at 6:45."

"Will do. Night."

"Night, and thanks, Michael."

"For what?"

"For everything." She closed the door to her bedroom, wishing she weren't so tired and could linger with her partner a little longer.

————

It seemed like only minutes before Emma heard a knock. She woke up with a sudden start, rolled over, and looked at the clock as Michael called through the door. "Breakfast in forty-five minutes."

"I'll be out in thirty," she said groggily.

"I made coffee, but I can't guarantee it's any good."

"At this point, anything will help." She tossed back the covers and, trying to clear the fog from her brain, sat on the edge of the bed. "Will I ever catch up on my sleep?" she mumbled as she got up, put on her robe, and opened the door to the sitting room.

"Good morning, sunshine," Michael said cheerfully. "The coffee's in the bathroom."

"Thanks." Emma smiled halfheartedly. She went to pour a cup and took a sip. "It tastes great. Have you been up for long?"

"About an hour. I've never required much sleep."

"That must have been an asset during your college days. I wish I could say the same thing. I'm not a morning person."

"Maybe a shower will help you wake up."

"God, I hope so."

Coffee in hand, Emma went back to the bedroom and closed the door. The hot water helped, and she was dressed and ready to go on time.

"You look great," Michael said when she emerged from her bedroom in a black pantsuit with a grey silk blouse.

"You clean up pretty well yourself. You're wearing Armani."

"Michael laughed. "I have to impress my New York audience, and no comment if you don't mind. Ready for breakfast? The wannabe-chicken last night wasn't very filling."

"As good as it tasted, neither was the duck. I finally understand the meaning of European portions."

Though the restaurant was crowded, they were given a table by the window. They both ordered the buffet. While they ate, they went over plans for the funeral.

"This was much nicer than the first time I saw you here," Michael said as they walked back toward the elevator.

"That's an understatement. Who woulda thunk?"

After freshening up, they met Lucio in front of the hotel at nine. "Will we get to San Pietro in Vincoli by 9:30?" Emma asked as he held the door open for her.

"Unless we have a problem with traffic, yes. It wasn't too bad when I drove over here, so hopefully we'll be okay."

"I don't want you to have an accident when you hear this, but would you tell us a little bit about the church?" Michael asked as they pulled out of the hotel drive.

"I'm surprised, sir. Are you sure? You were never interested before."

"That was the disinterested jerk called Michael," Emma said. "I guarantee you'll like the new model much better."

"I'm sure I will, and yes, I would be happy to tell you about San Pietro."

Michael leaned toward Emma. "I think knowing a little bit about a place before we go in for the funeral would be good."

"You're right, but come on. Own up to the real reason you're asking Lucio about San Pietro. After San Clemente you want to know everything about Rome."

"Fine. I admit I'm interested. Make you feel better?"

"Actually, it does." She looked in the mirror and saw Lucio grinning. "Give us a brief overview, Lucio."

"With pleasure," Lucio said. "San Pietro in Vincoli means 'Saint Peter in Chains.' According to legend, in the fifth century, the chains used to shackle Saint Peter in the Mamertine Prison were taken to Constantinople. Empress Eudoxia gave one of the chains to a church there and sent the other to her daughter in Rome. The young woman presented her chain to Pope Leo the First, who built the church to house it. Some years later, the second chain was brought back to Rome where, legend says, it miraculously linked with its partner. The entwined chains are in a reliquary in the confessio under the main altar."

"So people come here just to see the chains?" Michael asked.

"That used to be the case, but today the church is best known for Michelangelo's *Moses*. It's an amazing sculpture. If you have a chance, take a look. Be sure to notice Moses' long beard, which seems to be blowing and twisting in an unseen wind, and look at his muscles which bulge around the stone tablets containing the Ten Commandments. He gazes to his right at his people who betrayed his trust by worshipping the Golden Calf while he was on the mountain receiving the Torah from God."

"So the marble in *Moses* moves like it does in Bernini's *David*," Michael said proudly. He tapped Lucio on the shoulder. "See how far I've come?"

"Quite a ways, sir, and definitely in the right direction. Ms. Bradford has worked miracles."

"And believe me, it hasn't been an easy task." Emma smiled. "Tell us more about *Moses*."

"He is depicted with horns sticking out of his head."

"Horns on a human," Michael said with disbelief. "Was Michelangelo trying to be funny, or was he making some sort of symbolic statement?"

"Neither," said Lucio. "The horns came about due to Saint Jerome's mistranslation of the Book of Exodus, Chapter 34, verses 29 through 35. He mixed up the similar Hebrew words for 'radiated light' and 'grew horns.' During Michelangelo's day, the horns were a kind of iconographic symbolism that would have been understood by all who saw the statue."

"Iconographic?"

Emma responded. "It means a set of symbols or images used in art or music, or even in modern movies, which would be immediately recognized and understood by the viewer."

"Like a cape on a superhero," Michael said.

Emma laughed. "Exactly. The people looking at Moses would have understood the symbolic meaning and ignored the sculpted horns."

"And I would imagine sculpting marble horns would be easier than sculpting rays of light."

"You're definitely right in that regard," said Lucio. "Michelangelo felt *Moses* was his most lifelike creation. Legend says he was so impressed that he struck Moses's right knee with a hammer, commanding the statue, 'Now speak,' or possibly, 'Why won't you speak?'"

"That's not a true story, is it?" Michael asked.

"I don't know, but there's a scar on Moses' knee thought to be from Michelangelo's hammer."

When they pulled up in front of the church, Michael looked out the window. "This place looks more like a regular building than a church."

"You mean it's not magnificent?" Lucio responded. "The fifteenth-century portico is plain, but the interior is much more like what visitors to Rome expect in a church. You'll be impressed once you get inside."

Emma smiled as she got out of the car. "Thanks for the information, Lucio."

"You're welcome. Shall I wait for you?"

"Sure," Michael said. "Leave your cell on. I'll call you when the service is over."

As they walked toward the church, Bill was filming the guests. He gave them a thumbs-up as they went inside. Though it was still early, the church was already filling up with people. "Where shall we sit?" Michael said.

"Near the back, but not yet. I want to see the famous *Moses.*"

"Now?" Michael said with disbelief.

"What better time? Come on. And while we're at it, we'll go see Saint Peter's chains up close and personal. You might want to take a good look at the congregation while we're up there. We may be seen as ugly Americans, but who cares if we learn something from our stroll."

Emma removed her jacket, draped it across the two seats near the back on the side aisle, and led Michael up the aisle toward the front of the church. As they stood in front of Michelangelo's famous statue, Michael pointed to the horns. "Monsignor Masella's in front row," he whispered.

"I saw him. He's sitting by another monsignor. I wonder if that's Cardinal Amici's new secretary. They appear to be chummy."

"Let's take a closer look."

Though they didn't go all the way to the front of the altar, they lingered at the side, pretending to be discussing the lighted case. "Father Paul is sitting a few rows back," Michael said when they turned back to their seats.

"Shall we wave as we go by?" Emma said, "Better yet, let's say hello. You know how I love antagonizing people."

"Of course you do."

They walked along the side aisle toward the back of church, pausing briefly by Father Paul's chair. "Morning, Father," Emma whispered.

Father Paul was clearly bothered by the attention Emma was paying him. He shook his head. "Please," he mouthed.

"Sorry about your friend," Michael said.

Father Paul nodded and bowed his head, signaling he didn't want to talk.

"I think he was afraid to talk with us," Emma said as they walked to their seats.

"It looks that way."

When they were seated, Michael looked around. "There's Steven on the end of the left aisle near the front of the church," he said. "He's with another priest. I wonder who he is."

"I'm sure Steven will introduce us if he's anyone we should know."

Emma watched the two priests as they quietly conversed. A third priest approached them and whispered in Steven's ear. Looking concerned, Steven got up and walked with him to the church door. A few minutes later, he came back up the aisle next to their seats. As he passed their row, he nodded, acknowledging their presence.

"What's that all about?" Emma whispered.

"I don't know, but there's no time to figure it out. Here comes Cardinal Amici."

Emma watched the cardinal enter from a side door. "Even from this far back, he looks bad," she whispered. "He's hunched over like he was when he first joined the pope on the loggia."

Emma glanced behind her. A young altar boy carrying a towering cross was followed by two other white-robed boys holding large, gold candlesticks. Behind them was a casket covered in a white pall.

The cardinal signaled for the boys to wait. He left the altar, walked to the front row, and comforted a man and a woman who, Emma assumed, were Piero's mother and father.

"Is that normal behavior at a Catholic funeral mass?" Emma whispered to Michael. "I've never seen a celebrant talk with a family before a service, and for that matter, don't the priest and the family usually walk behind the casket as it goes up the aisle. Unless the cardinal did it earlier, and I don't see how since he's so restricted, he didn't sprinkle holy water on the casket before the service starts."

Michael looked puzzled. "How do you know all this?"

"My mother was member of the altar guild at our church, and I've been to enough Catholic funerals to know the services are very similar."

"Thankfully I haven't been to many of these things, but what Cardinal Amici's doing does seem strange."

The congregation stood as the casket moved slowly up the center aisle. When it reached the front, the cardinal said a prayer, motioned the congregation to be seated, and started back toward the altar. All of a sudden he stopped, turned, and stared out at the congregation.

"What's he doing?" Michael whispered.

"I think he's looking for me. If so, I have to let him know I'm here." Emma stood up.

Michael grabbed her arm. "What the hell are you doing?"

Emma shook free of Michael's grasp. She continued to stand and stare at the altar. Several members of the congregation, including Masella, turned to see what the cardinal was staring at so intently. Emma saw the cardinal nod. "He saw me," she whispered as she sat down.

"So did everyone else. Is that what you wanted?"

"I don't care about everyone else. I wanted the cardinal to know I'm here; that I realize he's in danger."

"So are you after that move."

"I'm not worried. I have you to protect me." Emma smiled, took Michael's arm, and leaned into him.

The Mass was about to begin when Angelo walked up the side aisle. He passed Emma and Michael, turned back, and nodded almost imperceptibly.

As the casket arrived at the altar and the Cardinal began the Mass, his voice was strained. There was none of the bravado he'd shown before leaving the loggia the day before. *He's grieving, but he's also scared,* Emma mused as she listened.

Throughout the service, she watched Ron and Bill do their jobs. While Ron filmed the Mass, Bill took footage of the congregants. Halfway through, he looked at Emma for direction. She pointed to her face and then Cardinal Amici. Bill nodded and zoomed in for a close-up. When he looked back at her again, Emma put up her index finger, signaling number one. Bill cocked his head. Realizing he hadn't understood, she pointed to others in her row. Bill grinned, moved toward the *Moses* statue and zoomed in on the faces of the priests and guests in the first few rows of the church.

When the mass was finally over, the cardinal, followed by Piero's family members, walked down along the center aisle to the rear of the church and formed a line going out the door. It took a while for the mourners in front of them to file out and greet the family, so by the time Emma and Michael finally got to the cardinal, he looked exhausted. His eyes were dull and lifeless, and his sensitive face was rapt with grief. *Considering his situation, it's not surprising*, Emma thought. *But what's more interesting than the cardinal's demeanor is the man standing beside him.* Masella was shaking hands with great gusto.

As Emma approached the pope's secretary, two men dressed in suits moved between and slightly behind Masella and the cardinal. Emma frowned and turned back to Michael. "I'm sick of this intrusive, overbearing priest," she whispered.

"I suggest you try to keep him from seeing your contempt."

"Just watch how charming I can be."

As soon as Emma greeted the monsignor, she realized she wasn't dealing with the man she met during the Bernini reception. He was no longer trying to hide his irritation. "What brings you to the funeral of a priest you never met?" he said gruffly.

"I'm following the story, Monsignor, and I wanted to express my condolences to the cardinal on the loss of his secretary."

As Emma started to move beyond Masella toward the cardinal, the two men, obviously the cardinal's guards, tried to block her approach. Michael took action. He stepped between her and the men, allowing her to advance toward the cardinal while they were concentrating on him.

"Eminence," Emma said as she took the cardinal's hand, "I'm so sorry for your loss."

The cardinal nodded. "Thank you," he said almost inaudibly.

As Steven had instructed, Emma raised her voice so everyone around her could hear. "This may not be the time to bring this up," she said. "If I'm being insensitive, I apologize, Eminence, but who knows when I'll be able to speak with you again. Mr. Kelsey and I received a great deal of positive feedback from our American audience about the interview I did with you on the opening day of the Bernini exhibition. Their e-mails and tweets say they'd like to hear you speak about Bernini again."

As she turned back to be sure Ron was filming, she saw Masella's frown. Instead of heeding his tacit warning and quitting, she raised her voice. "Would you consent to another interview for our American audience?"

Before the cardinal could respond, Masella moved forward to intervene. Michael took his arm. "You wouldn't want the cardinal to be rude to an ABC reporter on camera," he said as he pointed toward Ron, "or, for that matter, slight the American people."

Masella's eyes blazed, but he stepped back as Emma loudly addressed the cardinal again, "Would you meet us later this afternoon?"

Though Steven had suggested the interview take place by the obelisk, Emma suddenly realized it wasn't the right place to meet. The location had to be Bernini-related. "I'd like to interview you beside the Alexander Monument in Saint Peter's at five o'clock. I'm sure our audience would like to hear how Bernini's work remains relevant today, how it symbolizes the Counter-Reformation movement of which you're a part."

Emma wondered if she had gone too far. She glanced at Masella and had her answer. His expression screamed yes. *Maybe I'll be protecting the cardinal if I publicize his dilemma,* she thought as she continued. "Bernini used his art to promote the values and teachings of the church. Perhaps you can interpret the symbolism in the monument and do the same thing."

The cardinal's eyes finally showed a spark of life. "I'd be glad to grant you an interview, Ms. Bradford," he said, noticeably mustering all his reserved strength.

"We have your acceptance on camera, Eminence. We look forward to talking with you."

The man who'd been sitting with Masella during the funeral joined Emma. "Ms. Bradford, I'm Monsignor Giotto Tomai, Cardinal Amici's new secretary." As he spoke, Ron zoomed in to film the conversation. "I'm afraid His Eminence tires easily, so an interview is out of the question."

Emma refused to give in. "I won't keep him for long," she insisted. "Surely the Vatican wouldn't want to disappoint our American TV audience in New York and Boston, especially after the pope himself pledged to cooperate with ABC to promote the Bernini exhibition."

Monsignor Tomai appeared to be at a loss as to what to do. "Of course not," he finally said, his voice exuding irritation.

The cardinal smiled; his eyes brighter from the victory. Once again he took Emma's hand. As he grasped it tightly, she felt another paper. When he released her, she immediately deposited the note he left in her jacket pocket.

"Thank you, Eminence," she said. "Mr. Kelsey and I look forward to seeing you at five in front of Alexander's tomb."

"I'll be there or—how do you American's put it?—die trying."

Emma smiled, but she heard the grim message loud and clear.

CHAPTER EIGHTEEN

When Emma and Michael got to the end of the receiving line, Bill joined them. "I think Ron and I have everything you need," he said. "We're heading back to the truck. Want us to put what we have on a disk?"

"Please," Emma said.

Michael put his hand on Bill's shoulder. "Could you make two additional copies of the disk for me? I'd like to give a copy to a friend who might be able to shed some light on the people at the service. He'll know who should or shouldn't be there."

"Sure. We'll leave them for you at the concierge desk at the Excelsior."

"I'd rather you didn't," Emma said. "Michael and I are meeting the cardinal at the Alexander Monument at five. We can pick up the disks at the truck at 4:30."

"We'll see what we can do."

"Great." Michael took out his cell. "I'll call Lucio and tell him we're ready to go."

Before he could make the call, Angelo approached them. "Go back and take a closer look at the chains," he said as he walked by.

"Why would he want us to do that?" Michael asked. "It looks like he's leaving."

"He'll probably double back," Emma said. "Let's do as he asked."

The church was once again open to the public. Tourists milled around as Emma and Michael walked up the aisle toward the chains in the lighted glass case. "Maybe it's good we're not meeting Angelo in an empty church," Emma said as she saw him standing near *Moses*.

"But why would he want to meet in public place?"

"Probably because neither Masella nor Giotto would come back to a church filled with tourists."

"For your sake, I hope you're right."

"I hope so too. I'm not too popular at the Vatican, especially after my discussion with the cardinal in the receiving line."

"I heard what you said, Ms. Bradford," Angelo said as they walked up to him. "It took courage to do what you did. That is one of the reasons I wished to see you. I imagine you heard I am no longer in the cardinal's service."

"We know, but we don't know why or what happened," Emma said.

"Let me just say it was a mutual parting of the ways," Angelo said wistfully. "I came back into the church to say you are playing a dangerous game."

"I assure you we're not playing games, Monsignor," Emma said with great resolve. "We're trying to figure out what's going on."

"Probably little of which you are not aware. You must realize the cardinal is in danger. He is guarded twenty-four hours a day. I would be surprised if he comes to the basilica, despite your efforts to blackmail Masella."

"Blackmail?"

"You know what I mean, Ms. Bradford. You were not addressing only Cardinal Amici. You were speaking to your American audience. You were attempting to keep Masella from denying you access to the cardinal. You might have succeeded, but not in the way you wanted. You made an enemy of the pope's secretary, and that could be perilous for you and Mr. Kelsey."

"Really? You don't think Cardinal Amici will show up?"

"I have no idea. When you spoke with him, I observed energy and a renewed spirit which has clearly been lacking for days. Perhaps he will find a way, but if so, the meeting could become a problem for all of you. I believe Masella, not the pope, is behind the current problems in the Vatican. At the moment it is unclear whether or not the pontiff knows what is occurring."

"And what about you?" Michael asked. "Where do you stand on the issue?"

"Of course I prefer a conservative pope, but not this way. This is one of the reasons I will be leaving tonight. My new position is the Cathedral Church of Milan. Thank God I leave with the cardinal's blessing."

"But it wasn't his idea, was it?"

"Or yours," Emma added.

Angelo didn't reply. Instead, he took out a card and wrote on the back. "This is my cell number. Please call if you need my assistance."

Emma took the card. "Thank you, and good luck, Father."

Angelo nodded and turned to Michael. "I know you intend to continue with your investigation. In good conscience, I must tell you again: Cancel the interview with the cardinal. Report on Bernini. Piero's death was a warning to everyone."

"We appreciate your concern, but—"

"I am unable to change your mind."

"I'm afraid not," Emma said.

"Then God bless you both." Angelo made the sign of the cross, turned, and walked away.

Lucio was waiting when they left the church. "I saw everyone leaving and figured you'd be out in a minute," he said.

"We went back in to look at *Moses* and the chains," Emma said.

Michael smiled. "Yeah, I had to take a look at the iconographic horns."

Lucio shook his head. "I'm sure you did. While you were in the church, a priest came up to the car and asked me to drop you off at a souvenir shop near Saint Peter's Square."

"What did he look like?" Michael asked.

Lucio described the priest who was sitting with Steven during the funeral. "He's an old college friend," Michael said. "I saw him at the funeral, but we didn't have a chance to talk. I'm sure he wants to catch up."

Lucio held the door for Emma and Michael and got behind the wheel. As he pulled away from the church, he glanced back over his shoulder. "Shall I wait while until you finish your meeting?" he asked.

"No thanks," Michael said. "We'll have some lunch in the area and wait for Emma's interview with Cardinal Amici."

Emma wondered if it was her overactive imagination, but when she saw Lucio's face in the rearview mirror, she thought she saw him frown. *If he did, he quickly recovered*, she thought. "You have an interview with the cardinal?" he asked.

"You seem surprised."

"I suppose I am. Rumor is the cardinal is confined to his rooms."

"That's odd," Emma said, feigning ignorance. "Why would he be?"

"Because he opposes the liberal changes the pope is expected to announce. I know Pope John was unhappy with the statement Cardinal Amici made from the loggia."

"Michael and I heard him speak. I don't think he said anything to merit confinement. What about you, Lucio? Were you personally bothered by what the cardinal said? I figure you're a liberal—you left the seminary to get married. I imagine you support the pope's progressive agenda."

"In most areas I do. Certainly if celibacy weren't the rule, I'd be a happily married priest, so the prospect of eliminating the outdated practice is appealing."

When Lucio pulled up in front of the souvenir shop, Emma thought he seemed relieved the conversation was coming to an end. "Will you need me later?" he asked.

"I don't think so," Michael said. "I'll call if we do."

Lucio let Emma out of the car, and she and Michael entered the shop, where a smiling clerk greeted them. "You're the Americans," she said, leaning in conspiratorially. "I was told you might need of spiritual guidance."

Michael grinned. "I'm sure that's true, but it has to be from the right priest."

"I know just the monsignor to show you the way," she said. "Please follow me."

She led them to an office in the back of the store where Steven and the priest who had accompanied him to Piero's funeral were sitting behind a desk. Michael Kelsey and Emma Bradford, meet James McDonald," Steven said once the saleswoman had left. "He's a buddy from Notre Dame and the most recent addition to our team."

Michael shot Steven a skeptical look as he shook hands with the tall, red-haired, freckled-faced, green-eyed priest.

"Not to worry, my friend," Steven said when he saw doubt on Steven's face. "I trust James. We're on the same page, and because he's more liberal than I, he'll be able to help us find out what's going on in Masella's circle."

"I feel like I've known you for years," James said to Michael. "You and Steven certainly had some interesting adventures when you were growing up."

"I'm not sure 'interesting' is the word I'd choose to describe our escapades," Michael said, grinning broadly. "Nice to meet you, Father. Thanks for trying to help Emma and me solve this mystery."

"You're welcome, and it's James."

"Nice to meet you, James." Emma shook hands. "Steven couldn't answer my question. Maybe you can. Why are all off-the-market priests so handsome?"

When James smiled, a dimple formed in his right cheek, adding to his sex appeal. "If Pope John has his way, maybe we won't be for long," he said.

"I think we're finished discussing handsome priests," Michael said peevishly. He turned to Steven. "So, my friend, care to tell us what you've discovered?"

"The cardinal's being closely guarded," Steven said.

"Nothing we didn't know."

"How about this? His new secretary, Monsignor Giotto Tomai, is an up-and-coming power in the church."

Emma chimed in. "We figured as much. I assume he's a conservative."

"Not so, Emma," said James. "He's a moderate. We heard the pope appointed him to the position."

"By doing so, is the pontiff sending a message?" Emma asked.

"He believes he is," Steven said, "which doesn't sit well with the fringe elements of either faction. It's a little off topic, but before I forget to tell you, James learned the pope himself prohibited the autopsy on Piero Scala."

"Because he was afraid what he'd find would negatively affect the church?" Michael said.

"That's what James and I believe, though the official Vatican position is he did it for the sake of the grieving family. We think the pope believes left-wing liberals killed Piero to make a point."

"We've been told Pope John plans to make a major policy statement from the loggia on Wednesday," James said.

"Any truth to the rumor?" Emma asked

"There is, and that's the problem. The pontiff originally intended to issue a papal edict abolishing the celibacy rule."

"What's different now?"

"The way the changes, if they are made, will be implemented. Instead of issuing a decree, the pope will convene Vatican III to discuss the radical ideas he advocates."

"Really?" Emma said in disbelief. "Neither side will like that."

"That's an understatement."

"When did you find out about the new message?" she asked.

"Just before Piero's funeral began."

"When you left the church?"

"Yes, one of my colleagues delivered a note."

"Monsignor Cipriano must be furious," Michael said.

"I'm sure he is," said James. "God help anyone who stands in his way." He looked directly at Emma.

"How about you, James? How do you feel about what's going on? You're a liberal," Emma said, choosing to ignore what she assumed was a subtle warning.

"I'm not a liberal, but I am more liberal than my friend here. I believe change is necessary, but this isn't the time for a radical transformation. The effort to implement or avoid change is tearing the church apart. If some compromise isn't reached very soon ..."

"James is right," Steven said. "The Holy See is dissolving into a chaotic state. By convening Vatican III, the pope is acknowledging the situation and doing what he can to deal with the problem."

"Not to change the subject from the broad political picture to specifics, but were you able to find out anything about Dina Sandri's brothers or uncle?" Michael asked.

"The uncle's fraternal," Steven said. "All three have conservative leanings. I found out the older brother, Coreno, attended seminary with Angelo."

"He's the one who works in Florence?"

"Right."

"Anything new on Father Paul?" Emma asked.

"Only that he's being sent back to Chicago next week. Apparently the project he was working on in the Vatican archives has been terminated."

"Or someone's afraid to hear what he has to report and wants him out of here," Michael said. "My money's on Masella."

Steven nodded. "That's a pretty good bet. Did you two find out anything at the funeral?"

"A few things," Michael said. He told Steven and James about their meeting with Angelo.

"Everyone knows his departure wasn't voluntary," said Steven.

"Maybe so," Emma said, "but he doesn't seem too upset about escaping the fray."

"I don't imagine he is, especially in light of what happened to his predecessor." He paused. "So if that's it, James and I need to get back to the spy business."

"Before you do, I have something else." Emma took the cardinal's note from out of her jacket pocket. "When we shook hands, Cardinal Amici slipped me a note."

"You're full of surprises," Michael said.

"I wasn't keeping anything from you, Michael, nor am I making a dramatic revelation. I couldn't say anything about the note in front of Lucio. This is the first opportunity I've had to tell you about it."

"Forget Michael's fragile ego," Steven said. "What does the note say?"

"I have no idea. I haven't had time to read it."

"Don't keep us in suspense," said James.

Emma opened the note. "Wow!" she exclaimed.

"May I see?" Michael held out his hand, and Emma handed him the paper.

"Read it to us," said Steven.

Michael started to hand the note back to Emma. "No, go ahead," she said.

"Okay," Michael said. "There are five numbered statements."

1. *Pope John had Piero killed to stop me.*
2. *I am next.*
3. *You are in mortal danger.*
4. *Trust no one.*
5. *Help me.*

"There's nothing new in the note," Steven said.

"True," Emma said, "but the tone is frantic. What he was thinking has now become an overt statement. Cardinal Amici is accusing the pope of murder."

"Michael, have you seen anything to suggest you and Emma are in any kind of danger?" James asked.

"Oh yeah. Besides the attempt to get into Emma's room, we're being followed everywhere we go."

Steven stood up. "We have to get going. I'll fill James in on that and everything else. What's your plan?"

"Emma has an interview with Cardinal Amici in front of the Alexander Monument at five."

"If the cardinal shows, I'll be surprised, but in case he does, James will be there to keep an eye on the crowd."

"We'll have both Ron and Bill filming like they did at the funeral," Emma said. "We'll get the disk to you later. When and where?"

Emma turned to Steven. "Do you have another favorite restaurant where we could meet?"

"Sure, but you said you're being followed wherever you go. Are you sure it's a good idea?"

"We ditched the tail once. We can do it again. It would be natural for Michael and me to meet Helen after our interview with the cardinal."

"And you think you can pull it off again?" Steven asked.

Emma looked at Michael. "I don't see why not."

"Great. Whether you meet with the cardinal or not, James and I will meet you at Taverna Angelica at Piazza A. Capponi 6 at 8:30. It's a small restaurant near Saint Peter's. In fact it's so out of the way, it's almost subterranean."

"It sounds like a perfect meeting place," said Emma. "We should have enough time to do the interview with the cardinal, go back to the Excelsior to change, and head over to Helen's hotel."

"We'll see you there," Steven said. He directed his next comment to Michael: "I know you'll love the octopus salad on a bed of warm mashed potatoes with a basil-parsley pesto. It's my favorite, and we have similar tastes."

Emma laughed. "Any chance the restaurant serves burnt hamburgers and greasy, limp French fries?"

Steven slapped Michael on the back. "Nothing changes, does it, my friend?" He didn't give Michael a chance to defend himself. "Where are you going now?"

"To map out camera positions in the basilica before we meet the cardinal," Emma said.

Michael looked disappointed. "No time for lunch?"

"I saw a gelato stand on the corner. We could stop there."

"Think the guy sells hot dogs?"

Steven shook his head. "Same old Michael. James and I are going out the back door. We'll see you tonight. Hopefully we'll have more to report."

"Be careful," James said. "These people mean business."

Emma put her hand on James' arm. "You be careful too."

Emma and Michael left the store to the sound of blaring sirens and people running in the direction of the square. "What's happening?" Emma yelled over the noise.

"Apparently nothing good." As footsteps approached from behind, Michael grabbed Emma's arm. "Come on," he bellowed as they joined the rushing herd of humanity.

"Where are we going?" Emma shouted.

"To figure out what's going on in the square. You with me or do you want to wait here?"

"No way I'm staying behind, Geraldo."

The square was a scene of utter chaos. Several ambulances and police cars, their engines running and lights flashing, were parked at the barrier separating the Vatican from Italian territory. With Emma close behind, Michael raced over and pulled open the door to the news truck, which was still parked near the holy city. Ron and Bill were in the back, earphones on to block out extraneous noise as they edited the film.

"You guys can't hear what's going on in the square?" Michael yelled. "Grab the cameras and follow me. Shoot everything, whether it seems relevant or not."

"What do you know?" Bill called out as they raced out of the truck and headed toward the obelisk.

"Nothing. Let's go see what we can find out."

When they arrived outside the cordoned off area, Michael pulled out his Vatican press credentials. "Official business!" he declared. "Step aside."

"I hope these people think we're supposed to be here," Emma said as she held up her pass as well.

Luckily the crowd parted. They followed a group of medics who were approaching the body of a woman lying face down at the base of the obelisk. Emma stood aside so Ron could squeeze into the front row. "Film everything up close and personal," she directed.

As the EMT's rolled the body to reveal the woman's face, Emma gasped. "What is it?" Michael cried out.

"Oh my God!" Emma covered her mouth with her hand. "It's Dina."

"You're sure?"

"Absolutely."

"Is she dead?"

Ron turned back and shouted at Michael: "I'd say so, unless a person can live with a knife sticking out of her heart."

"Are you filming?" Michael yelled. "It looks like the EMT's are about to cover her up. Get a shot of the knife and her face before they do."

Michael turned around, spotted Bill, held up his arm, and waved. He made a circular motion with his arm and then pointed to his face.

"What are you doing?" Emma asked.

"I want Bill to film everyone in the vicinity to see if we recognize familiar faces in the crowd." He took out his cell. "David, call New York," he yelled over the noise. "Tell them to stand by for breaking news. Sure. I'll wait."

Emma was startled. "Are you sure you want to make this breaking news so soon? We'll no longer have the luxury of working in secret."

"If we don't go public right now, every other station will have reporters on the scene before we get back to the truck."

He waited for David to come back on the line. "Tell them to call the network. Emma and I will have extensive background information in a little while. Yes, Ron's with us now. He can have the first live report to you in fifteen minutes." He whirled around and addressed Emma: "We need to do this now while the body's in the square. You okay with it?"

"Sure, if you think it's what we ought to do. Give me a microphone."

Emma turned her back toward the obelisk so Ron could get Dina's body on the ground in the background and began:

This is Emma Bradford alongside Michael Kelsey. We're report-ing live from Saint Peter's Square in Vatican City, where, a few moments ago, a woman's body was found, a knife protruding from her chest. Could her death be another consequence of the growing tensions between Pope John and a group of right-wing conserva-tives led by Cardinal Amici? Michael, what's your take?"

Michael took the microphone.

It's possible, Emma. If this proves to be true, the woman's death could be the second fatality resulting from the philosophical disagreement. Just this morning, Piero Scala, Cardinal Amici's private secretary, was buried. Though no autopsy was conducted, many believe the monsignor, whose cause of death was officially listed as a heart attack, died under suspicious circumstances. Could the woman lying here in front of the basilica have anything to do with the major announcement Pope John is scheduled to make from there on Wednesday?

He paused so Ron could pan upward to film the loggia.

Our sources tell us it's possible that the Holy Father, in an effort to appease both conservative and liberal factions, will convene Vatican III to assist him in making major decisions concerning the direction the church will take in the years ahead. If this much-anticipated announcement takes place, neither liberals nor conservative will view it as a positive move.

He handed the microphone to Emma.

As of now we have few details about the dead woman. Perhaps we'll learn more during our interview with Cardinal Amici later this afternoon.

Michael shook his head. "No more," he mouthed. Emma nodded.

For now, that's it from Rome. Stay tuned to ABC for updates as the information becomes available, and be sure to watch when I interview Cardinal Amici, one of the major players in the current conflict.

"Excellent," Ron said. "Unless you need anything else, I'm on my way to the truck to send the video to New York and Boston."

Michael looked back toward the obelisk. "It looks like the body is being removed and the crime scene investigators are moving in. That's probably all we'll have today. We'll head back to the truck with you."

As they made their way back through the crowd, Emma felt her cell phone vibrate in her pocket. She took it out and checked the caller ID. "Who is it?" Michael asked.

She shrugged and answered. "Emma Bradford. Hello. Hello." She closed the cover. "It must have been a wrong number. Besides Helen, Ron, Giro, and Jack, who would know how to reach me on my cell?"

"Someone obviously misdialed."

They had moved a few more feet when the phone vibrated again. "Emma Bradford. Hello? Who is this?" There was nothing, so Emma hung up.

"Another hang up?" Michael asked.

"Yes."

They were almost at the barrier separating the Vatican from Rome when a large man wearing a clerical collar banged into Emma, causing her to stagger from the blow. Michael grabbed her so she wouldn't fall, but instead of stopping to see if she was okay, the man disappeared in the crowd. "What was that?" Emma said.

"I'm afraid nothing good. Are you all right?"

"I think so." Emma looked down. "Michael, there's a folded piece of paper on the ground. Do you think the man who ran into me could have dropped it?"

"There's only one way to find out." Michael bent down and picked up the paper.

"What does it say?"

"Seven words: 'Saint Agnes in Agony tomorrow at noon.'"

Before Michael could comment, Emma's phone vibrated again.

"Emma Bradford," she said, not knowing whether she was frightened or angry.

"Be there," was the response.

CHAPTER NINETEEN

Emma's muscles tensed. She stood quietly, her silence speaking volumes. After several minutes of waiting for her to talk about the call, Michael had to ask. "Are you going to tell me what just happened? Apparently the last call wasn't a wrong number."

"The caller, whoever he was, reiterated what the note said. He ordered me to be at Saint Agnes in Agony tomorrow at noon."

"Saint Agnes? Isn't that the church behind the Four Rivers Fountain?"

"It is, and whoever's been calling apparently knows when and where you and I are filming tomorrow morning. I'm supposed to do the shoot and casually stroll over to the church for a command performance."

"Did he tell you to leave me and the camera in the piazza?"

"Michael, he said two words: 'Be there.' He was delivering an ultimatum, not asking me to drop in for tea."

Michael continued to probe. "Was there anything familiar about his voice? Have you heard it before?"

"How could I possibly know?" Emma said impatiently. "I repeat: he uttered two words. Do you think whoever it is wants to frighten me into avoiding the tough questions during the interview?"

"There's no way we can be sure of anything at this point, but it's not out of the realm of possibilities. The message definitely says 'we know where you're going to be.' That's unsettling."

"The only way anyone could have the information would be if he looked at our schedule." Emma felt a strange uneasiness. "Could the man have been in my room? Unless Ron, Helen, David, or Bill have been talking about our plans—"

"Who would they tell? We haven't told Steven the specifics of our schedule, because there's no reason for him to know."

Emma shuddered. "Please tell me Dina didn't die because she had access to my room. You don't think a radical group killed her to send us a message?"

"I don't believe we had anything to do with her death, Emma, though it might be a good idea to find out how Dina happened to be the maid assigned to clean your room. She had to have security clearance to be allowed in a suite where expensive equipment was being stored. Who vetted her for the job?"

"Gusto should be able to tell us."

"I'm sure he could if he wanted to share the information, but so far he hasn't been forthcoming.

"Maybe that will change now that Dina is dead."

"Possibly, but I doubt it. I'll call Steven and tell him what happened. After that, we need to try and put Dina's death and your two-word call out of our minds and concentrate on the session with the cardinal. This is a crucial interview and we have to get it right."

"I wonder if he'll show up," Emma said. "Angelo doesn't think he will."

"Hold that thought. If I don't call Steven right away, I'll start scripting the interview and forget."

"What's the word?" Emma asked when Michael closed his phone.

"Steven knew about the dead woman in the square. Sante told him."

"Did he know who she was?"

"He just found out. Everything's under control, to whatever extent it can be, so let's sit in the truck and get ready for the interview. If humanly possible, I think the cardinal will show up. The question is; how far do you plan to go? Surely you're not going to stop with a few innocuous questions about Alexander's tomb."

"I'll push as much as I can, though it could be problematic. I'm sure the cardinal will be guarded like he was at the funeral."

"Then count on me to come to your rescue once again." Michel grinned. "I'll be wearing my iconographic cape when I step between you and the thugs."

Emma smiled. "Unfortunately, I don't think your cape will protect you from these guys, but maybe if you wore tights—"

"Forget it."

"The viewers would love seeing you in full Superman regalia."

"That ain't gonna happen." Michael hesitated.

"What?"

"I had a thought," Michael said, quickly becoming serious. "We should bring Bill along for the interview. While Ron films you and the cardinal, Bill can shoot from a distance. If I have a problem with the guards, he can document the encounter."

"You want him to film discreetly?"

"Actually, I'd rather he be obvious."

"So the guards will think twice before they try to strong-arm you."

"Exactly."

For the next hour, they sat in the truck, trying to anticipate the different scenarios they might encounter while talking with the cardinal. When they were as prepared as they could be without really knowing what to expect, they approached Ron and Bill.

"Good timing," Bill said as he handed Michael two disks and Emma one. "Here's the funeral footage. We also added the breaking news story we sent on to Boston and New York. Both stations aired the report immediately. It's running on all the news shows."

"If they ask, we'll provide more background after we finish with the cardinal. Think we can do it unscripted?" Michael asked.

"Absolutely, but we have to be careful not to say too much. We can't make accusations without proof." Emma stood up. "Shall we go, gentlemen?"

Bill moved back toward his seat in front of the monitors. "You too, Bill," Michael said.

"You want both of us to film?"

"We'll explain on the way over," Emma said. "But yes, we need you both."

"Then I'll get the camera and be right with you."

As they walked toward the basilica, there were few visible signs a murder had just occurred near the obelisk. The usual tourists were milling around, but there was no longer a police presence. Dina's body had been taken away, and a cleanup crew was hard at work.

"The Vatican police work fast," Emma said as they passed the obelisk.

"I'm sure they'd like to sweep our story under the rug just as quickly," said Michael.

At the back of the basilica near Alexander's tomb, they paused to explain the plan to Ron and Bill. "I don't care if it looks like nothing's happening," Michael said. "Keep filming. I'd like to have a record of everything that occurs and everyone who's looking on while Emma does the interview."

"You want me to take pictures of tourists too?"

Michael looked at Emma. "Please," she said. "Who knows if the onlookers really are tourists? I don't want to come back later and wish I'd taken a particular shot."

While Ron was putting masking tape on the floor so she and the cardinal would know where to stand, Emma moved away from the monument. She spotted James standing in a nearby chapel and touched Michael's arm. "James is here, but he's not wearing his collar," she whispered. "Would you believe he's wearing a Hawaiian shirt covered with huge red and blue flowers and pink flamingos? He's touristier than the average tourist."

"You got that right" Emma said as she caught James' eye and nodded. "No one would ever think he's a priest."

By the time they were ready for the cardinal, it was 4:45. Per Emma's request, Ron had taken preliminary shots of Truth with her foot on the globe, zooming in to show England, the country the Holy See was censuring at the time of the Counter-Reformation. Anticipating the cardinal would speak about the four crowning statues, she had Ron film them too.

"Now all we have to do is wait and hope," she said when they were ready to go.

"But not for long." Michael pointed toward the chapel to the left of the Alexander Monument. "The cardinal's here, and he's walking between two Incredible Hulks."

"They must be his guards, and it looks to me like they're doing more than escorting him. They seem to be holding him up. I don't know, Michael. Maybe this meeting was a mistake after all. The man's obviously a mess. Think he'll make it through an interview?"

"He pulled himself together at the last minute when he and the pope were out on the loggia. Hopefully he'll be able to do it again."

Emma crossed the short distance to meet the cardinal while Michael stayed behind. He signaled Bill, who was standing near the monument. "Start filming," he mouthed as Emma approached the party of three.

Bill nodded and began to shoot.

"Eminence." Emma extended her hand. "Thank you so much for coming."

"Cardinal Amici should be resting," the guard on the cardinal's right said irritably, as he moved slightly in front of his charge, blocking Emma's access.

Emma glared at the man. "I assure you the interview won't last long. When I'm finished, you can escort the cardinal back to his rooms and stand outside the door while he takes a nap."

She glanced at the cardinal for approval. He seemed to perk up a bit as he gave her an almost imperceptible nod.

He's warning me to be careful, she thought. *I'll heed his advice.* "Eminence," she said politely, "we're ready for you in front of the Alexander Monument."

One of the guards reached out to take Cardinal Amici's arm, but Emma stepped between them. "I'll help His Eminence," she said as she hooked her arm through his.

The guard reluctantly stepped aside. Michael leaned toward Ron. "The woman has balls," he whispered.

"You remember Michael Kelsey?" Emma asked when she and her charge reached the Xs taped on the floor.

The cardinal's smile was weak, his expression flat. "Of course," he said quietly. "Nice to see you again, Mr. Kelsey." He put out his hand. Michael bent to kiss his ring, but the cardinal shook hands instead.

He gave him a note, Emma thought when she saw the look on Michael's face. *That's why he wanted to shake hands.*

She continued the introductions. "This is Ron, our cameraman." She raised her voice. "And the gentleman filming everything from afar is Bill."

The cardinal nodded, and Bill waved in response. "If it meets with your approval, I'll give a short introduction," she said. "When I'm finished I'll ask for your comments."

"I'm ready," the cardinal said feebly.

As Emma began, she wondered if her first assessment had been accurate. Cardinal Amici looked too weak to be giving an interview. *But we'll see how this plays out,* she thought as she began.

She spent several minutes talking about the monument, ending with the four crowning statues:

> *The four statues crowning the monument represent the virtues practiced by Pope Alexander. In the foreground are Charity and Truth, and on the second level are Prudence and Justice. In this monument, Truth also symbolizes Religion.*
>
> *In the monument, Bernini makes a statement about the Counter-Reformation taking place during the seventeenth century. The symbolism continues to be relevant today as Catholic conservatives launch their own Counter-Reformation; this time it isn't a reaction to the Protestant Reformation, which was making serious inroads into the ancient faith, but rather to prevent changes they feel will undermine and destroy the church. With us this evening is one of the driving forces in the conservative movement, Cardinal Giancomo Amici.*

Emma turned toward the cardinal. "Good evening, Eminence. Thank you for joining us to explain how the Alexander Monument is as significant today as it was when Bernini designed it."

The cardinal made a conscious effort to stand straight. He breathed deeply and responded, "It's nice to be with you again, Ms. Bradford. We're standing in my favorite place in Saint Peter's. I often come here to contemplate and pray for guidance, particularly now, when the church faces yet another a difficult time in its history."

He smiled weakly, though his eyes remained clouded and sad as he continued. "You mentioned the figure representing Truth. Note her sorrowful expression. At the time of her creation, she was frowning about the state of the church in the seventeenth century, but her sadness could just as well be a reflection of what is happening today."

Emma started to ask another question, but the cardinal continued before she could get out the words. He spoke about Truth and Alexander's conflict with Henry VIII. "If Bernini were creating the statue today, it is likely that Truth's foot would be firmly planted on Rome, where plans are underway which will destroy Catholicism as we know it."

The cardinal winced as his guards moved in to stop the interview. Responding quickly, Michael stepped in front of the two men. He signaled for Bill to film the encounter and addressed the hulks. "Are you sure you want to intervene? Do you really want American Catholics to watch you manhandle a prince of the church?"

Apparently his words hit a nerve, because the two men backed off. Michael pointed toward Bill. He nodded and kept the camera focused on the two, obviously furious, men.

Watching the confrontation between Michael and the guards seemed to energize the cardinal. His voice was stronger as he continued: "The battle going on today is still about truth, but it is much more. Perhaps if Bernini were alive, he would find a way to add several more statues representing cardinal virtues to illustrate the issue."

"If you were Bernini's advisor, what would you suggest he include?" Emma asked.

The cardinal's eyes brightened. "Perhaps you were not aware, Ms. Bradford, but the word 'cardinal' comes from the Latin word 'cardo,' which means 'hinge.' The virtues Bernini portrays in Alexander's Monument are cardinal since morality hinges on them. We have talked about Truth. In the world today, the statue of Prudence becomes equally significant, so I would advise Bernini to make her larger. Prudence is the trait of understanding what is morally good to do in a particular situation and how best to do it. It is the ability to handle the circumstances of life in order to live in a morally good way. This is a virtue which should be practiced by the leaders of the church as they make decisions which affect church doctrine."

The cardinal flinched as he saw one of his guards take another step forward. Once again Michael intervened. He caught the man's eye and pointed to Bill. "I don't believe this," Michael said loudly. "The Vatican no longer allows free speech?"

The guard's jaw was clenched as he stepped back. He scowled, but said nothing.

Emma continued to probe: "You said you would advise Bernini to add other statues to the monument. What would you tell him right now were he standing in my place?"

This time when the cardinal smiled, his eyes smiled too. He had won this battle; he was no longer being driven by fear. "I would say add a statue of Hope," he said, his voice stronger. "Hope is our reliance on God's help as we attempt to attain the things He has promised, even in the face of difficulty or our initial belief that they're beyond our power. Today we must hope those to whom God has granted the power to lead the Catholic faithful will consider the ramifications of their actions."

When Emma saw the cardinal's guards make no overt move, she had renewed hope, hope that Michael could keep them under control until the interview was over. "Is there another statue important enough to be included in Bernini's monument?" she asked.

As he answered the question, Emma saw the same change come over the cardinal that she'd witnessed when he addressed the crowd from the loggia. He was no longer hunched or struggling to maintain his balance. Once again, if only for a moment, he exuded the power of his office. "I would add another virtue and, though you did not ask about them, one of the seven cardinal vices."

"Tell our audience what you would ask Bernini to create, Eminence."

"I would have him include a statue of Strength, which is the trait of persisting in or going after what is good and right in the face of difficulty, danger, harm, loss, or suffering. Now, more than ever, faithful Catholics must adopt Christian strength. As am I, they must be ready to undergo suffering or risk danger for the sake of doing God's will. Strength, given to all of us by God in Christ and by the Holy Spirit, allows us to endure pain and affliction."

Emma knew she was pushing the guards to their limit. Ron and Bill, cameras rolling, were the only reason the cardinal hadn't been dragged back to his rooms. "Would you stop with Strength?" she said, pushing the envelope once again.

The cardinal looked at the guards, but their sour expressions and threatening looks didn't deter him. On the contrary, they seemed to empower him to continue. "No, Ms. Bradford," he said. "I would have Bernini add one more statue, though it would be set apart from the rest. As I said before, I would ask him to sculpt one of the seven deadly sins—a personification of Pride. The medieval theologian Thomas Aquinas said of pride: 'Inordinate self-love is the cause of every sin. The root of pride is found to consist in man not being, in some way, subject to God and his rule.'"

Emma knew her next question would infuriate the already-irate guards. She looked at Michael, who seemed to know what she was thinking. He nodded, and she continued: "Are you accusing any particular person of having the sin of pride, Eminence?"

The cardinal hesitated; then he turned and glared at his guards. His voice was firm as he spoke. "I believe anyone who feels he has the right or the God-given power to make unilateral decisions regarding a doctrine which has existed for over two thousand years exhibits too much pride."

Emma kept prodding. "I don't mean to play the devil's advocate," she said. She watched the cardinal's lips curve upward in a weak smile as he acknowledged her intended pun. "If in a roundabout way you're referring to Pope John, our sources tell us he backed away from his original plans to make unilateral changes in church doctrine and now plans to convene Vatican III."

The cardinal seemed surprised. *God, he's been locked away with no access to the outside world,* she mused. *Could it be he hasn't heard of the pope's latest plan?* She took a chance. "I realize you've not been well and are spending most of your time resting in your rooms, but surely you've spoken with your fellow conservatives and they've told you about the pope's planned announcement tomorrow."

The cardinal looked mystified. "Since the death of my secretary, Piero Scala, I have had little contact with my friends and colleagues."

"You've received no e-mails regarding the pope's intentions?"

Before the cardinal could respond, one of the guards pushed Michael aside. "Film all you want," he said angrily. "This interview is over."

There was fury on the other guard's face as he approached Emma. Realizing Ron and Bill were filming, he made a concerted effort to smile as he spoke. "Ms. Bradford, Cardinal Amici has an appointment at 5:30, and we are nearing that time. I hope he provided the information you need for your report."

"An appointment?" Emma said. "Really? I thought you were taking the cardinal to his rooms so he could rest. I believe you said he's exhausted." She continued without allowing the guard to respond. "And yes, the cardinal gave me all the information I need, and you've helped confirm my suspicions."

She turned to the cardinal and took his hand. When she looked into his eyes, the spark was gone. Once again, his face was expressionless. "Thank you for your time, Eminence," she said. "I'm sure our American audience and Catholics around the world will be fascinated by what you had to say."

"Thank you for the opportunity to speak, Ms. Bradford. God willing, we'll meet again. Until then, be safe." He made the sign of the cross. "God Bless you." When the guard took his arm, he submitted to the man's wishes.

"And you, Cardinal Amici," Emma said loudly as he walked away.

"Good Lord, what just happened?" Michael asked as the two men virtually pulled the cardinal back the way he came.

Emma's knees were weak, and she shuddered involuntarily. "I think I've officially challenged Pope John and Masella Cipriano, and if you don't hold me up, I may fall."

"Let's sit down." Michael led Emma to one of the benches in the chapel through which the cardinal had passed. "Are you sorry you did the interview?"

"What could possibly make you think that?" Emma said irritably.

"How about the fact that you're pale and shaky?"

Emma took a deep breath. "I'm really fine, but I'm not sure anyone's going to be pleased."

Michael grinned. "Even Geraldo would be jealous. Good job."

"Let's hope our respective stations think the way you do."

As they sat in the magnificent chapel, Emma could feel herself beginning to relax. She closed her eyes, listening to the sounds and breathing in the smells of the basilica. "I need a little while to pull myself together," she whispered.

"I'm not surprised. You just did an emotional interview." For the next few minutes he sat quietly while Emma closed her eyes and breathed deeply.

Too soon, the glorious quiet was interrupted. Emma felt a tap on her shoulder. Startled back into the moment, she turned around nervously and saw James standing behind them, a guidebook in hand. "I don't mean to interrupt your prayers," he said loudly enough for anyone in the vicinity to hear. "I saw you doing an interview with some church bigwig in bright red robes. You're an American."

"We both are," Michael said as he struggled not to laugh out loud.

"Then maybe you can help me," James said. He took out his guidebook and opened it to the section on Saint Peter's.

Emma bit her lip to keep from giggling. "We'll certainly try."

James pointed to the Alexander monument. "My book doesn't say much about the tombs in the church. Would you mind if we return to the place you were just talking about? It is a tomb, isn't it?"

"I believe it's just a monument," Michael said. "I don't think anyone's actually buried there, but remember we're not experts on Saint Peter's."

"It sounded like the young lady knows her stuff."

"I apologize for being rude," Emma said. "I'm Emma Bradford. This is Michael Kelsey. We're in Rome covering the opening of the Bernini exhibition for ABC News. And you are?"

"James Jones." James pointed to his shirt. "Bet you can't guess where I'm from."

"Alaska?" Michael said.

James laughed. "No, I'm from Maui."

"Really?" Emma said. "We would have never known. Great Flamingos. How can we help you, Mr. Jones?"

"I'm an Episcopalian. I heard you say the monument is a criticism of the Church of England."

"That wasn't the primary purpose when Bernini created the design, but he did include a symbolic gesture. Come on and I'll show you what I'm talking about."

As they walked toward the monument, Emma looked around. It didn't appear there was anyone close enough to hear what they were saying, but just in case, she pointed toward the globe as she talked. "I assume you were close enough to hear my interview with the cardinal."

"I was. That was quite a zinger at the end. You okay?" James gazed up at Alexander's face.

"I am now, but when Cardinal Amici was escorted away, I could hardly make it to the chapel on my own power."

"You realize you stirred up a hornet's nest with your interview. Was that your intent?"

"I didn't have a specific plan, but I couldn't forego the opportunity to ask some tough questions. What good would it have done if I had asked Cardinal Amici to explain why Bernini created the figure of death coming out of the door below the tomb? Bernini's no longer the story."

James pointed upward toward Truth. "The cardinal's guards weren't happy," he said. He inclined his head toward Michael. "Who knew you could have played tackle instead of quarterback. Good block."

Michael grinned. "Did you see my iconographic cape?"

Emma rolled her eyes. "Please don't ask," she said to James.

"A wise suggestion," James responded. "If you're okay, I'm off to report to Steven. We'll see you tonight. In the meantime, watch your back."

"Gee, thanks for making me feel better," Emma said.

James's smile quickly turned to a frown. "I'm serious, Emma. After that interview, you've made enemies. There are already two dead bodies. From here on out, things are going to get a lot worse. Be careful."

Emma frowned. "And your follow-up statement did even less to assuage my fears."

"I'm just being honest." James raised his voice. "Thanks for the explanation, Ms. Bradford. You know a lot."

"You're welcome," Michael responded. "Enjoy the rest of your vacation in Rome." He leaned in. "But you may want to ditch the shirt. It's ridiculous."

"I'll take your advice and put on something more appropriate," James said, "but you should know my Hawaiian attire belongs to your buddy, Steven."

Michael shook his head. "Now why doesn't that surprise me? Thanks for being here, James."

"I wouldn't have missed the show for the world." He smiled at Emma and headed toward the exit at the back of the basilica.

Ron, who'd been standing in the background while Emma and Michael spoke with James, came over to the monument. "That was a hell of an interview, Emma," he said.

"You don't approve of my strong-arm tactics?"

"Quite the opposite. You were fantastic."

"You certainly were," Bill said as he joined them. "Speaking of strong-arming, you should have seen Michael in action."

"I got a glimpse of my superhero out the corner of my eye." Emma turned to Michael and smiled. "The guards were clearly annoyed."

Bill shook his head. "That's an understatement, which brings me to my next question. Do you want to include the footage of Michael's heroic actions in the feed we send to New York?"

Emma looked at Michael. "I don't know. What do you think, partner?"

"My first inclination is no, but Helen and David will have the final say. I'm thinking we need to hold something back until we need it. The cardinal was subtly accusatory, but we have nothing concrete. We need proof he's being held captive in his quarters." He turned to Bill. "Unless I'm overruled, let's hold your footage for now, but why don't you do some editing in case we need to use it down the line."

"I'll have it ready in an hour in case we need to send it off quickly."

Emma took hold of Michael's arm. "Am I right? Did Cardinal Amici slip you another of his infamous notes when he shook your hand?"

"Does anything get by you? I thought the message would give me a story of my own."

"Michael—"

"I'm kidding. He handed me a piece of paper. Let's see what he has to say." He unfolded a small square.

"Is it another list?"

"No. It says, 'Mention my name at the door of Taverna Angelica tonight at eight o'clock.'"

"That's all?"

Michael turned the paper over and looked at the other side. "That's it."

"Don't you think that's strange?"

"No stranger than any of the other notes he's slipped to us." Wait a minute." He paused, thinking. "Isn't the Taverna Angelica where we're supposed to meet Steven and James for dinner?"

"It is. Should we call Steven and tell him not to come?"

"We may tell him, but it won't make any difference, and, under the circumstances, I'll feel better if he was there. We have no idea what the cardinal has planned for us. When we get back to the hotel, I'll let Steven know about the note. We'll ask him to be at the restaurant before eight instead of at 8:30, but not to let on he knows us when we come in. I'm sure we'll be able to talk with him after—"

"After what?"

"Your guess is as good as mine."

CHAPTER TWENTY

While Emma picked up her key at the desk, Michael asked to speak with Gusto. The head of security had left for the day, but according to the night man, nothing unusual had happened in or around the vicinity of Emma's room.

When they got to the suite, Emma threw her purse on the table in the sitting room, kicked off her shoes, plopped down on the couch, and put her feet on the coffee table. "I don't know about you, but I'm exhausted," she said.

"That's not surprising. It's been a hectic day."

"And unfortunately it's not over."

While Emma called Helen and Giro, Michael poured a glass of red wine for her and opened a beer for himself. "What's going on?" he asked when she hung up.

"New York needs more background information. We're taping a follow-up segment at Saint Peter's tomorrow morning before we film at the Triton."

"Another command performance."

"Another?"

"We're meeting a mysterious person for dinner tonight, remember?"

"Then you'd better get dressed. I'll see you back here in twenty minutes, since I'm sure you won't let me meet you in the lobby."

"You got that right. Put on the security lock."

"Emma walked Michael to the door. "I know the drill."

———

"Red seems to be the color of the day," Michael said, when Emma opened the door twenty minutes later. He was wearing grey slacks, a blue blazer, a light blue shirt, and a red tie that matched Emma's red blazer.

"You'd think we're a couple dressing for a big dance," Emma responded impatiently.

Michael was momentarily taken aback. "Why so grouchy?" he said. "I thought you'd be energized and ready to go."

"I'm exhausted. I should have asked Cardinal Amici to pray I get a shot of adrenalin to get me going again. You're a Catholic. Is there a saint in charge of energy?"

"I'm no expert on saintly duties. You'll have to ask Steven or James. Once we're underway, you'll get your second wind."

When they reached the lobby, Emma handed the key-card to the girl behind the desk. "You know, it might not be a bad idea to rethink dropping your key off every time you leave the hotel," Michael said as they approached the revolving door. "When you do, you're all but announcing you're no longer in your room. It's too late tonight, but why don't you take the key with you when we leave tomorrow morning?"

"God, we're both sounding paranoid, but you're probably right."

The doorman whistled for a cab. "Quattro Fontane," Michael said.

"Speaking of being paranoid, can you tell if anyone's following us?" Emma asked when they were a block away from the hotel.

Michael looked around. "No, but that doesn't mean there's no one back there. Are you going to let Helen know we're on our way?"

"I am, but I'm going to tell her to wait for us in the lobby. Coming outside to greet us twice may be too much. We'll have her meet us near the door so if the goons are watching, they'll see us together."

"See, you're thinking like a smart reporter again."

"You mean in contrast to the zombie who was speaking with you a while ago."

Michael merely grinned.

Helen was by the lobby entrance when they got to the hotel. She greeted them warmly, if not a little too loudly, and accompanied them to the elevator. Without stopping to chat on the second floor, Emma and Michael took the back stairs down to the main-floor service entrance where Giro was waiting. "You're sure you weren't followed?" Michael asked as they got in the car.

"I don't think anyone was watching my house. I drove to the grocery store and took the back streets to the hotel. I never saw anyone following me."

"Then they already know where we're going," said Michael.

"You may be right," Emma said pensively "If that's the case, we need to be able to use the Quattro Fontane scenario again. I hate to put you through this for nothing, Giro, but Michael and I are going to go up to the second floor, take the elevator back down to the lobby, and grab a cab to the restaurant."

"Why would we do that?" Michael asked.

"Because someone may be out front watching the hotel. If we show up at the restaurant when we're supposed to be here, we're busted. I'll call and tell Helen to come back to the stairwell and bring a folder full of papers. They can be blank. Whatever she gives us is just for show. We want anyone who might be watching to think we made a quick stop to pick up some papers."

"I hate to rain on your parade," Michael said, "but why wouldn't Helen come out to the cab and hand us whatever it is we came here to get? Why would we go inside and let the cab leave only to catch another one moments later?"

"Too much analysis. I doubt our shadows will question why we went upstairs. We have too many valid reasons for doing so. We could need to view a segment, talk with Helen—"

"I get it," Michael said. "Sorry we wasted your time, Giro."

"Please don't worry," said Giro. "What time are you filming tomorrow and where? I want to pick you up early enough to get you there on time."

"I wish we knew," Michael said. "The original plan was to film at the Triton Fountain at nine and at the Four Rivers after that. We were just told we have to film first in Saint Peter's Square. I don't know how early Helen plans to start."

"I'll find out right now." Emma called Helen, told her about the folder, and asked what time she wanted them at Saint Peter's in the morning. "I'm afraid we have another

Borghese morning, Giro," Emma said when she hung up. "We're filming by the obelisk at eight. I'll need fifteen minutes in the truck before we start."

"Then I'll be at the hotel at seven. Should I wait for you to finish?"

"Plan to be available until at least one."

"I will," Giro said. "Good luck."

"Thanks," Emma replied.

Helen was waiting by the stairs. "Emma, when you have a minute, look in the folder. It's not filled with blank pages. I gave you copies of the e-mails ABC received since they aired your breaking news report about Dina. The audience is clamoring for more information."

Emma opened the file and glanced at the first few pages. "New York smells a big story," Helen said. "A half-hour ago, Ron and Bill sent the edited version of your interview with Cardinal Amici at the Alexander Monument. The plan is to go national as soon as they get the background material we're shooting in the morning. They want you to talk about why your focus changed from reporting on an art exhibit to investigating Vatican politics."

"Does this mean they won't air the additional Bernini segments?" Emma asked.

"They're going national with them too."

"That's great news. The exhibition should be promoted in the States."

"Then you'll be pleased to know they're rerunning the segments from the Borghese and the piece about Saint Theresa on *Good Morning America*, along with the continuing coverage of the Vatican story. Of course, this national exposure means you're going to have to stand by for live reports. I haven't received a schedule yet. I'll e-mail you both when I do. My guess is you'll start with Diane Sawyer, so be ready for a late night. Check your e-mail tonight when you get back to the hotel."

Michael laughed. "What's so funny?" Emma said.

"I was thinking. Maybe Jack won't think I'm just a Geraldo-wannabe after this."

"I wouldn't go that far," Emma teased. She turned to Helen. "Hopefully we'll have more to say tomorrow morning."

"Be careful."

"We definitely will," Michael said.

"I was surprised by your tone and the serious look on your face when Helen told us to be careful," Emma said as the cab pulled away from the hotel. "You don't want to quit."

"Of course not, but I'm worried."

"You're kidding," Emma said, feigning shock. "The great Michael Kelsey is worried?"

"Not about the story. When Helen told us to be careful, it finally hit me. What we're covering is significant and dangerous. With each new piece of information we uncover, I'm more worried about you."

"Me?" Emma said. "How could I possibly be in any danger when I'm sitting beside the man in the iconographic cape?"

Michael didn't smile. "I mean it, Emma."

"So do I. We'll both be fine. We have Steven and James working with us, and the illusive Sante is lurking in the background."

"You're sure you don't want to give up on this one? We can still report on Bernini—"

"And hand the story to another network or the cable news channels? No way in hell. I appreciate your concern, but nothing you say will change my mind. Are you with me or—"

"To the bitter end."

"I hope that wasn't a foreshadowing. You mean you're with me until our investigation comes to a successful conclusion."

"That too."

Near Saint Peter's they turned into a village-like area with narrow streets. "Steven couldn't have found a more isolated restaurant," Emma said as the cab pulled up in front of the Taverna Angelica.

"Our mysterious host had to be thinking the same thing when he chose this place for a meeting."

They entered a tiny, candlelit dining room containing about twenty tables. "What a cute place," Emma said as a man holding menus approached.

"Cardinal Amici sent us," Michael said to the man.

Emma laughed, and Michael looked at her quizzically. "What? Did I say something funny?" he asked.

"Think about it. I'm sure you'll figure it out."

Apparently the maître d' saw nothing humorous in the exchange. "If you'll follow me," he said somberly.

They weaved through the closely positioned tables, passing Steven and James near the back of the room. When they were beyond their table, Emma pointed to her neck. Michael nodded. Neither man was wearing his clerical collar.

The maître d' opened a door at the back of the room and stepped aside so Michael and Emma could enter. A short, slender man with silver-grey hair rose from a table to greet them. He was dressed in a simple black cassock with a scarlet skullcap. Only the bright red of the cap, the bejeweled cross around his neck, and the magnificent ring which sparkled on his finger when he extended his hand indicated his exalted rank.

"Ms. Bradford; Mr. Kelsey. Thank you for seeing me," he said, flashing a welcoming smile. "I'm Cardinal Camillo Remella."

"Our pleasure, Eminence," Michael said.

The cardinal motioned to the table. "I hope you don't mind. I've taken the liberty of ordering a light dinner."

"It smells delicious," Emma said. She smiled at Michael, knowing he wouldn't be pleased with the choice of food.

"It's the restaurant's specialty—lentil soup with pigeon breast. The waiter just brought the tureen to the table, so the soup should be hot." He pulled out a chair for Emma. "I'm afraid I don't have much time, so if you're not offended, I'll omit the usual niceties and get right to the point."

"Of course," Emma said. She sat down and motioned for Michael to sit beside her across from the cardinal.

"You may already know much of what I'm telling you, so forgive me if I am repetitious, but Cardinal Amici instructed me to tell you everything."

"You spoke with the cardinal?" Emma said. "We thought he's confined to his rooms."

"He is, but he is not prevented from attending Mass every day. I sat beside him this morning. During the peace, he slipped me a note."

"Another infamous note," Michael mumbled.

"I beg your pardon?" the cardinal said.

Emma gave Michael a warning look. "Nothing, Eminence. Did you bring the message with you?"

The cardinal seemed surprised at the question. "Of course not!" he said. "I destroyed the paper as soon as I returned to my room and read it."

Michael shook his head. "If you ask me, that's a sad commentary about the state of affairs in the Vatican."

The cardinal paused before responding. "You are right, young man. There was a time when communications between two cardinals would have been sacrosanct, but these are difficult times. You understand."

"I'm afraid we do," Emma said, "at least most of what's happening. Cardinal Remella, she said, "something's bothering me. You said we're skipping the niceties, so I'll get right to the point. You're an influential man, a high-ranking official of the church. I'm sure you're privy to rumors circulating in the Vatican. We know Pope John is very ill. Have you heard about what might happen if he dies from this mysterious strain of the flu?"

The cardinal didn't seem surprised by Emma's question. "Of course I hear gossip, but in this instance, there can be no truth to the rumor."

"Just the same, will you share what you've heard?"

With his head bowed as if in prayer, the cardinal contemplated Emma's request. A minute passed, and then another. Emma held her breath, knowing his response could be key to putting together the pieces of the puzzle they were trying to solve. "I suppose I could, though I rarely perpetuate rumors," he finally said. "Cardinal Amici asked me to be honest and forthcoming, so I shall deviate from my usual practice of keeping what I hear to myself. According to what I read in e-mails and have heard from other cardinals, there appears to be a behind-the-scenes movement to elevate Monsignor Cipriano to the papacy should Pope John die from his illness."

Emma gasped. "Tell me you're joking," she said.

"I am afraid not," Remella said soberly.

"Could that really happen?" Michael asked. "Masella's not even a bishop, let alone a cardinal."

"True, but technically, any baptized Catholic male is eligible to become pope as long as he is in good standing with the Holy See."

"Are you suggesting that tradition may be thrown to the wind if there's a need for a conclave in the near future?" Michael asked. "You said behind-the-scenes maneuvering is already occurring. Are backroom agreements allowed?"

"After the death of a pope, discussions prior to the conclave are common practice, but overt campaigning and lobbying is outlawed. Of course, cardinals have their ways of influencing their peers. They use facial expressions or avoidance of eye contact to make their points. Alliances are customary, but cardinals are forbidden to buy votes or make deals, and paper ballots are cast in secret and silence. The reality is, with the ease of air travel and the use of e-mails, cardinals can meet or communicate with one another on a regular basis. When they arrive for the conclave, their political opinions and beliefs, whether liberal or conservative, are well known."

"You mentioned e-mail. Would you be surprised to know Monsignor Cipriano was the driving force behind Cardinal della Chesia's election to the papacy?" Emma asked. "He used e-mails to achieve his objective."

"I am aware of Masella's efforts, Ms. Bradford," Remella replied, "but even though Masella mounted a massive electronic campaign, he did not break the rules. He never held clandestine meetings before the onset of the conclave."

"So it was acceptable for him to use a computer to convince his fellow liberals to support Cardinal della Chesia?" Michael said.

"Of course not," the cardinal said adamantly, "but remember, the rules for the election of a pope were drafted centuries ago."

"And electronic campaigning hasn't been addressed or prohibited?"

"Not yet. The Vatican moves slowly."

"That's paradoxical considering what's going on right now, isn't it?" Emma said.

"I suppose it is," the cardinal said pensively. "Using e-mail to advocate for election of Cardinal della Chesia is one thing, but though Cardinal Amici is convinced it is happening, I find it difficult to believe that a monsignor could sway a majority of the College of Cardinals to elect *him* as the next leader of the Holy See."

"Don't be so sure, Eminence," Michael said. "Here's my theory. Because he wasn't a cardinal, Masella's chances of becoming pope after Benedict's death were virtually nil, but he realized, through the use of e-mail, he could play on the liberals' desires for change and get his man elected."

"And by effecting the election of the cardinal of his choice, he'd have the thanks of a grateful pontiff," Emma said. "Think about it, Eminence. Masella is bright and ambitious. That, along with his technological savvy, would help him influence liberals looking for a pope who would guarantee radical change. It probably didn't take much to convince them that Cardinal della Chesia was the man for them."

"It's too bad we can't get our hands on a few of his e-mails," Michael said.

"I believe I can help in that regard," the cardinal said. "I saved most of Masella's messages. I will e-mail them to you when I get back to my rooms."

"Really," Emma said. "Thank you, Eminence."

"Yes, thanks," said Michael. "Cardinal Remella, this may sound like a strange question and I realize it's a little off topic, but do you happen to know anything about Monsignor Cipriano's background?"

"I'm afraid I am unclear as to what you want to know," the cardinal said.

"I believe Michael is asking if Masella had a major when he attended seminary, though I'm not sure you call it a major when you're studying to become a priest."

"For example," Michael elaborated, "I have a good friend who majored in religious studies at Notre Dame, and I studied communications and journalism at Yale."

"Ah, now I understand," the cardinal said. "I believe Masella earned a master's degree in psychology."

"So he'd know how to use subtle psychological coercion to achieve his goals. Individuals he's trying to persuade might not know they're being manipulated."

"I find it hard to accept what you seem to be suggesting, Mr. Kelsey. Working diligently for the election of a liberal cardinal is one thing, but coercion? We are no longer living in the Dark Ages, where cardinals were bribed or bullied into choosing one of their colleagues over another."

"This may be occurring today more than you know," Emma said. "Consider this: Masella facilitates Cardinal della Chesia's election to the papacy, thinking the man will be eternally grateful and advance Masella's liberal agenda."

"But his plan doesn't work," Michael said.

"Aye, there's the rub," said the cardinal. He sighed deeply, rested his elbow on the table, and leaned his head against his hand. "Everyone knows becoming the pope changes a man," he said introspectively. "Once elected, he no longer thinks of himself and those who supported his election. He begins to consider the universal church and the implications of his actions or, for that matter, of his inaction. When Cardinal della Chesia became pope, he decided he could not risk his service to God or the church by remaining faithful to the liberal faction. Now he wishes to be free of those who would unduly influence him."

"Meaning Monsignor Cipriano," Emma said.

"Yes," said the cardinal.

"We've heard the same thing from several other people," said Emma. "Eminence, are you aware a young woman's body was found near the obelisk in Saint Peter's Square earlier today?"

"I am," Remella said sadly. "The woman's uncle is my friend."

"Do you have any idea why your friend's niece was killed?" Michael asked. "Her death can't be mere coincidence."

"I agree with you, Mr. Kelsey. I imagine you believe Monsignor Scala's death was a warning to conservatives. I believe Dina was killed for the same reason. Her brother and uncle are part of a fringe conservative group. Though, for the most part, they are supportive of Cardinal Amici's viewpoint, they are more conservative than he."

"What you may not know is Dina was the maid who cleaned Emma's room at the Excelsior." Michael then told the cardinal about the attempted break-in. "Would Dina's uncle or brother have a reason to break into Emma's room?" he asked.

The cardinal didn't hesitate. "Definitely not to hurt you, but perhaps to warn you."

"Warn me to stop investigating?" Emma said.

"Or caution you to be careful. I find it hard to believe the conservatives are out to do you harm. The danger emanates from the liberal faction."

"Again, I apologize for being rude, Cardinal Remella," Emma said, "but why should we believe you? You're obviously a conservative."

"True, but I am also a Catholic who believes in the sanctity of life. *Thou shalt not kill.* Does that sound familiar?"

"And you're saying liberals have abandoned that commandment?" Michael asked.

"Certainly not all of them, but, sadly, it appears a few have done so."

"Forgive me, but if I don't understand why Cardinal Amici wanted you to meet with us, Eminence," said Emma.

"By now he knows we understand the seriousness of the situation. With all due respect, you haven't told us anything we didn't know or suspect."

"I am here because the cardinal needs your help, Ms. Bradford. He feels you might be deterred from reporting what you have seen and what you know to be true."

"And he wants to be sure we broadcast the Vatican's political dilemma to the world," Michael said," his voice exuding irritation. "Why? So his conservative allies can get the upper hand?"

The cardinal seemed genuinely surprised by Michael's question and his tone. "Not at all, Mr. Kelsey," he said indignantly. "Cardinal Amici fears for his life. He believes as long as you and Ms. Bradford continue to draw attention to the ongoing struggles in the Vatican, he will not be harmed.

"Because as long as he and the story are in the news, no one would dare kill him," Emma said.

"It is far more complicated than that, but you are fundamentally correct."

"I assure you we'll keep reporting the story," Michael said, "but because what's happening affects millions of people around the world, not to keep the cardinal from being murdered."

"Any idea how the cardinal plans to get out of this mess?" Emma asked before Remella could respond to Michael's statement.

"At the moment, no. As you said, he is cut off from the rest of the world. He is unable to send or receive e-mails, and everywhere he goes, he is accompanied by the guards put in place by Masella."

"It's mind-boggling that a monsignor could wield so much power," Michael said, his anger changing to amazement.

"Masella speaks for millions of Catholics who seek immediate reform in the church, and he has Pope John's ear."

"Not only his ear, but his gratitude," Emma said.

"Exactly." The cardinal removed a card from his pocket and gave it to Emma. "I would appreciate a call if you learn anything that could be of use to us."

"You mean to the conservatives?" Michael asked a little too sarcastically.

"No, Mr. Kelsey," the cardinal said, "to those of us who are trying to prevent an all-out schism in the church."

Emma took out her own card, wrote her cell number on the back, and handed it to the cardinal. "Please contact me if you hear anything which might benefit us as we try to report fairly, and keep us up to date about Cardinal Amici's circumstances. I'm afraid our interview at the Alexander Monument didn't help his situation. I was brazen in my questioning, and his answers were equally inflammatory."

"I will certainly do that, Ms. Bradford. My mission is to be sure the church's position in the world is preserved. There can be no more deaths."

"You're referring to Cardinal Amici," Emma said.

Cardinal Remella leaned forward. "I am also talking about you, Ms. Bradford. You are unquestionably in danger."

"But obviously not enough for you to ask us to stop investigating," Michael said.

The cardinal turned toward Michael. "We do what we must, Mr. Kelsey. Certainly I would hate to see anything happen to either of you—"

"Do I hear a 'but' coming?" Michael said.

"But I am asking for a reason greater than either of you or the cardinal."

"At Emma's expense?" he asked angrily.

Cardinal Remella's eyes flashed. "Young man, are you going to try and make me believe you and Ms. Bradford would abandon this story had I not asked you to continue? That is ridiculous. I am merely saying, what you are doing is far more important than the two of you, and I am advising you to be cautious as you continue to report."

Michael's irritation abated. "I apologize, Eminence."

The cardinal smiled. "We are both under a great deal of pressure. Please accept my apology as well." He looked down at the untouched food on the table. "It appears we have been unable to enjoy our soup. I must get back to my office. I hope the two of you will go out into the restaurant and enjoy a meal at my expense."

"We'll definitely eat, but not on you, Eminence," said Michael.

"One more thing before you go," Emma said. "Will you be able to tell Cardinal Amici about our meeting?"

The cardinal smiled. "Be assured my brother cardinal can expect a warm embrace from me during the peace tomorrow morning."

"Please find a way to give him my regards."

"I will. Thank both of you for meeting with me. Enjoy your evening."

"Wow!" Michael exclaimed when he and Emma were alone.

"My thoughts exactly. What's your take?"

"I have no idea, but I know two people who may be able to shed some light on what just happened."

"Steven and James."

CHAPTER TWENTY-ONE

"Have you ordered?" Michael asked as he and Emma sat down with Steven and James. "I'm starving."

Steven gave James a high five. "This is definitely an I-told-you-so moment. We saw a waiter take a tureen of soup and three bowls to the back room right before you got here. Since I know you so well, we waited for your meeting to end."

"Because you knew hamburger-man wouldn't eat the house specialty?" Emma joked.

"You got it," Steven said, smiling. "Did you eat the soup Cardinal Remella ordered, Michael?"

"No way."

"Neither did I," Emma said, "but it wasn't because the soup didn't look wonderful and smell delicious. The cardinal said he didn't have much time, which must have been true because we barely finished our conversation before he had to leave. By then the soup was cold."

Steven shook his head. "I don't think it was a matter of the cardinal not being able to stay. It's more likely he was nervous about meeting with you any longer. You two have become infamous."

"Not just infamous," James said. "I'm going to take it one step further and say your names are anathema in Vatican City."

"Then why are you two brave enough to meet with us?" Emma asked.

"Because we're stupid," Steven answered.

Michael laughed and slapped his knee. "You have no idea how many years I've waited for to hear you say that, my friend. Now I can die happy."

Steven put his hand on his friend's shoulder. "Under the circumstances, you might want to find different words to express your glee. Shall we order? I'm sure we're keeping our patient waiter from attending to his other customers."

"Sure, but I'm sure this place doesn't serve hamburgers, spaghetti, or lasagna."

"Enough about hamburgers." Emma addressed the waiter. "I apologize for my friend. He has a limited palate."

"There must be something on the menu you like to eat," the waiter said to Michael in broken English.

Michael looked embarrassed. "I'm sure there is." He looked at the list of entrees. "I'll have the fettuccine with tomatoes and the cheese I've never heard of."

Before the waiter left the table, he poured wine for Emma. Michael put his hand over the rim of his glass. "No thanks," he said. "There has to be one person at this table who has his wits about him."

Steven opened his mouth to comment. "Don't go there," Michael warned, with a twinkle in his eye.

"So you recognized Cardinal Remella," Michael said after the waiter left to put in their order.

"Of course," James said. "Everyone knows the cardinal. He's been a power broker for years."

"Did you learn anything new during your meeting?" Steven asked.

"Not much we didn't know," Emma said.

The continuing conversation was temporarily halted when the waiter delivered the meals. When they were all served and he was out of earshot, James continued: "So we were talking about what you learned from Cardinal Remella. Did he tell you why Cardinal Amici requested the meeting?"

Emma nodded yes. "The cardinal thinks as long as Michael and I keep reporting the story, he'll be okay. He believes he'll be in danger if we stop. In his mind, we're the reason the liberals are guarding him rather than killing him as a means of sending another message to conservatives."

"That's in keeping with what we've learned to date," Steven said. "Rumor has it both sides are gearing up for a showdown sooner rather than later. We know Cardinal Amici's being guarded. Today we learned the pope is also in forced isolation, at least until his speech on Wednesday."

"And they can do this how?" Michael asked. "Pope John is the supreme leader of the Holy See and the Vatican State. I thought that meant he has absolute power."

"He does, but remember, Masella told the world the pontiff is ill and needs his rest. There's been a suggestion the pope's contagious, which is why only Masella and his doctors can see him."

"It doesn't make sense," Emma said. "Are you suggesting Pope John's doctors are involved?"

"James and I wondered about that. We're looking into it, but as of now we don't have a definitive answer."

"Is it possible knowledgeable physicians could be fooled into believing their patient has the flu if he's being poisoned?" Michael asked.

"I suppose it's possible," Steven said. "Maybe there are poisons which present flu-like symptoms. I'm sure we could find out on the Internet."

"Probably, but definitely not using the Vatican server," said James. "I doubt if our efforts would enjoy the seal of the confessional."

"That's interesting," Emma said. "Does everyone who uses Vatican e-mail realize his correspondence could be read by unwanted individuals? I doubt Cardinal Remella knows, because he's using the Vatican server to send me copies of the messages he received from Masella before Cardinal della Chesia was elected pope."

"You're kidding," Steven said. "He actually kept the correspondence?"

"Apparently so."

"I'd like to see the messages, but for God's sake, don't e-mail them to me."

"We won't," said Michael. "I have a portable printer. Assuming the cardinal follows through with his promise, I'll print them for you. We'll be at the Orbit truck outside Saint Peter's Square tomorrow morning by 7:15."

"You're shooting at Saint Peter's again? Is there something we don't know?" Steven asked.

"We're doing a background shoot for the Cardinal Amici interview." A smile crossed Michael's face. "And speaking of that particular interview, please tell me James lied when he said the ghastly Hawaiian shirt he was wearing belongs to you."

"I'm proud to confess that it does."

"You've really worn that thing?"

"Proudly. I bought it for a fraternity luau senior year."

"I get it, but why in God's name would you bring it with you to Rome? You didn't expect to go to a luau in Vatican City, did you?"

"You never know," Steven said, grinning. "Despite your disdain, you have to admit the shirt came in handy. No one would have guessed James is a priest."

"If you two would stop talking about the hideous shirt, I'd like to get serious again," Emma said.

"Emma, I can't believe someone with your taste thinks my shirt's ugly," Steven said with feigned astonishment.

"Steven—"

"Okay. You obviously have something on your mind. What's bothering you? Though in light of what's going on, I suppose that's a stupid question."

"Tell me the truth. Is there a concerted effort underway to murder a pope and replace him with a monsignor?"

"You're telling us you think Masella expects to be elected pope should Pope John die?" Steven said incredulously. "I realize you're a journalist, which makes you a woman with an active imagination and a probing mind, but in my opinion, what you're suggesting is outside the realm of possibilities. Why would you think such a thing?"

"Cardinal Remella told us," Michael said, a matter-of-factly.

"You're kidding," James sputtered.

"Active journalistic minds or not, would we make up such a story?" Emma asked. "I was sure you'd heard the rumor."

"I haven't," Steven said. "James?"

"I haven't either. What exactly did the cardinal say, Emma?"

"That according to church doctrine, any Catholic male in good standing can be elected pope."

James looked skeptical. "He thinks Masella plans to murder Pope John and influence enough cardinals to change over seven-hundred years of tradition and elect him?"

"Not influence; coerce." Emma explained Masella's massive campaign to ensure Cardinal della Chesia's election to the papacy.

"I had no idea," Steven said. "When you mentioned e-mails, it didn't register. I figured the e-mails Cardinal Remella was sharing were communications between the Holy Father's office and the cardinals. I'd love to be able to disagree with you, but my gut tells me you're on the right track. If he has the audacity to ignore century-old rules and traditions, Masella's more dangerous than either James or I considered."

"I'm going out on a limb here with no 'if' or 'possibly,'" said James. "Pope John and Cardinal Amici aren't at odds. They're pawns in a bigger game. Masella's the problem."

"You're right," Steven said pensively. "The pope is Masella's puppet. If he continues to do what the monsignor wants, the poisonings will cease and Masella will, in reality if not in name, be the pope."

"But if the Holy Father doesn't do Masella's bidding and calls for Vatican III—"

"He'll go the way of Piero Scala, and Masella will use manipulation and pressure to get himself elected pope."

"You don't think that could really happen?" Emma said. "It's one thing for Cardinal Remella to suggest the possibility, but—"

"Oh, it could happen," said Steven. "The conservatives have been effectively shut down since the death of Piero and Cardinal Amici's imprisonment, for want of a better term. That leaves only the powerful liberals led by Masella."

"Where are the centrists in all this?" Emma asked. "A while ago, you said most Catholics fall somewhere in the middle when it comes to change, and Giro said the same thing when I asked him about the ongoing conflict."

"Apparently they're afraid to speak out for fear of retaliation from both sides," James said.

"What about Cardinal Amici's new secretary, Monsignor Tomai?" Michael asked. "Is it possible he's more involved with Masella than we first considered?"

Steven shrugged. "Anything's possible."

"So what do we do next?" Emma asked. "How do we prove what we believe to be true?"

Steven shook his head. "I have no idea. As of now, if we went public with our assumption, no one would believe it. It's almost impossible for me to comprehend. Why don't we talk again tomorrow after James and I have a chance to check with our sources?"

"That works. Anything else?" Michael asked.

"Maybe, but I hesitate to mention it."

"But it was important enough for you to bring it up, so what is it?" Emma said.

"I'm relatively sure I'm being watched. From time to time I've seen the same man parked across the street from my apartment."

"Why would anyone to be interested in what you're doing? You're not important," Emma said.

"Gee, thanks."

Emma laughed. "You know what I mean, Steven. How would anyone know you're associated with Michael and me? We've been so careful."

"Google? Research? Who knows?"

"But there's no way anyone could Google and cross-reference all the priests in Vatican City to find a link to Emma or me."

"We have no idea what Vatican security can or can't do. I have no doubt their systems are state of the art."

Michael sighed. "I can't believe I've drawn you into this mess. Though slight, I'm feeling a twinge of Catholic guilt."

Steven made the sign of the cross. "I absolve you of your sins. Feel no more guilt." He became serious. "Believe me, my friend, you aren't forcing either of us into doing anything we don't want to do. We're not involved because I want to help out an old friend. The story you're working on affects us and millions of other Catholics."

"He's right," James said. "To you, what's going on behind the scenes in Vatican City is a noteworthy news story. We're involved because, apart from our political leanings, what's occurring in the Holy See is horrific. If coercion and fear are being used to elect a pope, not to mention murder and attempted murder, what's happening has to be exposed and the church must begin to heal."

"But we have to be one-hundred-percent sure we're right before we make any of this information public," said Steven.

"As do we," Michael added. "We can't make rash and unsubstantiated statements without proof. So now that we're on the same page, back to the person you believe is watching you. Any idea who he is?"

"None whatsoever."

"Are you sure he didn't follow you to the restaurant?" Emma asked.

"No way he could have, at least not by car. I walked through the back streets, so I would have known if there was someone behind me. I even waited outside the restaurant to see if anyone rounded the corner from the same direction I came. No one did."

"What about you, James?"

"I haven't noticed anyone or anything unusual around my apartment, but from here on out, I'll keep my eyes open."

"And speaking about keeping your eyes open, I may need you to do that for me tomorrow at noon," Emma said.

Steven looked at her quizzically. "Why, what's happening?"

"It seems I have a command performance." She and Michael explained Emma's mysterious hang-ups followed by the two words, "Be there."

"That's all the man said?" Steven asked.

"That's it. Whoever it was wasn't kidding. As I told Michael, this isn't an invitation for tea."

"I don't like this," James said, frowning.

"Are you're planning to go?" Steven asked.

Michael rolled his eyes. "Do you even have to ask? Of course she's going."

"Because the two of you want the story, you're willing to risk Emma's life?" Steven said. "I've told you before. This isn't a game, my friend."

Michael scowled. "You know me better than that, or you should. Of course I don't want Emma to go. You try and stop her and see how far you get."

"Would you two stop talking about me as if I'm not in the room? Nothing either of you say can keep me from going to Saint Agnes, so give up and figure out a way to keep me safe."

"This is crazy, Emma," Steven said, "especially in light of what we've been talking about. You realize how dangerous these men are, and you're still going to show up?"

"Steven—"

"Okay! Okay! I'm on it. James and Sante will be at Saint Agnes by 11:30. I'll be there too, but you won't see my face. I'll be the priest praying for forgiveness with my head down."

Emma smiled. "You're already forgiven. What about whoever's following you? You can't coincidently show up where Michael and I happen to be."

"Don't worry about my shadow. I'll walk through the back streets. When I'm sure no one's behind me, I'll take a cab to Navona. Emma, do you have any idea who called you? Was there anything familiar about his voice? Could it have been Masella?"

"No to all your questions. It's hard to tell who's speaking when you hear only two words. All I know is his voice was deep and his tone threatening. Since Michael asked me the same question, I've given it a great deal of thought. Unfortunately, that's all I can tell you."

"Why Saint Agnes?" James pondered aloud. "It's out of the way. Why not stay close to Saint Peter's?"

"I'm inclined to think whoever called knows we're shooting at the Four Rivers Fountain in Navona Square in the morning," Michael said.

"How would he know that?" Steven asked. "I don't think you mentioned it to me, or if you did, it didn't register."

Michael shrugged. "I can't answer your question."

"Is there something about Saint Agnes which would make it a good location for a clandestine meeting?" Emma asked. "I mean are there numerous side chapels where two people could get together without being noticed?"

"Quite the opposite," said Steven. "I've only been to the church once, but if I remember correctly, the entrance is wide open and there are two large side chapels. One of them contains a statue of Saint Agnes. There's a chapel in the back with a lighted window displaying a small scull, but I believe there's only one way in or out of there. Why would someone who's obviously threatening you want to meet in a place where he could be trapped if you brought the police with you? It doesn't make sense."

"Maybe not," Michael said, "but hearing what Steven has to say makes me feel a little better."

"Why would it?" Emma said sharply. "I'm meeting with a man who, in no uncertain terms, insisted I show up. The layout of a church doesn't alter that fact."

"I beg to differ," Steven said.

"I know what Steven's saying, and I agree," said James. "If you'd been commanded to show up in Saint Peter's or one of the large basilicas like San Giovanni in Laterano or Santa Maria Maggiore, we'd have a hard time keeping our eyes on you. As it is, besides the back chapel with the skull, everything at Saint Agnes is out in the open. Our praying priest will be able to watch you while the tourist in the Hawaiian shirt sits and stares at the altar in awe, his camera in hand ready to take pictures of the magnificent church."

"You don't think the shirt might make you stand out a little too much?" Steven said. "You know we all love it, but—"

"You're saying I shouldn't wear it again?" James said, pretending to be shocked.

"Wear anything you want, but it might be a good idea if you chose something a little less touristy." He paused. "I realize we've been teasing you, but now that I think about it, what if someone was watching when you talked with Emma and Michael after the Cardinal Amici interview? He might not remember your face, but your shirt would be unforgettable."

"Good point. I'll wear something a little less noticeable."

"You mean a little less garish," Emma teased. "A wise decision." She turned to Steven. "Will Sante be there too?"

"Absolutely, though I also have concerns in that regard. Since we have no idea who you'll be meeting at Saint Agnes, we can't know if he'll be recognized."

"Then make him a priest," James suggested. "This is Rome. No one would pay attention to a priest wandering around a church."

"Good idea. He's about my size, though he's a little bit shorter. I imagine he'd be able to wear one of my cassocks."

Michael looked at his watch. "So now that we have a plan, it's time to say goodnight. Emma and I have an early call in the morning."

"You're leaving so soon?" Steven said. "I've never known you to be too tired to have dessert. The house specialty is mango Bavarian cream with a delicious kiwi sauce."

"Another reason to go. If I can't get my usual hot fudge sundae, forget it. I'll leave the kiwi sauce to the men who wear Hawaiian shirts. Kiwi is a tropical fruit, isn't it?"

"You're sure he's not forcing you to leave before you're finished, Emma?" Steven said.

Emma laughed. "By now you should know Michael can't force me to do anything. However, at the moment I'm running on pure adrenalin. What about tomorrow morning? If someone's following you, should you be coming to the truck for Cardinal Remella's e-mails?"

"I'll do it," said James.

"Didn't we just discuss the possibility that someone's keeping track of you too?" Steven said to James. "I'd rather you remain in the background." He turned to Michael. "I don't know who it will be, but someone will be there at 7:30. He'll identify himself as a priest from Notre Dame, a fan who wants to meet the great Michael Kelsey."

"Good idea. It shouldn't be hard to find someone who worships the ground I walk on."

"Maybe you don't understand, my friend. My courier won't truly be a fan. That will be his means of identifying himself."

"Your words cut to the core."

"Face reality," Steven teased.

Emma stood up. "Night, Steven; James. I'm going to take this poor, disillusioned soul back to the hotel."

"Not a minute too soon," Steven joked.

"Any idea when we're getting together again?" James asked.

"We'll see how things go," said Steven. "We'll talk when the need arises. We'll see you at Saint Agnes tomorrow at noon."

"Thanks, Steven," Emma said. "I'll feel better knowing you'll both be there."

"And don't forget Sante."

"Him too."

"We'll sit here until we're sure you're off," Steven said.

Michael grinned. "You can't fool me. You want me to believe you're staying because you're concerned for our safety? You actually want some of that Bavarian cream."

"Busted," Steven said, smiling. "You'll be sorry you didn't try it."

"I seriously doubt it, but enjoy. We'll talk."

"Yeah, see you tomorrow."

CHAPTER TWENTY-TWO

"I'm exhausted, but I'm afraid I won't be able to fall asleep," Emma said as the cab turned onto the Via Veneto. "Considering I'm going to need all my wits about me for the meeting at Saint Agnes tomorrow, not to mention the fountain shoot, that could be a problem."

"A problem I believe I can solve."

"Do I dare ask what you have in mind?"

"You doubt me," Michael jested. "I see it in your eyes."

"It's too dark for you to see anything."

"I know, I was kidding. When I'm too tired to sleep I sometimes take a short walk to help me relax, so I've solved your problem. I need cash, and I'd rather not get up even earlier to go to the ATM before we leave for Saint Peter's in the morning. Let's ask the driver to drop us across the street. If you're still wired after I get my money, we'll walk by the American embassy."

The driver dropped them at the same ATM had Emma used after first telling Michael about the potential story stemming from the conflict between Cardinal Amici and the pope. She stood by while Michael punched in his code. "You get what you need?" she asked as he put the money in his wallet.

"I did, and I got a little extra. I plan to buy a gelato at every one of those kiosks I've seen around town."

"So much for maintaining your boyish figure."

"You do have a way of throwing a wet blanket on a man's plans. Shall we take that walk to offset my planned gelato binge?"

"Why don't we skip the walk? Suddenly I'm feeling more relaxed."

Michael took Emma's hand and linked her arm in his. "Fine with me. I have great metabolism—"

"Is the old Michael emerging?"

"Never!"

"Good to know, because I was beginning to worry."

The traffic was sparse, but instead of jaywalking, they waited for the light to turn green before crossing the street to the newspaper stand directly opposite the hotel.

They waited for the light to change again. "Ready?" Michael said.

"I am."

They had just stepped into the street when a large black car flew around the corner onto Via Veneto. In seconds, Emma realized the careening machine was speeding directly at them. Michael appeared to recognize the danger at the same time. "Asshole," he yelled as he pulled Emma back onto the curb.

It was clear a few inches of cement weren't going to deter the driver of the black bullet. The driver hit the brakes, jerked the steering wheel to the left and, barely missing a passing car, angled his death machine toward the spot where Michael and Emma stood.

Emma's heart pounded in her chest. "Oh my God, he's coming at us again!" she screamed.

Michael grabbed Emma's arm and pulled her to safety behind one of the trees that lined the sidewalk.

Realizing the obstacle would prevent him from reaching his target, the driver slammed on the brakes. With tires squealing, he threw the car into reverse, swerved back on to the Via Veneto, and sped off past the hotel.

Only Michael's strong grip on her arm kept Emma from crumpling on the sidewalk. "That was no accident!" he yelled, his voice a mixture of fear and fury. "We have to get over to the hotel before he has time to turn around and come after us again. Let's go."

"I can't," Emma sobbed.

"Yes you can." Michael grabbed her hand. "That is, unless you want to die. Come on! Run!" He tightened his grip on Emma's hand. Dragging her behind him, he rushed into the street, dodging the few cars driving by as they made for the far side of Via Veneto and the safety of the hotel entrance. Breathing a sigh of relief, he paused to look at the clearly traumatized woman who dropped to the hotel steps. "Stay here!" he said sternly. "I'll go see if I can figure out who's trying to kill us."

When he got to the corner of Via Boncompagni, the attack car had circled the block and was once again racing in the direction of the Excelsior. The driver spied Michael standing vulnerably on the sidewalk outside the hotel. The sound of tires screeching and the smell of burning rubber filled the air as the car veered across two lanes of traffic, aiming in a straight line toward its quarry.

Michael abruptly turned and darted back toward the safety of the hotel entrance. Aware he'd lose a battle with a concrete wall, the driver swerved onto Via Boncompagni and raced away into the darkness. "Damn," Michael shouted angrily as he ran back to the street.

With no hope of learning who had tried to run them down, Michael loped back to the curb to help Emma. When he rounded the corner, he panicked. Emma wasn't on the steps where he'd left her. He froze in his tracks as horrifying thoughts crossed his mind: *Was the speeding car merely a diversion? Did someone grab Emma while I was on a wild goose chase?* He ran to the street again, but he saw nothing but the normal flow of traffic passing by the hotel. *If someone did take her, it would be too late for me to do anything about it,* he thought with alarm as he anxiously ran up the stairs to the revolving door.

"Emma, where the hell are you?" he shouted as he entered the empty reception area.

His legs feeling like he was moving in slow motion, Michael climbed the stairs into the opulent lobby. *Please be in here,* he prayed as he looked around. "Thank you, God," he whispered when he saw Emma on a settee to the right of the door. She was hunched over at the waist and staring down at the floor. A woman knelt beside her.

Michael hurried over to the couch. "Who are you?" he said irritably when the woman looked up.

"I'm ... I'm the receptionist, sir," the startled woman stammered. "I'm trying to help Ms. Bradford? I asked her what happened, but she didn't answer."

Making a concerted effort to calm down, Michael took a deep breath. "Unfortunately, Ms. Bradford and I were conversing and not paying attention when we started to cross Via Veneto. We were almost hit by a speeding car."

"But you weren't."

"Physically we're fine, but we're obviously shaken by the incident. I appreciate your help and apologize for lashing out at you. I'll sit here with Ms. Bradford until she calms down."

The woman stood. "Is there anything I can do for either of you?"

"There is. Would you bring us the keycard to Ms. Bradford's suite?"

"Of course. Should I call a doctor?"

"There's no need. I'm sure she'll be fine once I get her upstairs."

"I'll bring the card right away."

Michael sat down on the couch beside Emma, put his arm around her, and pulled her toward him. "You're safe now," he whispered into her hair.

A shudder passed through Emma's body. For a moment she didn't respond. When she finally spoke, her voice was weak. "I was so scared, Michael."

"I know. I was too. If it makes you feel any better, whoever tried to run us down is long gone."

At that moment, the receptionist returned. "Here's Ms. Bradford's key," she said, "and I brought her a glass of water."

Michael took the glass. "Thanks."

"Would you like to speak with one of our security agents? Gusto isn't here, but—."

"No, we're all set. The incident took place out on the street, so there's nothing Excelsior security can do. Again, I appreciate the assistance you've provided Ms. Bradford."

The receptionist nodded and turned away. "Emma, we're going upstairs," Michael said, once she'd left the lobby, "but first take a drink of water." He handed her the glass.

Without responding, Emma took a sip and put the glass on the table.

"Are you ready to go?" he asked.

Emma nodded. Michael helped her off the couch, holding her arm to steady her as she stood. "I've got you," he said. "How are you doing?"

"Better. At least I think so."

When the elevator door closed, Emma began to shake uncontrollably. Michael took her in his arms. "It's okay, Emma," he whispered.

"Then why can't I stop shaking?"

"Your body's in shock."

"Please don't let go," she whispered as tears ran down her face.

When the elevator door opened on the fourth floor, Michael put his arm around Emma's waist and held her tightly as they walked toward her room. Still holding on, he inserted and removed the key, opened the door, flipped on the lights, led her to the couch, and helped her sit down. "I'm going to go get you another glass of water," he said.

Emma reached out to stop him. "No, please stay with me."

He sat down beside her. She put her head on his shoulder and shut her eyes. Michael waited quietly. It was ten minutes before her shaking subsided and he could feel her body begin to relax. "Instead of water, I'd really like a glass of wine," she said, her voice still weak. "I'm sorry, Michael."

"For what?"

"For being such a wimp."

"We were almost killed. I'm surprised you're doing as well as you are."

Emma took a deep breath, but she didn't move away from Michael's embrace. Instead, she held on more tightly, feeling safe and secure in his arms. "You didn't fall apart," she whispered.

"Maybe not on the outside, but I was so scared."

Despite the stress she was feeling, Emma couldn't miss the opportunity. She looked up and smiled weakly. "You were scared? A big football jock and famous investigative reporter?"

"Now there's the Emma I've come to know and love," Michael said with relief. "You must be feeling a little better."

"Not really. I'll take that glass of wine." She reluctantly sat up, signaling Michael could let go.

"Coming right up," he said as he got off the couch. He opened the mini bar, took out a half liter of white wine, and poured a glass for Emma and another for himself.

Emma took a gulp, leaned back, and curled her feet up on the couch. "God, I need this." She took another sip.

For a little while they sat quietly. When Emma finally spoke, her voice was stronger, but there was pleading urgency in her words. "Someone just tried to kill us, Michael. Who was it?"

"A question I've been asking myself. When I left you on the curb, I ran out to try and get a look at the license plate. The car was speeding toward me, so I retreated to the corner of the hotel, knowing the driver wouldn't slam into the building to get to me. Instead of continuing along the Via Veneto, he rounded the corner. By the time I got back to the street, he was too far away for me to read the plate, but it was definitely the same kind of car I chased from in front of the hotel."

"The one with Vatican plates."

"Right. Now we know how far these people will go. They would kill us to bury the story."

"Are you sure they weren't just warning us?"

"No way. We were targets. If we'd been a few seconds later or a little slower crossing the street, the headlines tomorrow would be: 'Two ABC Reporters Killed by Hit and Run Driver on Via Veneto.'"

Emma shuddered. "Not a headline I'd like to read."

"I assure you—if the driver had his way, neither of us would be reading anything. Are you feeling calmer?"

"The wine's helping. Why?"

Michael stood up. "I thought I'd—"

"You're not leaving—"

"I'm not going anywhere." He moved closer to Emma and took her hand. "I was going to say I'll call Steven and tell him what happened."

"Sorry. I guess I'm not as calm as I thought I was. Mind if I keep thinking out loud? Maybe if we keep sharing ideas, we'll figure it out."

"Talk away."

"I'm wondering how whoever tried to run us down knew we were out for the evening. When we left, we didn't see anyone watching the hotel. Giro wasn't driving, so they weren't following our car. A cab dropped us off at Helen's hotel, and we took another one to the restaurant. Stop and think. We didn't see anyone watching the Excelsior, but that doesn't mean anything. It was rush hour, so there were lots of cars on the street. My guess is whoever was waiting in the black car knew we'd gone out, though he probably had no idea where we were going. He was waiting for us to come back."

"But he had no way of knowing we'd stop across the street," Michael said. We decided at the last minute."

"Maybe his decision to run us over was also spontaneous. The driver of the car was waiting for us to return and saw the cab drop us at the ATM. He watched until we were finished—"

"Saw his chance, and gunned the engine. So if we'd come straight to the hotel ..." Michael paused. "God I'm stupid," he said angrily.

"What are you talking about?"

"Since all this started, we've been so careful. All of sudden I threw caution to the wind and put both our lives in danger."

"You had no way of knowing some maniac would try to run us over."

"I didn't know someone would try to kill us, but I should have heeded Steven's warning. Masella will stop at nothing to have his way. I blame myself for what happened. I knew it was possible that whoever's watching us could try to stop our investigation one way or another."

"That may be true, but anticipating this particular scenario would have been impossible. What do you think would have happened if we had come straight to the hotel instead of getting out of the cab across the street?"

"Probably nothing. The opportunity wouldn't have been there. We would have come directly inside, and the driver of the death car, knowing we were in for the night, would have left."

"You realize all of this is mere speculation."

"I do, so why don't we stop hypothesizing?" Michael stood up and took his phone out of his pocket.

"You're calling Steven to tell him what happened."

"I am."

Emma listened while Michael talked to his friend. "What did he say?" she asked when he hung up.

"Of course he's worried."

"He didn't suggest we should quit investigating?"

"No. Even if the thought crossed his mind, he wouldn't have said anything. He knows me and, by now, he realizes how stubborn you are. The only change in plans is that Sante will bring another policeman with him to Saint Agnes tomorrow."

"Also dressed as a priest?"

"I didn't ask, but I'm sure Steven knows what's best under the circumstances. Why don't you go to bed?"

"I can't sleep yet. We have e-mails to check first."

"They'll wait until tomorrow morning."

When Emma stood up, her knees still felt slightly wobbly. Michael reached out to steady her, but she waved him away. "I'm fine, and no, the e-mails won't wait. I'm hoping Cardinal Remella forwarded Masella's correspondence." She crossed the room and sat at the desk.

"I'll be right with you," Michael said. He waited to see if Emma would object to his leaving the room to change clothes, but she was fixed on reading her e-mails.

"Look at this," she said when Michael reappeared in sweats and a T-shirt.

"I take it the cardinal kept his word."

"He did. Masella wasn't even subtle in his campaigning."

"Summarize for me?"

"In a nutshell, he says only Cardinal della Chesia can bring the church into the twenty-first century, that the election of a conservative cardinal would keep the church firmly entrenched in the Middle Ages."

"There's nothing new. He's preaching the liberal platform."

"True. The message is the same. What's surprising is the e-mails are being sent to cardinals—princes of the church. Who the hell is this guy?"

"Someone who's egotistical and very dangerous. We found that out tonight."

"That we did." Emma paused, and Michael waited for her to collect her thoughts. "I think I know, but tell me why these e-mails make you even more certain it's Masella and not a conservative fringe group behind the attempt on our lives. I know we all decided at dinner, but—"

"Because of something Cardinal Remella told us. He said, 'Thou shalt not kill.' It's about the sanctity of life. I think many of the older men, and my guess is this is the group which makes up the conservative element, still believe in traditional Catholic values. Sure, they don't like what's going on, but they're not going to break a sacred commandment to advance their agenda. 'Thou shalt not kill.' Do you really think they're willing to risk their immortal souls to stop our investigation?"

"But Masella believes in the same Ten Commandments."

"No doubt he does, or he did at one point, but he's out of control; he's drunk with the prospect of power, and he'll stop at nothing to achieve his objectives. He's a narcissist who greatly overestimates his own abilities. He's megalomania-cal. He believes his is the only way. That conviction informs his life."

"So you believe he's mentally ill and not just power hungry."

"I'm no psychiatrist, but he'd have to be sick to try and pull this off. Would a sane man with the rank of monsignor violate the traditions of the church and openly campaign for the election of a particular cardinal to the papacy? Would a sane man kill Piero Scala, a member of the opposition, as a warning? Would a sane man try to poison a pope?"

"Would a sane man kill a maid as a warning and try to kill two American journalists?"

"I rest my case." Michael sighed. "This man is beyond dangerous, and, under the circumstances, though you won't like hearing it, I believe it would be best if you skip the meeting tomorrow."

"You can't be serious," Emma said in disbelief. "There's no way I'm backing off."

Michael shook his head. "I knew that's what you'd say. I only wanted to point out the potential danger. While you get ready for bed, I'll call Steven and tell him about Masella's e-mails."

"I'll go, but first I want to see what Helen has to say."

Emma opened Helen's e-mail. "Well, a little good news," she said. "We're going live on *ABC World News* tomorrow evening." She looked at the clock. "Or, rather, this evening. It's going to be another late one; that is if we survive tomorrow's meeting at Saint Agnes."

"We will," Michael said. "We have to. Think you can sleep?"

"I hope so. Thanks for sleeping with me."

Michael grinned. "I can't think of anything I'd rather do."

Emma shook her head. "You know what I mean."

"Unfortunately I do." Michael grinned. "Sleep well."

CHAPTER TWENTY-THREE

When Emma woke up, Michael was laying on the couch in the sitting room going through his notes.

"Did you sleep well?" he asked.

"You know, surprisingly, I did."

"Good. Breakfast should be here in a few minutes."

"If you want to shower and get dressed, I can wait for the food."

Michael didn't hesitate before responding: "No way, he said resolutely. "Do you really think I'm stupid enough to let down my guard again? You know the old cliché: fool me once ... I'll take a quick shower after we eat."

"Talk about paranoia. It's room service coming with food, Michael, not an invasion by Vatican liberals who plan to kill us."

"You're sure? After last night, I'd think you'd want to be extra cautious."

There was a tap on the door. "Saved by a knock," Emma said, grinning. "May I at least let the guy in?"

"I suppose, but I'm right behind you, umbrella in hand."

"You're kidding," Right?"

Michael held up the umbrella. "Does it look like I am?"

Rolling her eyes, Emma opened the door. "Buongiorno," the waiter said cheerfully as he pushed the table into the room.

"Buongiorno," said Emma.

"That's okay, we'll take care of it," Michael said as the man started to uncover the plates. "We'll call when we're finished eating." He handed the waiter five euros, followed him to the door, and, when he was out, flipped the security lock.

Emma sat down at the table. "Funny thing, we weren't accosted, so you didn't have to defend me with your trusty umbrella after all. Should I say I told you so?"

Michael made a face as he pulled two chairs up to the table. "It appears you already have."

As Emma poured Michael's coffee, the teasing stopped. "I don't know how you feel, but I'm worried," she said.

"You're anxious about the meeting with your mysterious caller."

"Going to Saint Agnes is actually number three on my list of concerns."

"Wow! If that's the case, I'm afraid to ask about numbers one and two."

"You're hearing them anyway. First and foremost, we have absolutely no idea what we're going to say during the background shoot this morning. We were going to make plans when we got back to the hotel last night, but for a reason I'd like to forget, we never got back to it."

"We can figure everything out while we eat. What's number two?"

"I haven't scripted the Four Rivers segment, and you haven't worked on your spiel about the Triton."

"You're half right. I did the Triton copy last night before I went to sleep."

"Really? I thought you were exhausted."

"I was, but I figured I wouldn't have time this morning. As for the Four Rivers report, I'll bet you could do the spiel without any prep work. Everything Nicola said will come flowing back to you when you get to the fountain."

"That might be true under normal circumstances, but considering what's going on, I'm having trouble concentrating."

"You're referring to number three on your list."

"I am, though I wish I could find a way to put the meeting out of my mind."

"I know, but back to number two. If you want to review for the Four Rivers shoot, stay in the car while I'm shooting the Triton segment, or, if you prefer, I'll call Lucio and we'll drive separately."

Emma nodded no. "As far as I'm concerned, the second option is out. Under the circumstances, let's stay together. If worse comes to worse, rehearse the Navona copy while you're doing the Triton segment."

"That works for me."

"Good. So now all we have to worry about is the Cardinal Amici interview background. How far do we go? We told Steven and James we wouldn't report anything we don't know for sure."

"Then we can't mention the people following us, the attempt on our lives last night, the noon meeting at Saint Agnes, Dina's murder, Cardinal Amici's imprisonment—"

"And we can't hint that Piero might have been murdered or the pope isn't really suffering from the flu."

"Nor can we reveal Masella's e-mails to Cardinal Remella or our hypothesis that our favorite monsignor is angling to be the next pope. You know, when we say all of this aloud, it appears we have nothing but a bunch of theories. We both believe we're right in our thinking, but we can't prove anything."

"Then what do we say this morning?"

"We give the audience the facts as we know them—the reforms the liberals want, and the response from the conservatives."

"Should we mention Masella? All we can say for sure is he's the pope's secretary. We have our suspicions, but we have to have proof before we make accusations."

"I think we need to bring him up so when we come back to do a full report as the story unfolds, we won't be springing him on the audience."

"Sort of a verbal foreshadowing."

"Exactly, and putting his name out there might make him think twice before he tries to kill us again. He could figure he'd be a suspect."

"Possibly, but if he is a megalomaniacal narcissist with a God complex, he probably thinks he's above the law. If that's the case, he won't give up."

"Wow, that's some psychological diagnosis. Are you sure you majored in journalism?"

"Actually I majored in art history, but I took Psychology 101."

"Of course you did. "So, *Doctor* Bradford, do you or don't want to mention Masella's name?"

"I think you should. I merely wanted you to know the risks involved by doing so."

"It's a chance I'm willing to take. What's next?"

"I'm afraid that's it."

Michael frowned. "What we have to say isn't earth-shattering, which is sad because if truth be told, what we suspect, but can't yet prove, is crucial; even historic."

"So I guess that's our report, and because I did the intro to the interview with the cardinal, you do the intro to the intro."

"You're sure?"

"I am. While you shower and dress, I'm going to work on my Four Rivers copy. I should be able to outline what I want to say in fifteen minutes and run through it a couple of times on the way and while you're filming at the Triton."

While Michael got ready, Emma skimmed Nicola's notes.

"Are you ready?" he asked when he returned twenty minutes later and saw Emma putting her papers away.

"I am. While you were dressing, I forwarded Cardinal Remella's e-mails to your computer. Before we leave, we need to stop by your room and run copies for Steven and James."

"I'm glad you remembered." Michael looked at his watch. "We should have enough time."

"I'm sure Giro will wait if we're a few minutes late. Think I should keep the room key with me or leave it at the desk?"

"The former. If one of the bad guys sees us leave without dropping off the key, he may assume we'll be right back and think twice about trying to break in."

"You're thinking Gusto might be Masella's man at the hotel?"

"I have no idea, but after last night, everyone's suspect."

Michael pushed the room service table into the hallway, and they took the elevator to the third floor. While Emma waited, he printed Masella's e-mails and put them in a manila folder. "I'm all set," he said, "and we're still on time."

As they passed through the lobby, Emma waved to the receptionist, but she kept her key. They pushed through the revolving door and saw Giro waiting in the limo area. "Did you have a nice dinner last night." he asked as he got out and opened Emma's door.

Emma looked at Michael who nodded no, silently telling her not to mention the event on the Via Veneto. "We did, she said. "The food at Taverna Angelica was excellent. However, we were out so late that I didn't finish my script for today's shoot. You'll have to forgive me if I don't talk with you during the drive."

"There's nothing to forgive," Giro said.

As they drove, Emma looked over the Four Rivers copy and Michael reviewed his material for Saint Peter's and the Triton segment. When Giro dropped them by the basilica, they both felt ready to report.

"You go to makeup first," Emma said as they entered the truck. "Then while my face is fixed, you can go out and wait for Steven or his messenger."

"It sounds like a plan."

While Emma waited for the woman to finish applying Michael's makeup, she looked through her Four Rivers report one last time. "All set?" Michael asked as he approached the place where she was sitting.

"With the segment; I think so. Now the miracle worker begins, though I have no idea how she'll get rid of the dark circles under my eyes."

Michael leaned in and studied Emma's face. "I don't see any dark circles."

"Then you need glasses. Go wait for Steven or whomever."

Michael went outside to wait by the truck. It wasn't long before a young, shiny-faced priest who looked like he'd recently graduated from seminary approached him. "I'm Father McCarthy from Notre Dame," he said. "I'm a fan. I've always wanted to meet you, Mr. Kelsey."

"It's great to meet someone who appreciates my work," Michael said, grinning.

The young priest seemed confused. "You have something for me?" he asked, without asking Michael to explain.

"I do." Michael pulled out an autographed picture and handed it to him.

"Is this what I'm supposed to be taking back to Monsignor Laurent?" he asked warily. "He said something about a folder."

"Then you really aren't a fan, Father? You'd rather have some meaningless papers than a signed photo?"

Father McDonald was clearly flustered. "I … I am, and sure, but …" he stuttered.

"I'm joking," Michael said. He put his hand on the priest's shoulder. "When you get back to Monsignor Laurent, hand him the picture first. I'm always looking for ways to play a joke on my friend. Could you join me in the truck for a moment?"

"Sure, but why?" the young man asked, looking even more confused.

"Come on in and I'll tell you."

Father McDonald followed Michael into the truck, and Michael handed him the information. "I'd like for you to put the folder under your cassock."

"I don't understand."

"It's best if you don't. The less you know, the better off you are. If anyone, and I mean anyone, from a cardinal to Pope John himself, stops you and asks why you were talking with me, show him the picture. Don't mention the folder or Steven."

"Then the picture's not just a joke on Monsignor Laurent."

"It is, but in case you're stopped, it's a gift to you from your hero." Michael grinned. "Okay, that may be taking it a bit too far. How about if it's a picture of an American journalist you've seen on TV a few times?"

"Very good. Before I go, Monsignor Laurent said to say he would see you later today. He also said he's doing his best to convert you to the true faith, so you should be at the church on time."

"Tell him we'll be there."

Michael shook hands with the young priest. "Thanks for helping us out, Father."

The priest hadn't been gone for long when Emma came out of the truck. "You all set to do the intro to the intro?"

"As ready as I'll ever be. I just handed off the e-mails to Steven's currier. God, I feel old. The priest was a baby."

When they got to the obelisk, Helen and Ron were waiting. Emma spied Bill, camera in hand, filming the few tourists in the square.

"Know what you want to say, Emma?" Helen asked.

"Michael's doing the report."

"Really? His idea or yours?"

"Mine. We're both working on the story, so he should get equal screen time."

Helen smiled and turned to Michael. "Ron marked the place where he wants you to stand."

"I'm on it literally and figuratively."

"Why don't you do a run through before we film? I'd like to hear what you plan to say."

"You don't trust me?"

"Of course I do, but I'm the one who has to take the fall if you say something we can't substantiate."

"We worried about the same thing when we did the prep work," Emma said. "I think we're in the clear in that regard, but it's probably a good idea if Michael does a run-through so we can eliminate anything that might be questionable."

When Ron gave the signal, Michael began. Taking into account what he and Emma had decided, he did the entire report, giving only the facts. "What do you think?" he asked Helen when he was finished.

"I think we're through. Your report was verifiable, so there's no need to cut."

"Really?" Michael said proudly. "Then we're ready to film?"

"I shot the run-through," Ron said, "so, as Helen said, we're done here."

"I'm finished too," Bill said as he approached from the colonnade area. "It's really too early for hordes of tourists to be out. I filmed a few priests who were milling around. Not one of them seemed to be paying much attention to what you were doing, but I'll put the footage on a disk just in case."

"Thanks, Bill," Michael said.

"Lucio, Vezio and Giro are waiting," Helen said. "Shall we head right over to the Triton fountain? Who's doing the segment? Or are you reporting as a team?"

"Michael's doing the Triton. I'll report on Four Rivers," Emma said.

During the drive to the fountain, Michael went through his copy. "Are you staying in the car or watching the shoot?" he asked when they arrived at the site.

"As I said in the truck, I think I'm ready, so I'll watch."

"Then be prepared to see genius."

"Oh my God. He's baaaack."

Michael laughed. "Not to worry. As I told you before, the 'he' you're referring to is gone forever. I wish Nicola was around so I could thank her. She's the only reason I can do this. I haven't had time to do any background research."

"You can tell her when you see her. So let's hear what you have to say."

Bill positioned Michael beside the fountain and gave him the signal to begin. Michael nodded and started:

Bernini created a new style in sculpture. As you've seen during our previous reports, he possessed the extraordinary ability to reproduced movement of human bodies in stone. The Triton, the first of Bernini's famous fountains, exemplifies this talent and is an exceptional example of Baroque art.

As Bill filmed, Michael used Nicola's notes to describe the fountain, concluding with: "This is Michael Kelsey, reporting from Rome."

"Excellent," Emma and Helen said in unison.

"I hope our friend in the black car on the other side of the street agrees," Michael said. "Hopefully he'll believe we're no longer investigating Vatican politics and are only reporting on Bernini."

Emma looked toward the car. "Is that the same one that came at us last night?"

"It could be. I didn't have time to look for identifying marks. All I cared about was keeping both of us from being run over. Shall we go ask the driver if he was the one who tried to kill us?"

"You're not serious."

"Watch me." As Michael started toward the car, he turned back. "Film this, Ron," he called out.

"Sure thing." Ron picked up his camera, turned it toward the street, and started after Michael.

When the driver of the black car saw Michael head into the traffic, he put up the tinted window and sped away.

"Déjà vu," Emma said when Michael returned. "These guys don't want a one-on-one confrontation."

"Right. They're cowards." He turned to Ron. "Did you film the almost encounter?"

"I did, but I didn't get much."

"I didn't expect you to. Did you at least get a shot of the car as it sped away?"

"If it helps, I did."

"It may. Who knows?"

"What's going on?" Helen asked.

"We'll fill you in later," Michael said.

"I've heard that before. This time, I hope it's true. All this cloak-and-dagger business over the past few days has me worried."

"With reason," Michael whispered under his breath.

"What?" Helen said.

"I was going to ask if we need to do the Triton segment again."

Helen turned to Bill. "What do you think," she asked.

"There's no need, but I want to take a few different angles of the dolphins and Triton before we leave here. We'll meet you at the Piazza Navona."

"Nervous?" Michael asked Emma when they were in the car.

"If you're talking about the meeting, I'm trying to concentrate on one thing at a time. If I think about who might be at Saint Agnes, I'll never get through the Four Rivers segment."

"While you're filming, I'll go into the church and take a look around. I'd feel better knowing what we're walking into."

"Good idea. That way we won't be going in blind."

When Helen and Ron reached the fountain, Michael left the group and headed for the church. "Any idea where you'd like to stand?" Ron asked Emma.

"Actually, yes. Position me so you can see the fountain with the façade of the church in the background."

"Want to do a dry run?"

"It's not necessary unless you want to consider camera angles."

"No need. Let's see if we can do this in one take." Ron pointed. Emma took a breath and started to talk:

This is Emma Bradford, reporting from the center of Piazza Navona beside Bernini's Fontana del Quattro Fiumi, *or, in English,* Four Rivers Fountain, *which is considered to be one of the artist's most famous and beautiful works.*

Emma talked about the history of the fountain and the four river gods before Ron gave her a cut sign. "My preliminary shots were from a distance," he said. "I want to be sure I have film of everything you mentioned. Let's walk around while you point to each of the objects you talked about."

"Sure." Emma pointed to the central rock formation, each of the river gods, and the various animals.

"Alright, I'm up to speed," Ron said when they got back to the spot he'd marked on the pavement. You ready to continue?"

"I am"

"Then go for it."

Emma waited for the red light, smiled and began again:

Certainly the Four Rivers Fountain is famous for its incredible beauty, but it's also well-known because it perpetuates the legendary rivalry between the two great Baroque architects of the time, Bernini and Borromini. Bernini is said to have expressed his disdain for Borromini's façade of Saint Agnes in Agony, the church directly behind the sculpture. When visitors to the square observed the placement of the demigods in the fountain, a legend was born.

Emma repeated Nicola's story about famed rivalry. When she finished, Ron put up his hand, signaling her to wait. "Give me a minute before you wrap," he said. "I took a few shots when Helen and I were out the first afternoon we were in Rome, but that was before I heard your rivalry spiel."

He took pictures of the façade of the church, the statue of Saint Agnes, and the positioning of the figures in the fountain. "Alright," he said. "Let's finish this." He pointed to Emma.

Is there any truth to the legends? Probably not since the fountain was completed in 1651and the church in 1657, so obviously the stories of the symbolic placements and expressions of the river gods couldn't be true. As for Saint Agnes, I guess you'll have to make up your own minds about whether or not Borromini was sending Bernini a message. This is Emma Bradford, reporting from the Fontana del Quattro Fiumi in Piazza Navona, Rome."

"Excellent!" Helen said. "You and Michael are doing a great job tying everything together."

"I think so too," Michael said.

"You're back," Emma said. "You watched the segment?"

"The part about the rivalry between Bernini and Borromini. I like rivalries that eventually turn to friendships." He winked at Emma.

"I don't think that happened in the case of Bernini and Borromini."

"But—"

"Shall we head over to the elephant obelisk?" Helen interrupted. "I think we've exhausted the rivalry topic.

"We're shooting Bernini's chick today?" Emma asked, wondering how she could stall her producer until after the meeting in Saint Agnes.

"If that's the sculpture with the elephant, we are. You didn't know?"

"I was running late this morning, and didn't check the schedule. I'm afraid I need a few minutes." She looked at her watch. "It's 11:30. Helen, why don't you and Ron take a lunch-break. Michael and I will grab something to eat, I'll go through Nicola's notes, script the segment, and we'll meet you by the Neptune Fountain in ninety minutes."

"You brought notes with you?" Michael asked.

Emma turned so Helen couldn't see her face. "Of course I did," she said as she raised her eyebrows.

"I'll help Emma with her copy," Michael said. "We'll be ready to film at one, Helen."

"You didn't bring notes, did you?" Michael said when Helen and Ron had packed up and left the fountain area.

"No, but I didn't want to tell Helen we couldn't leave now because we have a mysterious meeting in Saint Agnes in a half-hour. What did you see in the church?"

"Steven and James were right. It's a strange choice for a clandestine meeting. There's no place to be alone."

"So you're thinking whoever wants to meet with me only wants to talk."

"In my opinion, yes, and if it helps, I don't think your mysterious caller will try anything with all the tourists milling around."

Emma looked at her watched. "We'll know if you're right in twenty-five minutes."

CHAPTER TWENTY-FOUR

To pass the time, they went to a gelato stand next to Saint Agnes. While they waited, Emma watched the church door. Several priests went inside, but she didn't see Steven or James. "Try to relax," Michael said as they neared the front of the long line.

"Easy for you to say. This could be my last meal," she said joking, yet paradoxically serious.

Michael laughed. "Then if you believe what the sign says, you'll die happy."

It seemed like forever, but they finally got to the counter. "Two tartufo al cioccolato and two coffees," Michael said.

"Make that one tartufo al cioccolato and two coffees," said Emma.

"Are you sure?"

"I am. My stomach's getting ickier by the minute. I'll just take a taste of yours."

"You're assuming I'm willing to share."

"I have no doubt my hero in the iconographic cape will take pity on a nervous Nellie and give her one tiny bite of his chocolate truffle gelato."

"That's hitting below the belt, but when you put it that way, I suppose I have no choice."

They found a table and moved the chairs so they could both see the church. "I want to be inside by 11:55," Emma said. "If we're late, whoever gave me the emphatic order to 'be there' probably won't be pleased."

"Without doubt, so we'll be on time." Michael tasted the gelato and pushed the bowl toward Emma. "Take a bite, but just a little one. I feel my cape is falling off my shoulders."

Emma picked up a spoon and took a taste. "Mmmmm. It's delicious," she said.

Michael jokingly jerked the bowl away. "Now you'll probably want more."

"Not to worry. It's rich and I'm rattled. If I ate any more, I'd probably throw up all over our mystery man."

"Maybe that's not a bad strategy." Michael pushed the bowl back toward her. "Take another bite."

Emma laughed nervously. "No thanks."

She sat quietly and watched Michael inhale the gelato. "Please tell me you're not going to lick the bowl," she said when he scraped off the last remaining trace of chocolate.

"I'm tempted, but I'm in Rome representing ABC. I wouldn't want some American tourist to take a picture of my tongue attacking the bowl and e-mail it to *Good Morning America*. Can you hear George Stephanopoulos talk about the gauche reporter who's giving Americans and ABC a bad name?"

"I'm mentally writing my e-mail as we speak. Believe me—you wouldn't like what I have to say. Admit it. You were relieved when I didn't want another bite."

"Maybe I was pleased, but, though it was slipping slightly, I assure you my cape was securely attached to my jacket and I would have shared." He looked at his watch. "Okay, enough of this. If we're going to be on time, we should go. Ready?"

Emma stood up. "As ready as I'll ever be. I can't decide if I'm curious, nervous, or flat-out frightened."

"I don't think you have reason to be afraid. As I said before, Saint Agnes isn't a place I would choose if I intended to inflict bodily harm on the person I was meeting."

"I hope you're right." Emma took a deep breath. "I'm so nervous."

Michael squeezed her hand. "I know you are."

"I didn't see Steven or James go in, did you?"

"No, but I'm sure they're in there."

They climbed the stairs to the church door, passing ascending columns of pious nuns in ancient penguin habits. At 11:55, they entered the church.

Emma took another deep breath. Struggling to calm down, she looked around. "There's Steven," she whispered when she saw a priest with his head bent low in prayer. As if on cue, James, who was near the altar, turned around and gave Emma an almost imperceptible nod.

"I see Sante," Michael said. "He's wearing Steven's cassock. Look there. He's to our right near the huge sculpture of Saint Agnes. The burly guy with him must be the other policeman he talked about bringing. What do you want to do? Should we pretend to be tourists and wander around?"

Emma nodded no. "Let's stand here in the center aisle. I want to be out in the open and obvious."

Two priests entered the church, but neither came toward them. "I feel ridiculous standing here," Emma whispered. "Shall we walk toward the altar?"

Suddenly a voice came from behind them. "Beautiful church, isn't it? Instead of looking at the altar, perhaps you might like to take a closer look at the statue of Saint Agnes in the chapel to your right."

Stunned when she recognized the voice of the man who was addressing her, Emma spun around to face Monsignors Cipriano and Tomai. Standing to Masella's right was also a hulking giant with a sour expression on his face.

"I believe you met Cardinal Amici's new secretary at Piero's funeral," Masella said, "and this is my bodyguard, Tito."

Emma struggled to remain calm and poised. Surprised as she was to see Masella himself, she was suddenly less concerned and felt safer than she had only seconds before.

She was about to respond when Michael spoke: "A bodyguard," he said contemptuously. "I'm surprised a monsignor would require protection. I've seen lots of bishops and a few cardinals walking around the Vatican by themselves. None of them had bodyguards."

"Under normal circumstances, increased security would not be necessary," Masella said, "but these are not ordinary times, and I am Pope John's private secretary."

Michael's eyes twinkled mischievously. "Did you hear that, Emma?"

"I did."

Michael turned back to Masella. "Thank God these are atypical times. If murder, attempted murder, and imprisonment were the norm around here, I'd really be concerned about the state of the Catholic Church."

"I already am," said Emma. She turned toward Tito. "Speaking of unusual times, aren't you one of the two men who was guarding Cardinal Amici's door?" As Tito began to answer, she put up her hand. "No need to respond. I'm sure you were person who prevented me from keeping my scheduled appointment with the cardinal. I believe you said he was resting. Now you're here with Monsignor Cipriano. Interesting."

"You have no reason to accuse Tito of anything, Ms. Bradford," Masella said. "He was following orders."

Emma sensed a chink in Masella's armor. "Whose?" she asked. "Yours?"

"Of course not," Masella said indignantly. "I have no authority to place men outside the cardinal's room."

"If not you, then who the hell's responsible for imprisoning Cardinal Amici?" Michael said.

Masella looked composed, but Emma could tell he was agitated. "What you appear to be suggesting is ridiculous, Mr. Kelsey. I assure you, the cardinal is not being held against his will, and, I might add, no crimes are being committed in the Vatican. One reason I came to Saint Agnes is to make that clear."

"Really?" Michael's voice dripped with sarcasm. "Maybe you *are* speaking truthfully. Frankly, I'd be shocked to find out you have the balls, excuse me, Emma, to show up here after you sent your hired thugs after us last night. Sorry. Did I get the term wrong? Maybe priests, aka holy men, aren't referred to as thugs regardless of what they do. Oh well, whatever they're called, a concerted effort was made to kill Ms. Bradford and me last night."

Masella verbally expressed shock, but his facial expression didn't change. "I have no idea what you mean," he said in contrived disbelief.

Michael seethed when he saw the smirk on the monsignor's face. "I'm sure you don't." He turned to Tomai. "From your astonished expression, Monsignor, I assume Masella hasn't told you everything."

"Stick around," said Emma. "Michael and I are just getting started. When we're finished everything will be clear."

Michael glared at Masella. "Ms. Bradford's right," he said. "We've only scratched the surface. "Let me ask you a question, Monsignor Cipriano. Is telling a lie a mortal sin? Honestly, I can't remember. As we say in the U.S., I'm a fallen Catholic. But even though I don't go to Mass, unless Pope John has recently made a radical change in church doctrine, I'm certain murder still remains a cardinal sin."

Masella was clearly making a concerted effort to appear unfazed by Michael's words. He inhaled deeply, gathering his thoughts, before speaking. "I came here to refute what you and Ms. Bradford obviously believe." He motioned to a nearby row of unoccupied chairs. "Shall we act like civilized human beings and sit while we talk?"

"We prefer to stand," Michael said with irritation. "Emma, would you please tell Monsignor Cipriano what we *know* to be true? And, Monsignor, please note I used the word *know* and not believe. It wasn't by chance."

He turned to Emma, his back to Masella. "Go for it," he whispered before raising his voice so Masella could hear him. "And don't leave anything out. I'm sure what you have to say will ring true to our friend here, but Monsignor Tomai may be surprised by the revelations."

Giotto was clearly uneasy. "Please tell me what all this is about, Ms. Bradford," he said in seeming disbelief. "I have no idea what you are implying."

"Not implying, Monsignor. Let me give it to you numerically. I want you to grasp the implication of my words." Emma turned to Masella. "Feel free to comment after each point I make, Monsignor."

"I'm sure Monsignor Tomai will learn a great deal from your contribution to the conversation, Emma," Michael added. "He's a smart man."

"There's nothing to understand," Masella said angrily.

He was clearly trying to mask his fury as Emma began. "First, we *know* Monsignor Scala was murdered, most likely on your orders. Care to comment, Monsignor?"

For a split second, Masella looked flustered, but he quickly recovered. He reached into the pocket in his cassock. "Anticipating you might have a question about Piero, I brought this." He handed Emma an envelope. "It is a letter from Piero's family to the pope asking that there be no violation of their son's body."

"Of course it is," Michael said derisively. "Did you already have a handwriting expert verify it for us? No need to waste our time with this garbage. Go on, Emma. Tell Masella what else we *know*. Perhaps he'll have more show-and-tell to share."

"We *know* Michael and I are being followed," Emma said. "Whether we go out in our car or take a cab, there's always someone right behind us."

"In this instance, you are correct, Ms. Bradford," Masella said, a sneer on his face. "Our people are following you, but you should be pleased, not upset. These men mean neither you nor Mr. Kelsey any harm. On the contrary, they are in place for your protection."

Michael smirked. "Is this type of *protection* available to all journalists who come to Rome to cover the opening of an art exhibition, or are Ms. Bradford and I special?"

"We would do the same for any reporter who interferes in the internal politics of the Holy See. The pope wants to make certain nothing happens to you while you are on Vatican soil."

"You expect us to accept this ridiculous notion?" Michael said angrily. "We're supposed to believe that Pope John ordered his thugs to shadow us? He has time to be concerned about the two *interfering* journalists, which seems to be the label you've given us? That's a bunch of crap."

"Of course he does," Masella said irritably. "Do you think I could arrange for your security detail on my own?"

"Oh, so now it's a security detail," Michael said, his anger intensifying. "I might point out that we're not only being *protected* when we're in Vatican territory, unless Rome has suddenly been assimilated into the Holy See. Has the pope suddenly made the entire city a part of the Vatican?"

"Now you are being absurd," said Masella.

"We're not the ones offering preposterous suggestions," Emma said. "Apparently you expect us to believe Pope John is so concerned about our *interference*, as you put it, that he's taken time from his busy schedule to worry about our safety."

"He would make time if those two journalists were causing problems for the church."

"How nice of him to want to see we're safe," Michael responded sarcastically," but I'm wondering why our security detail races away each time I approach their car. It's happened twice now."

"I am afraid I am unable to explain their behavior."

"But if they're acting on your instructions—"

"You mean Pope John's orders."

Michael chuckled. "That's right. I forgot."

Masella flashed a bogus smile. "Now that I have covered what I wanted you to know, do you have any questions, Ms. Bradford?"

"Oh, like I told Monsignor Tomai, I'm only getting started," Emma said with contempt. "Back to the subject we touched on when you introduced Tito. Why is Cardinal Amici being held against his will?"

Out of the corner of her eye, Emma thought she saw Giotto cringe, but Masella didn't blink. "The cardinal is being guarded for his own safety," he said without pause. "There are crazy fringe groups who are trying to advance their own agendas. He is free to go to Mass every day, and, if you recall, he attended Piero's funeral."

"Fringe groups like your liberal compatriots?" Michael said.

Without waiting for Masella to respond, Emma continued: "And then there's the matter of the pope's illness. We haven't addressed that disturbing topic."

Masella reached into his pocket and handed Emma another letter. "I anticipated this question too, so I also brought a report from Pope John's doctors."

"Another carefully arranged show-and-tell," Emma said. "I'll bet these learned men confirm your assertion that the pope has the flu."

"Of course they do," Masella said indignantly. "What did you expect? If you read their comments, you will learn that what began as a bad case of influenza has progressed into pneumonia."

Emma glanced at the report. "Are the pope's doctors forced to do your bidding as well, Monsignor? Are they harming rather than trying to heal the pope? Are they in your pocket?"

Masella scowled. "If by 'in my pocket' you mean do they work for me, that is a ludicrous suggestion. The pope's doctors would never be complicit in such a plot. They took an oath to save lives, not take them."

"I'm an Episcopalian, not a Catholic, so I'm not privy to your religious practice, but I believe you also took an oath, Monsignor. Did you violate yours by actively campaigning for Cardinal della Chesia's election?"

Masella momentarily lost his cool. Emma wasn't sure the others saw him cringe, but she definitely did. "Ah, you know what I'm talking about," she said, "but that's a subject for another time. Back to what I *know*. If the pope should die from his so-called pneumonia, you will actively campaign to be his successor."

Masella's eyes narrowed. "That is absurd, Ms. Bradford.

This time Giotto's distress was apparent to everyone in the group. *Either he's a great actor, or he doesn't know what he's involved in*, Emma mused as the monsignor took hold of

Masella's sleeve. "Masella, is this true?" he asked, his face contorted with concern.

Masella pulled his arm from Giotto's grasp and ignored the question. "Where do you come up with these outrageous ideas, Ms. Bradford?" he said indignantly. "I am a monsignor, not a cardinal. Cardinals become popes.

"Ms. Bradford and I aren't stupid, *Monsignor*," said Michael. "Please don't insult our intelligence. Everyone here knows choosing a pope from among the College of Cardinals is just a long-established tradition. It is not church doctrine. You're as eligible to be pope as any other Catholic in good standing. If I went to church a little more, I could run for election myself."

"That's utterly ridiculous," Masella said disdainfully.

"For once, you and I agree," Michael said, "but you also know it's not beyond the realm of possibility. You could be the next pope."

Emma steeled herself and confronted Masella again. "Can you deny you sent e-mails urging or, perhaps to use more accurate words, coercing or intimidating the cardinals into voting for Cardinal della Chesia?"

"I categorically deny using any threats or coercion."

"Really. Would you be surprised to know we have copies your e-mails? However, being at a decided disadvantage because I didn't know who commanded me to show up at Saint Agnes, I'm afraid I didn't come prepared. Unlike you, I can't suddenly produce written evidence to support my claims."

Masella hesitated before responding. It was the first time Emma had seen any clear sign of weakness. "You are full of surprises, Ms. Bradford," he said. "You may have copies of e-mails, but it seems you have misconstrued my message. I was merely the spokesman for those who believe change is necessary. These men believed that Cardinal della Chesia was the man to implement the much-needed new policies."

"So after the new pope is elected, the spokesman became the power behind the throne. Cardinal della Chesia's election didn't hurt you, did it, Monsignor? Let's see. What did you gain? Oh yes! You're now the pope's private secretary."

"I assure you, I did not actively campaign for my position, Ms. Bradford."

Michael glared at Masella. "You're lying!" he said. "You achieved your first goal. That wasn't enough. Now you're after the bigger prize."

"I will not waste my valuable time addressing such an outrageous accusation."

"And I suppose it's too far-fetched for us to think you tried to kill us last night," Michael said. "Come on, Monsignor. You might not have been behind the wheel of the car, but you definitely gave the order. Deny it all you want."

"Why would I want to kill you?" Masella said a little too cunningly.

Michael slapped his forehead. "Duh! Could it be to keep our story out of the news? If the world knew what you're up to, would you be able to pull off your coup? I doubt it. There are too many middle-of-the-road Catholics who would be appalled by your actions, let alone liberals who may want change but would never condone murder to make it happen."

"And while we're on the subject of murder, what can you tell us about Dina's death?" Emma asked.

"Who is Dina?" Masella asked the question, but his facial expression didn't show any confusion.

"That would be Dina Sandri. She has two brothers who are priests," Michael explained slowly, as if to a child. "Coincidentally, Dina was Ms. Bradford's maid at the Excelsior. Did I use the word coincidently? Funny thing—I don't believe in coincidence. We're relatively sure it was Dina who gave someone, perhaps her brother, the key to Emma's room and he tried to break in."

"And you believe I did all this?"

"I know you weren't the one driving the car that sped toward us on the Via Veneto last night. I'm equally sure you didn't personally make the call ordering Dina to break into Ms. Bradford's room. Your goons did it for you."

"That's preposterous."

"Is it? Those are personal issues. Let's widen the scope. I'd bet my life you're the driving force behind the pope's announcement on Wednesday, and it's equally probable you're leading the charge to block his efforts to convene Vatican III."

"I would be careful about gambling your life on suppositions, Mr. Kelsey," Masella said coldly. "It would not be a wise wager."

"It that a threat?"

Masella smirked. "Your choice of words, not mine."

Michael looked at Giotto. The monsignor's eyes were wide and, in spite of the cool church, he was perspiring. "You seem surprised by what we've been saying, Monsignor," he said.

"Come to think of it, why did you come here with Monsignor Cipriano?" Emma asked Giotto. "It's apparent you're not bosom buddies. I've been told you have diverse philosophies."

Giotto spoke boldly, but he looked confused and conflicted. "I agreed to come with Masella in order to correct your misconceptions."

"And yet, ironically, your efforts have made us even more determined to find out what's really going on and report the truth," Emma asserted. "I don't know about Michael, but with everything you say, I'm convinced we're on the right track. In essence, you and Masella have confirmed our suspicions, Monsignor Tomai."

Giotto looked down, but Masella stared directly at Emma, his eyes like cold steel. "Let me make it clear so there are no misunderstandings between us, Ms. Bradford. My purpose in coming here was to offer valid explanations for your concerns, to answer your questions. Instead of accepting my words, you have chosen to refute everything I say, so I shall no longer waste my time. However, let me make it perfectly clear. If you continue to pursue this non-story, there will be consequences."

Scowling, Michael moved closer to the monsignor. "That sounds like a threat."

Masella didn't back down. "Consider it a warning from a friend," he said. "I guarantee the consequences of your actions will be far-reaching. I cannot allow you to damage the church with your ludicrous accusations."

"There's something in your tone which says you're about to give us some unsolicited advice," Emma said.

"It is not advice—call it a strong recommendation. If I were you, I would look both ways when crossing the street, and be very careful when walking along the deserted Excelsior hallways."

"That's not a recommendation, it's another threat," Emma said angrily.

Masella smirked. "You are wrong, Ms. Bradford. I am merely saying it would be difficult for you to mislead me. You asked if I think you are stupid. Do you believe I am? Let me give you several reasons why you should heed my warning. You assume your friends who are observing our conversation would be available to assist you should the need arise. They are neutralized."

He pointed to several brawny men positioned in strategic places near Steven, James, and Sante. "Ah, I see Monsignor Laurent." Masella grinned and waved toward the place where Steven was kneeling. "If your friend failed to notice my friendly greeting, please give him and his fellow priest, James McDonald, over there in the blue shirt, my regards. I know you and Steven are old friends, Mr. Kelsey. Is the fact you are a 'fallen Catholic,' as you say, the reason you left San Clemente before Mass began?"

He turned to Emma. "And Ms. Bradford, did you enjoy dinner last night at Taverna Angelica after your meeting with Cardinal Remella? Perhaps you have yet to hear, though I would be surprised since the Vatican gossips were active today. It seems our beloved cardinal had a mini-stroke after returning home from the restaurant last night. At this point his prognosis for a full recovery is excellent, though the doctors still worry that he might suffer a second stroke which could kill him."

This time Emma didn't try to conceal her shock. "Cardinal Remella had a stroke?"

"Sadly he did. I could give you more reasons to heed my warnings, but I believe I have made my point. Report on Bernini, Ms. Bradford—nothing more. If you continue to interfere where you have no business, I will be unable to guarantee your safety." He glared, and without further comment, turned and walked out of the church with Giotto trailing close behind.

Oh my God!" Emma exclaimed when Masella and his crew had exited the church.

Michael took her arm. "Do you want to sit down?"

"No. I'll be fine. Do you think all of Masella's men are out of here?"

"It looks like it, but who knows. The man obviously has eyes everywhere."

Michael motioned for Steven, James, and Sante to join them. "What was that all about?" Steven asked. "You're clearly upset."

"More shocked than upset," Emma said. "Let's get out of here and find a place to talk. Masella may have left some of his spies around. I don't want to be overheard."

"Spies? What do you mean?"

"Not now, Steven," Emma said. "We'll tell you everything when we get outside. Bring Sante."

"Shall I bring my friend, Colombo?" Sante asked.

"Of course, if you trust him."

They left the church and found an empty corner table on the edge of the Gelato stand. Sante introduced Colombo, who shook hands with everyone in the group. When they were all seated, Michael and Emma filled everyone in on the conversation in Saint Agnes.

"How could the monsignor know all that?" Steven said when Emma finished her account.

"I've asked myself the same question dozens of times over the past fifteen minutes," Michael said.

"Could Giro be one of Masella's men?" James asked.

Emma shook her head. "There's no way. I'm not basing my opinion on fact, only a gut feeling, but I trust Giro."

"I agree with James," Michael said. "Gut feeling or not, it makes sense. Besides knowing our schedule and listening to what we've been talking about during the drives to and from the shoots, Giro was complicit in our scheme to throw off the men who were following us."

"I still don't buy it."

"Then if not Giro, who?" Michael asked.

Emma thought for a moment. "What about Lucio? I could more easily picture him as Masella's spy. He has liberal leanings. He's also angry because he had to leave the seminary in order to get married, so he would likely support a pope who promises change."

"How could Lucio know you're trying to expose Masella?" James asked.

Michael turned to James. "For one thing, he and Giro are friends. They're together when they wait for us to finish shooting. It would be natural for them to talk. If Lucio probes and Giro thinks they're making conversation, there's no reason for him to be anything but honest."

"What about Vezio, Helen and Ron's driver?" Emma asked. "He knew we were shooting today at the Four Rivers Fountain."

"I don't think he's the problem," Michael said. "I've only seen him from a distance. He's shown no interest in either of us. Have you spoken with him, Emma?"

"Only to say hello, goodbye, or give him a message from Helen." Emma paused. "So we're back to Lucio. Steven, can you connect him to Masella or to Dina's family?"

"I'll give it my best shot."

"What about Cardinal Amici?" James asked. "I'm sure he's alive because Masella can't figure out a way to kill him and make it look like he died of natural causes."

"Which brings me to Cardinal Remella," Michael said. "Masella as much as said back off or he'll suffer another stroke."

"I know Elio Mantia, the cardinal's secretary," said James. "I'll give him a call and see what I can find out."

From the first moments of the call, it was clear that James wasn't talking to Elio. The conversation was short and formal, not the way two acquaintances would communicate. "Is there a problem?" Steven asked when James hung up.

"You probably figured out I wasn't speaking with Elio. Supposedly he's at the cardinal's bedside."

"Oh Lord!" Emma exclaimed. "Did Cardinal Remella have another stroke? I heard you ask if the cardinal is expected to pull through. What were you told?"

"The exact words were: 'That all depends on you and your friends.'"

"That's it?"

"Yes. Whoever was speaking made the threat and hung up."

"So what do we do now?" Michael asked. "I'm open to any and all suggestions."

Steven shrugged. "I have no idea, but we'd better think before we act. Now Cardinal Remella's life could depend on whatever decision we make. Unfortunately, we're going to have to solve this problem ourselves. We can't bring anyone else into the mix."

"I agree," James said. "We have no idea who we can or can't trust."

"So all by ourselves we have to rescue two cardinals," Emma said skeptically.

Michael shook his head. "Not just two cardinals. You're forgetting something. The pontiff is in as much if not more danger than Cardinal Amici and Cardinal Remella. We're facing a daunting task."

"I repeat—what do we do?" Emma said. "Should we forget the story?"

"No way!" James and Michael said in unison.

"Okay, if we're running with the story, do any of you have a plan?"

"Not specifically," Steven said. "First, James I will see if there's a connection between Masella and Lucio."

"And while you're at it, see if you can connect Masella to a man named Gusto Baldi," Michael said. "He's the head of security at the Excelsior."

"You think he's Masella's man at the hotel?"

"I don't know, but it's definitely possible."

"When should we get together again?" Emma asked.

"You know, I'd feel better if we all stayed together," Michael said. "We can stay in Emma's suite."

Steven grinned. "Oh good! We'll have an old-fashioned slumber party."

"Be serious, will you?" Michael said. "Masella knows we're friends, which puts you and James in danger. Piero's dead—"

"I know, I know, but James and I can take care of ourselves, and, unlike Piero, we're not directly involved in the struggle between Masella and Cardinal Amici."

Michael put his hand on Steven's shoulder. "You're wrong, my friend. You *are* involved and Masella knows it. You were right about someone following you. It had to be one of Masella's minions. You're clearly in danger."

"I agree," Emma said. "Remember, Masella identified all of you when we were in Saint Agnes, and speaking of that less than pleasant meeting, what do you think Monsignor Tomai knows?"

"If he knows much, he's a hell of an actor," Michael said. "He seemed genuinely surprised by what we had to say about Masella."

"I still think we should try to find out what role he's playing in all this," Emma said. "Could Masella rather than the pope have made the appointment? Could Monsignor Tomai think what Masella's doing, despite the means he's using to achieve his goals, is right for the church?"

"We'll try to find answers to your questions," Steven said. "Hopefully we'll have news later today." Steven frowned. "And though I hate to admit it, you may be right about staying together."

"Really? You think I'm right?" Michael jested.

"Don't push it, my friend. James and I will go back to our apartments, get what we need for our slumber party, and meet you at the Excelsior. Are you headed back now?"

"We have one more segment to shoot," Emma said. "We should back by 2:30. Will you be okay until then?"

"We'll be fine," said James. "It's broad daylight, and Sante and Colombo will be with us."

"Don't worry about them," Sante said. "We'll get them to the hotel safely before we return to the Vatican."

Michael slapped Sante on the back. "I have another brilliant idea. Why don't you and Colombo stay at the Excelsior so you'll be close by if, God forbid, we should need you?"

Colombo shook his head. "Your hotel is much too expensive for a man on a policeman's salary, Mr. Kelsey."

"That's not an issue. I have a room I don't use. Since the attempted break-in, I've been sleeping on the couch in Emma's sitting room. I'm not offering because I'm a nice guy and want you to have a couple of luxurious nights." He paused and grinned. "Well, maybe I am, but, seriously, I'm worried about you as much as I am Steven and James. Clearly Masella knows you're working with us. It's not safe for you to go back to the Vatican."

"Then we're all in agreement," said James. "Accompanied by Sante and Colombo, Steven and I will go to our apartments, pack up, and meet you at the hotel at 2:30. Call us if you're going be late."

"Should we try to be secretive about what we're doing or where we're going?" Sante asked.

"I don't see a need for secrecy," Michael said. "Despite our best efforts, Masella knew pretty much everything we'd been doing. And remember, he identified all of you at Saint Agnes. I'm sure we've all been under surveillance. Why bother?"

"Michael's right," Steven said. "No more hide and seek. However, I think it's a good idea if we travel in pairs, and let's agree to stay out in the open as much as possible. No more walking down the back streets to avoid being seen. If we're visible, we're less vulnerable."

"Good thinking." Michael said. He looked from person to person. "Thanks, all of you. We appreciate your help and support."

"Haven't I always had your back, old buddy?" Steven said.

"That's debatable."

Steven started to protest, but Michael cut him off. "I'm kidding. Of course you have. We'll see you in a while, hopefully with pertinent information."

"Promise to be careful," Emma said. "Masella's dangerous."

Steven nodded. "We know. Go do your thing and don't worry about us."

CHAPTER TWENTY-FIVE

"How are you?" Michael asked as they walked toward the Neptune Fountain.

"I think I'm okay, but in my wildest dreams, I never expected Masella to show up in person. Pretty brazen, don't you think?"

"I could say the same thing about you. I'm sure the meeting turned out the way it did because we both dug in our heels and looked Masella directly in the eye. We wouldn't back off and negotiate, so the monsignor had no choice but to spit out idle threats."

"What if they aren't idle threats? We may have overplayed our hand by revealing what we know."

"I don't think we did. Masella knew what we had on him long before the meeting. At least everything's out in the open, but whether or not he realizes we can't prove our accusations is another story."

When they reached the fountain, Helen seemed impatient to begin. "Did you finish the Elephant Obelisk copy?" she asked without a preliminary greeting.

Emma looked at Michael. "Oh my God! With everything that's happened over the past hour, I forgot to call Nicola. I can't do the segment without talking with her first."

Helen's irritation showed both on her face and in her tone. "I thought you had your notes with you," she said. "What kept you from finishing your report?"

Michael made an instant decision. He looked at Emma for approval. Knowing what he was thinking, she nodded and he turned to Helen. "Emma's failure to complete the Elephant Obelisk copy has to do with story real story we're pursuing, Helen. I guarantee, what happened over the last hour and what we've discovered over the past few days is more significant than these mundane Bernini segments. When you hear the particulars, you won't be disappointed in Emma. You'll be excited."

"Michael's right," Emma said. "I'm not exaggerating when I tell you what we're investigating has the potential to be the story of the decade. We don't have all the facts. That's why we've played it close to the vest until now. When we fill you in, it's vital that our discussion stays among the six of us. No hints to New York or Boston until we give you the go-ahead, and no talking between yourselves in front of anyone, especially Lucio."

The journalist in Helen quickly emerged, her irritation giving way to curiosity. "Tell me what you're talking about," she demanded. "No excuses, no more procrastinating. I want to know about this huge story right now."

"'Interesting' isn't the right word," Michael said. "'Fascinating' is a better way to put it, maybe 'frighteningly fascinating.'"

"I think 'shocking' is a better term to describe what's going on in the Holy See," Emma said, "but however you choose to explain what's happening in the Vatican, when we break the story it will definitely have worldwide repercussions."

"Let's take a walk." Michael took hold of Helen's arm. When Emma started to follow, he shook his head. "Maybe you should stay back and work on your copy."

Understanding Michael wanted alone-time with Helen, Emma nodded. "Good idea," she said. "I'll plan the camera shots with Ron."

"We've hesitated to say anything for two reasons," Michael said as he and Helen walked away from the fountain. "First, until noon today, we were only pursuing a theory. To some extent we still are, but the pieces of the puzzle are falling into place. We now know what we believed to be true actually is, through proving it may not be easy."

"And the second reason?"

"A primary rationale for our silence is concern for you and the crew. We were afraid that, by making you a part of our investigation, we'd be putting you in danger. The only reason we decided to share the information today is because you won't let it go. And if you start an independent investigation, you could cause problems for all of us."

"I'd be stepping on your toes and alerting people you don't want to know what you're investigating."

"They already know what we're doing, but not where we are in the process. So would you be willing to postpone our conversation with my *assurance* that we'll answer all of your questions in good time, just not here and now? It's not safe."

"What do you mean, it's not safe?" Helen motioned to the area around them. "We're standing in a public square in the heart of Rome."

"Look at the people within earshot. I'm sure one of these innocent tourists works for Monsignor Masella Cipriano."

"Pope John's private secretary? Why's that significant?"

"It's more than significant. It's key to what Emma and I will tell you later today. All I can do right now is reiterate what Emma said earlier. From now on, anything we discuss, whether it seems trivial or not, is said in private and stays strictly among you, Emma, me, Ron, Bill, and David. Again, don't say anything about what we tell you in front of Lucio."

Helen frowned. "If I didn't know you better, I'd believe you've lost it. Lucio? You don't trust a man who was randomly hired to drive you around Rome?"

"If Lucio was driving me around by chance, he isn't anymore. Emma and I don't have concrete proof, but we're reasonably sure he works for or is in some way associated with Monsignor Cipriano. Later this afternoon, we'll be able to confirm or reject our premise."

"I certainly hope so," Helen said. "This new investigation of yours is beginning to interfere with what we were sent to Rome to do."

"Then I suggest we film Bernini's elephant," Michael said, smiling. "When we're finished, ask Vezio to drive you and Ron to the truck and then to the Quattro Fontane. Giro will drive us directly to the Excelsior."

"You can't believe Giro's involved too?"

"We don't think he is, but for the moment everyone's suspect. After the shoot, Emma and I will be meeting with our Vatican sources."

"The man you went to meet after you left the Four Rivers Fountain."

"Him and a fellow priest, along with two Vatican policemen. Hopefully they'll have learned more about Lucio since our last conversation. You, Ron, Bill, and David come to Emma's suite at four?"

"This sounds like the plot of a bad mystery novel. I've been doing this for a long time, and here's what I think. Whatever it is you're pursuing, you and Emma realize you're in way over your heads. You've kept quiet, not because you're afraid for our safety, but because you figured I'd quickly bring this investigation to a close."

"I assure you, the possibility never crossed my mind, and I'm being truthful when I tell you this is neither the time nor the place for further discussion. So could you please exercise some patience and wait until we get together this afternoon?"

"More than once, you and Emma used me in your cat-and-mouse games so you could meet secretly with your friend. Are Ron, Bill, David, and I supposed to play the same game when we come to meet with you at the Excelsior this afternoon?"

"Ironically, there's no need for game-playing anymore, and nor was there at that point, though we didn't know it at the time. Despite our efforts, we were unable to keep Masella from discovering our plans. He knew where we were and who we were seeing. Everything's out in the open now, so there's no need to hide. That said, I suggest you come as a group."

"Is that your subtle way of saying it's dangerous to come alone?"

"Not necessarily. I'm hoping Masella will think we're getting together for a production meeting."

"To what purpose? To plan for our final Bernini shots? If, as you say, the monsignor is keeping tabs on you and Emma, he knows you're almost finished filming the segments. As I hear myself talk, I'm increasingly anxious for all of us."

"We'll address all of your concerns at four. When you hear what we have to say, the producer and journalist in you will want to run with the story, so please be patient for a few more hours."

Helen exuded exasperation. "I suppose I have no option but to do as you ask. So, if I'm forced to abide by your time schedule, let's do as you suggest and finish the elephant shoot."

"Good decision." Michael put his arm around Helen's shoulders, and they headed back toward the Neptune Fountain.

"Don't try to make nice. I'm not happy," Helen said as they walked.

"I know—"

Helen stepped out of Michael's embrace. "And no more efforts to appease me. As soon as Bill sends the segment to New York, we'll be leaving for the Excelsior."

"We'll be waiting for you."

"Have you two worked things out?" Emma asked when Michael and Helen joined her and Ron.

"For now, but—"

"I told Helen we'd bring her up to speed later today. She graciously agreed to wait."

"I'm not sure 'gracious' is the word I'd use," Helen said irritably. "I'm sure you both know waiting's not my forte."

"Mine neither," said Emma. "In this case, though I hate to admit it, I agree with Michael. This is neither the time nor the place for a serious discussion. Thanks for understanding."

Helen frowned. "I'm not sure I do, but it seems I have no say in the matter." She turned to Ron. "Where's Bill now?"

"He's in the truck editing the Triton and Four Rivers reports. Since Giro and Vezio were unavailable, I called Lucio. He picked him up. I believe he plans to drive over to the Piazza della Minerva in case we need him later. Anyway, when I spoke with Bill a few minutes ago, he was adding in the additional footage I shot of Saint Agnes and the Nile god."

"Call him on the way to the elephant shoot, Michael said. "Tell him to stay in the truck after he's finished. Tell him you and Helen will drop off the Elephant Obelisk footage on the way back to your hotel. How much time do you estimate he'll need to edit and send it to New York?"

"I'd say about an hour."

Michael looked at Helen. "Then we have a plan. You can fill Ron in on the particulars. Right now I need to let Steven know what's going on." He took his cell phone out of his pocket, punched in the number, and waited for Steven to answer.

Steven didn't bother with the usual greeting. "This is an unexpected call," he said. "Don't tell me there's already a problem."

"Possibly, and so you know, you're on speaker phone."

"You're sure no one will overhear the conversation?"

"There's no one close enough, and we're huddled together."

"Then, talk to me."

When Michael finished telling Steven about the planned meeting, he didn't immediately respond. "You there?" Michael finally asked.

"Yeah. I was thinking, to be safe, Sante and Colombo will meet you at the Excelsior and walk you to Emma's room. Sante will remain there while Colombo picks Bill up at the truck and escorts him back to the hotel."

"Why doesn't Colombo go straight to the truck from his apartment?" Michael asked. "There's no need for both him and Sante to meet us at the Excelsior."

"Did you not hear me, my friend? Sante and Colombo will wait for Giro to drop you outside the hotel. Both of them will walk with you to Emma's room. If we're all finished about the same time, James and I will be with them. If not, we'll be along soon."

"Come on," Michael said. "Two escorts? Or possibly four, if you and James show up? Isn't that overkill? You can't be concerned about an attack on us in a public hotel hallway, or have you forgotten I'm a big, strong football jock?"

Steven laughed. "I try to put it out of my mind, and as for being concerned, if I recall, you had a rather frightening experience on the Via Veneto last night. Under normal circumstances, I wouldn't have given your quick trip to the ATM machine a second thought. Get the picture?"

"Perfectly."

"And maybe you've forgotten Masella's threat during your meeting in Saint Agnes. Didn't you say he specifically referenced the long, deserted hallways at the Excelsior?"

"He did, but—"

"But nothing. Let me give you one more cause for caution. Weren't you the one who asked me to do a background search on Gusto to see if there was a connection between him and Masella? So the monsignor's veiled threat and his possible connection to the head of hotel security must have concerned you too."

"I get the point."

"I thought you might," Steven said smugly.

"I've heard enough. See you in a while."

"You didn't say anything about a frightening occurrence on the Via Veneto last night," Helen said when Michael put the phone in his pocket. "Nor did you mention veiled threats Masella made toward you and Emma."

"Look around, Helen. There are ears everywhere and we're no longer huddled together. I was taking a chance putting Steven on speaker phone. You agreed to trust me."

"I know, but the more I hear, the harder it is for me to wait."

"Unfortunately, in this instance, you'll have to be patient."

"But it's so damn frustrating." Helen glared at Emma. "I'm inclined to forget the elephant shoot, and, as your boss, compel you to go to the hotel so we can talk. However, I suppose we should stick with the original plan. So it's your turn to make a call. If you can't reach Nicola, you won't have the information to do the report from the Piazza della Minerva."

"Failing to reach Nicola doesn't mean I can't do the segment. That was an excuse. What I say won't be quite as interesting, that's all. I need her to wow the audience once again."

Emma dialed the number. "Come on," she said under her breath as the phone rang for the fourth time. She sighed when Nicola finally picked up. "I'm glad you answered. Hang on a minute." Emma put her hand over the phone. "She's there. Helen, you and Ron go on, and we'll meet you at the obelisk in fifteen minutes."

"We're on our way," Helen said. "The faster we finish this segment, the closer we are to hearing about the really important story."

"And remember, don't say anything to anyone," Michael warned.

"You got it. Mum's the word."

Seeing Ron's puzzled look, Helen shrugged. "You'll know what's going on when I do. For now it seems our assignment is to keep our mouths shut."

While Michael waited, Emma sat on a bench near the fountain and took notes. "I take it you have what you need," he said as she stood up and closed her notebook.

"Everything came back to me. I only needed to be sure of the names of the artist who interpreted Bernini's design and the Dominican friar who was on Bernini's shit list."

"Excuse me?"

Emma laughed at Michael's puzzled expression. "As you told Helen, all will be become clear in due time."

CHAPTER TWENTY-SIX

W hen Giro dropped them at the Piazza della Minerva. Lucio was standing with Vezio beside the cars. "Helen and Ron are waiting by Bernini's chick," he said.

"Thanks," Emma said, wondering if they were off base thinking Lucio could be reporting to Masella.

They walked the short distance to the obelisk. "If you're ready, let's get this over with," Helen said as Emma and Michael approached. "It seems we have more important matters to discuss."

"Any particular place you'd like to stand?" Ron asked as Helen touched up Emma's makeup.

"Since you asked, I suggest we start with a long-distance view of the elephant so the audience sees entire the obelisk as well as the animal's body. Once I've mentioned the part about the elephant being designed to hold the pillar, move in so only that the sculpture and I are in the frame. Maybe it helps to know I won't be mentioning the obelisk again."

"It does."

"After a few general statements about Bernini's commission, etc., I'm going to talk about the animal's rear end. When I do, I'll move around to the back. Go with me. I'm also planning to mention the building directly behind the animal's butt. Bernini was making a political statement by placing the elephant the way he did, so you'll want to take a picture of the sculpture as it's positioned with the building in the background. Also, in my first few sentences I'm going to mention Santa Maria Sopra Minerva. Should you take a picture before I begin?"

"No. When you mention the church, I'll take the shot. Want to do a preliminary run-through?"

"It's not necessary."

"Then I'll film your first effort. We'll do the whole thing again if you're not happy with the results."

"Sounds good." Emma approached the elephant. She moved around until Ron was satisfied with the shot, and he gave her a signal to begin.

This is Emma Bradford, reporting from Rome. I'm standing just behind the pantheon in the Piazza della Minerva, directly in front of the only Gothic church in Rome. Santa Maria Sopra Minerva was so named because it was built on the foundations of a temple dedicated to Minerva, the Roman goddess of wisdom.

Emma talked about the church before moving on to Bernini's chick.

Though the church is interesting and worth visiting, the focal point of the Piazza della Minerva is an endearing sculpture of a cheery baby elephant carrying a small, sixth-century Egyptian obelisk on its back. The pillar was found in the ruins of a temple dedicated to the goddess Isis which once stood nearby. Pope Alexander the Seventh asked Bernini to design something to support the obelisk. The result is typical of Bernini's endless imagination. The artist originally intended for the sculpture, which the Italians affectionately call Pulcino della Minerva, or Minerva's Little Chick, to be a joke, a tongue-in-cheek reference to the Carthaginian leader Hannibal's war elephants that, in 218 BC, carried tall siege towers across the Alps to attack the Roman Empire.

Emma then related the story of Bernini and his Dominican nemesis. She ended:

The elephant's position was Bernini's final salute and last word on the feud. It's mine too. This is Emma Bradford, saying goodbye for now from Rome.

"That's a great story," Michael said.

"I thought the same thing when Nicola first told me about Bernini and Father Paglia." She turned to Ron. "Did you get a good shot of the friar's window?"

"Not while you were reporting. I focused on the elephant's tail. I'll do it right now."

"Good. Then if you think we're done here, we're heading back to the hotel. We'll see you all at four."

Helen nodded. "We'll definitely be on time."

Giro was talking with Lucio and Vezio when Emma and Michael arrived at the car. "I didn't expect you back so soon," Giro said as he opened the back door for Emma to slide in.

"The shoot went well," Emma said. She turned to Vezio. "Helen and Ron will be here as soon as they finish packing up the equipment."

"Then you don't need me this afternoon?" Lucio asked.

"No," Michael said. "I'll go back to the hotel with Emma."

"Any idea where Helen and Ron want to go?" Vezio asked.

"Helen said they'll be dropping off the disk at the truck before going to the Quattro Fontane. Michael and I won't need Giro and Lucio again today, so I assume they'll give you the afternoon off as well. I do know they'll need you early in the morning. We're shooting inside Saint Peter's at seven."

Emma wasn't sure, but she thought she saw a change in Lucio's facial expression when she mentioned the plans for the morning. The question she had about Lucio's involvement with Masella was quickly answered. *There's something going on,* she mused as she slid into the backseat of Giro's car, *and Lucio knows what it is.*

Lucio and Vezio were still standing by the cars when Giro pulled away from the Piazza della Minerva. Michael immediately flipped open his phone and punched in Steven's number. "Tell me what you know," he said. "Yeah, hello to you too. We're on our way."

For the next five minutes, Michael listened. The extent of his response was an occasional "I see" or "okay." The conversation ended with a terse "we'll be there shortly."

"Steven must have had something interesting to say to keep you quiet for so long," Emma said.

"I'll ignore your insult this time because, actually, he was full of news. He discovered our friend Lucio attended seminary with Masella, and—are you ready for this?"

"I don't know, am I?"

"Here it comes."

"Michael!"

"Okay, okay. Lucio is married to Masella's sister."

"You're kidding," Emma said, a look of disbelief on her face. "When Lucio drove us to Dal Bolognese, he told us he left the seminary to get married. To Masella's sister? No wonder he feels so strongly about the celibacy issue and the right of priests to marry. Why didn't he tell us?"

"I don't mean to interrupt," Giro said, "and I don't want you to think I intentionally listen to what you say, but I could have told you that. I know a lot about Lucio."

"In that case, I'm asking," said Emma. "Are you and Lucio close friends? More than once he referred to you as my 'good friend Giro.'"

"We're not *good* friends, but we worked together a few times before driving you and Michael. While you were filming, we had time to talk. He told me about his private life."

"Care to share?" Michael asked. "I wouldn't ask you to violate a trust."

Giro laughed. "Our talks were not bound by the seal of the confessional, and Lucio didn't ask me keep quiet."

"Okay," Michael said. "Are you privy to information about Lucio's relationship with his brother-in-law?"

"He mentioned Masella once or twice. I think they are good friends. I know that Masella used to eat at Lucio's home once or twice a week, but I guess he hasn't been around much lately."

"Do they share the same political philosophy? What I mean is, do you think Lucio is a radical liberal?"

"Lucio is very liberal. He doesn't like the rule that keeps him from being both a priest and a father. He said if priests are told they can marry, he will stop teaching and go back to the seminary."

"You think he still wants to be a priest?" Emma asked.

"He said he wants to be the first married Catholic man to be ordained, so I guess so. With Masella's help, he might be. I don't know if he was just talking, but I think he expects the pope to do away with celibacy very soon." Giro paused. "May I ask you a question?"

"Of course," Emma said. "Ask away."

"Do you have a problem with Lucio?"

Emma looked at Michael. "Might as well tell him," he said.

"We don't know anything for sure, but it's possible Lucio has been reporting our schedule and activities to Masella."

"And you believe I've been giving him the information? I promise you—"

Michael shook his head. "We're not accusing you of anything, Giro. We assumed you and Lucio talked, but you did nothing improper. How could you have known Lucio was reporting to Masella, if that's what he's been doing? We began to suspect Lucio when we met Masella at Saint Agnes in Agony today at noon. Someone had to tell the monsignor we were filming in the vicinity."

"Masella came to the church to see you?"

"You seem surprised," Emma said.

"I am. Monsignor Cipriano is a powerful man. Why didn't he have you come to him?"

"The thought crossed my mind," Emma said. "When I turned around and stared into Masella's eyes, I was more than a little surprised."

"Back to Lucio for a minute," Michael said. "During your conversations, did you happen to mention our Quattro

Fontane caper? Our methods to ditch the men following us probably made for an amusing story. You might have said something during one of your seemingly meaningless conversations."

"I did. I'm sorry." Giro looked miserable as he continued. "Lucio asked so many questions, and I didn't think. . ."

Emma reached forward and patted Giro on the shoulder. "Of course you didn't. Why would you consider you were doing anything but making polite conversation to pass the time?"

"Did I say something to put you and Mr. Kelsey in danger?"

"It wasn't your conversation with Lucio that caused our problems," Michael said.

"Then you do have problems with the monsignor," said Giro.

"Sufficed to say Masella is not pleased with us, but as Emma said, there's no way it's your fault. The monsignor finally realized we know a great deal about him and even more about his plans, but he didn't hear about any of this from Lucio. The only information the monsignor might have gotten from him was our schedule, so please don't worry. Can you remember anything else about your conversations?"

"Not much, but I remember Lucio was interested in what you were doing every day. He asked a lot of questions like: What time are they leaving the hotel? Are you driving them to a restaurant this evening? Which one? What time is their reservation? When are you picking them up to go back to the hotel?" Giro shook his head. "I thought he wanted to know so he could plan his schedule."

"That a fair assumption," Emma said.

"Then you're not angry with me for having, as you Americans say, loose lips?"

Emma laughed. "Absolutely not. We appreciate your openness and honesty." She turned to Michael. "What else did Steven say? Was he able to find a connection between Gusto and Masella?"

"Not directly, but interestingly, Gusto's brother is a member of the Vatican police force."

"Wow. Another coincidence."

"You heard what I told Masella," Michael said. "I don't believe in coincidence."

"We should ask Sante if he knows anything about him," Emma said.

"Steven already called. The phone went to voicemail. He probably went to his apartment to pick up what he needs for our slumber party. I'm sure he'll call back when he gets the message."

"What about Dina? Did Steven say anything about her?" Emma asked.

"Her older brother, the one who's currently assigned to the church in Florence, also attended seminary with Masella, so it's likely he knows Lucio too."

"The more you talk, the more I believe the push for radical change isn't just political for Masella," Emma said. "It's personal. I find it interesting that everyone in this drama so far is connected in some way, though we still don't know why Dina was killed. If her brothers are members of Masella's liberal—"

Michael interrupted. "That wasn't what Steven said. He told us the older brother went to seminary with Masella. He's not part of the monsignor's inner circle, which makes me wonder if he's involved with one of the conservative fringe groups. I'm sure Steven and Sante are looking into it."

"You said you won't need me again tonight," Giro said as they turned onto the Via Veneto.

"I don't think we will," Emma said, "but in case our plans change, don't turn off your cell."

"I'm always standing by. I hope you can trust me. I didn't mean to be disloyal."

"We know," Emma said, "and you weren't disloyal. We never asked you to keep secrets, especially not from Lucio."

"From here on out, I'll keep quiet, so please call if you want the car."

"We will. Thanks," said Emma.

When Giro pulled into the circular drive in front of the hotel, another of the ever-present black cars was parked on the street to the right of the driveway exit.

"This really pisses me off," Michael snarled. He yanked open the door, jumped out, and raced toward the idling vehicle.

"I'm right behind you!" Giro yelled and he leaped out of the front seat.

"Michael! No!" Emma yelled. "We know these people are dangerous." She opened the back door and go out to take a closer look at what was happening.

Still running, Michael looked back. "Go inside, Emma" he yelled.

For some inexplicable reason, Emma was anxious as she shut the Mercedes door, but unlike the previous episodes when Michael had run off without concern for his safety, this was different. Though she couldn't figure out what it was, there was something strange about the scenario unfolding in front of her. The driver of the black car wasn't speeding away. He seemed to be baiting Michael, waiting for him to come closer.

Focusing intently on the goings-on at the curb, Emma paid little attention to a black stretch limo that pulled up close to Giro's idling Mercedes. She gave the driver a momentary glance, assuming he was merely dropping off his passenger, and closed Giro's door so it wouldn't be nicked.

As Michael neared the car at the curb, the back door of the limo opened, blocking Emma's access to the street, so she turned back to go behind the two cars. As she craned her neck to see what was happening with Michael, two men leapt out of the backseat of the limo and moved toward her.

In an instant, Emma realized something significant was happening, and it wasn't good. She willed her feet to move, but they seemed to be glued to the pavement. Despite her desire to remove herself from harm's way, they wouldn't take away her from the impending danger.

Blood pounded in her temples, and her heart beat rapidly in her chest as one of the men grasped her arm and dragged her toward the still-open back door of the limo. He tugged her behind him into the backseat as the second man forcibly shoved her toward the middle. He then jumped in, sandwiching her tightly in the middle between them.

At that moment Emma knew only one thing for certain: she was in trouble. "Michael!" she screamed just as the door closed.

At the sound of Emma's cry, Michael whirled around. "Oh my God! Emma!" he yelled.

It took a few long seconds before he fully realized what was happening. He turned away from his objective and raced toward the now-moving limo. Instead of slowing down, the driver of the car gunned the engine and headed straight for him, forcing him to jump back onto the curb. Tires screeched as the limo shot forward onto the Via Veneto. Weaving in and out of traffic, it sped away with the decoy car following close behind.

Michael raced back toward the sidewalk, but the two cars had disappeared in the distance. He bent over at the waist, his head in his hands. "Emma. Oh My God," he cried out.

All of a sudden, his phone vibrated. He pulled it out of his pocket and looked at the caller ID. With a mixture of fear and excitement, he answered. "Emma," he said breathlessly. "What's going on? Tell me you're okay."

It wasn't Emma's on the other end of the line. A man with a deep voice responded: "She is for now. If you want her to stay that way, you had better listed to me. If you continue with your investigation, you will regret your decision."

"Let me talk to her," Michael pleaded, but the line went dead.

Michael froze. Staring at the traffic passing by the hotel, he tried to think, but to no avail; his mind went blank.

The blaring horn of a taxi exiting the circle jolted Michael back to reality. Giro grabbed his arm and pulled him onto the curb. Struggling to assuage his own fears and make sense of what happened, he turned to see Giro's pale face. "What do we do now?" he pleaded.

Before Giro could respond, a familiar voice came from the direction of the street. "What do you mean, what do we do now?"

Michael turned around as Steven, James, and Sante approached. "Sorry Sante wasn't waiting when you arrived," Steven said. "We were all ready at the same time, so we shared a cab. Per my instructions, I assumed you'd wait in the lobby until Sante got here."

Steven saw the panic on Michael's face. "For God's sake, what's the matter, man?" He looked around. "Where's Emma?"

Michael inhaled deeply and exhaled as he spoke. "Masella has her."

Steven grabbed Michael's arm. "What do you mean, Masella has her?"

"You heard me. Masella's men took Emma less than a minute ago."

Michael began to pace up and down on the driveway in front of the revolving door. His thoughts were jumbled and his mind was reeling. "Emma's been kidnapped, and it's my fault," he said, anguish in his voice. "Masella knew I'd act like an ass, and I didn't disappoint him. When we got back to the hotel, one of his men was sitting in a car right over there." He pointed to the curb. "Like an idiot, I reacted without thinking. I left Emma in the car and raced over to confront the driver—"

"And when you did, someone grabbed her?"

"That's right." Michael struggled to organize his thoughts. "Masella banked on my need to confront his men."

"It's not your fault. It's mine," Giro said, his voice vibrating, and a look of horror on his face. "Why did I leave Emma to go after you?"

"Neither of us had any idea our actions were putting Emma in danger, Giro. We were parked in front of the hotel in a well-lit area. Who in his right mind—?"

"Exactly," said James. "None of us thought Masella could be this brazen."

"But we should have," Michael said frantically. "So again—what now? I can't imagine the outcome if we don't come up with a plan."

Steven frowned. "I wish I had the answer to your question, but getting worked up to the point where we can't think straight won't help Emma. Let's go upstairs and figure out a plan of action. It's possible Masella will try to contact you with his demands."

"If it helps at all, I don't think the monsignor plans to kill Emma," Sante said. "He would have too much trouble explaining the kidnapping and murder of an ABC journalist."

James nodded. "I agree with Sante. Masella's not naïve. He has to realize you've told Steven and me everything. He wouldn't try to eliminate all of us."

"Don't be so sure," Michael said grimly. "We never imagined he'd make an attempt on our lives last night, and we never dreamed he'd kidnap Emma in broad daylight."

"I hear you," Steven said, "but I really think you're giving Masella too much credit. He might be able to kidnap one woman, but even a man with a gigantic ego like his couldn't think he'd be able to pull off mass murder and get away with it. I believe Emma's okay, at least for the moment."

"And I'm equally sure she's not the target," James added, trying to sound calm for Michael's sake.

"So if she's not the target, then why did Masella grab her?"

"She's the bait," Steven said. "She's the means to an end, though at this point I'm not sure what that means. Our immediate objective is to make some sense of this, so let's go upstairs and try to figure out what to do next."

Giro had a somber look on his face. "If only—"

"No 'if onlys,' I'll say this one more time, Giro. What happened to Emma isn't your fault. We both had a momentary lapse in judgment."

"If anything happens to her, I won't forgive myself."

"We won't let anything happen to Emma," said Steven.

"Shall I wait here in case you need the car?" Giro asked. "Please let me help."

"I have a better idea," Michael said, seeing the anguish on Giro's face. "Have the valet park the car and join us upstairs. You might be able to provide some much-needed insight. Maybe you'll remember something significant that Lucio said. Emma was sure he reacted when she mentioned tomorrow's schedule."

"You think Lucio knew about the plan to kidnap Emma?" Steven asked. "I find that hard to believe."

"I don't know, but it's certainly possible. So come on, Giro. We could use your input."

Giro sighed. "Thank you, Michael. I want to help any way I can."

"Then take care of the car. We'll wait for you in the foyer."

"Oh God!" Michael said when they pushed through the door. "I insisted Emma bring her key with her this morning. It's in her purse."

"I'm sure you can get another one," James said. "Come on. I'll go with you."

"The girl at the desk, I think her name is Maura, knows Emma and I work together, but I don't want all of you waiting around in the lobby while I speak with her." He handed Steven his keycard. "Go up to my room and wait for me to call. Then come upstairs to Emma's room—suite 4201."

"We're not in imminent danger, Michael," Steven said. "The bad guys have gone, so we don't have to hole up in your room. We'll wait for you by the elevator on the fourth floor."

"You might be more comfortable if you had a place to sit. I'm going to have a little talk with Gusto too, so I might not be right up. Our discussion may take a little while."

With a stern look in his eyes, Steven took hold of Michael's arm. "That would be unwise, my friend. In fact, it would be downright stupid. Get Emma's key. You're not going to say or do anything until we've all weighed the pros and cons of our actions. We need to get together and talk about what's best for Emma. There will be no decisions made while we're standing here in the lobby. Let's go upstairs. You can call Helen, Ron, and David while Sante calls Colombo and lets him and Bill know what happened. I want everyone in Emma's room as soon as possible. There's no need to wait until four, and no more charging ahead without thinking."

"Though I hate it, you're right. If I confront Gusto, he'll realize we know he's involved, and, if what we suspect is true, he'll get in touch with Masella. What was I thinking? If you hadn't been here being logical for both of us, I could have put Emma in even more danger."

"Like we all are, you were worried about her, so get the key and let's make a plan."

CHAPTER TWENTY-SEVEN

As the black limo weaved in and out of traffic, Emma struggled to maintain her composure. *I can't let these men see how terrified I am,* she thought as she fought back tears. Mustering all her strength, she turned to speak to the man who had pulled her into the car. "You realize you just kidnapped an American journalist," she said, her voice filled with feigned anger to hide her fear. "You made a foolhardy decision. My colleague saw what happened. Are you sure you want your actions splashed all over the ABC network and their affiliates?"

"Do you think being a reporter for an American news station makes you invulnerable, Ms. Bradford?" the burly man answered. "And as for the kidnapping allegation, you're confused."

"You're an American," Emma said. "I don't believe it. Who do you work for? Who ordered you to kidnap me?"

A nervous grin broke across the man's face. "You weren't kidnapped, Ms. Bradford. We took you from the hotel for your protection."

"My God! You're unbelievable!" Emma exclaimed. "You expect me to believe your ridiculous justification for forcing me into this car against my will? Where are you taking me?"

"You'll know soon enough."

Emma tried to play on the man's apparent discomfort. "And then what? Do you plan to kill me?"

The other side of the sandwich smirked as he spoke: "We won't harm you, Ms. Bradford; at least not now."

Emma felt tightness in her chest. *I can't let them know how scared I am,* she thought again as she spoke up. The sharpness in her tone quickly wiped the bogus grin off the man's face. "I gather 'for now' is the operative phrase," she said emphatically. "In order to stay safe, I'm going to have to behave myself. Is that what you're saying?"

"We're saying nothing of the sort," said the American. "We're doing what we were ordered to do: taking you to Monsignor Cipriano."

"Ah, there's the line I've been waiting to hear: you're following orders. That's the oldest justification for inappropriate behavior in the books." Emma's stared at him defiantly. "Nazi criminals come to mind. Ever hear of the Nuremberg trials? If I recall, every one of the defendants used that feeble excuse, but they were hanged anyway."

"I assure you—"

Emma ignored the man's attempt to justify his actions. "Why would the monsignor possibly need to see me tonight?" she asked. "We had such a pleasant and productive meeting at Saint Agnes."

"Apparently you continue to interfere into matters which are none of your business. Instead of heeding Monsignor Cipriano's warnings to stop investigating, you continued in an irresponsible manner, causing potential harm to him and the church. The monsignor said to say he will be writing your story from here on out."

"What does that mean?"

"I'm sure the monsignor will tell you."

"Do you work for Masella or his liberal cause?"

"Both, Ms. Bradford."

When the driver stopped the car at the fence separating Vatican City and Rome, the American opened the door. Before exiting, he turned back to look at Emma. "I suggest you keep quiet on the way to the basilica," he said menacingly. "Do I make myself clear?"

"It's clear you're threatening me."

"You're mistaken, but at the moment I don't have enough time to convince you. The monsignor eagerly anticipates your arrival, and, as you know, he's not a man to be kept waiting."

"If he only wants to talk, why drag me here? He could have called and made an appointment."

"Apparently his last effort to meet with you on neutral ground failed to deter you from reckless reporting. Let's go."

As she slid out of the car, Emma saw her chance. Mustering all her strength, she tried to pull away. She'd only gone a few steps when strong hands grabbed her, jerking her backwards. "Don't be a fool, Ms. Bradford," her Italian captor growled.

Emma winced as he increased the pressure on her arm, but she couldn't concede defeat. "Or what?" she asked defiantly.

"Trust me; you don't want to find out," said the American.

Emma moved on rubbery legs as they walked alongside the right colonnade toward the stairwell leading to the entrance. They weaved in and out of the downward-moving crowd toward the main door. The basilica was closing as they approached the portico. The men ushering out the last group of visitors stepped aside when Masella's men flashed their IDs.

There was an eerie silence in the church as Emma, wedged tightly between the two men, began the walk up the nave. As she looked through Bernini's magnificent baldachino toward the Cathedra Petri, bathed in light from the windows on either side, she silently prayed, *God help me be strong as I go through this.*

Suddenly she realized the irony in what she was viewing. The altar was created to symbolize the power of the pope, yet at that moment in time Pope John literally had no power. The authority of the church was in the hands of the man she was going to meet—Monsignor Masella Cipriano.

——

Twenty minutes after Emma's kidnapping, Michael, Steven, James, Sante, and Giro arrived at Emma's suite. As they approached the door, Michael noticed an envelope protruding from the crack between the two doors. He handed the keycard to Steven, grabbed the envelope, and tore it open. With feelings of anticipation and trepidation, he unfolded the paper, read, sighed, and refolded it immediately.

"That didn't take long," Steven said. "Come inside and tell us what the note said."

Michael followed the others into the room. "Okay, tell us," said James.

"The note says: 'Expect a call in thirty-minutes.'"

"Is it signed?" Steven asked.

"No, but I'm sure it's from Masella."

Sante looked puzzled. "Who could have left it here?"

"The same person who's been helping Masella from inside the hotel, Gusto Baldi, the head of hotel security. I'd like to go downstairs and kill him with my bare hands."

"If he left the note, he likely left the hotel right away," Steven said. "He wouldn't wait around to see what you're going to do next."

"He's irrelevant," said James. "He's only the messenger, not part of Masella's inner circle. We need to concentrate on Masella himself." He looked at his watch. "Let's call Helen and David and get them over here. We have twenty minutes before Masella calls. We need to start making plans."

"No need," Michael said. "We have no idea what's happening with Emma. I don't mean to be rude, but no more talking. I'll call Helen. After that, let's sit quietly and wait. Maybe the silence will help us all gather our thoughts."

"Before we begin the quiet thing, what did Helen say?" Steven asked when Michael hung up.

"She, Ron, and David are catching a cab as we speak. Depending on traffic, they'll be here in ten or fifteen minutes. Bill and Colombo will come from the truck."

Michael stood, walked to balcony door, pushed aside the sheers, and stepped outside. Lost in his own demons, he stared down at the traffic on the Via Veneto. He kept checking his watch, as the same thought raced over and over through his mind: *Let Emma be alright! Let Emma be alright!*

When the minute hand was on the appointed time, he came back into the room. "Will the phone ever ring?" he asked, fear and frustration in his voice.

Steven walked across the room and put his hand on Michael's shoulder. "It will. Masella's just playing you; he's exacerbating your fears."

Michael began to pace. He had just checked his watch again when the shrill ring of the hotel phone on the desk shattered the silence. Everything seemed to be moving in slow motion as he walked toward the sound and picked up the receiver. "What have you done with Emma?" he began.

"She's safe for now," was the gruff response.

Michael immediately recognized Masella's voice. "What you're doing makes no sense, Monsignor Cipriano. What could you possibly hope to gain by kidnapping Emma?"

Michael could picture the contemptuous grin on Masella's face as he responded. "The attention of the world and the beginning of change in the church. Ms. Bradford will be the catalyst for both of those goals."

Suddenly Michael's anger turned to fear. "What do you mean?" he asked hesitantly.

"It is quite simple. Ms. Bradford is going to kill Cardinal Amici while he celebrates Mass in the Blessed Sacrament Chapel tomorrow morning."

Michael stood stunned and speechless for fully fifteen seconds. Struggling to find the appropriate words, all he could think of to say was: "You've got to be kidding."

"I assure you, I'm not, Mr. Kelsey. At Ms. Bradford's hand, the cardinal will die, and with his death will come the demise of the conservative movement."

"You're deluded if you think you can pull this off," Michael said as he struggled to remain calm and rational. "If the cardinal dies, another conservative will step in to take his place. Think about it. Sympathy for your cause will instantly evaporate."

"Quite the contrary," Masella said smugly. "I will be seen as the savior of the church."

"What about Emma?" Michael argued. "She'll never let you railroad her into killing the cardinal."

"She won't fire the deadly shot, but when the chaos subsides, the murder weapon will be in her hand. Everyone will believe she committed the act."

Michael gasped. "You're crazy," he said hostilely, trying to hide the panic he was feeling. "No one would believe she pulled the trigger. Why would she?"

"Because like the martyrs of the past, she will be acting for the good of the church. She will give her life so much-needed changes are implemented immediately."

Michael's fear intensified. *I have to remain rational if I'm going to get through to this man,* he thought. "I don't understand," he said, struggling to sound composed. "How do you plan to make Emma a martyr?"

Masella laughed nervously. "It is obvious, Mr. Kelsey. The Swiss Guard will hear the shot, enter the chapel, and, realizing what occurred, kill the cardinal's murderer. But do not worry, after Ms. Bradford's death the pope will quickly proclaim her a hero and a martyr because she killed the man who was poisoning him in order to prevent change. Of course, you realize the guards will also kill anyone who might try to come to the murderer's rescue."

"And if we don't rush to save her: If we go along with your plan to sacrifice Emma?"

The monsignor, obviously surprised by the question, paused before answering. "You would never do that," he said tentatively. "I know you, Mr. Kelsey. After all, I realized that you would leave Ms. Bradford alone in front of the Excelsior to go chasing after the car? You fail to think, my friend. You act impulsively."

"You're not thinking straight, Masella," Michael said coolly, resisting the impulse to lash out angrily. "The Swiss Guard may kill us, but by then we will have reported your plan and intentions to our stations in New York and Boston."

"Who would believe you when they witness the events taking place in the chapel tomorrow morning? I will have my own camera running. You are not the only one who has the ability to film for a national broadcast. I have the Vatican network at my disposal, and before you think this will work in your favor, you must realize I am not committed to the concept of unbiased reporting."

Michael played on the monsignor's narcissism. "I'm impressed," he said. "I can see you've done your homework."

Masella obviously relished what he perceived to be a compliment. When he spoke, there was a lilt in his voice. "Though ABC news strives to report objectively, you should know it is not my intention to present my version from both sides. Quite the contrary. My cameraman will focus on the proof I will need to support my story. Your theory of how the crime was committed will be negated when the Vatican network breaks into programming with the words: 'ABC Reporter Murders Cardinal Amici in Cold Blood.' The entire episode will be caught on tape—my tape."

With every statement Masella made, Michael felt more anxious. How could he make the man see his plan would succeed? Flattery hadn't worked. *No more games,* he decided. "You're deluded, Masella," he said. "Take a minute to think about what you just told me. There's no way in hell an ABC reporter would come to Saint Peter's with a gun, pull it out during Mass, and shoot the celebrant."

"She would if she believed it was the only way the Catholic Church could survive. In our reporting *we* will say that, during her investigation, Ms. Bradford realized radical change is necessary. She came to believe Cardinal Amici was singlehandedly preventing the reforms. I will find a note to that effect in her pocket."

Michael had a sudden flash of insight. "Aren't you forgetting something, Monsignor? Ms. Bradford is Episcopalian. She's not Catholic. Why would anyone believe she cared enough about change in the Catholic Church to murder a cardinal?"

Masella chuckled. "I have taken that into consideration, Mr. Kelsey. Because of the trip to Rome, Ms. Bradford will have had a miraculous epiphany. My people have watched her reports. She is clearly moved by Bernini's works and his efforts to halt the Reformation. Her own words illustrate the awe she felt when looking at the majesty and grandeur of Saint Peter's. Those feelings have converted others, so why not Ms. Bradford—our newest convert to Catholicism?"

Michael laughed nervously. "That's a huge leap in logic," Masella. Do you really think sane people will buy your explanation?"

"Perhaps not at first, but after the pope confirms her last-minute conversion, of course they will. Even more so after he praises her as the savior of the church, which he will do from the loggia on Wednesday, at the same time he makes several major announcements brought about, in part, by Ms. Bradford's brave and selfless acts."

A knot formed in Michael's throat, and he felt nauseous. His suspicions had become fact, his fears reality. His next words were both a statement and a question. "And with the cardinal's death, the pope will suddenly be well enough to speak to the crowd in Saint Peter's."

"He will be speaking to the world as well. Perhaps ABC will carry the speech live. Think about it. There will be a report on Ms. Bradford's death and perhaps, at the same time, an announcement about the unfortunate demise of another of their reporters, as well as his friend, an American monsignor who graduated from Notre Dame."

"How do you plan to explain our deaths?"

"That has yet to be decided. Perhaps you will be shot by a Swiss Guard who misinterprets your efforts to keep Ms. Bradford from attacking Cardinal Amici. I suppose it depends on when you arrive. If you are in the chapel before the Cardinal's death, that line will work. If our conservative friend is already dead ... Well, I will figure out something."

"I noticed you said 'I' instead of 'we.' You didn't refer to the pontiff. Now I understand why you're doing this. You finally realized your preposterous plan to be elected pope if Pope John dies won't work. Why? Because you're a lowly monsignor. Despite your electronic campaign and terror tactics, the conclave might decide not to break centuries of tradition. So you must retain your power by other means. By killing the leading conservative opposing the radical change you seek, you hope to frighten his colleagues into submission. The cardinal will no longer be poisoning Pope John, so he will suddenly and miraculously recover. Though not in name, you will have papal power."

"Apparently you figured it out, Mr. Kelsey. I hope you know my actions are for the good of the church."

"You mean for the good of Monsignor Masella Cipriano," Michael said angrily. "You're crazy!"

"Believe what you would, Mr. Kelsey, but if you want to live, surprise me and do not act as I anticipate you will. Accept that Ms. Bradford is being sacrificed for the greater good and stay away."

"Like hell I will," Michael bellowed, but Masella had hung up.

His head throbbing, Michael dropped to the couch.

"Alright. Tell me the worst," Steven said, seeing the look on his friend's face. "I got the gist of the conversation. Be specific. What did Masella say?"

"The man's a certified lunatic, and that doesn't bode well for Emma. So listen to this and draw your own conclusions. Masella plans to kill Cardinal Amici and make it look like Emma pulled the trigger. Then loyal members of the Swiss Guard will kill her because they'll think she killed the cardinal."

Sante's eyes flew open, and he gasped in disbelief. "Are you serious?" he choked out.

"Unfortunately, I am."

"Tell us everything Masella told you," said James.

A knock on the door prevented Michael from beginning. Giro walked over and opened it to admit Helen and the others.

"What's up?" Helen said. "Why'd you want to meet earlier? You were adamant about getting together at four."

When she saw Michael's pained expression and body language, the color drained from her face. "Where's Emma?" she said tentatively. "What's going on?"

"Sit down and we'll give you a quick overview," Steven said. "We'll add specifics as we go along, and then we'll collectively try and figure out what we're going to do."

Michael made the necessary introductions. When the group was seated, he and Steven began. Between the two of them and James, it took only minutes to bring the rest of the group up to speed. As soon as they finished, Helen jumped into action. "There's obviously no time to waste," she said as she, removed her cell from her purse. "I'll call New York. We'll go live with Emma's kidnapping. Telling the world will keep the monsignor from going forward with his plan."

"It makes sense." Bill reached for the camera. "We can be ready in ten minutes. Right, Ron? Where should we set up?" He answered his own question? "How about in the front of the hotel where Emma was abducted?"

"Hold on," Steven said. "Unfortunately, it's not that easy. We can't go public."

"Steven's right," Michael said. "One leak and Emma's as good as dead. We're dealing with a narcissistic sociopath."

Helen put her phone on the table. "Then we have to make a plan. Michael, did Masella tell you when or where Emma is supposed to commit the murder?"

"In the Blessed Sacrament Chapel tomorrow, but he didn't say when."

"I believe I know," Sante said. "Several days ago I received a memo saying that Cardinal Amici will say Mass at seven tomorrow morning in the Chapel of Blessed Sacrament. He celebrates for his family every year on the anniversary of his mother's death."

"Where's the cardinal now? Can we get a message to him telling him to cancel the service and stay away?" Helen asked.

"As far as I know, he's in his rooms," said Sante. "I can find out, but I doubt if we can contact him."

"Sante's right," Michael said. "Angelo told us the cardinal's computer was confiscated, and I doubt he'll have access to a phone."

"What about Cardinal Remella?" James asked. "He seems to have access to Cardinal Amici?"

Michael nodded no. "He told Emma and me the only way he and the cardinal communicated was by notes handed back and forth at Mass during the peace, and the murder will be over before the peace is offered."

"And you're forgetting Cardinal Remella had a so-called stroke," said Steven.

"You're right," James said. "So now we have to worry about the two cardinals, not to mention Emma."

"I'm sure Cardinal Remella will be fine if we can resolve the issue of Emma and Cardinal Amici," Steven said.

Sante flipped open his phone. "Let me confirm where both cardinals are at the moment."

"What about talking with Giotto Tomai?" Michael asked as Sante made his call. "I know he was at Saint Agnes with Masella, but he seemed surprised by what Emma and I told him. And you said he's a moderate, so if we told him what's going on—"

"We'll do that as a last resort," Steven said. "I don't know if we can trust him. We have no idea what he was thinking when he accompanied Masella to the meeting at Saint Agnes, and even if he disagrees with Masella's philosophy and actions to promote his cause, it's questionable how far he'll go to oppose him. I imagine he'll be thinking of his predecessor, Piero Scala."

"Which would be a definite impetus for remaining neutral at best, and at worst, joining him" said James.

Helen shook her head. "None of this makes any sense."

"Can an insane man make sense?" Michael said.

Before Helen could respond, Sante snapped his phone closed. "Cardinal Amici is in his apartments. As of noon today, his guard has been doubled. Two men are standing outside the door, and two are stationed in his anteroom."

"And Cardinal Remella?" Michael asked.

"He remains hospitalized, though I was unable to get an update on his condition."

"What about the pope? Is there anything new in his regard?" James asked, looking almost afraid to hear the answer to his question.

"Not that I know of, but I didn't ask."

For a long moment, no one said anything. Steven finally broke the silence. "Obviously we have to get into the basilica before the cardinal says Mass tomorrow morning."

Michael stood up. "No way we're waiting until then. Sante, how can we get into the basilica right now?"

"I don't know what excuse we could use to get in once the basilica is closed to the public, and I don't think we should try," Sante said.

Michael glared. "Why not?"

"Think about it," James said. "We don't know who's reporting to Masella. He's clearly receiving information from numerous sources. I understand how you feel, but let's not take a chance. It's not worth the gamble. I don't think we should risk contacting anyone at this point, and it won't do us any good to barge into the basilica tonight. We probably wouldn't find Emma, and if we did, we'd be outnumbered by Masella's men. Hard as it's going to be, we have to wait."

"James is right," Steven said. "The basilica doors will probably open early for the cardinal's family and select guests. We'll be there by six and settled in the chapel before the Mass begins. Sante, could you and Colombo find three or four men you can trust?"

Colombo answered quickly, "I'm sure we can." He paused. "At least I hope so."

"I hear what you're saying, but I still think we should act right away," Michael said. "What if, for some unforeseen reason, Masella realizes his ridiculous plan has no chance of succeeding and decides to kill Emma tonight? I'm going to Saint Peter's. Come with me or stay here, but I'm outta here."

As Michael stood up, Steven grabbed his arm. "There's no way in hell you're walking out of this room. Do you honestly think Masella stopped watching us because he has Emma? Didn't he say he knows you? He expected you to leave Emma in the car to accost the men waiting in front of the Excelsior. Don't you think he's counting on you to panic, do the same thing, and rush off to rescue her? He wants to draw you out. You know he won't hesitate to kill all of us. We assume Emma's at Saint Peter's, but where is she being held? If we barge in to rescue her, we won't come out."

"Aren't you being overly dramatic?" Michael said, clearly not wanting to believe what was happening. "Can Masella really kill two ABC reporters and a couple of priests and get away with it?"

"Of course he can. Saint Peter's isn't Saint Agnes in Agony. Remember all the nooks and crannies in the building in contrast to the openness of the Navona church?"

"Yeah, but I don't believe Masella will kill us in the basilica. How would he explain our deaths to the world?"

James thought out loud: "He wouldn't have to. Our bodies wouldn't be discovered in Saint Peter's. We'd be victims of some terrible accident in another part of Vatican City."

"Or in Rome," Giro said.

"I don't think Masella would leave Vatican territory," said Steven. "He wouldn't want the Italian police to take over the investigation. He can't control them."

"The man has to know modern forensics will eventually reveal the truth," Michael said.

"You're not watching CSI," my friend. You're involved in a real-life drama, and, may I remind you, there seems to be problem with truth in Vatican City. Think about Piero. We'll never know what happened to him."

"And no one will ever know for certain what happened to you, either," Sante added. "Masella will find a way to hide the cause of your deaths."

"Masella has to know Helen and David could go live with the story," Michael said.

Steven shook his head no. "He knows they won't. They have no proof. They can't report a theory, especially with the Vatican and the Holy See doing their spin thing. In a short time, the pope will miraculously recover and refute anything they're reporting. He'll declare Emma a martyr, and you, Emma, and your story will be painted in a negative light. Masella will have won. You'll be American journalists who tragically died while reporting on the Bernini exhibition."

"And poor Cardinal Remella will suffer another stroke and pass away," James said.

"Steven and James are right," said Helen. "ABC won't run with the story unless we have definitive proof. We're not taking on the Holy See unless we can prove our accusations."

"So we have to figure out a way to rescue Emma and the cardinals and, at the same time, expose Masella and his plan," James said. "Steven's right, Michael. Racing off to Saint Peter's now won't help any of us."

"Then what do we do?" Michael groaned.

A moment of uneasy silence passed before Steven answered: "God only knows."

CHAPTER TWENTY-EIGHT

The two men paused outside the wrought-iron entrance to the Chapel of the Blessed Sacrament. From behind the grating, a silhouette of a man appeared in the shadows. It moved toward them. "Ms. Bradford. Thank you for joining me," Masella said, a leering grin on his face. "I had a productive conversation with Mr. Kelsey. He and Monsignor Laurent send their regards."

Masella stepped into the dim light of the basilica. Though his tone was cordial, his mouth was frozen in a thin line and his eyes were cold. "Welcome to Saint Peter's."

Not wanting to show weakness, Emma struggled to pull herself together. "Welcome to Saint Peter's?" she said angrily. "You sound like coming here is *my* choice."

Masella cocked his head. "I fail to understand. Perhaps we have a language problem. I merely asked these men to invite you to see me. If you refused to do as they asked … Well, you are here now, and you are about to be a part of a process much more important than either of us."

Emma forced herself to maintain eye contact. "I have no idea what you're talking about, Monsignor," she said. "So far all I've heard are the ramblings of a deranged man."

"I assure you I am quite sane, Ms. Bradford. Let me explain. As I told Mr. Kelsey only moments ago, from now on I will be writing your story for you. I imagine the ABC network will air your tragic tale without commercials. That is the usual procedure when covering an important story, is it not?"

Not sure how to respond, Emma took a deep breath. "What you say is intriguing," she said. Enlighten me."

"My pleasure. Perhaps I can make you understand by providing the introduction for the breaking news."

"Don't keep me in suspense."

Masella smiled, but his demeanor was hostile and cold. "You will hear …" He paused. "Let me revise my previous statement. You will not hear. I wonder which of the journalists of ABC will report. Will it be Diane Sawyer who says: 'One of our own reporters murdered Cardinal Giancomo Amici during Mass in Saint Peter's'?"

Emma's felt her knees go weak and she took hold of the back of one of the nearby chairs to steady herself. "What are you saying?" she asked, horrified at what she was hearing. "Why would I kill the cardinal, and who in his right mind would believe I did?"

"That has all been worked out."

"And when I go on air to refute your explanation? What then?"

"You will never be in a position to do that, Ms. Bradford. Remember, I said you would be unable to hear the headlines. Let me clarify. Throughout the history of the church, individuals have committed great and selfless acts. Many have made the ultimate sacrifice for the greater good. You will be our newest martyr."

Emma felt like she was suffocating. "You're not serious," she moaned.

"You will soon discover I am deadly serious—no pun intended."

"Do you truly believe you can get away with this preposterous plan?"

"Without question."

"But why? What do you possibly hope to gain?"

Masella moved in closer. "Change, Ms. Bradford, which has always been my goal. Without you and Cardinal Amici around to hinder our plans, Pope John will announce unilateral changes. There will be no reason to convene Vatican III."

Though she doubted her tactic would work, Emma tried to reason with the irrational man. "Why are you so fearful of change that evolves slowly?" she asked. "What would be wrong with convening Vatican III?"

"Simply this, Ms. Bradford; Vatican II. For three years, learned churchmen, and you will note I use the term 'learned' with great disdain, debated religious freedom, the celibacy of priests, and other proposed changes. At the end the church was altered; some say not enough, and others say too much. I would fall in the much too little category."

"And now you think you can singlehandedly bring about the changes you personally desire? You won't succeed. I *know* and can *prove* that you killed Piero Scala and Dina Sandri. I *know* and can *prove* that Gusto Baldi works for you, as does Lucio Pietro, who's married to your sister. I *know*, and will soon be able to prove, that you're poisoning the pope. You will determine whether he lives or dies. As I told you in Saint Agnes, I have e-mails in my possession which *prove* you broke the rules and campaigned for Pope John's election. Finally, I can *prove* you're involved in a movement to do away with centuries of Catholic practice. You plan to be the next pope—you, a lowly monsignor."

Apparently Masella wasn't used to such disrespect. His eyes widened, and his voice exuded irritation. "You say you can *prove* all of this." He chuckled. "If you are dead, it could be difficult."

For the first time, Emma saw a chink in the monsignor's armor. Knowing she had nothing to lose, she continued: "If I *know* and can *prove* my allegations, why wouldn't my partner, Mr. Kelsey, and the rest of our staff be able to do the same thing?"

Emma felt a surge of elation when she saw Masella's expression change. *He understands,* she reflected. *I have a chance.*

For a few moments, Masella didn't answer. When he finally spoke, all of Emma's newfound hopes were quickly dashed. "You are right, Ms. Bradford," he said broodingly. "Perhaps my grand scheme will fail. Nevertheless, I shall proceed as planned. Even if I fail, the death of Cardinal Amici, followed by your demise, will make a profound statement." His eyes grew wide. "One way or another, change will take place. When that happens, I will get the credit."

Masella seemed to be in an almost trance-like state, and Emma waited for him to continue. When he said nothing, she addressed him again, her voice soft and her tone conciliatory. "But none of this makes sense, Masella. You know it. I see uncertainty and skepticism in your eyes."

Again Masella didn't respond, so Emma continued. "Why can't you admit you went too far? Accept responsibility for your actions. You'll be the martyr. You'll be telling the world how far you're willing to go to achieve the changes you feel are vital to the survival of the church."

Masella hesitated. "I'm not sure ..." he said tentatively.

Not wanting to interrupt Masella's thought process, Emma remained quiet. When he finally spoke, a wave of nausea swept through her. "Though you make a point, I have come too far to turn back now, Ms. Bradford."

Emma didn't want to hear the answer, but, as an icy numbness came over her, she asked the question anyway: "What are you going to do?"

"Exactly what I planned. So allow me to show you, using a term often heard on American television shows, 'the scene of the crime.'" He chuckled as he took Emma's arm. "Did you enjoy the tidbits about Rome and Saint Peter's which Nicola provided?" he asked as they walked.

"I did," Emma said, wondering where Masella was going with his question.

"Good. Were you able to spend time in the Blessed Sacrament Chapel when Nicola took you on your initial tour of Saint Peter's?" He paused, looking puzzled. "Ah," he said, seconds later, "now I remember. Instead of coming here, you spent your last minutes in the basilica viewing Saint Longinus, so this is your first visit to this special and holy place where you and Cardinal Amici will die; your friends too if they are imprudent enough to ignore my warnings and burst in to save you." Suddenly, he chuckled.

"You find your threat amusing?" Emma asked.

"It is not a threat, Ms. Bradford, but to answer your question. What I find amusing is the irony of what I just said. You decided not to spend the last minutes of your *tour* in the chapel. Now you will spend the last minutes of your *life* in the place you chose not to visit."

———

Everyone in the group gathered in Emma's sitting room was baffled. "I know I've said this before and my idea was categorically rejected, but I think we need to go live right now," Helen said. "If the world knows Emma was kidnapped—"

"We'll be backing Masella into a corner, and Emma will be in greater jeopardy than she is now," Steven said.

David nodded in agreement. "I concur. My first inclination is to air the story, but in this case Emma's life is at stake."

"Then what do you suggest?" Helen said impatiently. "It seems no one has a workable plan."

"I have an idea," Steven said.

"Don't keep us in suspense," Michael grumbled. "If we can't come up with something very soon, to hell with you— I'm going to Saint Peter's."

"Then you'll have to go through me to get there," Steven said. "Now be quiet and listen. Everyone entering Saint Peter's early tomorrow morning has to be a member of the clergy or a member of the cardinal's family."

"Will there be a list of guests at the door?" Helen asked.

"Let's hope that's a detail Masella overlooked," Steven said, wondering how many more potentially disastrous details they would fail to consider.

"So assuming there's no list, except for you and James, none of the rest of us will be able to get in," Michael was saying. "And the two of you might find it difficult. You're not exactly on Masella's happy list."

"That's true, but I don't think the monsignor will look twice at two monks praying in the chapel."

"Monks?"

"Cardinal Amici has two brothers who are monks. They're currently in a monastery in Sicily, so it's unlikely they'll be attending the Mass for their aunt. Michael, you and I will each dress in a monk's robe complete with cowl. Masella might be fooled into thinking we're the brothers. I'm sure I can get the appropriate attire."

"Only two brothers? There's no way you're leaving me out of this," James said.

"Relax. You'll dress in civilian clothes." Steven turned to Helen. "You think makeup can make James look like an ugly old man?"

Helen smiled. "Easy, but we'll need a wig or hair dye."

"Leave that to me," Giro said. "I can go out of the hotel through the staff entrance and get whatever you need."

"Great!" Steven said. "Helen, make a list."

"Will do. I'll need for you to go to the truck too, Giro. The makeup case is there. Do you have a dark suit?"

"Not that an old man would use, but my father does. He lives a few miles from me. I'll stop by and borrow one of his jackets and a hat. How about a cane?"

"That works for me," said James. "It may come in handy."

"What about Colombo and me?" Sante asked.

"Your job is vital to the success of our plan," Steven said. "Find us enough Swiss Guard and Vatican police to subdue Masella's cohorts before they enter the chapel and kill Emma.

Replace Masella's men with your allies. Michael, James, and I can't fight a battle in Saint Peter's by ourselves, especially since we'll have no idea who's on whose side."

"We'll get started as soon as we finish here," Sante said. "When the Swiss Guard enters the Blessed Sacrament chapel tomorrow morning, it will be the good guys."

"We're counting on that," said Michael. "You're going to have to be careful when you leave the hotel. Masella's men will be watching the main entrance. The Doney restaurant has a separate entrance leading from a sidewalk café. I know because Emma and I had a drink there when we first began our joint investigation. Go through there."

"Good idea," Sante said. "Let's pray Masella's men aren't waiting in the lobby."

"Your mouth to God's ears," Michael said.

"What about us?" Helen asked. "You can't expect us to sit idly by while all this is going on."

"And how can I help?" Giro said. "Please let me do something besides go for makeup and a jacket. I was in the Italian army for four years. I have a black belt."

"That's a plus for us," Steven said.

"Think you can get another one of those monk's robes?" Michael asked Steven.

"Sure, but too many monks might arouse Masella's suspicions. How would you feel about being a very large nun?" Steven asked Giro. "You'd be accompanied by another nun from your convent, Sister Mary Ronetta. She's going to have bulky, flowing robes to hide her camera." He looked across the room. "You're going to have to film everything, Ron."

"I can do that."

"What about Sister Mary Bill? What will she be doing?" Bill asked.

Bill's question eased the tension in the room as everyone laughed. "You're much too tall to be a nun, my friend," Steven said "You'd make a better priest."

"You're still ignoring me," Helen said.

"I'm not. You'll be in the truck watching the feed. If things don't go well, go live."

"How will I know when to act?"

"Believe me, you'll know," Michael said. "If the cardinal dies, or if Masella seems to be winning, for want of a better word, send the feed. As for commentary, do a short intro. The footage will say the rest. Let's pray this doesn't have to happen. Before we go in tomorrow, give New York a heads-up, but don't be specific. Tell them to expect breaking news around one a.m. I know they don't have reporters on duty—"

"I'll give them reason to have someone standing by. Hopefully we'll be able to go live with a good ending on *Good Morning America.*"

"I pray we will," said Steven.

"Can you really get all these uniforms, or whatever you call them?" Michael asked.

"Of course I can. I ask again: after all these years, how could you doubt me? I'll make a few calls and go pick them up."

"This time I'm putting my foot down," Michael said. "You're not leaving this room. You're the one who chided me for not realizing Masella's men are still watching us. If they spot you, I'm afraid you wouldn't come back."

"I can go," Giro said.

Michael shook his head. "You have enough to do, and Masella knows you're our driver. I hate to ask, but David, will you do the honors? You're the least likely to be recognized."

"Tell me where and when, and I'll be there."

"Thanks," Steven said. "I'll make the arrangements. At least we know how we're getting into the basilica and the chapel. Now we have to figure out what to do when we get there."

———

Masella led Emma through the opening into a lovely chapel filled with the scent of flowers and incense. "This will be the scene of your martyrdom, Ms. Bradford," he said. "Perhaps you would like to hear something about the place where you will give your life so millions will be freed from the tyranny of a conservative Catholic Church entrenched in the Middle Ages."

Though his voice was decisive and strong, Emma saw fatigue in Masella's eyes. *I have to stay strong,* she thought. *It's the only way I have a chance.* "A church you think will change with my death," she said.

"Do not flatter yourself, Ms. Bradford. Your death is secondary, though you will be the one who is praised. It is Cardinal Amici who must die, and with him his conservative movement."

"Do you seriously believe Cardinal Amici's death will stop his fellow conservatives from moving ahead with their agenda?"

"Perhaps not, but it will certainly give them pause. By the time they reorganize, the major changes will have been made."

"And you will have consolidated your power base."

"Ah, you finally understand. How unfortunate you failed to see the entire picture earlier. Had you stayed out of our politics from the beginning…" Masella paused. "Well, this is no time for what-ifs. Perhaps your persistence made my goal easier to achieve."

Emma was at a loss for words. She stared at Masella in disbelief, wondering what ludicrous comment he'd make next. She wasn't surprised when he changed the subject.

"So Ms. Bradford," he said, a leering grin on his face, "shall I be your Nicola this time? Would you like to know about the site of your martyrdom? Perhaps, in time, a statue will be erected to you. Where would you like it? By your favorite place in the basilica, Pope Alexander's Monument?"

Torn between confusion and fright, Emma shivered. "You have to know your plan won't work," she said somberly.

"It may not, but let me say again, you will not know if it did. So shall I tell you about the chapel?"

"I'm not interested."

"But it will help us pass the time. I am surprised that ABC failed to include the chapel in your reports." He turned to the American and Italian who had grabbed Emma at the hotel. "You may leave," he said imperiously. "My guards are outside the door, and I imagine you need to prepare for tomorrow morning's Mass."

The men nodded and left the chapel. When the door closed, Masella began again: "So, Ms. Bradford. We are alone. Would you like to pray before I begin? This chapel is designated as a place for prayer."

As Emma looked behind her, Masella snickered. "With great surety, I can say that no one will rush through the door to rescue you." He took out his cell phone, flipped it open and pressed a button. "Is Mr. Kelsey still in Ms. Bradford's room at the Excelsior?" he asked. "I see. Good. If they come to the basilica, kill all of them."

Emma shuddered. "You'd kill innocent people to achieve your goal?" She glared at Masella. "Right," she said with contempt. "You already have."

"Casualties in a holy war," Masella said. "Apparently you find no need to pray, so I shall continue with my narrative. Did you notice the Baroque wrought iron at the chapel entrance? It was designed by Francesco Borromini. My sources tell me you stressed the rivalry between him and Bernini when you reported from the *Fontana Dei Quattro Fiumi*. Ah, my dear, you seem surprised. Did I not say I know everything about your activities?"

Emma said nothing.

"I assume you are aware of my authority and influence, Ms. Bradford. Despite my warnings, you refused to abandon your investigation and concentrate on the Bernini exhibition, but as you television reporters say, this is old news."

Though Emma looked away, indicating her disinterest in what Masella was saying, he continued: "The Blessed Sacrament is exposed here for the continuous adoration of the faithful. Did you see the notice outside? Only those who wish to pray may enter. The Eucharist is frequently celebrated in this chapel, as it will be by Cardinal Amici tomorrow morning. At least, he will begin the Mass. Perhaps I will grant an exemption and allow you to take communion before you kill the cardinal and are, in turn, killed."

Does he expect me to thank him? Emma wondered. She eyed the monsignor with defiance and continued to remain silent.

Masella was growing more irritated as he continued: "Allowing you the sacrament is the least I can do considering what you will be doing for me. Shall I tell you about the art that decorates the chapel?"

Emma ignored the monsignor's question.

"You are stubborn, Ms. Bradford," Masella said, his eyes flashing. "I shall take your lack of response as a yes. The most precious work, the Tabernacle to hold the sacramental Host, was designed by your friend, Bernini. See the two lovely gilded bronze angels kneeling in reverent prayer. They are filled with joy as they invite the faithful to forget the deafening noise of the world, if only for a moment or two. Think about it, Ms. Bradford. The angels may be the last figures you see as you joyously depart this life."

Emma looked away.

Clearly growing more frustrated, Masella rambled on as he tried to intimidate Emma and gain the psychological upper hand. "You are not enjoying my descriptions as much as you did the explanations Nicola provided at San Clemente," he said. "However, I shall persist in an effort to make you appreciate the beauties of this special chapel, the place where you will spend your last moments before ascending to the Lord."

Before Masella could begin again, the American goon reentered the chapel. "I'm sorry to interrupt, Monsignor," he said from just inside the iron grate. "The cleaning crew is coming toward the chapel. Maybe you and Ms. Bradford would like to go elsewhere so you aren't disturbed while they do their jobs?"

Masella seemed both confused and angry. *Something he didn't count on in his carefully orchestrated plan,* Emma thought. She spoke for the first time. "I'm beginning to enjoy the chapel, Monsignor," she said. "Perhaps those who clean the magnificent place will want to listen to what you have to say. Why don't we stay and talk while they work?"

Suddenly Masella was back in control. "Do you truly believe I am stupid, Ms. Bradford? I thought I showed you how smart I am at the end of our meeting at Saint Agnes." He turned to the American. "Thank you. We will go elsewhere. Please accompany us."

Masella took Emma's arm. "It seems we will have to find another place to wait while you prepare for your sacrifice. I had hoped the beauty of the Blessed Sacrament chapel would give you peace, but apparently that is not to be. Shall we go?"

"Do I have a choice?"

Masella sneered. "You know the answer to your question is no."

CHAPTER TWENTY-NINE

The atmosphere in Emma's suite was tense. Michael ordered food for everyone, but no one ate much. When the cart containing the half-empty plates had been rolled into the hallway, the assembled group continued to make plans.

"Let me play devil's advocate," Michael said. "Steven, you talk and we'll point out any problems we have with our plan."

"Good idea," Steven said. "We need to anticipate anything that could happen and have a tentative solution for whatever problem we may encounter. So when we get into the basilica—"

"You must mean *if* we get inside," Michael said. "We can't assume we'll be able to waltz up to the door and be admitted without suitable IDs. It's possible the guard will have a list of invited guests. Then what?"

Sante raised his hand like a student wanting to be recognized. "Sante, you apparently have an idea," Steven said.

"Maybe. I won't be able to get your names on a guest list, but I *think* I can help. I recently met a man who works in the Vatican credentials office. His name is Domenic, but I don't know his last name. Maybe I can get him to issue some sort of credential or invitation that will look real enough to get us into the basilica for the Mass. If I can reach him, and if he is willing, I could go to his office and work with him."

"Are you sure you want to do this?" Steven asked. "You could be putting yourself at risk. If you find Domenic, it's possible he could intentionally or inadvertently report your request to one of Masella's allies. You could be detained the minute you walk into his office."

"And trust me—Masella's men are swarming around like flies on shit," Michael said; "something Emma and I learned during the Saint Agnes meeting. I'd hate for you to have a mysterious heart attack."

"I'm willing to take the chance," Sante replied. "I have two advantages Monsignor Scala didn't have: I know the enemy, and I'm a policeman. Think about it. What if we get to the door and can't get in because we don't have the right identification? You and Michael will probably have to prove you're the cardinal's cousins, and Sisters Mary Giro and Mary Ronetta will need to show they are connected to the Amici family."

"And Father Bill may be turned away if he doesn't have a reason for being in the basilica before hours, especially if Masella has beefed up security," Michael added.

"Which I'm sure he has," said Steven.

"What could possibly make you believe you can trust Domenic?" James asked. "You said you just met him."

"I am not sure if I can trust him, but I know he's conservative."

"And you know this how?" Michael asked.

"I don't think my answer will make you feel better."

"Tell us anyway," James said.

"After a couple of hours of drinking, Dominique began to criticize the changes the pope—"

"You're joking," James said incredulously. "You're gambling your life and possibly ours on the ramblings of a drunk?"

"Yes, unless you have a better idea. At the moment we don't have a better plan.

"Unfortunately, Sante's right," said Steven.

"I agree," Michael said. "At the moment, Domenic's our best chance. So, Sante, how much are you going to tell the guy?"

"I won't know until to talk to him. I will try to tell him something that won't give away our real reason for needing the credentials."

Helen, who had been quietly listening to the conversation, chimed in. "I'm not particularly comfortable with the plan, but as you said, at the moment it looks like it's all we have."

"Is everyone on board?" Michael asked. He looked around the room. No one said anything, but everyone nodded yes. "None of you appear to be any more enthusiastic than I am, but I guess we're a go." He turned to Sante. "Try to get Dominic to design an invitation rather than an ID, and it would help if the guard sees the cardinal's seal. Maybe that will keep him from looking more closely and discovering we're imposters."

"Any idea how I can convince Domenic to add the seal?"

"I don't know. Tell him the cardinal's cousins and his nieces, Sister Mary Giro and Sister Mary Ronetta, decided to come to the service at the last minute and the cardinal didn't have time to mail the necessary invitations. He personally asked you to take care of the matter. Make James one of the cardinal's childhood friends, though I'm not sure he'll be believable if he's dressed like a grubby old man. Cardinal Amici can be Father Bill's mentor."

"What if Domenic asks me why he didn't invite these people earlier?"

"Tell him he sent e-mails," Steven suggested, "but because Masella recently increased security, all guests need written invitations. There was no time to send them via snail-mail. The cardinal had local invitations delivered, but not those which had to be mailed out of Rome."

"That might work. At least it's worth a try," said Sante.

"Anything else?" Michael asked.

"There may be another problem," Sante said hesitantly.

Steven groaned. "Then let's talk about it now and not when we're standing at the basilica door. What is it?"

"What if Domenic knows the cardinal is isolated and can't receive e-mails? He could figure out what I'm asking—"

Steven interrupted. "Even if he realizes the cardinal's movements are restricted, he'd likely accept the premise that a Vatican policeman has access to him, though, if he asks, I'm not sure how you'll explain why it's you and not a member of the Swiss Guard. Anyway, you're going to have to see how Domenic responds to your request and your reasons for needing the credentials and go from there."

"I'm afraid to ask, but is there anything else?" Michael said. He looked from person to person and got no response. "Then we're a go."

"I'll call Domenic," Sante said. "Pray only one person with that name works in the credentials office."

"Call from Emma's bedroom," Michael said. "We want Domenic to believe you're making the request on your own. He might not think so if he hears us talking."

"So if we can get inside the chapel, then what?" Giro asked Steven as Sante left the room.

"It will be early in the morning, so I doubt members of the cardinal's family or any of Masella's men will have arrived. We should have our choice of seats. We'll position ourselves so we have a clear view of the altar."

"All of us need to sit on the aisle so we can get out if need be," Ron said, "especially me since I'll be filming. I'll have to sit in the last row so I can get wide-angle shot of the altar through the hole I'll cut in my habit."

"Once we're in position, then what?" Bill asked.

Michael answered: "We'll have to plan as we go,"

"Damn, that's frustrating," said Ron.

Michael put his hand on Ron's shoulder. "I agree, but we have no idea who'll be escorting Emma, though it's safe to assume Masella will be with her. Nor do we know if the cardinal will walk up the aisle or if he'll be left alone once he's at the altar."

"If I'm hearing you right, the key phrase here is 'we don't know,'" Bill said. "We have to be ready for anything." He inhaled and exhaled deeply. "That's hardly comforting."

"We'd all feel better if we could make definite plans," Helen said, "but there are too many variables."

As Helen spoke, Sante rejoined the group. "But we have one less problem—at least I hope so."

"You talked with Domenic?" Michael asked.

"I was lucky there was only one Domenic in the office. I did what Steven suggested. I told him Cardinal Amici needed last-minute passes for his two nieces, nuns from Florence; a priest he mentored who is assigned to a church in Naples; two cousins, monks from Sicily; and a childhood friend who knew Mrs. Amici, the cardinal's mother. Either Domenic didn't know the cardinal couldn't have made the request or he didn't care. He is willing to help create some sort of acceptable invitation."

"Sante, is it possible that Domenic's eager to help you because he heard rumors about Emma's kidnapping?" Michael asked.

"I don't think so, though I imagine everyone believes something big is about to happen."

Suddenly Michael stood up. "I have an alternative plan," he said enthusiastically. "Let's get the jump on Masella and put out our own e-mail about Emma's kidnapping and Masella's intentions."

"No way in hell!" Steven said harshly.

"Why not?" Despite the resolute look on Steven's face, Michael persisted. "It could help."

"Help whom? Emma? Be sensible, Michael," Steven said, frustration in his voice. "Are you willing to risk her life?" When Michael opened his mouth to respond, Steven put up his hand. "No, let me finish. Even if I agreed to issue some sort of statement, what would I say? Do you really want me to expose Masella's plan? No doubt he'd hear about my e-mail as soon as it hit cyberspace. With nothing to lose, Emma's as good as dead."

Michael still wasn't ready to give up. "On the other hand, it's possible the cardinal would learn about Masella's intentions and stay away from the Blessed Sacrament chapel. If he's not there, Masella's scheme won't work; Emma couldn't kill him."

"Come on, my friend. You're not thinking straight. You know Masella would immediately implement an alternate strategy."

"Which he might not have, so he'd have to get creative," James said. "That doesn't bode well for Emma."

"I know you're disappointed, Michael," Steven said, "but we're not dealing with a moron. Granted, Masella is delusional, egomaniacal, and narcissistic, but he's also a brilliant man."

"I know, but—"

"Aren't you forgetting the cardinal can no longer send or receive e-mail?" James said. "Even if we put out some sort of statement or tried to create a rumor, it wouldn't reach the intended target. We have to let the drama play out and deal with issues if and when they arise."

"I agree with Steven and James," Helen said. "An e-mail would do Emma and the rest of us more harm than good."

"And we can't forget Cardinal Remella," said Sante. "Masella would immediately kill him."

Michael grimaced. "God, I hate this."

"Believe me, we all do." Steven said.

"Since we all agree this flawed and risky plan is our only option, Colombo and I will go." Sante stood up. "We have a lot to accomplish before tomorrow morning."

"While Sante works with Domenic, I will try to put together a team from the Swiss Guard and the police," Colombo said.

Michael shook hands with both men. "Good luck to both of you," he said. "If you have any problems, please call either Steven or me right away."

"God go with you," Steven intoned as he made the sign of the cross over the two men.

"And with you," Sante said. "If I have enough time, I will deliver the invitations myself. If not, someone I trust will come."

"Remember, whatever you come up with has to be here by five," Michael said.

"I'll do my best. If it's too late to get the invitations to the hotel, someone will be waiting by the news truck in the morning. Either way, I won't let you down."

"You two take care of yourselves," Steven said as he walked Sante and Colombo to the door. "We don't need the added burden of coming up with a way to rescue you."

Colombo looked back. "There will be no need," he said, "Sante and I will be fine." His tone hardly exuded confidence.

———

Emma's nonstop nightmare continued. Masella and the two new guards walked her down into the grotto containing the tombs of deceased popes. When they reached the bottom step, Masella immediately embarked upon another of his rambling diatribes about Saint Peter's.

"For Christ's sake," Emma muttered as he began his spiel. "I can't do this all night."

"Did you say something?" Masella asked, a puzzled look spoiling his otherwise calm demeanor.

"No, nothing."

"Then I shall tell you about the crypt."

Before giving Emma the facts she dreaded hearing, he cocked his head as though he'd come to a sudden realization. "I would like to be able to say you will be buried down here, but though your deed will be glorious and benefit all Catholics, you *are* an Episcopalian." He lowered his head, deep in thought. "Perhaps that won't be a problem after all," he said, looking up at Emma. "After the pope hears your story, I am certain he will grant you a special dispensation."

Oh my God! The man's going to kill me with his rambling before the Swiss Guard kills me with their guns tomorrow. Emma shuddered at the thought. "You know, I'd really rather not hear about the crypt right now, Monsignor," she said, mustering all of her resolve to remain calm. "If this is my last night on earth, I'd prefer to spend it in quiet reflection."

"Not *if* it is your final night, Ms. Bradford. You *will* die tomorrow morning in the Blessed Sacrament chapel. Of course you would like some private time to prepare. You will have your opportunity to make peace with God, but first, the crypt. Is that not what all reporters desire—the facts? Had you reported factual information about the Bernini exhibition and nothing more, you might not be in this predicament."

Emma opened her mouth to respond, but Masella gave her a dismissive wave. *He's going off on another tangent again,* Emma reflected, and she stifled a groan.

"Ninety-one popes, kings, and queens, including Bernini's patron, Queen Christina of Sweden, are buried below the basilica." Masella's face lit up as though he had unexpectedly come to yet another surprising conclusion. "Do you know Pope John Paul the First is also buried here in the crypt? Shall we walk over to his tomb?" He pointed to an arch on the right side of the grotto.

Grasping Emma's arm tightly, he continued to ramble as they walked. "You might wonder why I chose to single out this particular pope. It is because his reign lasted a mere thirty-three days. He died thirty-one years ago on September 28, 1978. If our current Holy Father should be unfortunate enough to die from influenza, his time in office will be of a similar duration." He hesitated again, as if coming to another significant realization. "Is it ironic, is it not?" he said thoughtfully. "John Paul died in September, as will Pope John if the episode in the chapel fails to go my way. Perhaps this is an omen."

"Your way! You've got to be—"

Masella ignored Emma's outburst. "So you see, Ms. Bradford, your sacrifice will preclude another pope from departing this life before he has the opportunity to make his mark on the church."

I'll never get through to Masella, Emma though. Suddenly she made a decision. Going along with the monsignor's twisted reasoning was her last best chance to survive. Michael and Steven would never find her down in the crypt. She'd have to take her chances in the chapel. She managed an insincere smile. "Monsignor, hearing you speak has finally made me see the light. I will accept my role to ensure the Catholic Church survives and thrives in the modern world."

Masella was definitely surprised. "Really?" he said with seeming disbelief. "Are you finally saying you accept your fate?"

When he reached out to put his hand on her arm, Emma shied away. Smirking, Masella pulled back. "Are you telling me the truth, Ms. Bradford?" he asked. He sighed. "Well, whether or not you are being honest or attempting to fool me is of no import."

Once again Emma tried to sound sincere, hoping Masella would accept her sudden change of heart. "If you don't mind, I'm exhausted," she said. "Now that I've made my decision, I feel the weight of my task. I'd like to rest and pray."

Masella laughed as if she'd told a side-splitting joke. "Your words are both illogical and ironic, Ms. Bradford."

"I'm afraid I don't understand what you mean."

"Then let me enlighten you. You said you want to rest tonight. Think about it. By 7:30 in the morning, your rest will be eternal."

Emma couldn't stand the ludicrous conversation any longer. "Please leave me alone," she pleaded, no longer pretending to be strong.

Masella scowled. "Oh, very well, I will permit you your much-desired privacy. I shall retire to my private chapel and pray for a successful conclusion to my plan and for your soul." He bowed, turned, and headed for the stairs.

"Thank God for a few moments of quiet," Emma whispered as the sound of Masella's footsteps faded in the distance.

When she heard the door to the grotto open and close, she looked around. *Be careful what you wish for*, she mused as the silence enveloped her and she realized she was alone among the dead.

A moan escaped her lips when, for the first time, she had the opportunity to ponder what would soon take place in the chapel above her. Suddenly the thought that she might really die in Saint Peter's seemed surreal. It was like the final curtain falling after Act I of a two-act Broadway play. She walked back and knelt in front of Pope John Paul's tomb. With her index finger she traced the carved name, "IoAnnes Pavlus PP.I," and the monogram of Christ below it. As she looked at the two ancient reliefs of open-winged angels praying on either side, a tear fell down her cheek. Though she was not particularly religious, she began to pray.

———

While Helen slept in Emma's bed, the men camped out in the sitting room. When the alarm rang at 4:30, Michael was already dressed. The clothes David had successfully procured the night before were piled on the floor by the door.

Michael picked up the nuns' habits, the monks' cowls, and the priest's cassock and carried them to the desk. He placed them beside Giro's father's coat, the gray wig, and the makeup bag from the news truck.

"Sante called," Steven said as he emerged from the bathroom. "His messenger is on the way over with the credentials. He says they're crude but passable if the guard on the door doesn't look too closely."

"And if he doesn't have an access list. Did Colombo find a few policemen to help us out?"

"He hadn't heard from Colombo, but if you have any credit with the man upstairs, pray he accomplished his mission."

The conversation was interrupted when Helen came in from Emma's bedroom. "You two look like you've been up for a while," she said to Michael and Steven. "Any news?"

"Nothing," Steven said. "I wish I could say I'm feeling more confident. The truth is I'm more apprehensive than when we turned in last night; or should I say early this morning?"

"We all are," Michael said. "I couldn't sleep. I wrestled with what we might or might not face in the chapel the morning."

"So did I," Steven said. "Once or twice I considered throwing caution to the wind and charging over to Saint Peter's, but when I came to my senses, I realized that even if we could get into the basilica and figure out where Masella's holding Emma, our actions might provoke him into killing her outright."

"It's mindboggling," Michael said. "I can't believe I came to Rome to report on an artist I'd never heard of and now ..."

"I know," Steven said. "So let's go over the plan one more time, at least as much of it as we can without knowing what we're going to find in the chapel."

CHAPTER THIRTY

The sound of a door opening and footsteps descending the stairs startled Emma. Her mind clouded with the fog of sleep, for a moment she forgot where she was. She glanced at her watch. "Oh my God, it's already six," she whispered. "Unless a miracle happens, I have a little over an hour to live."

She listened as the footsteps drew nearer. "Ah, I see you came back to pray at John Paul's tomb," Masella said serenely as he approached. "How appropriate you should say your final prayers here in this spot. But now the time for your petitioning is over. The hour of your martyrdom nears."

In spite of herself, Emma laughed, in part due to the absurd and terrifying dilemma in which she found herself, and to some extent from an intense case of nerves.

Masella scowled. "You may find this humorous, Ms. Bradford, but let me assure you; it is anything but comical.

Despite her efforts to control her emotions, Emma laughed again. "You've lost your mind," she said.

"You are mistaken, Ms. Bradford. I suggest you spend your final moments focusing on your immortal soul and not on my supposed state of mind or my triumph."

"Triumph?" Clearly flabbergasted, Emma gazed at Masella. "What a ludicrous choice of words. Do you really believe you're some sort of crusader charging into battle against the infidels?"

Masella had a faraway look in his eyes. "A superb analogy, Ms. Bradford. It would have made a first-rate lead-in to your news broadcast. Would you mind if I use your excellent comparison during my own analysis of the morning events on the Vatican network? Rest assured I will give you full credit." He laughed nervously. "Should I say 'rest in the assurance' rather than 'rest assured'? After all, in a little over an hour, you will be resting for all eternity."

Emma couldn't laugh at Masella's last remark. She made another attempt to make him change his mind. "Please reconsider this absurd plan, Monsignor," she urged.

Masella shook his head vehemently. "I cannot do that, Ms. Bradford, and unfortunately, I have no more time to convince you my actions are valid and proper."

Emma's resolve quickly evaporated. "What if I promise not to broadcast the story?" she implored.

"Had you stopped with your investigation after we met in Saint Agnes, perhaps my strategy would have changed, but you persisted, which necessitated immediate action on my part. So you see, Ms. Bradford, the cardinal's death, as well as your own, was brought about by your failure to follow my advice."

"No one has to die," Emma said with desperation in her voice. "We can work this out."

"Of course we can," Masella said. "It is really quite simple. You will kill Cardinal Amici, or so it will seem. In turn, you will attain martyrdom."

Emma's head dropped to her chest. She was out of ideas and through arguing. *Let Michael and Steven be safe,* she prayed as Masella took her arm and led her away from John Paul's tomb.

She quickly decided not to give Masella the satisfaction of seeing her defeated. *I'll be damned if I let this sicko see me cry,* she decided. She mustered all her strength, and, head held high, walked toward the stairs to face whatever fate awaited her in the chapel.

———

"Frankly, I'm surprised you didn't sneak out and try to rescue Emma singlehandedly while the rest of us slept," James said to Michael as Helen began the process of turning him into an old man.

"You forget. You're dealing with the new Michael. That's what Emma calls me."

"That's the understatement of the year," Steven said. "The twenty-four-thousand-dollar question, or maybe it's a million-dollar question now, is what prompted this miraculous change?"

"You're in the miracle business. You tell me."

"Let's see," Steven said, smiling. "Could it be the perpetual and uncatchable playboy has finally met his match?"

"That doesn't merit a response." Michael thought for a moment. "Well, maybe it does, but I can't think of an appropriate answer right now. I have more important things on my mind."

The conversation, which had brought a few moments of normalcy into a tense situation, was interrupted by a knock on the door. Michael walked over and peered out through the peephole. "Is it Sante's messenger?" David asked.

"God, I hope so!"

"What the hell is that?" Ron asked as Michael picked up the umbrella and held it over his head.

"It's an umbrella."

"That's obvious," Helen said. "The question is what are you going to do with it?"

"I'm taking appropriate precautions." Brandishing his weapon, Michael pulled open the door.

Seeing the raised umbrella, the courier stepped back. "Take it easy," he said. "I'm here to deliver a package from Sante." He held out a manila envelope.

"Ignore my crazy friend," Steven said, stepping forward to take the envelope.

Michael put the umbrella on the entry table. "Sorry if I startled you. One can't be too careful these days."

"I suppose so," the messenger said as he continued to back away. "If that's all, I will be going."

"Did Sante give you any other messages for us?" James called from the sitting room.

"He just told me to deliver the envelope."

"Again, I apologize for the umbrella," Michael said.

"At least you didn't use it on me." The messenger turned and hastily retreated down the hall.

"That went well," said Steven.

"You wouldn't be so quick to criticize if the messenger had turned out to be one of Masella's men." Michael picked up the umbrella, raised it above his head, and swung it around like a lariat as he spoke: "I pictured dozens of Vatican policemen swarming out of the stairwell, charging into the room, and subduing us before we could help Emma. The only thing available to save her was this." He lowered the umbrella and put it back on the table.

"That may be a slight exaggeration, but he does have a point," Helen said.

"I'm glad you finally understand," Michael said as he removed the invitations for the Mass from the envelope and handed one to Steven. "You and I are now officially Cardinal Amici's cousins from Sicily. We're the monk brothers."

"Is my invitation there too?" Giro asked.

"Yes, sister, as is Sister Mary Ronetta's." Giro took the card and handed one to Ron.

"I hate to mention another potential problem," Ron said, "but won't it seem odd when our invitations are different from the others?"

Steven sighed. "It's possible, so we'll have to be the first ones to go inside. When the crowd begins to arrive, the guard won't have time to leave his post to report any discrepancies."

"He could text or phone Masella," Ron said.

"Here we go again with ifs and suppositions," Steven said, shaking his head. "Hopefully the damn guard will think we're from out of town and don't need special papers. Honestly, we have no idea what he'll think, what he'll do, or how he'll handle the matter. What I do know is we can't worry about all the little things that could go wrong. We have to look at the bigger picture. If it makes you feel any better, I think we're okay in this regard. The man on duty will likely assume you're family."

"Then we'd better finish getting ready so we can be the first ones inside the basilica," James said as he donned the grey wig and tattered jacket.

"I hate to add another what-if to your list," said Helen. "Bill may be okay, but won't a grubby old man, two monks, and two very large nuns look out of place in the Excelsior lobby? I'd go so far as to say you'd be suspect. What if the night receptionist calls security and you're detained? I'd hate to think what will happen at Saint Peter's if you're not there."

"Another thing we overlooked," Steven said. "Any suggestions, Helen?"

"As a matter of fact, yes. David and I will go downstairs and see who's in the lobby. I'll distract whoever's behind the desk so you can walk through. I'm hoping we'll only have to deal with one person at this early hour."

"What about security cameras?" Michael asked. "I insisted they be up and running twenty-four/seven."

Steven groaned. "The minute we think we have a plan, something else comes up to make me wonder how the hell we're going to pull this off. To answer your question, let's hope no one is monitoring the cameras at this early hour or, if someone is on duty, we'll look like a group of monks and nuns and an old man going to early mass."

"Assuming you're right, what's your plan?" James asked Helen.

"At the moment I have no idea, but David and I will come up with something on the way down." She looked at Giro. "You and Ron need to shave before you put on your habits. If anyone stopped you … nuns with beards?"

"Actually, it's not unusual." Giro grinned. "When I was in school I saw many nuns with mustaches, though I think ours are a little thicker. I'll take care of my problem right now," Helen.

"And Sister Mary Ronetta is right behind him," Ron said.

———

"May I use the ladies' room?" Emma asked after Masella finished conversing with the guards.

Obviously this was a request the monsignor wasn't prepared to hear. His eyes narrowed as he addressed the American: "You take her," he ordered, "and do not let her out of your sight. My plan will not work if Ms. Bradford fails to appear in the chapel."

He turned to Emma. "And we would never wish to deprive you of the chance to make a profound contribution to the well-being of the church, would we, Ms. Bradford?"

"You don't need to remind me," Emma said, her voice oozing contempt.

The escort grasped Emma's arm tightly and guided her out of the basilica and down the stairs to the public restroom, the same one Emma had used before she and Nicola went up the stairs to see Bernini's amazing statue of Constantine. *A lifetime ago,* she thought. "I'll be out in a minute," she said, thinking the man would wait for her outside in the hallway.

"I'm afraid that won't do," he said. "I'll be coming in with you."

Emma stared at the guard in amazement. "You're not serious," she laughed nervously. "You think I'll try to climb out of a bathroom window?"

"There are no windows, but just the same, I'll be waiting inside."

Emma wasn't sure if she ever really believed she'd have an opportunity to get away, but at that moment, she was forced to accept her fate. She was going to the Blessed Sacrament chapel. How she came out was the only thing in question.

———

Helen called from the lobby. "I sent the woman on duty to housekeeping for extra towels. I'm watching the desk while she's away. You guys don't have much time."

"We'll take the stairs," Michael said. "Did you look out front?"

"No, but I can. Why?"

"Giro said Masella will be expecting us to come for Emma. I'm sure he told his men to call when we leave."

"What do you want us to do?"

"You go outside and take a look. Have David wait in the lobby. If Masella's men are out there, I don't want them to see the two of you together. As soon as you've cleared the revolving door, throw up your arms."

"Excuse me?"

"Pretend you've forgotten something and come back inside. I don't want to take a chance these guys will grab you like they did Emma. We'll wait on the landing above the first floor until we hear from you."

"I'm putting the phone in my pocket and heading out right now."

There was silence on Helen's side of the line. Moments later she came back. "You were right," she said. "There's a black car out there with two men sitting in the front seat. So what now?"

"Check the door to the Doney. It's early, but the chef and maître d' should be preparing for breakfast."

"Then what?"

"If the door's unlocked, let me know. If not, knock and tell whoever comes to see who it is that your friends are attending a special memorial Mass at Saint Peter's. They're hungry. They forgot to hang the room service card on the door, and there's no place to get food at such an early hour. Ask him to give you a couple of Danishes. We're heading down the last flight of stairs right now. If this works and the man goes into the kitchen, let the phone ring once and we'll come through. Be sure to leave the door unlocked."

"What if the guy closes it?"

"Step inside before he does. Unlock it when he goes into the kitchen. If the pastries are already out, he may tell you to help yourself. Hopefully he'll go back into the kitchen and leave you alone."

"Since we're back to the what-ifs, what if Giro can't get to the car without being seen? I think it was parked in the limo area to the right of the exit."

"Steven had the same concern, so he called for two cabs. We'll meet them in front of the wine shop around the corner on Via Lombardia. Send David over to wait for them. We can't have the drivers leave because we're not there. To be safe, have him go through the Doney."

"Do you want him to come back and go with me to Saint Peter's?"

"No use wasting the time it will take for him to get back to the hotel. He can go with us. Give us five minutes and go through the Doney as well. I'll have our driver contact dispatch and have a taxi waiting for you outside the sidewalk café when you get there. David will be waiting for you in the Orbit truck when you arrive."

"We'll be monitoring Sister Ronetta's feed," Helen said. "I just hope we don't have to go live to New York."

"Believe me, so do I," Michael said wistfully. "So do I."

———

The guard gripped Emma's arm as they rejoined Masella in the tombs. "Feeling more refreshed?" the monsignor asked.

"I'm not sure 'refreshed' is the word I'd use to describe how I feel," she said somberly.

"I too must say my prayers and attend to a few last-minute details before the Mass begins. My friends here will remain with you." Masella turned to leave, but looked back, grinning haughtily. "Be sure I will return on time." He paused, and Emma could almost see his brain working. "Were you a Catholic, I would administer last rites, but because you are not, I will bless you." He made the sign of the cross. "Lord, receive this woman's soul into your caring. Her sacrifice is for the many and for the good of your church."

He spun around and headed up the stairs.

No one was behind the registration desk when, after receiving a single ring signal from Helen, the small group got to the concierge desk. They quickly passed the elevators and rounded the corner. When they reached the end of the hallway leading to the restaurant, Steven breathed a sigh of relief. The door to the Doney was slightly ajar, and there was no one in the restaurant.

"Thank you, Helen," Michael said under his breath as they hurried through the room and out the door leading to the street. When they reached the patio, although the morning was mild, he felt a sudden chill and he shivered. They turned right, and, realizing two running monks, a priest, a grubby old man, and two very large nuns would attract attention, walked slowly toward the corner.

David was waiting by the cabs in front of the wine shop. The motley crew climbed in, Michael, Steven, and David in one car and Giro, Ron, James, and Bill in the other. With little traffic on the road, they quickly arrived at the barrier separating Vatican City from Rome.

"Good luck," David said as the cabs drove away. "I wish I was going into the basilica with you."

"I know, but you need to stay with Helen," Michael said. "You two could have important decisions to make about what or what not to send to New York."

Steven shook David's hand. "I agree with Michael," he said. "We'll see you soon."

David put his other hand over Steven's. "Be safe," he said.

"As Steven often says, 'your mouth to God's ears,'" said James.

"Here we go," Steven said. He turned and made the sign of the cross. "May God keep you safe."

"And you," James said as he blessed Steven.

"Don't forget Emma," Michael pleaded.

"That goes without saying, my friend."

"Say it anyway, would you?"

"Dear Lord," Steven began, "please bless Emma, Cardinal Amici, Cardinal Remella, and your servant, Pope John. Help them endure their trials with strength, secure in the knowledge that you will protect them."

"Thanks," Michael said with a nervous smile on his face.

They were just beyond the fountains when they heard a cab pull up to the truck. Michael turned around as Helen was paying the fare. She gave him a thumbs-up and went to join David.

Keeping his eyes trained on the Via della Conciliazione, Steven waited until he was sure no black car had followed Helen's cab. *They must still be waiting for us to leave the Excelsior,* he reflected as he caught up with the group approaching the basilica steps.

"Everything under control?" Michael asked.

"So far so good," Steven answered. "Apparently no one followed Helen."

"Then let's rescue Emma and save the cardinal."

As expected, a member of the Swiss Guard dressed resplendently in his ceremonial uniform waited at the door. "God, I hope there's no list and these invitations work," Michael whispered as they approached the sentinel.

"What if they don't?" Ron asked.

Steven frowned. "We're ignoring what-ifs, remember?"

Keeping his head low with the cowl covering much of his face, Steven removed his invitation from a pocket in his robe. Holding his breath, he handed it to the guard. Relief washed over him when the man made no move to check it against a guest list.

Masella blew that one, he reflected as the guard glanced at cardinal's seal. He handed the card to Steven and waved him through. Without pausing, Michael, James, Bill, Ron, and Giro flashed their identical invitations and were allowed to pass with no further scrutiny.

Except for a few priests attending to their business, the cavernous basilica was empty. "My God, the place is huge," Michael whispered. "You don't know how big it is until you're here with no tourists milling around." He took a deep breath, coming back to the moment at hand. "So, the first part of our plan went off without a hitch."

"I hope the rest of our task is as problem free," said Steven. "I hate to think what would have happened had the guard detained us."

"It's simple. We'd have stormed the place," Michael said, trying to show less concern than he was feeling.

Steven rolled his eyes. "Of course that's exactly what we would have done."

As they walked by Michelangelo's Pieta, Michael thought about how excited Emma was when she talked about seeing the sculpture for the first time. "God, please let her be safe so she can see it again," he whispered as they neared the Chapel of the Blessed Sacrament.

When they reached the iron gating, Michael took a deep breath, trying to calm his nerves. "It's going to be fine," James said, as he pushed through the gate.

"I know," Michael said, not wanting to discourage the others by telling them how little faith he had in what he was saying. He stared into the dimly lit chapel. The Eucharist candles were burning and the altar had been set for the Mass, but no guests had arrived.

"Let's take our positions," Steven whispered. He pointed toward two chairs in the next-to-last row. "Michael, you and I will sit here on the aisle. Ron, position yourself so you can aim the camera between us. You might want to put a few missals on your seat so you're sitting up higher."

"Will do," said Ron. "When I shaved, I cut the hole in my habit. The camera lens just fits."

"Good. James, you go to the other side. The front row has been roped off, so that's probably where Masella will bring Emma. Sit two rows back."

"Where do you want me?" Giro asked.

"Halfway up, in front of Michael and me," Steven said. "Bill, sit opposite him."

"Is there anything we can do while we're waiting?" Michael asked.

Steven nodded. "Pray, my friend. Pray!"

CHAPTER THIRTY-ONE

By 6:15, Steven and Michael were kneeling near the back of the chapel, cowls up and heads bent low as if deep in prayer. Ron sat behind with the camera pointed between them. Giro, James, and Bill were in place.

As the minutes dragged by, Michael kept glancing at his watch. It took all he had to maintain a superficial calm during the seemingly unending wait. From his bowed position, he occasionally glanced at the people filling the chapel. Most were old. *Probably the cardinal's real family,* he thought as he waited for the inevitable: Emma's entrance. He leaned toward Steven. "I can't stand this waiting. What can we do?"

"There's nothing more to be done. Patience, my friend."

"You know patience isn't one of my virtues."

"You're kidding."

"Come on, Steven," Michael implored. "Do we have a chance of stopping this from happening?"

"Honestly, I have no idea. I know you're worried, Michael. I am too, but we have to wait for Masella to make his move or all of this will be for nothing. Until he acts, it's only our word against his. We have to expose him and his insidious plot. We can't screw this up."

"And Emma? Do we sacrifice her for the sake of the story?"

"Of course not, but if you aren't patient, you'll be doing just that."

Michael tried to put negative thoughts out of his mind, but to no avail. He bowed his head to hide the tears which were welling up in his eyes. "God," he prayed, silently, "keep the woman I love safe. There, I've said it. Please take care of Emma so I can tell her how I feel."

At 6:45, Monsignor Masella pushed open the iron gate. Following behind him were two burly men with Emma securely sandwiched between. Despite Steven's admonition to keep his head down, Michael couldn't help himself. He peeked up from beneath the cowl. He figured Emma would look disheveled, but he hadn't expected to see the haunted look on her face. She looked like a deer caught in the headlights; her eyes were wild with dread and fear.

Hardly able to breath, Michael was frantic, his mind in such turmoil it was difficult to think straight. He made a sudden move to get up, but Steven pulled him down. "Where the hell are you going?" he whispered. "Listen to me. Keep your head down, and don't let Emma see you. All of our lives may depend on her not recognizing you."

Feeling helpless, Michael sighed deeply. He reluctantly sat down and bowed his head as the two men dragged the pale and trembling woman up to the front row. They moved in, positioning Emma between them while Masella sat on the aisle.

Michael looked up and stared at the back of Emma's bowed head, willing her to turn and look at him. "Help is coming, Emma," he whispered. "Hang on for a little while longer. Turn around so you can see I'm here."

"Damn it, Michael," Steven said quietly and firmly. "Look at the floor or you'll blow this." Michael shut his eyes and, again, reluctantly bowed his head.

At exactly seven, the procession gathered at the back of the chapel by the wrought-iron gating. Cardinal Amici, dressed in vestments the color of blood, started slowly up the aisle behind an altar boy carrying a cross.

Despite Steven's admonitions, Michael glanced up again. Strangely, unlike Emma, who was clearly terrified, the cardinal looked calm and serene. "The man looks as if he's in complete control of the situation," he whispered to Steven.

"Or resigned to his fate."

"If you don't mind, I prefer the former."

Cardinal Amici reached the altar and turned around to bless the assembled group, concentrating first on the people sitting in the front row. From his vantage point, Michael could see a change come over him when he spied Emma. He seemed to stand straighter as he looked at her.

This is the ultimate irony, Michael mused. *Little does the cardinal know that Masella is using the woman he believes is here to save him as the means of his downfall.*

When his eyes came to rest on Masella, the cardinal's calm demeanor changed to an expression of unmitigated hatred. He stared for a moment, turned to the altar, dropped to one knee, and kissed the fair linen before turning back again to face the congregation. With candles flickering behind him and genuine passion in his voice, he said loudly: "Blessed Mary, ever Virgin, pray for me."

Simultaneously, Michael and Steven realized the cardinal's words weren't part of the Mass. There was trouble ahead, and not just from Masella. "Something's wrong," Steven whispered.

"I agree," Michael said, angst in his voice and alarm on his face. "What do we do?"

"Nothing yet."

Michael watched Masella as he leaned forward. "What's he doing," he whispered to Steven.

"I have no idea." Steven put his hand on Michael's arm and held him firmly. "I know you want to charge up there, but we have to wait."

For Michael waiting was hell. The seconds crawled by like hours. He was wide awake but living a nightmare. He wanted to look away, but he was transfixed on the scene playing out in slow motion in front of him. Only Steven's continuing grasp on his arm kept him from racing out of his seat and tackling the monsignor.

At 7:05, the actual Mass began. Masella settled back in his seat, apparently feeling more comfortable and confident when the cardinal's words once again followed the traditional script.

Giro turned around in his seat, looking for a signal to spring into action. Steven nodded. "Not yet," he mouthed. "Wait."

Steven heard the sound of Ron's camera rolling during a Gospel reading by a young man, who was introduced as the cardinal's great nephew. When the reading was over, Cardinal Amici shuffled to a portable lectern set up to the right of the altar, directly in front of Masella and Emma. "He's delivering a homily," Steven whispered.

"Is that unusual?"

"No, but look at your program. It's unscheduled."

"He's put himself at risk by standing right in front of Masella," Michael whispered. "It's almost as if he realizes what's about to happen. He's daring the monsignor to kill him. Is that possible?"

"You should know by now, anything's possible."

Michael's stomach was in knots. This was one what-if they hadn't considered. "If he is privy to the plan, why would he be here?" he whispered.

"Shh. Listen," Steven admonished.

It quickly became apparent the previously calm and composed cardinal was becoming increasingly jittery. He nervously twisted his seal ring as he spoke. "He's worried," Michael said uneasily. "We have to move."

Steven grasped Michael's arm more tightly and continued to hold him down. "Damn it, Michael. Not yet."

The cardinal began to talk about his mother, for whom he was celebrating Mass, and the role she had played in his decision to become a priest. With every word he uttered, Emma became more aware of Masella's rising anxiety. His body tensed as he nervously clasped and unclasped his hands and restlessly squirmed in his seat.

Oh my God! He's really going through with this, she thought, terror overwhelming her. She leaned forward to look at the monsignor's face. His appearance confirmed her worst fears. His eyes were large and glazed over, and his brow was damp with nervous sweat. *There's no turning back,* she thought as she leaned back in her chair. Surprisingly, she was no longer frightened. She was going to die, and so she prayed.

The cardinal was about two minutes into his homily when Masella leaned toward her. "I had hoped to give you the privilege and comfort of receiving the sacrament of communion before your death," he whispered, "but at the time I had no idea Cardinal Amici would waste my time with a homily about his dear departed mother. I can delay no longer." He made the sign of the cross over Emma. "I absolve you of your sins," he said a little too loudly, causing the congregants on the other side of the aisle to turn their eyes from the cardinal and focus on him.

"It's happening," Michael whispered with urgency. "Masella's about to kill the cardinal."

Steven released his grip on Michael's arm. "I agree—go!"

The two men leaped from their seats at the exact moment when Masella rose. The guard who had been sitting between him and Emma forcefully jerked her out of her chair and pulled her toward the altar. A leering smile on his face, Masella boldly confronted the cardinal. "I will not allow you to destroy the church," he yelled. "This is the only way." He quickly stepped aside so the guard, gun pointed at the cardinal, could get a clear shot.

Masella's cold, cackling laugh penetrated Emma's senses, momentarily drawing her eyes away from the cardinal's face. She stared at her captor. He was indeed a madman, his face a mask of hate, and his eyes ablaze with passion.

To take the shot, the cardinal's assassin was forced to release his grip on Emma's arm. Though rigid with fear and her brain in a fog, she realized no one was holding her. This was her chance to run. She turned, but though she willed her feet to move, her knees buckled.

Realizing what was occurring, the guard who'd been seated to her right leapt out of his seat, grabbed her right arm to steady her, and forced her to stand.

The cardinal didn't flinch. "On the contrary, I will resurrect it," he bellowed resolutely, his dark eyes radiating determination.

Though it seemed like an eternity, the final act of the drama played out in only seconds. Without warning, Cardinal Amici pulled a gun from under his robe, aimed, and fired a single shot at Masella's head. Like a gymnast, he whirled and discharged a second shot into the hand of the guard who was holding the gun. The guard dropped the weapon and cried out in pain as Masella fell, surprise flooding his face. "May God forgive me," the cardinal cried as he fired again, this time into the monsignor's heart.

James dropped his cane, leapt out of his seat, and raced toward the man who was holding Emma. He jerked her captor away and delivered a hard blow to his jaw as Emma fell to the floor.

There was a surreal quality to the scene as a monk, his eyes focused on Emma, raced toward the altar. "Emma!" he cried. "Emma! It's Michael!"

Through the chaos, Emma heard her name and saw James kneeling beside her. Terrified, she kept her head down, instinctively curling in fetal position.

Michael dropped down onto the floor beside her. "It's over, Emma," he said as calmly as possible. "Masella's dead. Cardinal Amici's alive, and you're safe." When he put his hand on her shoulder, Emma recoiled.

It took several minutes before she glanced up at the man seated beside her. "Michael," she cried out.

To the surprise of everyone around, a large nun who'd been sitting in front of Michael and Steven left her seat, raced up the aisle, and grabbed the wounded guard who was trying to stand, throwing him to the floor. "Make a move and I'll break your arm," Giro roared in a gravelly voice. Suddenly, a second nun who had been sitting in the back row stood up, jerked the camera from beneath her robes, and proceeded up the aisle.

Confused, but sensing the situation was under control, Cardinal Amici lowered his gun as Steven approached him, holding out his hand as he walked. The cardinal was dazed, but he handed over the weapon without protest. "It's finally over," the man in scarlet said quietly. "May God forgive me." The hand which killed a fellow priest and wounded a guard clutched his pectoral cross.

"I'm sure he already has," Steven murmured in response.

The cardinal nodded. "And to think it came to this."

Before Steven could respond, a cadre of Swiss Guard, replete in their Michelangelo-designed striped jumpsuits, blasted through the door. They were not carrying halberds, their signature long-handled axes. Instead, they were brandishing Berettas.

"Oh, God!" Steven exclaimed. He put himself between the cardinal and the armed men as Michael pushed Emma back down on the floor and covered her with his body.

Michael looked up at Steven. "What now?" he asked, panic in his eyes. "We're no match for these armed men."

Steven exhaled deeply. "Thank God I don't have to answer your question. Here come Sante and Colombo."

As members of the Swiss Guard stood alertly at the gate, Sante moved out from behind them. "I told these guys I needed to go first," he said, "but they wouldn't listen."

James went to meet Sante and the Swiss Guard, leaving Emma and Michael on the chapel floor. Emma was no longer crying, but Michael could tell she was distraught. Her shoulders were trembling as she covered her face with her hands.

Michael pulled her to him and put his arm around her shoulder, endeavoring to comfort her and let her know the danger had passed. "The nightmare's over, Emma. Do you understand?"

Confusion and fright in her eyes, Emma looked up and nodded blankly. Hugging her to him, Michael waited.

"I wasn't sure what you'd do," she finally said as her breathing began to return to normal, "but I figured you'd do something. That thought helped me get through this ordeal. Thank you for coming to my rescue." She smiled weakly, and her voice shook with emotion as she spoke: "Though those monk's robes aren't exactly what I had in mind when I imagined you arriving in your iconographic cape."

Michael felt his spirits lift for the first time since Emma was snatched from the Excelsior. "That's the Emma I love," he whispered.

If Emma heard what he said, she didn't respond. Still hanging on tightly, she watched the chaotic scene, as the Vatican police swarmed in and surrounded the cardinal, and members of his family struggled to figure out what was happening.

"Steven's here too," Michael said to Emma. "Somebody had to watch out for me while I was watching out for you. And in case you didn't recognize him, James was the old man who got to you first. Sister Mary Ronetta is filming and Sister Mary Giro's here, though you might not recognize him." He motioned to the man-nun, who, alongside a Vatican policeman, was standing over the downed guard. "Sister Giro will sit with you until I get back," he continued. "I'm sure the Swiss Guard will have questions."

"You have to go?"

"I do. We're worried about the pope. Steven, James, and I have to figure who else was involved in Masella's scheme and neutralize them."

"Please be careful," Emma pleaded.

"We will. Even if the Vatican police finish their interrogation, stay here in the chapel until you hear from me."

Steven handed the cardinal's weapon to a policeman. "The Swiss Guard and the Vatican police seem to have everything under control," he said when Michael joined him by the chapel door. He motioned to James, who walked back to the chapel entrance. Seconds later, Sante joined all three.

"What do you know?" Michael asked Sante.

"One of my friends in the Swiss Guard told me that Masella doubled Pope John's guard early this morning. They were told the only people who were to given access to the pope were two of his doctors and, of course, Masella himself."

"So here's the problem," said Michael. "Masella had to realize his harebrained scheme might fail. What orders did he leave with the guards and the doctors, and who did he tell to carry them out?"

"What about Monsignor Tomai?" Steven asked. "He was with Masella at Saint Agnes."

"But he's Cardinal Amici's secretary," Sante said.

"Appointed by Masella," said Steven.

The cardinal, walking between two of the Swiss Guard, bent and blessed Emma as he passed by. He proceeded toward the rear of the chapel, nodding to Michael, James, and Steven as he passed. At the door, he turned and looked back pensively at the chaotic scene. He shook his head and walked into the basilica.

"Think he's under arrest?" Michael asked.

Steven answered: "I'm sure he'll have a lot of questions to answer, but whether he'll be arrested or not, I have no idea. It depends on what happens in the next few minutes. We have to be sure he's not taken into custody, and I'm afraid whatever we do is going to involve Emma."

"Emma's in no shape to do anything, even answer questions the police are already asking," Michael said in disbelief. "Surely you don't expect her to be part of our plan." He paused. "For that matter, what is our plan?"

"I'm afraid we're flying by the seat of our pants," Steven said. "Okay, we'll leave Emma here for the moment. I'm sure the congregants will confirm her story, so she shouldn't be detained for long. Sante, go ask Giro to turn on his phone. Tell him to stay with Emma and stand by in case we need her."

"What about Colombo?" Sante asked.

"He can come with us."

While Sante went to get Colombo and talk with Giro, Steven walked over to one of the policemen who had entered the chapel immediately after the shooting. He spoke with the man for a few minutes before returning to Michael.

"What did you say?" Michael asked.

"I told him what was happening and that I'd explain everything as soon as we make sure the cardinal's safe."

"We have no idea where he was taken," Michael said anxiously.

"Of course I don't know anything for sure, but I imagine he was escorted to his rooms."

"Why would you assume that?" Michael asked.

"Where else would they take him?"

"Good point, and it's safe to say he's being guarded. The question is, by whom? By Masella's men or the good guys?"

"A question I'm afraid I can't answer. Maybe Sante can help in that regard."

"Did I hear my name?" Sante asked as he and Colombo approached.

"You did," said Steven. "We need to get to Cardinal Amici before someone tries to finish what Masella started. I'd like for you to come with us."

"Of course. I'll bring along two men I know I can trust."

In a few seconds, Sante returned with his cohorts. "As Monsignor Laurent said, we need to get to Cardinal Amici's rooms as quickly as possible," Michael said. He looked back at Emma, wishing he could stay with her instead of racing off to rescue the cardinal. *But I can't,* he thought as he turned and, with the others, left the chapel.

As Sante led them through passages unknown even to Steven, Michael's heart raced. Would they be in time to save the cardinal or, even in death, had Masella managed to achieve his objectives?

When they arrived at the cardinal's door, there were no guards on duty. "What the hell?" Steven said as he tried the latch. "The door's bolted from the inside."

"Could the rooms have been sealed? Could someone have taken the cardinal somewhere else? Could he be in danger?" Michael asked anxiously.

"How?" Steven said sharply. "I told you, the door's bolted from inside."

Steven turned to Sante. "Any chance there's a passageway from the outside into the cardinal's room?"

"If there were, wouldn't the cardinal have used it to escape his captors?" Sante said.

"Point made." He knocked on the door and waited for a response. Hearing nothing, he knocked again.

Suddenly, the quiet in the hall was shattered by the sound of a gunshot emanating from behind the cardinal's locked door. "What the hell's happening in there?" Michael shouted.

Steven pounded on the door. "Eminence," he called out. "It's Monsignor Laurent. If you're in there, please open the door."

Feeling tense and helpless, the men waited. "Do you think one of Masella's men finished the job the monsignor started in the chapel?" Michael asked anxiously.

"I wish I knew." Steven pounded on the door again. "Eminence, please open the door."

Time dragged by as the men waited to discover what had happened in the cardinal's room. Suddenly, they heard the sound of the latch being lifted. Instinctively, the two Swiss Guard aimed their Berettas toward the opening.

"Don't fire unless we're threatened," Steven ordered. "We have no idea who's behind the door or what went on in there."

As they saw the door open a crack, they heard a familiar voice: "It's Cardinal Amici."

"Eminence, it's Monsignor Steven Laurent. I'm here with Michael Kelsey and Father McDonald. Are you all right?"

"Masella was an evil man," the cardinal said from behind the cracked door.

Michael took a deep breath. "We know. Monsignor Cipriano is dead."

"Of course he is," said the cardinal, his voice sounding stronger. "I shot him."

Steven couldn't believe how unemotional the cardinal sounded. "But you're okay, Eminence?" he asked anxiously.

"I am. Is Ms. Bradford alright? She was an innocent pawn—"

"She's fine," Michael called out. "She's on her way."

Michael looked at Sante. "Call Giro and tell him to get Emma here as quickly as possible."

"I'll go get her myself," Colombo said. "If she's not through answering questions, I may have to call my superiors to get her released into my custody."

"Do whatever you have to," Steven said, "but hurry. Emma may be the only person who can get the cardinal to open the door."

"Can't we pull it open?" one of the guards asked.

"Not a good idea," said Steven. "We have no idea if the cardinal has a gun or who else might be in the room. He may be the captor, or he could be the captive. Whichever, it's safe to assume he's spooked, so let's not push him. We'll wait for Emma."

"Cardinal Amici, Emma's on her way," Michael repeated calmly to the man behind the door. "I know she'll want to talk with you."

"Is she bringing the camera with her?" the cardinal asked tentatively.

Steven looked at Michael. "What's that all about?" he whispered.

"I have no idea. Ask him."

"Would you like a camera, Eminence?" Steven asked.

There was another pause. "I would," he finally said. "All of this must be part of the official record. I know I am to be interrogated, so bring a member of the Swiss Guard or the Vatican police with you. Perhaps there will be no need for further questioning when he hears what I have to say."

Steven turned to James. "Call Colombo. Tell him to bring Bill, and have Bill bring the camera. Hopefully Ron's still filming. I don't want him to stop. For the record, Sante can listen to what the Cardinal has to say."

"Will do." James punched in Colombo's number and spoke briefly. "Colombo's almost at the chapel," he said. "As you might imagine, it's chaotic in there."

"I hope he hurries," Michael said.

"I'm sure he's moving as quickly as circumstances allow," said Steven. "Pray the Vatican police allow Emma to leave."

"Should we keep talking to the cardinal?" Michael asked as they waited.

"Truthfully, I have no idea what we should be doing," Steven said, his tone of voice exuding the frustration he was feeling. "In this instance, there isn't a precedent I can reference."

James put his hand on Steven's shoulder. "It's okay, my friend. We're all jumpy." He turned to Michael. "To answer your question, I think we need to find out as much as we can before we go barging in there."

"James is right," Steven said. He walked closer to the door. "Eminence, are you alone?"

"I am now," the cardinal said.

"Who was with you?" Michael asked.

"Another of Masella's men. He tried to kill me."

Before Steven could probe further, Colombo entered the hallway with Emma and Bill following close behind.

Though she still looked disheveled and pale, Michael saw the familiar resolve in Emma's eyes. He walked over and took her hand. "You okay?" he asked.

"Considering the circumstances, I am."

"Did you finish answering questions?"

"For now. The police are in the process of interviewing everyone who attended the Mass. She assessed the situation in the hall. "How bad is it?"

"It's difficult to say," Steven said. "We think Cardinal Amici's alone, but there was someone with him."

"Was?"

"Yes. We heard a shot," Sante said.

"The cardinal shot someone else?"

"It seems so," Michael said. "Colombo brought you to us because the cardinal wants to see you."

Bill looked puzzled. "Why am I here?"

"Because he asked for you, or rather he asked for your camera."

"He wants me to record what happens next?"

Michael nodded. "That's what he said. Is Ron getting the footage of what's going on in the chapel?"

"He was still shooting when I left to come up here."

"Is he sending the feed to the truck?"

"Everything."

"Then let's get this part of the story before we decide what to do next."

"We don't have much time if we want an exclusive," Emma said. "I saw a swarm of news crews coming across the piazza as we left the basilica. I think they'll be kept from entering while the investigation's ongoing, but it won't be long before they have enough to interrupt their broadcasts with breaking news."

"So what do you want to do?" Bill asked.

With a concerted effort, Emma jumped into action. "Stall the cardinal a little longer. I'll do a quick intro. Helen can send this footage to New York along with the uncut and unedited video Ron took in the chapel."

"What he sends is going to be awfully graphic," Bill said.

"Then I'll add a warning at the end of my spiel."

"You sure you're strong enough to do the intro?" Michael asked.

"If you mean am I going to collapse, no, though I'll admit my knees are still weak."

"Then let's go for it," said Bill.

Emma moved in front of the wall to the right of the cardinal's door. Bill nodded, and she began:

*This is Emma Bradford, reporting live from Vatican City, where
only moments ago, there was a startling occurrence. Events are
still unfolding, so this report will be brief. What you're about
to see is uncut footage of the scenario which took place inside
the Chapel of the Blessed Sacrament in Saint Peter's Basilica.
As Michael Kelsey and I have been reporting for the past few
days, there has been an ongoing struggle between Cardinal
Giancomo Amici and Pope John. The subject of this contentious
relationship—the direction the Catholic Church will take in
the years to come. What you will see, unedited and uncut, is
the pope's private secretary, Monsignor Cipriano Masella, in a
failed attempt to use violence to impose his liberal agenda. His
plans were thwarted when he died at the hand of Cardinal
Amici, who fired in self-defense. I warn you, the scenes you are
about to view are extremely graphic and disturbing, so parental
discretion is strongly suggested. This is Emma Bradford. Stay
tuned to ABC. I'll be back with exclusive information as these
constantly fluctuating events continue to unfold.*

"Good job," said Bill, stopping the camera.

"Thanks. Did Cardinal Amici say anything else while I
was filming?" Emma asked.

"Nothing," James said.

"Shall I try to talk with him?"

Steven nodded. "It seems you're the only one who can get
him to let us in."

Motioning Bill to follow, Emma walked to the cardinal's door and knocked. "Cardinal Amici, it's Emma Bradford. I'm here with our cameraman, Bill Stevens. You remember him. He was the man who was filming the guards during our interview at the Alexander monument."

For a moment there was no response, so Emma tried again. "Cardinal, it's Emma."

"Ms. Bradford," the cardinal called out. "I saw you in the chapel. I knew how Masella planned to use you."

"You did?" Emma asked in disbelief. "Will you open the door and tell me how you knew?"

The assembled group waited. Emma turned around and saw the drawn Berettas. She addressed the cardinal again. "Eminence, are you armed? Michael told me he heard a shot. Do you have a gun?"

"I do, but it's on my desk across the room."

Steven signaled for the two guards to put their guns away. Sante turned and nodded his approval.

"Will you open the door so we can talk?" Emma asked. "Bill will begin filming as soon as you do."

"I will, but only for you, Bill, and a policeman. No one else."

"I'd like to bring Monsignors Laurent and McDonald with me," she said calmly, "as well as Michael Kelsey, my partner from ABC. These men are the reason I'm still around to speak with you. If we're going to report this story accurately, I'll need their help. Also with us will be Sante and Colombo, Vatican policemen who will take your statement."

The cardinal didn't immediately answer. "Fine," he eventually said, "but only you, Monsignor Laurent, Mr. Kelsey, Sante, and, of course, Bill with his camera."

Emma looked at James and Colombo. "We're going to have to do it his way," she said.

"All right, Eminence," Emma said. "Open the door. We're coming in."

The cardinal didn't respond, but seconds later the door opened enough for him to see outside.

"See, it's just us," Emma said reassuringly.

The cardinal opened the door all the way and the group entered. "Oh my God!" Steven exclaimed as he looked beyond the cardinal through the large anteroom and into the bedroom. "There's a body lying on the floor."

Emma didn't have time to react. "Come in," the cardinal said calmly. "I have a great deal to say. Are you filming?"

Emma looked at Bill, who nodded. "We are, Eminence," she said.

"Then please join me."

CHAPTER THIRTY-TWO

T he cardinal led Emma and the group through the anteroom and into his bedroom. *A fight to the death occurred
here,* was Emma's first thought.

"Ms. Bradford, come in," the cardinal said graciously,
as if asking friends to join him for a social occasion. "Mr.
Kelsey, Monsignor Laurent." He looked at Bill. "Thank you
for filming, young man. You did an excellent job during the
interview in the basilica."

"Thank you, Eminence," Bill said.

"This is Sante," said Steven. "I trust him, Eminence. You
can too."

The cardinal nodded and pointed to the body on the
floor. The man lying face down, obviously dead or gravely
wounded, wore clerical robes. There was a gun on the floor
near his right hand. Emma glanced at the cardinal's desk. As
he said, a gun rested on the shiny mahogany surface.

Steven approached the body. "May I turn him over,
Eminence?"

"Of course," the cardinal said calmly. "Once he is
removed, this horrendous episode in the church's history will
be over once and for all."

Steven bent and rolled the body. He gasped when he saw
the gaping bullet hole in the center of the man's forehead.
"It's Giotto Tomai."

"And Masella's second in command," the cardinal said with remarkable composure.

"I don't believe it," Emma said. "Monsignor Tomai seemed genuinely surprised by what Masella said during our meeting in Saint Agnes. Of course, I considered the possibility he was acting, but ..." The cardinal had a puzzled look on his face. "It's a long story, Eminence," she said. "One I'll share with you later. You're certain Monsignor Tomai was working with Masella?"

"Without question!"

"Will you tell us what happened?" Steven asked.

"I will, but back in my anteroom. I am sure all of us would be more comfortable in there. When we have finished, Sante, your men may remove the body."

When they had gathered in the anteroom, the cardinal closed his bedroom door.

"Eminence, are you ready to make a statement?" Emma asked.

"Of course." The cardinal looked directly at the camera. "I shot Masella, and I shot Giotto," he said a matter-of-factly. "I wasn't always a cardinal, a man of peace. I am an expert hunter. All along I knew what Masella was planning, so I carried a gun hidden under my robes when I entered the chapel. I used it to thwart the monsignor's evil scheme."

"We know, but what happened up here?" Steven asked. "How did you know about Monsignor Tomai?"

"One question at a time, Monsignor." The cardinal motioned toward the sofa. "If you will all sit down."

Emma preferred to stand, but there was firmness in the cardinal's voice which compelled her to do as he asked.

When she, Michael, and Steven were seated, the cardinal sat opposite them. Sante remained standing at his side.

"Now, Eminence, talk to us," Emma urged.

"Certainly," the cardinal said. "Are you filming, Bill?"

"I am, Eminence," Bill replied.

"And you, Sante, I would like for you to accept this as my formal statement. Please reserve your astonishment while I talk. What you are about to hear will seem more baroque as I continue to relate my story."

Emma smiled. "Excellent choice of words, Eminence. Please continue."

"I was escorted to my room by the Swiss Guard. They let me in, and I bolted the door from the inside. When I turned around, Monsignor Tomai was standing behind my desk pointing a gun directly at me."

"You're sure he realized it was you?" Emma asked.

"Of course he did! He addressed me by name."

"What else did he say?" Emma asked.

"Five words: 'Masella failed! I will succeed!'"

"Obviously he didn't fire right away," Emma said. "Were you carrying a second gun under your robes?"

"No. The pious monsignor was unable to deny his fellow priest the opportunity to save his immortal soul. I asked him if I could pray before he killed me, telling him I needed to confess my sins and ask God's forgiveness. Incredibly, he offered to hear my confession and give me absolution. He was both deluded *and* foolish."

"What happened next?" Michael asked, feeling like he was reading the last pages of what Helen had called a 'bad mystery novel.'

"I pointed to my prie-dieu, indicating I wanted to kneel on the cushion in front of my Bible."

"And he let you?" Steven said in amazement.

The cardinal smiled. "He actually encouraged me to pray. Another imprudent move on his part."

"So you went to your prie-dieu. Then what?" Emma asked.

"I reached down to adjust the cushion, pulled out another gun, spun around on my knees, and shot the monsignor in the head. That is it."

"That's it?" Emma asked in amazement.

"What more can I say? The evidence will prove I am telling the truth. Masella and Monsignor Tomai were going to kill me. Had Masella succeeded, Pope John would have been a puppet pope. Had Masella failed, yet lived, he would have given the pope the final dose of poison."

"That's what we figured," Emma said, "but how could you have known about Masella's intentions?"

The cardinal smiled. "If you were able to find out, I certainly could, Ms. Bradford."

"But you've been cut off from the world," Steven said.

"That is not true. I had Cardinal Remella and all his resources at my command."

"How?" Steven asked. "You didn't have access to e-mail."

"And you couldn't have passed lengthy notes during the peace at Mass," Emma said. "I can see how the cardinal could have given you short messages, but how could he have revealed Masella's entire plan?"

"I shall show you in a minute, Ms. Bradford, but first let me apologize."

"For what?" Emma asked.

"For putting you through your ordeal yesterday afternoon and last night, and, more particularly, for letting the situation play out this morning, though, I must say, the events in the chapel were not what I expected."

"What do you mean?" Emma asked.

"Surely you recall Masella's plan, Ms. Bradford."

"Unfortunately, with great clarity."

"Then you know Masella intended to make my death look like it was your idea, not his. He would then use the Vatican Network to report his version of the story."

"Right," Emma said pensively.

"Under the circumstances, that might have been difficult to do," said the cardinal.

"I don't understand—"

"At the last minute Masella's egotism got the best of him, and, if you recall, he announced that he would not allow me to destroy the church."

"So he was actually confessing to the intended murder; and after all that planning to make it look like Emma committed the crime, he was absolving her," Michael said.

"He was, so had I died at his hand, his plan would not have worked after all, but back to what Masella *hoped* would happen. It was never to be."

"How do you know that?" Emma asked, still trying to make sense of what the cardinal was saying.

"As I told you, I have always known what Masella planned to do. I also knew you would be safe, Ms. Bradford. The American who took you from the Excelsior is one of my men. He was prepared to kill Masella last night had he made a move to harm you."

Emma was astonished. "The American works for you?"

"He does, and I find the need to apologize yet again. I am sorry Father Paul was forced to treat you with such insensitivity. He is a former Green Beret who found his calling and became a priest. I bring him to Rome from time to time when I require his special talents."

"Special talents?" Emma shook her head. "You often need to use force, Eminence?"

"Of course not, at least not regularly, though, of late, special circumstances have necessitated the special brand of protection Father Paul provides."

"Where's *Father Paul* now?" Emma asked.

The cardinal looked at his watch. "He should be at Fiumicino, ready to board his flight to his parish in Baltimore. He asked me to apologize for his conduct. If he had acted differently—"

"He couldn't have told me something to make me worry less?" Emma said.

"Unfortunately, no—"

"Why the hell not?" Michael demanded, furious that all of them, Emma in particular, had to go through what they did for no apparent reason.

"Because it took over a month for Father Paul to earn the monsignor's trust. Had he been discovered, I guarantee, Ms. Bradford would be dead, and I would have no way to prove what I am telling you now. It would have been Masella's word against mine, and remember, he had the pope on his side; at least he believed he did."

"Are you telling us Pope John's been faking—that he isn't sick?" Michael asked in disbelief.

"Not entirely. Initially he had a severe case of influenza, but once his doctors realized he was being poisoned—."

Steven finished the cardinal's sentence. "They stopped administering the drug, and he pretended to be getting sicker."

"Exactly. Once Cardinal Remella explained what was occurring, the doctors became willing participants in our plan to save Pope John and thwart Masella's plan."

"Speaking of Cardinal Remella, Masella told me he had a stroke," Emma said.

The cardinal smiled. "The only stroke in this case was our stroke of luck when I discovered Masella's plan to poison him as well. My people put out the statement about his sudden illness. For his safety, he was swiftly taken to the hospital, where he has been guarded by the Vatican police."

"So he's all right?" Emma asked.

"Now that Masella and Giotto are dead, he will be released with a clean bill of health."

"So Cardinal Remella was being kept on ice," Michael said.

"I beg your pardon?"

"What Michael means is you had him isolated so if you had failed to stop Masella—"

"He would have stepped in to lead the conservative movement. He has all the necessary evidence to expose Masella's plan."

"Then why go through with the charade?" Michael asked, still irritated.

"Would you have believed me had I told you about Masella's outrageous scheme?"

"Probably not, at least not at first," Michael said.

"I agree," said Emma. "What about Monsignor Tomai, Eminence?"

"His appointment was my suggestion. You know the old adage: 'Keep your friends close and your enemies even closer'? That's what the pope and I have been doing. He has been listening to and watching Masella—"

"And you've been watching Giotto," Steven said.

"Yes."

"Was this going on when you and the pope appeared on the loggia?" Emma asked.

"It was."

"Then you're a damn good actor." Michael quickly realized he'd been disrespectful. "Sorry, Eminence."

"About what? I appreciate the compliment."

"What do you plan to say about Masella?" Steven asked.

"I'll simply tell the truth. Masella is dead, and his insidious plot, which in his last moments he confessed, died with him. Are you hearing all of this, Sante?"

"I am, Eminence."

The cardinal turned toward Bill. "When we have finished with this initial discussion, I would like for you to film another report. This time I'll join Ms. Bradford and Mr. Kelsey to explain the recent occurrences to the world."

"You're sure Pope John approves of what you're doing?" Steven asked.

"Of course he does. We decided I should speak so he can remain above the fray."

"His Holiness will corroborate your statement?" Sante asked.

"He will."

"Speaking of communicating with the pope, you haven't told us how you manage to get information to him and vice versa," Emma said.

"Through Cardinal Remella, of course."

"But how?"

"Before I answer, I should apologize one last time, Ms. Bradford. I used you from the beginning. I hinted there was a story to pursue and found a way to make you pursue it."

"So all of this was planned from day one?" Michael said. "How could you have known Emma and I would follow through?"

"I am not the only one who can do his homework, young man. Thank God for Google. I believe your producers were told how important the Bernini's exhibit is to the Vatican?"

"They were," Emma said.

"Well, it was and is, but not just because Bernini was a great artist, who, as you said in one of your reports, forever changed the face of Rome. The exhibition was the catalyst for getting you here, though we initially had no idea who your stations would send to cover the exhibition."

"Why the two of us?" Emma asked. "I mean, why one reporter from Boston and another from New York? Why not a nationally or internationally known investigative reporter?"

"Because if our plan was to work, we had to establish a rivalry between two local ABC stations and their reporters."

"So we'd work harder and, hopefully, uncover the real story," Michael said.

"Yes, Mr. Kelsey. Pope John pledged his cooperation, so suddenly Bernini became significant. Once you and Ms. Bradford arrived, we waited to see which one of you would learn there was a more important story than the Bernini exhibition. Imagine our pleasure when you joined forces."

"What about the other players?" Michael asked. "There's Lucio and Gusto—"

Emma interrupted. "And Dina, my maid, who was killed?"

"Ah yes, Dina, a sad consequence of the conflict. The cardinal bowed his head in a silent prayer. "Masella ordered her death for the same reason he killed Piero, to prevent me from opposing Pope John's plans to unilaterally modernize the church. Dina was a member of the Vatican police, a woman I strategically placed at the Excelsior to keep an eye on you. When Masella found out from Enrico Baldi—"

"Gusto's brother," Michael interrupted.

"Yes, Enrico was Masella's man. Gusto told him about Dina and he told Masella, who had her eliminated. She knew the risks when she accepted the job. She will always have my gratitude, and daily masses will be said for her in perpetuity."

"Then she wasn't the one who tried to break into my room?" Emma said. "Nor did she send her brothers?"

"No, that was Gusto. My sources report it was he who had a woman call housekeeping to say you needed towels. Though he stayed in the background when she went to the desk, he accompanied her to your room."

"Who was she?" Michael asked.

"We have yet to discover her identity, though I assure you we will. Gusto is currently being interrogated by the

Vatican police and Enrico is under arrest. In any case, when Gusto and the woman were unable to get in because you engaged the security lock, he called Masella, who ordered him to wait for a better time."

"Any idea what they planned to do if they got in?" Steven asked.

"I'm good, young man, but not that good, though I plan to find the answer to your question."

"What will happen to Lucio?" Emma asked.

"We are still looking into what role he played. He is Masella's brother-in-law, but, as of now, we have no proof his involvement went beyond reporting on your activities. If it did, he will be dealt with, as will all the others who have played their parts."

"So now what?" Steven asked.

"Now I will show you how I managed to keep track of what was going on."

The cardinal rose and walked to a bookcase on the wall. He pulled out a book on the end. "One of my favorites," he said, as he handed the book to Emma.

She read the title aloud: *"Bernini and the Counter-Reformation.* Appropriate," she said, smiling.

The cardinal pushed a button in the space between where the book had rested and the side of the cabinet. The bookcase swung inward, exposing a corridor. "In the old days, when the passage was designed to be an escape from this room, this case had to be pulled out manually. For some reason, my predecessor in this apartment had it electronically wired. Perhaps he feared for his safety at the hands of a potential enemy."

Emma went over and peered inside. "Where does the passage lead?"

"To a door in the rear of the Vatican gardens. The exit is partially hidden by shrubbery."

"And Masella and his men had no idea it was there?"

"Apparently not. Cardinal Remella was the one who told me about it. He was told by his friend, Cardinal della Chesia, who occupied this room before it was given to me."

"Cardinal della Chesia?" Emma said, surprise on her face. "These were Pope John's apartments?"

Cardinal Amici nodded. "They were."

"Could he have wired the door because he feared Masella?"

"Even before he was elected, Pope John knew that Masella was a dangerous and powerful force, Ms. Bradford, so it is possible that was his motive."

"And you never thought you'd be found out; that someone would come in to check on you?" Michael asked.

"We were able to use the passageway after I was locked in for the night. As you learned when you came up here from the chapel, the door can be bolted from the inside. Remella, who, for some reason, was not closely watched until you met with him at Antico Arco, would come through the passageway to my anteroom."

"When things settle down, would you take Michael and me through the passage?" Emma asked. "It would be a great place to do a follow-up report."

"Of course," the cardinal said, though you realize you will be exposing my secret means of escape."

"Hopefully you won't find the need to break out again," Emma said.

"To use an American phrase one of my brother cardinals often uses, 'your mouth to God's ears.'" The cardinal smiled.

"A phrase I've heard or uttered several time over the past eighteen hours," Michael said "So what now?"

"Now I need to find a new secretary, someone I can trust." The cardinal pointed to Steven. "Monsignor, you are that man."

Steven was clearly taken aback. "I appreciate the vote of confidence, Eminence but—"

"A long career in the Vatican is of no interest to you. I am not asking you to dedicate your life to me for as long as I live, though at my age, it might not be asking too much."

"Eminence—"

"Let me finish. I am not requiring a long-term commitment, but I need you now; you and your friend James, who will be asked to assume the position of Pope John's interim secretary until all of this is sorted out. Six months. Will you give you that?"

"My pleasure, Eminence," Steven said. He shook his head in disbelief. "I never saw this coming."

"Life is full of surprises," the cardinal reflected.

"That it is, Eminence," Steven said. "May I bring James in so you can ask him about serving the pope? Though I'm sure I know what his answer will be."

"Bring everyone in, but we are not going to say anything to your friend about his new assignment. The Holy Father will ask him. Would you open the door? That is, after you make sure the Swiss Guard put their Berettas away."

"That's the least a good secretary could do for his boss, Eminence." Steven went to the door, stepped out, and, several minutes later, returned with James and Colombo. Steven introduced Colombo to the cardinal.

"I am glad to meet you, Colombo," the cardinal said, "and it is a pleasure to see you again, Monsignor McDonald. Thank you for all you have done for me, for the pontiff, and for the church."

"You're welcome, Eminence," said James. "We're all glad you and Emma are safe."

"Thanks be to God," the cardinal said.

Five minutes into the conversation, the cardinal's phone rang. He nodded to Steven. "My new private secretary will answer."

"Of course," Steven said. "My first official duty."

James was clearly surprised. "You're Cardinal Amici's new secretary?" he said.

"Interim secretary," Steven said, "and I won't be for long if I don't do what my boss asks." He picked up the phone, his face exuding pride as he spoke. When he hung up, he looked at Emma. "The Holy Father wishes to see you, Michael, and James."

"He can have you in a minute," the cardinal said. "I realize the police will want to collect evidence from my bedroom to corroborate what I have said. That process can begin in a moment. How long do you think it will take for you to send this interview and your next report to New York?"

"Not long," Emma said. "My producer, Helen Taylor, is in the truck outside the square. I can do my report immediately. Helen has the footage we shot earlier. Do you want it edited? We sent the events in the chapel live and uncut."

"I would prefer you do some editing this time. It is not necessary for the personal parts of our conversation to be aired; report the facts."

Emma grimaced, and the cardinal, obviously concerned, asked: "Have I said something to upset you, Ms. Bradford?"

"When you said you wanted me to report the facts, I thought about Masella. He told me I would die because of my persistent need to report the facts. He said if Michael and I had stopped investigating after the meeting at Saint Agnes—"

"None of this would have happened," said the cardinal.

"You knew about the meeting?" James asked.

"I did. Some of the men Masella boasted about just before he left the church are loyal to me and our conservative cause."

"How could you have known?" Emma asked. "I had no idea who demanded the meeting."

"You think the Vatican is a medieval state, Ms. Bradford? I assure you, with the help of your CIA and FBI, our equipment is state of the art. We can certainly tap a man's phone line and trace his cell usage."

Michael was clearly irritated. "I ask you again, Eminence: Why did any of this have to happen? Why didn't you and the pope get together, make a joint statement to the world, arrest Masella for treason, or whatever you guys in the Holy See call it, and be done with it?"

"With no proof? We could have done so, but the church would remain in a state of turmoil. The two sides would continue to fight. This way, though painful for Ms. Bradford and the rest of you, the conflict ends."

"Are you sure?" Steven asked. "Or is a private secretary not allowed to question his boss?"

"Always ask, young man. It is part of the job description, but let me answer your question. By letting the drama play out the way it did, liberals and conservatives will see the need for working together. No doubt there will still be fringe groups on both sides, but they will lack the power to act. Pope John and I have agreed to convene Vatican III. More learned men than we will make the decisions."

"Will there be an announcement from the Benediction Loggia tomorrow?" Emma asked.

"Yes, but not the announcement the world expects. The pope will say that sanity has returned to the Holy See; that the church has survived another dark chapter in its history."

"Excellent," Emma said. "Michael and I will cover the event for ABC. It will be great to look up and see both you and Pope John standing side by side on the loggia, this time without pretense."

"You will not be looking up, Ms. Bradford. You and Mr. Kelsey will be standing behind Pope John and me on the loggia. In addition, you, your producers, and your cameramen will have exclusive access to the pope. He will grant you an interview before our appearance, and I will be available to answer whatever questions you may have. Now, it is not wise to keep His Holiness waiting any longer. Are you ready to report, Ms. Bradford?"

"Any chance you have a place where I could freshen up before I go on air?" Emma asked.

"Believe it or not, I have all the conveniences of home." The cardinal pointed to a door. "Right through there."

"I'll be ready in less than five minutes."

The cardinal smiled. "We will be waiting."

CHAPTER THIRTY-THREE

Looking less disheveled, Emma emerged from the cardinal's bathroom. Her wan look had all but disappeared, and her eyes were bright. "I'm ready to report," she said.

"Where do you want me?" the cardinal asked Bill.

"If you'll stand just out of camera range, I'll signal when it's time for you to join Emma."

"Fine," the cardinal said.

Bill gave the signal, and Emma began:

This is Emma Bradford, reporting from the private apartments of Cardinal Giancomo Amici, a central player in the drama playing out in the Holy See over the past few days. As the curtain comes down on the final act of the play, it's safe to say the past few hours have been some of the most extraordinary in recent Vatican history and certainly in this reporter's life. But let me begin at the beginning and set the stage for you.

When I and my ABC partner, Michael Kelsey, arrived in Rome, our purpose was to report on the opening of the Bernini exhibition. Little did we know our focus would quickly change. The mysterious death of Piero Scala, Cardinal Amici's private secretary, combined with the cardinal's confinement to his rooms and the continuing health issues of Pope John, prompted us to initiate an investigation. Suddenly, as fantastic as the Bernini exhibition proved to be, it took backseat to the political struggle taking place among the hierarchy of the Holy See, which, contrary to Vatican policies, was being acted out in the media.

Many occurrences, which we will be reporting on in great detail over the days ahead, including an attempt on Michael's and my lives as we crossed the Via Veneto outside the Excelsior hotel, led us to believe that both the pope and Cardinal Amici were in grave danger. These assumptions proved to be true, as I quickly learned yesterday. Upon my return to the hotel after a day of wrapping up the Bernini shoot, I was forcefully taken by two of Monsignor Masella's men, dragged into a car, and driven to Saint Peter's Basilica. Throughout the next fourteen hours, I personally learned of the monsignor's incredible plan. From his own lips I heard of his intention to murder the cardinal in hopes of suppressing the conservative movement. Incredibly, he planned to make it look like I was the one who committed the crime, which, in turn, would have precipitated my death at the hands of the Swiss Guard who would, he planned, enter the chapel, see what I'd done, and shoot me.

I imagine many of you are smiling either from shock or disbelief. Believe me—I too have experienced numerous emotions ranging from incredulity to outright terror as I spent last night, my final hours on earth according to the monsignor, in the papal crypt beneath this magnificent basilica.

Early this morning, I was taken to the Chapel of the Blessed Sacrament, where the final scene in my life was to be performed. Every year on this date, the anniversary of his mother's death, Cardinal Amici celebrates Mass for family and close friends. At seven a.m., as you will see in the unedited film clip, the cardinal entered the chapel and began the service. Shortly thereafter, Monsignor Cipriano stood and confronted him, as did one of his men, who aimed a gun at the cardinal's chest. His intention—to kill the cardinal. How he planned to plant the murder weapon in my hand so the world would think I pulled the trigger is something I'm glad I didn't have to discover. What I do know is Masella's justification for my actions was my supposed-miraculous flash of insight, my realization it would be an honor for me to sacrifice my life and become a martyr for his cause. However, and I'm saying this not as a reporter but as one of those with a starring role in the drama, thank God Cardinal Amici had a different idea. He pulled his own weapon from beneath his robes and shot the monsignor twice, killing him. He also wounded the guard before he could return fire.

Though I had no idea at the time, Michael Kelsey and our ally in the investigation, Monsignor Steven Laurent, an American graduate of Notre Dame who is currently assigned to the Holy See, were in the back of the chapel disguised as monks. Monsignor James McDonald, another American who was masquerading as an old man, sat just behind me. Our cameraman, Ron Sullivan, who, through a hole he had cut in the nun's habit he wore as a disguise, shot the amazing footage you'll soon see, occupied the back row, and my driver, Giro, who has been instrumental in bringing my ordeal to a successful conclusion, sat near the altar, ready to sacrifice his life to save mine and the cardinal's. With me now are two of my personal heroes and stars in the drama: Monsignors Laurent and Michael Kelsey. Will you please join me, gentlemen?

Emma greeted both men and again addressed the audience.

As you can see, they're still dressed in their monk's robes, the disguises they used to gain access to the chapel in an attempt to rescue me and Cardinal Amici. They, and my aforementioned driver in his nun's habit, rushed to my rescue and now, a little over thirty minutes later, we are here with Cardinal Amici. Eminence, will you tell our audience how Act I of the drama which took place in the chapel became Act II here in your private apartments?

The cardinal stepped in front of the camera.

First, Ms. Bradford, may I give you, Mr. Kelsey, Monsignors Laurent and McDonald, as well as all of the other individuals who risked their lives to rescue you, protect me, and, in essence, save the church, my personal thanks and the thanks of Catholics everywhere? Your role in this drama, which I believe is a marvelous extended metaphor for what has occurred over the past days and weeks, will be discussed for years to come.

As the interview continued, the cardinal talked about the rift that was tearing the church apart and Masella's role in exacerbating the violence, including the murder of Piero Scala and Dina and the attempt to poison the pope.

Deciding she needed more interaction with the cardinal instead of a continuing monologue, Emma began to ask questions: "Was Monsignor Masella working alone?" she asked.

"No, Ms. Bradford," said the cardinal. "His ally in this endeavor was my secretary, Giotto Tomai. When I returned to my rooms after the ordeal in the Blessed Sacrament chapel, Monsignor Tomai was waiting for me, gun in hand, the barrel pointed toward my head."

"You never suspected your secretary was involved in Masella's plot?"

"On the contrary—I knew he was, though I had no idea he would confront me with the intention of finishing what Masella had begun in the chapel. I hoped that once Masella had been stopped, Monsignor Tomai would see the error of his ways. Unfortunately, that was not to be."

"How were you able to prevent the monsignor from carrying out his plan to kill you here in your apartments?"

The cardinal smiled weakly. "It was easy, Ms. Bradford. I played on my secretary's religious convictions by asking him to let me confess my sins and make my peace with God before my death. When, as I expected he would, he allowed me to do so, it gave me the opportunity to go to my priedieu. He had no idea I had another gun hidden under the cushion on which I knelt."

"Why so many guns, Eminence? You're a man of God, a man of peace."

"I am, but under these extreme circumstances I had to be prepared for anything that could occur. I have always owned guns. In my youth, I used to hunt, shoot skeet, and target practice with my father. When Masella's intentions became obvious, I asked one of my brothers to bring my handguns to the Vatican."

The cardinal looked around the room. "If you were to search this room and my private quarters, you would find several more hidden weapons. To save my own life and the life of the pope, I was forced to act. I pulled out the gun and shot Monsignor Tomai. Before today, Ms. Bradford, I had never taken a human life. Now I have killed two men, fellow brothers in Christ, and wounded another. My heart is heavy, even though their deaths were necessary and my conscience is clear."

"It's not ABC's practice to go on the air without proof of what we're reporting," Emma said, "but in this instance, I can personally corroborate your story, Eminence. Will Pope John do the same?"

"I assure you he will, Ms. Bradford. He will give you and Mr. Kelsey an exclusive interview tomorrow morning before he and I speak to the crowd from the Benediction Loggia. That is the least we can do to express our thanks. After that, we would like for you to join us as we make several major announcements."

"Thank you, Eminence, it will be our pleasure.

The cardinal, Steven and Michael stepped aside. Bill pointed the camera toward Emma.

We will now air the footage of the events which took place in the Chapel of the Blessed Sacrament and in this room only moments ago. Michael and I will be back later this morning, throughout the afternoon, and tonight with updates. Be sure to join us for our exclusive interview with Pope John. This is Emma Bradford, signing off for the moment from Vatican City. Stay tuned to ABC for breaking news as we continue to report details in this shocking drama.

"Did I cover everything you wanted me to say?" Emma asked the cardinal as Bill turned off the camera.

"You did, though I know the questions are just beginning. As promised, I will be available for whatever you need."

"I hope you mean it, because I'm going to make my first request," Emma said.

"Anything. I told you that."

"Would you please call Cardinal Remella and make him available to Michael and me when he's released from the hospital? Since you mentioned his name in your comments, I'd like to include him among those we interview."

"My secretary will do it immediately."

"What time do you want to meet Cardinal Remella, Emma?" Steven asked.

"It depends on when he's out of the hospital and the length of our meeting with Pope John. How long do you think that will last, Eminence?"

"I would imagine fifteen to twenty minutes."

"If possible, I'd like a little while to freshen up and collect my thoughts before we go live again," Emma said. "If the cardinal is available, how about ten o'clock? It's possible Helen and David will want us to do local interviews for our respective stations. With breaking news like this, *Good Morning America* may be exempted or go on an hour earlier than their usual seven o'clock airtime."

"Any idea where you want to set up?" Bill asked.

"Michael, what do you think?"

"How about the papal tomb?"

Emma looked toward Cardinal Amici. "Could we do that?"

"Again, my secretary will call the appropriate people and ask that the crypt be closed to the public."

"That's fantastic. Thank you."

"You are very welcome, but now we must end this conversation. Sante, you may ask the police to come in to continue the interview and to remove the body. Ms. Bradford, you and the others must go. The pope is waiting. Monsignor McDonald will escort you to the pope's private library in east wing of the papal apartments." He looked at James. "Will you be able to find your way, Monsignor?"

"I will, Eminence," James said.

The cardinal removed a card from a drawer beside the sofa and handed it to James. "This will allow you, Mr. Kelsey and Ms. Bradford to pass through the various rooms on the way to the papal apartments. Under the circumstances, I am sure security has been tightened, and you would be prevented from entering the second floor reception rooms and the third floor apartments.

The cardinal turned to Steven. "I am going to ask you to stay here with me, Monsignor. I would like for you to witness my conversation with the police and help me prepare for my part of the announcement from the loggia tomorrow. Would you also stay, Sante?"

"Of course, Eminence. I am sure what I tell the police will expedite the matter."

"I appreciate that, young man. As soon as this unpleasantness is over, we can get on with the business of healing the rift Masella sought to extend." The cardinal took Emma's hand. "For all you have done, my eternal gratitude, Ms. Bradford." He shook hands with the men. "You too, gentlemen. Please give Pope John my regards. Tell him I will speak with him later this morning."

"We will, Eminence," James said.

"Enjoy your visit," the cardinal said.

When James turned to leave, Cardinal Amici smiled knowingly at Emma.

CHAPTER THIRTY-FOUR

"**I** can't believe what I just heard," James said as they approached the entrance to the papal apartments on the third floor of the Apostolic Palace.

"You're talking about Steven," Michael said.

"Among other things. I never thought he'd take a position here in the Vatican, let alone one as important as being a private secretary to a cardinal."

"I've gotta say I was surprised," Michael said, "but even if Steven hadn't wanted the job, there was no way he could have refused. The cardinal's a force to be reckoned with. I might have said yes had he asked me."

James laughed. "Thank God he didn't. You're right about the cardinal's indomitable presence. I suppose I'm a little taken aback because Steven was ready to go home until you and Emma arrived in Rome. Now he's stuck here, for want of a better word, for at least six months."

"If I had to guess, I'd say longer," Michael said, "and I don't think he's unhappy about the possibility. The only thing that worries me is his dislike of structure. He's never been one to abide by rules and time schedules."

"Well, whether he likes rigidity or not, that's going to be his life from now on. One of the first things I learned when I came here is that the Vatican functions on rules, ceremony, and protocol.

"It's possible Emma's ordeal made Steven realize what a mess things are around here," Michael said. "He seems he's willing to give up his personal desires for the greater good, at least for now."

"I'm not sure my kidnapping had anything to do with Steven's about-face," Emma chimed in. "I agree with Michael; he had to accept the appointment." She looked at Michael. "Remember when you first introduced me to Steven? You said he joined the priesthood to do something meaningful."

"I also told you he could have found a different way to contribute."

"Now he has. Cleaning up the mess Masella left would be a meaningful way to serve the church."

Michael looked at James. "I get the idea you don't think Steven should be working for the cardinal," he said.

"On the contrary—I think it's great, though I confess I've had a few twinges of jealousy. I'd give my right arm to be involved in the clean-up and healing process."

"Maybe Steven will find a way to involve you," Emma said.

"Trust me. Clean or dirty, I'll use every trick in the book to plead my case." James chuckled. "Michael, you guys have been friends forever. Can I count on you for blackmail material?"

Michael laughed. "Absolutely! Before I'm finished, you won't be helping. You'll be bossing Steven around."

"I'll hold you to it, but I'll have to pick your brain later. We're here." He presented his card to one of two Swiss Guard. The man opened the door and stood aside.

"I'll wait out here while you go in," James said, disappointment on his face.

"No you won't," Emma said. 'You heard the cardinal say the pope wants to see you too."

"Really?" James said. "In all the excitement, I must have missed that part of the conversation."

Another member of the guard was standing just inside the door. "Follow me please," he said to the trio.

Emma, Michael and James followed the man through rooms filled with incredible Gobelins tapestries hanging on the wall and covering the floors, as well as priceless paintings that Emma had viewed on slides in her art classes. "Wow," she whispered to Michael. "The paintings in these rooms alone could keep all the parishes in the States open forever."

Michael frowned. "Not a good place for yet another controversial discussion," he whispered back.

"I suppose you're right."

After passing through several more opulent rooms, they were led through two smaller areas. "This is the Antecamera Segretta," James said. "It's just outside the pope's personal library."

Two more armed members of the Vatican police force stood at attention by the pope's door. "Do they always carry guns when they're guarding the pope?" Emma asked James, nodding toward the guards.

"I honestly don't know," James said. "I've only been in the pope's apartments once, and he was on his summer holiday, so there was no need for guards at the door. I assume that under the circumstances they're taking extraordinary precautions."

James didn't have to present his card. Obviously anticipating the arrival of the pope's guests, one of the men opened
the door. Emma went in first. "I assumed there would be a
huge entourage attending the pontiff," James whispered as
a lone man in a black cassock immediately appeared in the
doorway."

"Maybe they're keeping the pope separated from his
usual staff because they still don't know who they can trust,"
Michael said quietly.

"Ms. Bradford, Mr. Kelsey, Monsignor McDonald. I'm
Father Dominic, Father General of the Society of Jesus," the
man said, stone-faced. "Follow me please. His Holiness prefers to receive you in his personal library this morning. It's
smaller and more suitable for private conversation."

Father Dominic opened the door. Light poured into the
room from three large windows. Not far from the entrance,
Pope John was sitting behind an unpretentious writing desk,
his head down as he concentrated on the papers in front of
him.

While he continued to read, Emma quickly looked
around the room. In the center was a broad, mahogany table
several yards long. Library cases ran along the four walls, and
above them, hung twelve exquisite paintings of animals. *The
fittings of the room combine in perfect harmony,* she thought. *What
an ideal place to work.*

Emma's musings were interrupted with Father Dominic
intoned: "Holiness, may I present Monsignor McDonald, Ms.
Bradford, and Mr. Kelsey?"

Pope John was dressed in a simple white cassock and
a white skull cap. A rather nondescript gold crucifix hung

around his neck. When he looked up from what he was reading, there was a pained expression on his face, and his eyes were troubled. The pontiff put down the papers and stood. "Pax vobis," he said quietly.

"Holiness." James bent and kissed the ring on the pontiff's extended hand. In English, he introduced Emma and Michael. The pope offered the ring to Michael and Emma. He acknowledged Father Dominic. "For centuries, the Jesuits have been responsible for the behind-the-scenes security for the pope," he said. "Father Dominic just arrived from his office at Collegio di San Roberto Bellarimino."

"His Holiness has been informed in full about the events of the morning, including the deaths of Monsignors Cipriano and Tomai," Dominic said. "I have temporarily assumed the role of secretary until a permanent replacement is named."

"Which we will talk about in a moment." The pontiff motioned to the table. "Shall we sit?"

They walked over to the table. The three visitors remained standing until the pope sat down, and they sat opposite him. "Now we will speak about my new secretary, the pontiff said, looking at James. "I am asking you to assume the role, Monsignor McDonald, on an interim basis, of course. If things go well and you and I get along, the position could become permanent. Since I assumed this office I have functioned with only one secretary." He looked down and Emma knew he was thinking of Masella and the chaos his last secretary had caused. "As of now, I will continue as before," he said, "though if the burden becomes too much, I will consider adding someone else to my staff."

"I'm honored, Holiness?" James said, a look of amazement on his face. "I hope to handle my duties to your satisfaction."

"I am sure you will," the pope said, smiling weakly.

"May I ask a question, Holiness," James asked hesitantly.

"Of course," Pope John said. He smiled again and Emma noted there was no joy in his eyes. "Why have you chosen me for the position? There are certainly more qualified and experienced members of the clergy—"

"I am sure there are," the pope said introspectively, "but right now, anyone else I would ask is involved in Vatican politics and has likely taken sides in the liberal/conservative controversy. Honestly, I no longer know whom I can trust. Will Masella's followers suddenly rise up and attempt to force through their liberal agenda? Will those linked to ultra-conservative fringe groups take advantage of the current situation to try and drag the church back to the time before Vatican II? Each is a possibility, and I worry. Just before you arrived I learned your friend, Monsignor Laurent, has agreed to serve Cardinal Amici as his private secretary."

"That's true," James said, still looking puzzled and not ready to abandon his inquiry. "Of course I understand your safety concerns," Holiness," he said. "I'm not arguing with you, but—."

Pope John put up his hand, silencing James. "I know Cardinal Amici implicitly trusts Monsignor Laurent. He tells me I can trust you. At this time in the church's struggle to find compromise and resolution to our differences, it is important to me that neither you nor his secretary has a political agenda. Am I right in making that assumption?"

"You are, Holiness."

"The cardinal also assures me you are dependable and honest. Today this alone would qualify you for the position. Is he correct in this regard?"

"He is, Holiness."

"Perhaps even more important to me than your political affiliation or your qualifications at this crucial time, is that you and Monsignor Laurent know each other well, which, I assume, will be advantageous as the cardinal and I struggle to heal the damage this political rift has caused. So, I shall ask again. Will you serve me and, by doing so, serve God?"

"It would be my honor and privilege, Holiness," said James.

"Good. Before we make an official announcement, I have one request, Monsignor."

"Anything," James said.

The pontiff smiled, and, this time, his previously dull eyes brightened. "I am told that you have in your possession a garish Hawaiian shirt. Am I correct?"

James laughed. "You are, Holiness. Would you by chance be asking me if you can borrow it sometime? Or perhaps, as your secretary, you would like for me to arrange a luau downstairs in the state reception rooms?"

"Ah, a sense of humor. I like that," the pope said, seemingly glad to inject a little levity into an otherwise bleak state of affairs. "Quite the contrary," he said. "I request, no, I demand that you send that particular shirt home with Ms. Bradford. We cannot have another scandal emanating from the pope's office at this point in time."

"I'll be more than glad to take the shirt home with me," Emma said. "I'll keep it, but not so Monsignor McDonald can wear it again. It will forever remain a symbol of the help he and Monsignor Laurent gave Michael and me."

"You will have to tell me how my secretary's shirt played a role in your investigation," the pontiff said. Emma began and Michael added details during the light and often-amusing conversation which continued for another ten minutes. When the pontiff clasped his hands in front of him on the table, Emma sensed the interview was over.

"Would you like for me to remain with you, Holiness?" James asked as Emma and Michael stood up and prepared to leave.

"No, thank you, Monsignor. Your duties will officially begin tomorrow morning. No doubt Ms. Bradford and Mr. Kelsey will want you for their interviews, and you will need time to clear your calendar before assuming your new duties. Father Dominic and a few select members of my staff will remain with me until then. I have been told that the nuns who prepare my meals are no longer suspect." He smiled again and Emma noted the pleasure he'd shown during the conversation was gone as, once again, he dealt with the crucial issues facing the church. "When you leave, I will be making a formal statement to the Swiss Guard exonerating Cardinal Amici," he said somberly.

The pope turned to Emma. "I will be available prior to the conciliatory announcement from the loggia tomorrow, Ms. Bradford. My new secretary will coordinate with Monsignor Laurent to arrange a time and place for our joint interview, though I imagine it will be held in this room."

"Thank you, Holiness."

"No. Thank you for all you have done."

"While you were mitting with His Holiness, Monsignor Laurent phoned. He asked me to tell you that Cardinal Remella has left the hospital," Dominic said to Emma. "When you are finished here, he will meet you in the crypt."

"Thank you," Emma said. She bowed to the pontiff. "If you'll excuse us?"

The pope rose. "Of course," he said. "Until tomorrow."

"Congratulations, James," Emma said as they left the Antecamera Segretta.

"You knew?"

"We did, but Cardinal Amici swore us to secrecy."

James grinned "I can't believe what just happened," he said, exuding excitement. "So I guess I won't have to bribe you for information after all, Michael."

Michael laughed. "If I were you, I'd keep my options open. With Steven you never know."

As they entered the square, Emma looked up at the pope's open shutters. *I can't believe I was just up there in the inner sanctum,* she thought as Colombo approached from the right colonnade. *Was it only a few days ago when I stood out here with Nicola and stared up at the pope's apartments? I never though. . ."*

Suddenly, realizing what was ahead, Emma was all business. "I'll need a few minutes to make myself presentable before we go on air," she said as she as they neared the truck.

"That's why I'm here," said Colombo. "Steven phoned a short while ago. I'm to tell you, while David waited in the truck, Helen went to the hotel and picked up changes of clothes for both of you."

"Am I supposed to change in the truck?" Emma asked.

"No. Steven said you can shower and change at his apartment. He said to hurry. His exact words were: 'You are not to spend time primping like women usually do.'"

Emma laughed. "Isn't that the ultimate irony? A celibate priest talking to me about women's bad habits."

"I suppose it is." Colombo grinned.

Colombo, Michael, and James waited in Steven's small living room while Emma showered and changed into a grey pantsuit with a robin's egg blue silk blouse. "I feel like a new woman," she said as she emerged from the bathroom.

"The old one looked pretty good to me," Michael said, "though I admit the new you looks fantastic. If we didn't have the footage to prove it, no one would believe you were involved in the Blessed Sacrament fiasco."

Emma shuddered. "I wonder if I'll ever be able to put this nightmare out of my mind."

"Emma, it's been three hours," Michael said as he headed for the bathroom. "Give yourself some time."

Michael was ready to go in ten minutes. "I had to skip the shower," he said, smiling. "Hopefully Steven's cologne will cover—"

"Steven wears cologne?" Emma joked. "He's a priest."

"Emma, men don't slather on the smelly stuff to attract women," Michael said.

"Why don't we let Steven explain," James said. "I'll admit his answer might be amusing. Right now we have to get to the crypt."

The piazza was packed with news crews. So she wouldn't be recognized, Emma kept her head down as they approached a phalanx of Swiss Guard positioned across the bottom of the stairs. "The basilica is closed to the public," one of the men said as he stepped forward to keep the foursome from entering. "There is an ongoing investigation occurring inside."

James and Colombo showed their IDs. "I'm escorting Ms. Bradford and Mr. Kelsey, the ABC reporters who were involved in the Blessed Sacrament chapel incident," James said. "They'll be interviewing Cardinal Remella."

"I'm afraid I don't have my identification with me," Emma said.

"That is not a problem, Ms. Bradford," the guard said. "You have the most famous face in Rome. I am honored to meet you. You too, Mr. Kelsey."

When they entered the portico, Emma glanced to her right. "God, I can't believe how much has happened since Nicola and I stood here in front of the Constantine statue." She took a deep breath. "Back then, all I could think about was kicking that arrogant Michael Kelsey's butt so I'd get national recognition."

Michael laughed. "Well, you got your wish, but certainly not like either one of us would have anticipated when I initiated our absurd competition."

"Ah, so you do admit to being the instigator?"

"I suppose I could have been a little less arrogant when we were on the plane."

"A little …?"

"Okay, a lot less."

"While we're confessing, I probably did my part to perpetuate the rivalry. Thank God we became a team and stopped trying to outshine one other."

Michael smiled and squeezed Emma's hand. "You okay?" he asked as they entered the basilica.

"I'm not really sure. Coming through this door and walking up the nave toward the baldachino doesn't conjure up fond memories. You may think I'm nuts, but the twisted pillars of the baldachino make me think of Masella's twisted mind."

"I'm sure lots of things you see in here will be upsetting," Michael said. "Don't be so hard on yourself. Let your feelings take you where they will."

Emma nodded, paused, and rubbed Saint Peter's foot.

"What was that for?" he asked.

"Maybe it was my way of injecting some element of normalcy into my otherwise chaotic life."

Michael took Emma's arm. "You know, you don't have to do the interview with Cardinal Remella in the crypt. Why make this any more difficult than it has to be?"

Emma leaned into him. "If I had my druthers, I'd never walk down those steps again, but I have to try and put aside my fears. If I run away from what happened, I'll never get beyond it."

"You think facing your ghosts down there will be cathartic?"

"I can only hope."

"Then, as Ron often says, 'let's do this.'" He let go of Emma's arm and rubbed Saint Peter's foot.

"I'll ask you the same question you asked me. What was that for?"

Michael smiled. "In a word, luck!"

When they reached the bottom of the steps, there was no time for Emma to dwell on her past experiences in the crypt. Cardinal Remella was waiting. He was dressed in a black cassock with a scarlet sash and skullcap. His jewel-encrusted pectoral cross hung from a thick gold chain around his neck. "Ms. Bradford," he said as he extended his hand. "Though there are no adequate words to express my feelings, may I offer my personal thanks for what you endured here in the crypt and later in the chapel?"

Emma shook the cardinal's hand. "I don't know how to respond, Eminence, so let me say I'm glad we're all safe. Michael and I are so relieved you weren't really ill."

"Happily there was no stroke, though I believe my supposed illness was a stroke of genius on Cardinal Amici's part. Had I not been hospitalized, it is doubtful I would be standing here with you." A cloud came over the cardinal's face as he continued. "But we must put what happened behind us. It is time for all of us to concentrate on the future." He turned to James. "Congratulations on your new position, Monsignor. I look forward to working with you and Monsignor Laurent as we all strive to repair the damage Masella inflicted on the church."

James kissed the cardinal's ring. "I'm honored, Eminence."

"I believe you know my secretary, Monsignor Ezio Mantia. He is a fine young man who has helped me immensely in the sad days we have all been forced to endure."

"I've met him, Eminence," James said, "but I don't know him well."

"I am sure you will get to know him better very soon. Ezio shares your sense of humor, though I have never known him to wear a Hawaiian shirt."

James laughed. "That shirt seems to be the talk of the Vatican. I promised Pope John I'd send it home with Emma." He paused. "You know, maybe I should keep the shirt with me. It may come in handy if I have to do more spying for the pontiff."

The cardinal shook his head. "My prayer is that the intrigue in the Holy See is a thing of the past and you will have no need to wear *the* shirt. Send it home. Perhaps that will be an omen for positive progress in the future."

The cardinal turned to Michael. "Forgive me for ignoring you, young man." He extended his hand. "Your efforts were instrumental in bringing this sad chapter in the church's history to successful conclusion, and I thank you."

Michael kissed the cardinal's ring. "You're welcome, Eminence."

"I know Cardinal Amici explained our ruse to involve you and Ms. Bradford. I apologize for our deception, but it was necessary. Your work has exceeded our expectations."

Michael sighed. "Mine too. In my wildest dreams, I never anticipated a routine report on an artist I'd never heard of until last week could set in motion the events that took place over the past twenty-four hours. I can't say I haven't been angry from time to time as we've heard the entire story, but I'm sure I'll get beyond those feelings."

"With time, I hope you will. Perhaps if you keep the results rather than the ruse in mind, it will help."

"I'll try to do that, Eminence."

"Good," the cardinal said. He turned to Emma. "So where would you and Mr. Kelsey like to film?"

Emma didn't hesitate. "By Pope John Paul the First's tomb."

CHAPTER THIRTY-FIVE

E mma was pleased with the Remella interview. During the discussion, he reiterated what Cardinal Amici had said and added more information about Masella's intentions. "Eminence, thank you so much for your time and insight," she said when the camera stopped rolling.

"You are very welcome, Ms. Bradford. Under the circumstances, it was the least I could do for you. So are you ready to see our secret passageway?"

Emma didn't look back as the cardinal led the way up the stairs and out of the basilica. When they arrived at the outside entrance to the passageway in the Vatican gardens, Cardinal Amici and Steven were waiting for them. "What a pleasant surprise, Eminence," she said. "I expected you'd be waiting in your apartments."

"That was the original plan, but Cardinal Remella and I thought you might like to have both of us show you our secret way in and out of his rooms."

As Bill and Ron filmed from two different angles, the two cardinals, speaking about their clandestine meetings as they walked, took Emma and Michael along a well-lit corridor from the entrance behind the shrubs to Cardinal Amici's apartments.

"You two have become the stars in your drama," Cardinal Amici said when Emma concluded the interview.

"Quoting Shakespeare, though 'all's well that ends well,' it's a role I would have gladly turned down had it been offered," Emma said.

"Of that I have no doubt," said Cardinal Amici. The cardinal again addressed Emma. "To celebrate the successful ending of our play, I would like to take the entire cast to dinner. How long will you be in Rome?"

"Until Sunday," Emma said.

"Then how about Saturday night? I believe the Excelsior has a private dining room. I would like to thank everyone who has been a player in your drama, though at this point we are probably overextending the metaphor."

Emma counted the number on her fingers. "There will be eleven of us: Michael and I; Steven and James; Helen, David, Ron, Bill, Sante, Colombo, and of course Giro. We couldn't have succeeded without all of them."

"Then Steven will ask for a set-up for the eleven of you, myself and Cardinal Remella. That makes our number thirteen." The cardinal hesitated. "Are you superstitious, Ms. Bradford? If so, Cardinal Remella will bring Monsignor Mantia."

"I'm not usually a superstitious person, Eminence, but in light of what happened recently, why take a chance?"

"Good. Pope John and I will see you tomorrow morning. I imagine you have a great deal to do before then."

———

Two hours later, Emma and Michael were exhausted and tired of talking. Michael had interviewed Giro, Ron, and

David, and they had both fielded a wide range of questions and given interviews to other networks and representatives of the print media.

"God, I'm glad that's over," Emma said as the last of the news crews left the basilica. "I'm not used to being on this side of the camera. Now that I know what it's like, maybe I'll be less pushy with the people I'm interviewing."

"Yeah, like that's going to happen," Michael teased. "You'll always be a killer, and don't try to convince me otherwise."

"Who's a killer?" Helen asked as she joined them.

Emma appraised her producer. She was obviously exhausted. Her hair was in disarray, her clothes disheveled, and, Emma noted, she was missing her trademark cardigan around her waist.

"Emma was telling me that after being on the other side of the interviews, she'd be nicer to her guests in the future," Michael said.

"If I see that, you'll be covering Mayor Marino again."

"Oh God! I take it all back."

"I figured you would." Helen looked from Emma to Michael. "Congratulations to both of you. The raw footage Ron shot in the chapel, Emma, your interview with Cardinal Amici and Cardinal Remella, and, Michael, your segment with Giro and the others were well received in New York. This was the lead story on every American network, and it's being repeatedly aired around the world."

"You'll put a montage on a disk so I can look at everything once all of this is over?" Emma asked.

"Of course," said David, who had joined them while Helen was doling out the praise. "Would you like to take a look and see what you do or don't want to keep?"

"Normally I'd say yes, but right now all I want to do is take a nap. Despite the makeup covering the dark circles under my eyes, you can probably see I'm beat. An hour or two of sleep by Pope John Paul the First's tomb wasn't enough."

"No nap yet," Helen said. "As usual, there's no rest for the weary, at least not yet."

"Please tell me there's no more today," Michael groaned.

"I'm afraid I can't say the words you want to hear, so let's touch up your makeup to be sure those dark circles Emma just mentioned don't show up on camera. You have an interview with *Good Morning America*. After that, we'll tape the segments for *ABC World News*. You also have interviews with WABC and WCVB. Right now, Robin's standing by."

"We really have to do this?" Michael mumbled.

"Yes, unless you can figure out a way to say no to New York. You've been announced in the teaser for this segment."

"Then let's get it over with," Emma droned.

———

"Would you believe I'm glad we did all the interviews?" Emma said a half-hour later when Ron finally turned off the camera.

"I'm sure you are," said Helen. "So that's all for now. In case we don't have an opportunity to talk business tonight, Giro will pick you up at eight in the morning. We'll meet at the truck at 8:30 to go over your questions for the pope and Cardinal Amici. Did you bring a black suit with you, Emma?"

"I have a dark pantsuit, but I didn't bring a skirt." Emma grinned. "I suppose a low-cut little black dress wouldn't do for a meeting with the pope."

"Remember, Catholic priests are celibate," Michael teased. "I'm not sure they'd be able to keep their vows if you show up in an outfit like that."

"Then I'll save it until the pope and Cardinal Amici announce that Vatican III has abolished the rule. Trust me— thousands of women all over the world will be smiling when they hear that proclamation. Steven and James will quickly move to the top of the most-desired list."

Michael shook his head. "I can't believe you said that."

"You started it with your ridiculous comment about my dress."

"Would you two cut it out?" Helen said. "Emma, give me your sizes. I'll go shopping and have the maid put whatever I find in your room if you're not there. You'll need a mantilla too. I'm not sure that's what they call that lacy thing, but you get the picture. You can't use your ordeal as an excuse to be inappropriately dressed when you see the pope this time. Considering the circumstances, this morning was an exception. You wouldn't have been expected to follow protocol. What about you, Michael?"

"I have a black suit with me, but I'm not sure my bright red tie will do."

"Then I'll pick up something appropriate for you too."

————

It was after four when Emma and Michael got back to the Excelsior. When they entered the lobby, Mr. Ferrari was behind the concierge desk. He motioned for Emma to come over to him. "I am so pleased to see you, Ms. Bradford," he said, his eyes twinkling. "You too, Mr. Kelsey."

"I'm glad to see you too," Emma said. "There were times when I didn't know if I'd be returning to this lovely hotel."

"I am sure your experience was terrifying. You should know that Gusto was arrested for trying to break into your room and for his part in the plot to kill Cardinal Amici."

"That's one less thing for me to worry about," Emma said.

Mr. Ferrari looked down, obviously embarrassed. "I would like to apologize on behalf of the entire Excelsior staff," he said.

"There's really no need," Emma said, "but thank you. Are you on duty tomorrow?"

"I am."

"Then we'll talk again. Right now my body's screaming for a shower and a nap."

"Of course," Mr. Ferrari said, smiling. "A domani."

"A domani," Emma said.

When they got into the elevator, Michael pushed the button for the fourth floor, and Emma quickly pushed the third floor button. "I hope you're not offended, Michael, but I need some time to myself," she said. "Before I do anything else, I want to call my parents. I'm sure they know I'm fine from watching the news, but I'd like to talk with them. After that, I'm going to lie down. I'll meet you downstairs at eight."

"You don't want me with you?"

"What am I dealing with now, the fragile male ego? If Steven can get away, how about dinner with him and Michael tonight? I heard the pope say that James' duties will begin in the morning. This may be the only opportunity for the four of us to get together before you and I leave Rome. I hoped we'd be able to take them out Saturday night, but with the cardinal's cast party—"

Michael laughed. "A command performance. I'll call Steven and have him get hold of James. I'll let you know if we're a go, but I'm putting you on notice. I have a few personal things I want to say to you."

"And I want to hear everything, but not now and not tonight. I plan to go to bed and sleep until I'm forced to get up tomorrow morning. You must be exhausted too."

"I am. Honestly, I can't remember the last time I slept. I certainly didn't last night—"

"A time I'd like to forget. During dinner I want to hear how you guys came up with your rescue plan. I mean, Sisters Mary Giro and Ronetta? Now that's creative."

"Honestly, we were flying blind. We couldn't make definitive plans. As I told you, there were too many ifs, but that's for another time. It appears we're on my floor. You're sure—"

"Bye, Michael. Call me when you've talked with Steven and James."

Emma waved as Michael reluctantly left the elevator.

CHAPTER THIRTY-SIX

E mma checked her e-mails and called her parents. She was just about to take a nap when the phone rang. "What did Steven say?" she answered.

"Hello to you too. He and Steven will meet us at El Toulà on Via della Lupa at eight."

"Sounds good. Bye."

"Just like that?"

"Call me at seven."

"Yes, ma'am."

"Bye, Michael."

———

The shrill ring of the phone by her bed startled Emma out of a sound sleep. For a moment, she lay there, trying to get her bearings. When she realized where she was, she picked up the phone. "It can't be time for dinner," she groaned.

"You're not much for greetings, are you?" Michael said. "Did you sleep well?"

"I slept the sleep of the dead." She paused. "Under the circumstances, that might not be the best way to describe my nap."

"Probably not. I'll pick you up—"

"I'll see you downstairs at 7:45."

"Exactly what I was going to say."

Emma dragged herself out of bed, showered, dressed in her little black dress, and took the elevator to the lobby.

Michael was waiting by the concierge desk. "You look incredible," he said. "I'm glad Pope John hasn't eliminated the celibacy rule."

Emma laughed. "I told you Steven and James will be at the top of women's most-wanted list."

"Your most-wanted list?"

"Me and every other smart woman, so why don't you stop while you're ahead?"

Steven and James were waiting outside when the cab pulled up to the restaurant near the Spanish Steps and Piazza del Popolo.

"Emma, you're gorgeous," Steven said. "Looking at you makes me hope the pope and Cardinal Amici decide to—"

"See, I told you," Michael said. "I knew Steven would rue the day he took the vow of celibacy."

"I may be a priest, but I'm also a man," Steven teased.

"A man who wears cologne, I might add," Emma said. "James told me you'd explain."

Steven laughed. "Sometimes it gets rather hot in the confessional. I wear cologne—"

"Enough said. I'll use my imagination. Hi, James."

"Hi, gorgeous!" James said.

"Not you too?" Michael said, rolling his eyes. "Shall we go in?"

"Good idea," said Emma. "This conversation has obviously run its course."

"Another place you stop after saying Mass at Santa Maria del Popolo?" Michael said, smirking.

"Actually, El Toulà's near the top of my favorites list," said Steven. "It's expensive, but since you're paying—"

"Expensive? And you come here? If I recall, besides your celibacy vow you also took a vow of poverty. So how would you know about this fabulous expensive restaurant?"

"I've heard my rich parishioners talk about the good food. I've never—"

"Careful, my friend," Michael said. "If you lie, you'll be confessing your sins to your friend James."

"If you two don't stop, we'll never get to the table, let alone enjoy the expensive food," said Emma.

"Amen, sister," James said.

They followed the maître d into a welcoming, vaulted-ceilinged, white-walled room filled with antique furniture and framed prints.

"Definitely not the Bernini Café," Michael said. "I hope they serve something I can eat."

"Oh Lord, I thought we'd gotten beyond this," Emma groaned.

"We definitely have," Michael said, grinning. "I just thought I'd interject a little humor into the conversation."

Emma ordered a bowl Venetian-style fish soup and raved about the linguine with lobster, cherry tomatoes, and sweet red peppers. When Steven ordered expensive caviar, Emma laughed at Michael's expression.

The evening was delightful, and though her ordeal in the Blessed Sacrament chapel continued to press on her mind, the stories the men shared about their agonizing night gave Emma new insight, and their humorous tales about Sister Mary Ronetta and Sister Mary Giro made her laugh. "I never thought I'd find anything funny about what happened," she said. "Apparently I was wrong."

"Believe me, it wasn't amusing at the time," James said.

"For any of us," Emma said quietly.

"Enough of this," said Steven. "Let's talk about James and me."

During the rest of the meal, the two men talked about their jobs and what they hoped would result from the cooperation between their bosses. It was after midnight when the group said good-bye at the door of the Excelsior. Michael walked Emma to her room. She inserted and removed the keycard, opened the door, and turned back. "I'm going to miss having you in the next room tonight," she said quietly.

"Come on," Michael said. "You never knew I was around. You shut the door and went right to sleep."

Emma grinned. "I can't lie, you're right, but now that I think about it, it was nice to close my eyes knowing you were out there in your iconographic cape."

Michael smiled. "I still am." He bent and kissed her lightly on the mouth. "You're sure—"

"Kiss me again and I might lose my resolve."

"Then—"

"Night, Michael."

"Double lock your door."

"Always. I learned my lesson. Thank you."

"No thanks necessary. How about breakfast downstairs at seven?"

"Make it 7:30."

"Shall I pick you up?"

"Michael!"

"I get it, so as Mr. Ferrari said, a 'domani.'"

———

Emma's phone rang at 6:45. Thinking it was her auto-mated wake-up call, she picked up the receiver and slammed it back down. She lay back and covered her head with the pillow. *I'll doze for ten more minutes,* she thought as she closed her eyes.

A minute later, the phone rang again. *I just got the damn call.* She reached toward the sound. "Emma Bradford," she said crossly.

"Are you going to hang up on me again?"

"Michael?" Emma tried to think through the fog of sleep. "Of course it had to be you. I forgot to arrange a wake-up call."

"Then I'm glad I phoned. Sleep well?"

"I did, but not long enough, and if I'm going to be on time, I have to get going. I'll see you downstairs in forty-five minutes." She hung up before Michael could reply.

God, I never checked to see if Helen brought the appropri-ate clothes, Emma thought as she walked by the closet. She opened the door. Hanging in a plastic bag was a black silk suit. "Wow, ABC went all out on this one," she said when she saw the Armani tag. "I wonder if I have to give it back when the interview's over." She took out the lace mantilla and examined it closely. "Another work of art."

Forty-minutes later and feeling elegant, Emma entered the restaurant. Michael stood and waved. "You look fantas-tic," he said as she approached the table.

"Anyone would look good in Armani, but then you must already know that. Aren't you wearing the same label? Though the tie isn't what I've come to expect. Grey and black aren't your best colors."

"You mean because they don't reflect my vibrant personality?" Suddenly Michael burst out laughing.

"What's so funny?" Emma asked.

"I was picturing us as we walk up to the pope's office, on a red carpet, of course. As we approach the door, a famous entertainment reporter stops us, sticks the microphone in our face, and wants to know *who* we're wearing."

Emma smiled. "As ridiculous as it sounds, ABC had to believe it's a possibility. If not, why the designer label?"

"They obviously want us to look impressive on camera. So much for cost-cutting."

During breakfast, they decided that rather than make a specific list of questions to ask the cardinal and the pope, they'd let events dictate what to say. Neither doubted they would be at a loss for words.

After going back to their respective rooms for a short time, they met in the lobby. Giro was waiting when they got to the car. "What, no nun's habit this morning?" Michael asked as Emma slid into the backseat.

"My days of being Sister Mary Giro are over. I hope I've had my last moment in the spotlight."

"It can't hurt business," Michael said. "Let's see, your new ad could read: 'Drive with Giro, the man-nun who singlehandedly saved the Catholic Church.'"

Giro laughed. "That's an exaggeration, but if I need new clients, I'll remember what you said."

When they pulled up to the news truck, there were reporters everywhere. Vatican policemen opened the Mercedes' doors for Emma and Michael. "We'll park the car for you," one of them said as he opened Giro's door.

Giro looked at Emma. "Am I going with you?"

"Of course you are," Michael said. "Even though we joked about it, you were an integral part of our rescue effort. So let these men park the car. I'm sure Steven left instructions for all of us."

Instead of leaving a message, Steven was waiting in the truck. "You two look much better this morning," he said with a grin on his face. "Apparently you slept well."

Emma realized the implication in Steven's comment. "I did," she said. "How about you, Michael?"

The exchange went right over Michael's head. "I already told you I did."

"I'm glad." Steven winked at Emma. "You look gorgeous."

"Didn't we go through this last night?" Michael said, frowning. "If you're not careful, I might have to report you to your boss."

"And if you're not careful, you'll have a run for your money. If—"

"This conversation could get me back to church," Michael teased. "I'll be praying the conservatives win on the celibacy issue."

Steven laughed. "Enough of this," he said. "Morning, Giro."

"Good morning, Monsignor."

"Monsignor? What happened to Steven?"

"I don't think it's right for me to call Cardinal Amici's secretary by his given name."

"What if I prefer Steven?"

"Then I'll call you Steven," Giro said, a grin on his face.

Helen and David came to the front of the truck. "All set?" Helen asked.

"We are," Emma said.

"Then I'm outta here." Steven headed for the door. "I wanted to be sure you got here. I have a few things to do, but I'll be back for you at 9:45."

"Your boss keeping you busy?" Michael teased.

"You have no idea, but I'm enjoying the work."

Michael dropped down in a nearby chair. "Oh my God! This is not my friend. What have they done to you? Since nursery school I've *never* heard you say you liked to work."

"I didn't say I like to work. I said I'm enjoying the job."

"And there's a difference?"

"Go get your faced fixed so you look better. You have dark circles under your eyes." Steven turned and left the truck.

From a roped-off area near the obelisk, Emma and Michael gave interviews to the BBC, numerous Italian television stations, and the Vatican Network, and they taped a segment for Good Morning America. At nine 9:45 Steven returned with several members of the Swiss Guard. Surrounded by security, they made their way past the gathering throngs in the square through the reception and anterooms to the pope's library.

When they approached the door, Emma donned her mantilla. "I wasn't nervous yesterday," she said, "but today I'm terrified."

"Yesterday you were running on adrenalin," Steven said. "Today you're going in cold. It's natural for you to be nervous. I still shake in my boots when I come into these rooms. It's not the pope, per se, but the power and majesty of the office."

This time it was James who opened the door to the Antecamera Segretta. "Bill and Ron are ready to go, as is a cameraman from the Vatican network," he said as he led them to the library. He paused by the door. "Shall we go in?"

Emma sighed deeply. "No time like the present."

Dressed in their clerical finery, the cardinal and the pope were seated side by side at the mahogany table. They rose as Emma and Michael approached. "Good morning, Ms. Bradford; Mr. Kelsey," the cardinal said. "His Holiness and I are ready for you."

"Thank you, Eminence," Emma said.

When the pope spoke, his voice was stronger than it had been the previous morning. "I hope a good night's sleep helped you to recover from the horrors of yesterday and the night before," Ms. Bradford.

"It certainly helped," said Emma.

"Then if you are ready, Cardinal Amici and I would like to give your audience an idea of what we plan to announce in two hours. After we finish, we invite you to attend a small reception the Sala Degli Agrazzi." He looked at Emma. "With your art background, you will appreciate the three Gobelins tapestries presented to the Holy See by Louis the Fifteenth of France."

"I'm sure I will. Thank you," Emma said.

"You are welcome." The pope turned to Bill and Ron. "Please leave your cameras behind," he said politely. "All of your associates are welcome to join you at the reception.

"I'm sure they'll appreciate the invitation, Holiness," Bill said.

"I'm not sure how you wish for us to conduct the interview, Eminence," Emma said.

Cardinal Amici looked at the pope. "We discussed the matter and would prefer to be given the opportunity to speak in lieu of a question-and-answer session."

"Of course," Michael and Emma said in unison.

After Emma's introduction, the cardinal and the pope began. During their nearly ten-minute conversation, they said little about what had gone on, but rather concentrated on what would be. They planned to work together to make necessary changes while preserving the values and practices of the church which had existed for centuries. The men mutually agreed to put the issue of celibacy on the table. *Wow, that's a step in the right direction,* Emma mused as they concluded their presentation.

"You do the wrap-up," she whispered to Michael.

Michael thanked the pope and the cardinal and, after several additional comments, signed off.

"Steven and I will remain here, but my assistant, Father Paolo, will escort you to the reception," James said. "I'll be there to take you to the loggia."

The pope handed Emma an envelope. "I wanted to express my appreciation in writing," he said.

"Thank you, Holiness."

"Pope John and I will see you later," the cardinal said as Emma and Michael turned to leave the room.

Though there were no cameras at the reception, Emma and Michael did several informal interviews with reporters using pens and pads. When they were finished, Emma did as the pope suggested and took a close look at the tapestries, glad she had enough knowledge to appreciate their beauty.

At 11:45, Steven arrived and guided them and other invited guests to the loggia. As they stood in the back row, Emma thought about the first announcement she'd heard from the balcony. "I can't believe the cardinal and the pope were working together all the time," she whispered to Michael. "They were excellent actors."

"They certainly fooled us," Michael said.

When the pope and the cardinal arrived, the crowd roared their approval. They continued to respond positively as the pope made his announcements, including the one about Vatican III. The applause reached a crescendo when the cardinal expressed his support for the plan. After the short speeches were over, the pope blessed the crowd, and then the two men departed. By the time Emma and Michael were back inside, there was no sign of either of them.

Steven led the way back to the truck through the now-clearing crowd. "That was fantastic," Helen said when they were inside and the door had closed, blocking out the noise. "Just so you know, Ron was able to get a close-up of you standing in the row behind the pope and the cardinal. This is going to be the lead story all day and probably all week. You'll have one more press conference and a few streaming-live interviews from the hotel."

"Are we actually close to being finished?" Emma asked.

"For today, at least as regards this story. We're still doing the Bernini wrap-up tomorrow. Since the broadcasts are going national, New York wants us to complete the project."

"After that we're on our own?" Michael asked enthusiastically.

"You are." Helen paused. "That is, until I need you again."

"Try not to need us, will you?" Emma said. "I need sleep."

Emma headed for the door. Suddenly she turned back. "Any idea where Bernini is buried?" she asked David.

"No, why?"

"Just a thought. Let's end the broadcasts by his tomb. We began at the Borghese with his early works."

"Hang on. I'll get the answer to your question." David went to the computer. "He's buried in Santa Maria Maggiore."

"Another place on my must-see list," Emma said, "though I realize it might not happen this trip."

"I like your idea of wrapping the series at Bernini's tomb," Ron said. "Unless you want to film from the church, I can go over and take pictures of the tomb. We'll show the footage while you're doing your wrap-up."

"Sounds like a plan," Emma said. "Thanks, Ron."

As Emma approached the truck door, there was a knock. She looked back at Helen. "As you so aptly put it, there's no rest for the weary."

Michael opened the door. "Another baby," he whispered when he saw the young priest who stood outside.

"Mr. Kelsey, Ms. Bradford, I'm Father Kilpatrick. Monsignor McDonald is waiting for you. I'll take you to him if you're ready for your press conference."

"Lead the way," Emma said. 'I'm ready for my close-up."

CHAPTER THIRTY-SEVEN

Ron and Bill were waiting by the obelisk. "This is strictly a question-and-answer session," Ron said.

"No formal statement?" Emma asked.

"Nope."

"Good," Michael said.

For the next half-hour, Michael and Emma took questions together and separately from television reporters and the print press from all over the world. "Everything they ask sounds the same now," Emma said as they walked back to the truck. "I see many of the same faces out there. Aren't they tired of all this by now?"

"It must be a slow news day," Michael joked.

At the truck they said good-bye to Helen and David. When they got to the barrier, Giro was waiting. "I'm ready to get out of here," he said. "I hope I have done my last interview."

"You're not enjoying your moment in the spotlight?" Michael asked.

"Definitely not."

During the ride back to hotel, Emma drifted off. As they pulled into the circular entrance, Michael instinctively looked for familiar black car waiting, but it wasn't there. "Thank God," he whispered as he tapped Emma on the shoulder. "We're here."

"Would you like the car before dinner?" Giro asked as he opened Emma's door.

"I don't think so," Michael answered. "We're both exhausted. I imagine you are too, Giro. Why don't you try to get some rest?"

"That's my plan, but if you change your mind, I am close by."

"Near the Spanish Steps on one side of the triangle," Emma said, smiling.

As they walked toward the elevator, they waved to Mr. Ferrari, who was at the corner of the concierge desk assisting another guest. Emma had no argument from Michael when she pushed buttons for both third and fourth floors.

Michael got off on his floor. When the elevator reached the fourth, Emma trudged down the hall. As soon as she entered the sitting room, she kicked off her shoes. She changed out of the Armani suit, put on pj's, and called Nicola, who agreed to meet them in the lobby at one o'clock for their first afternoon of sightseeing.

Before going into her bedroom, Emma took the pope's letter out of her bag. She turned out the light in the sitting room, plopped down on her bed, and carefully opened the envelope. She read:

My Dear Ms. Bradford,

Realizing I have verbally articulated our appreciation for your service to the Catholic Church and to me personally, I am obliged to express our gratitude in writing, realizing all too well that mere words will never adequately convey my personal feelings. You will be included in my daily prayers for as long as

I live, and will always have my eternal gratitude. Should you
ever need anything, please do not hesitate to ask. As you were
for me, I shall be available to you.

   May you put all of this unpleasantness behind you, and,
with God's help, find peace, strong in the knowledge that your
service will never be forgotten.
God bless and keep you.
PP Servus Sevorum Dei
IoAnnes P.M. XXIV

"Pastor of Pastors and Servant of the Servants of God,"
Emma said aloud, "an impressive title."

Tears came to her eyes as she put the letter back into the
envelope. She didn't know if she would ever be able to put
the unpleasant incident, as the pope called it, behind her, but
it was certainly comforting to know she'd be in the prayers
of the leader of the Roman Catholic Church. "If that doesn't
help, nothing will," she whispered as she turned off the light.

———

Emma slept soundly until the phone rang.

"I woke you up," Michael said when she answered sleepily.

She looked at the clock. "Thank God you did. I'll meet
you downstairs in thirty minutes."

"Your coffee's waiting."

"With that incentive, I'll be there in twenty."

Emma quickly showered, dressed, and was downstairs
on time. "I spoke with Steven," Michael said while Emma
sipped her coffee, "and he left me a text this morning. He
made the arrangements for the cardinal's dinner party."

"Excellent. Now we just have to get through today."

While they ate, Michael went through the material he planned to use in his part of the reports. As Emma read through her Saint Longinus notes, the information seemed trivial in light of what they'd gone through over the past few days. Unfortunately, she'd lost some of her enthusiasm for Bernini. She was sure she'd get it back when they got to Longinus, but whatever she felt, she would report.

———

When Giro dropped them at the truck, Emma looked at the square. It was still early, so there weren't many tourists milling around. The basilica was open, and the scene looked normal. When she saw a group of nuns admiring the obelisk, she smiled, thinking of Sister Mary Giro and Sister Mary Ronetta.

When the makeup had been applied, Emma and her crew, and Michael and his, headed across the square to the steps. A few people stared, but no one stopped them. Michael and Bill filmed at baldachino and the Cathedra while Emma and Ron did the Saint Longinus segment. As Michael had suggested, everything Nicola told her came rushing back, and when she finished, her appreciation for Bernini, which had waned during the ordeal in the chapel, had definitely returned.

"The final program looks great," Helen said when they got back to the truck.

"So we're finished?" Michael asked.

"We are if you want to skip Bernini's tomb," said Ron. "I definitely think it merits mention."

"I can't believe I forgot about how I wanted to end the series," Emma said. "Give me a minute to look at the guidebook. Where do you want me?"

"It doesn't really make any difference since we're showing the shots I took of the tomb while you talk. You've already done the wrap-up, so I'll stick this part in right before your closing statements."

"You know, I'd rather film my final words again. I'll talk about the tomb and then say a few words about Bernini and his contributions to Saint Peter's and the city of Rome."

Ron looked at Helen for approval. "To use Ron's favorite phrase, 'go for it,'" she said.

Emma looked at the pictures and read the brief blurb about Bernini's simple tomb. "I'm ready to wrap this up. Michael, will you stand with me while I talk?"

"If that's what you want."

Emma took Michael's arm. "Of course I do," she said. "We're partners, remember?"

The three left the truck. "If possible, could you position me so you can get shots of the columns and the statues on top of the roof?" Emma said to Ron. "After I talk about the tomb, I'm going to mention those and the basilica. As Nicola always says, 'follow what I'm saying with your eyes,' though in this case, with the camera." They chose a place, and Emma began:

Ironically, the man who changed the face of Rome with his elaborate structures is buried in a tomb so simple that it takes a sleuth to track it down. A discreet floor tomb very close to the high altar in Santa Maria Maggiore marks the great artist's final resting place. It's ironic that the tomb of someone who created some of the largest, most flamboyant monuments in Rome rests in such an unassuming location in the important and magnificent basilica.

As Michael and I stand here in Saint Peter's Square, only a short week since we arrived to begin our report on the Bernini, it's hard for us to fathom what has happened and how the narrative shifted from Bernini's sculptures to the story we've been covering for the past twenty-four-plus hours. Now, as the dust settles and Pope John and Cardinal Amici begin the healing process, we return to our original task, which was to report on this fantastic exhibition. Hopefully over the year ahead, many of you will have the opportunity to come to Rome and see firsthand what Michael and I have been talking about this past week. I'm sure when you do, you'll come to think of Gian Lorenzo Bernini as your favorite artist. I know we have.

Emma handed the microphone to Michael, who said: "This is Michael Kelsey alongside Emma Bradford, signing off from Bernini's magnificent square in front of Saint Peter's Basilica."

"I'm sorta sad we've taped our last Bernini report," Michael said as Ron turned off the camera. "I came here with a chip on my shoulder—and no comment from you, Emma. I'm going home with a genuine appreciation of Baroque art and Bernini in particular."

"I'd say that's real growth," Emma said. "And now we're free! We are free, aren't we, Helen?"

"For the moment, but just in case, I'd like for you leave your cell phones on. You're off duty until I call you again.

Giro will drive you on your excursions. So while I go back to work, you enjoy!"

"Nothing you say will make me feel guilty," Emma said. "After a quick trip back to the hotel to change, we're off for a great afternoon."

"Any idea where you're going?" Ron asked.

"I don't know. Michael?"

Michael shrugged. "I'm just along for the ride."

"In that case, since I'm free to make a unilateral decision, we're meeting Nicola at one, and then heading to the Forum and the Coliseum. Tomorrow morning I want to be at Navona Square to see the street cleaners before the crowds arrive, and I want to visit Saint Agnes in Agony without worrying about meeting the mysterious man who left me the 'be there' message. After a visit to the Parthenon, I plan to throw a coin in the Trevi Fountain. My next-time-I'm-in-Rome list is getting longer by the minute. There's a lot I haven't seen in the basilica, and we haven't set foot in the Vatican museums. The tossed coin will ensure my return to see it all."

"Then you'd better get going," Helen said. "But before you do, I want to tell you both how impressed I am with your work. Though I was worried at the beginning, especially about you, Michael, and your cowboy reputation, I quickly discovered you're both consummate professionals. This has been a pleasure."

"Believe me, we feel the same way," Emma said. On an impulse, she hugged Helen. "I hope we'll work together in the future."

"Bring me to New York with you, will you?"

"New York?" Emma said, her eyes wide with anticipation.

"I guarantee you'll be doing investigative reporting for the network in no time. I've already heard rumors to that effect. I'm sure you'll love working with Emma on a regular basis, won't you, Michael."

"Sure, but—"

"Think about it, Michael," Emma joked. "You're going to be Geraldo, not just a Geraldo- wannabe."

———

During the afternoon, Nicola, Emma, and Michael wandered through the Forum and the Coliseum. Emma loved seeing the ancient senate, Caesar's supposed gravesite and the Temple of the Vestal Virgins. From the look on Michael's face and the questions he asked Nicola about the gladiators in the Coliseum, she knew Michael was enjoying himself too.

They got back to the hotel at seven. "I'll call a cab to take us to dinner," he said to Giro. "I imagine you'd like a good night's sleep."

"I'll be happy to come back for you," Giro said as he opened Emma's door.

"I don't think that will be necessary," Emma said. She turned to Michael. "If you don't mind, I'd rather eat here at the hotel. I don't even want to think about changing again." She took Michael's arm. "Let's order room service though I forbid you from ordering a hamburger. My new quest is to open your mind to different foods."

"You heard the lady, Giro," Michael said. "I'm still a work in progress. Not only am I an art aficionado and a fan of ancient Rome, I'm also going to be forced to become a gourmet."

"Good luck, Emma," Giro said, smiling. "You definitely have a lot of work to do."

"I succeeded before. I will again."

As they waited for Giro to drive away, neither said anything. Emma was thinking about the night when they escaped the death car and the afternoon when she was snatched from that very place. From the serious look on Michael's face, she knew he too was remembering both horrific events.

"I'm going to go take a shower and change," Michael said as they got on the elevator. "If you're sure you want to eat in, I'll see you in about an hour."

"I definitely do," Emma said, trying to shake the feelings she had experienced minutes before. "I'm still tired, and more importantly, I'd like to spend some alone-time with my partner."

"What a good idea." Michael kissed her lightly on the lips. On an impulse, Emma reached up, put her hand on the back of Michael's neck, pulled his face to hers, and kissed him passionately. She smiled as she let go. "I'll see you in a while."

"That's it?"

"For now," she said seductively, as the elevator door closed.

As she walked toward her room, Emma was confused. It was apparent where she and Michael were headed, but was this what she wanted? *There will be complications,* she thought, *especially if, as Helen suggested, we'll be working together. But yes,* she told herself confidently, *it's definitely what I want.* She slid the keycard into the slot and opened the door.

———

Dinner was wonderful. Though he frowned at first, Michael enjoyed the batter fried shrimp and potato wedges Emma ordered for him, and her skewered sturgeon with charcoal grilled artichokes was delicious. For dessert they shared a wild berries mousse with raspberry sauce. When Michael finished the last bite, he leaned back. "Not quite as good as a hamburger, fries, and a hot fudge Sunday," he said, smiling, "but not so bad."

"Ah a takeoff on a Bernini comment," Emma said. When Michael looked at her quizzically, she explained: "I wasn't able to use one of my favorite quotes in the presentations. It seems Bernini was a humble man—"

"So you're saying I'm humble," Michael teased.

"Far from it, so shall I continue or not?"

"By all means do."

"Thank you. When Bernini evaluated his extraordinary works of art, he would say, 'at least it's not bad.'"

"He truly was humble," Michael said seriously. "I would have said 'what I've created is extraordinary.'"

"And you would have been right," Emma said.

When they were finished and the table was in the hall, Michael poured the last of the wine. As she drank, Emma thought of the first time she tried the Cerritos Blange in the Doney, the night she revealed her true identity to Michael. She rested her head on his shoulder. "I couldn't have asked for a nicer evening," she murmured.

Michael put his glass down, took hers, and put it down on the table as well. He put his arm around her and pulled her toward him. I love you, Emma," he whispered into her hair. "I didn't realize how much I cared until I sat in the back of the Blessed Sacrament chapel, waiting for you to come in with Masella. Okay, I'm rambling. What I'm trying to say is I think I've loved you from the first moment I laid eyes on you."

Emma sat up and laughed. "Really?" she said incredulously. "If that's the case, you had a funny way of showing it. You were a real jerk."

"Oh, that!" he said, grinning. "Over the past few days, I've given the plane ride to Rome a great deal of thought. Would you like a psychological analysis of my behavior? I'm sure you'll understand. If I recall, you took Psychology 101 at Wellesley."

"You're right, I did," Emma said, "so don't keep me in suspense, give me your professional analysis."

"I'm trying to," Michael said, feigning exasperation. "I put my carry-on in the overhead bin, sat down, and immediately knew I loved you. I acted like an ass so you'd hate me because I was afraid of commitment."

Emma laughed. "Right. You took one look at me and thought, 'wow, this woman's out to get me. I'd better act like a jerk so I don't have to commit to a long term relationship or, God forbid, marriage.'"

"Makes sense, doesn't it? So when did you realize you were in love with me?"

Emma stared at Michael, a surprised look on her face. "You think I'm in love with you?" she said. "What could possibly give you that idea?"

"You know you are. Don't deny it. I'm not merely your hero in the iconographic cape."

Emma shook her head. "I'm sure you mean my hero in the iconographic monk's robe?"

"That too." Michael's smile disappeared. "Now I'm being serious," he said. "I was blind at first, but it didn't take long for me to realize you're not just a beautiful face. You're intelligent, sensitive, caring, bright—"

"Don't stop now," Emma joked.

Michael laughed. "I don't have to say anymore. You know how I feel and what I want. Now it's up to you. I realize you've been through hell, and I don't want to rush you; that is, assuming you want the same thing I do. Am I rambling again?"

"You definitely are, and apparently there's only one way to shut you up." Emma leaned in and kissed him tenderly and then with more ardor. "Is that answer enough?"

There was a moment of awkwardness as Michael kissed her forehead, her eyelids, her nose, her cheek. He nuzzled her neck as he helped her off the couch and led her to the bedroom. Each comfortable with their choice to take their relationship to the next level, they undressed and slid beneath the sheets. "I love you," Michael whispered as he continued where he left off, nuzzling her neck and caressing her breasts.

"Oh, God, I love you too," Emma murmured. She arched her back as his teasing tongue brought her to the brink. "Make love to me."

"All in good time," Michael whispered as he continued to give her pleasure.

When Emma didn't think she could stand it any longer, Michael rolled over on top. "You're so beautiful," he said as he began to move, slowly at first, and then with more urgency.

As her passion reached a peak, Emma dug her fingernails into Michael back. "Michael!" she called out as she exploded in waves of pleasure.

"Oh my God!" Michael cried as he felt his release. Spent, he rolled off and pulled Emma to him. She rested her head on his shoulder and closed her eyes.

———

Wrapped in Michael's arms, Emma slept soundly. At six, she rolled over and looked at the clock. She snuggled against him again and began to kiss his face and chest. He sleepily moaned as she worked her way down his body, giving him the pleasure he'd given her only hours before.

"No," she whispered as he started to roll on top. "Lie back and enjoy."

Slowly and seductively, she lowered her body to his. As he caressed her breasts, she began to move, watching his face contort with exquisite joy. As her passion built, she writhed, and, once again, exploded in intense waves of ecstasy. Michael rolled on top and, minutes later, cried out her name.

"Why don't we skip breakfast and spend another hour in bed?" he said as he nuzzled her neck.

"Though tempting, there's no way," Emma murmured. "I'm seeing Rome." Suddenly wide awake, she threw back the covers.

"God, you're beautiful," Michael said. "Take pity. Unless you come back to bed, I'm not going to make it through the day."

Emma looked down at Michael's well-toned, muscular body. "You're not so bad yourself. Hold that thought until tonight. Right now I'm going to take a shower. After that, you can feed me. For some unknown reason, I'm starving."

"A shower sounds great. I'll join you."

"Not if you want to explore—"

"Oh, I'd love to explore."

"If you'll let me finish my sentence—not if you want to explore Rome."

"I'd rather explore you."

"Again, I'm tempted, but you'll have to wait. So get up." Emma grinned. "Though I guess you already are."

"With you around, that's a given, so come back to bed."

"Take a cold shower in your own room. I want to be at Navona Square before the street sweepers finish working. By now it may be too late."

They had breakfast, and afterwards, Emma glimpsed the street sweepers in the stillness of the morning in an almost empty Piazza Navona. Thankfully, she was able to walk through Saint Agnes without too many thoughts of the meeting with Masella. She realized Nicola was right—it took more than a few minutes to see the Pantheon. When they'd seen it all, she became the ultimate tourist and threw coins in the Trevi Fountain.

"I can't wait to come back here with you," Michael said. "How about a honeymoon in Rome?"

"Aren't we we're getting slightly ahead of ourselves? If I recall, you were the one who said we've only known each other for a week."

"But you'll consider it."

"Of course," she replied. Michael took her hand and they went to meet Giro.

When they got back to the hotel, they held their breaths as they checked their messages. There were no voicemails, but Helen had left an e-mail. "I hate to open this," Emma said. "The thought of working our last evening in Rome isn't particularly appealing."

"Shall we pretend we lost our internet connection?"

"That probably isn't a good idea." She double clicked the e-mail and read.

"What'd she say?"

"She and David are enjoying Rome."

"Then there's nothing for us to do?"

"Apparently not," Emma grinned. "At least not when it comes to work. However, I can think of something I'd like to do."

They made love and, again, fell asleep wrapped in each other's arms.

———

Emma was still a little groggy when they arrived at the private dining room. However, she perked up as she greeted the cardinals and their other guests.

Setting the casual tone, the two cardinals, dressed in black suits with white clerical collars, showed no hint of the magnificent trimmings of their offices. Steven wore a short-sleeve, button-down shirt and grey slacks. Emma and the others laughed when James showed up in the forbidden Hawaiian shirt. "My new job doesn't start until tomorrow," he joked. "I brought a change of clothes and, as the pope ordered, will leave my beloved shirt with Emma."

"Whose shirt?" Steven said.

"You really want to admit ownership?" James said, grinning.

Emma felt like she was having dinner with a group of old friends. The conversation was lively and the laughs plenty. There was no talk of Vatican politics, Masella, or the ordeal in the chapel.

As he gave a final toast, Cardinal Amici read aloud a note from Pope John He finished: *I and the Catholic Church will always be grateful to all of you for your service. From my rooms in the Apostolic Palace I raise my glass in a toast to you all.*

"To the pope," they all said as they raised their glasses.

"And to your swift return to Rome," the cardinal said as he raised his glass again.

"Thank you, Eminence," Emma said. "We will definitely be back soon." She looked around the table. "We have good friends we want to see."

After everyone left, James and Steven stayed behind. "How about a nightcap?" Michael suggested.

"Sounds great," said James. "It's a beautiful autumn night. Shall we sit outside?"

As Michael led the way to the outdoor café, Steven put his arm around Emma's shoulder. "You look happy," he said.

"I am. How'd you know?"

"Could it be the light in your eyes? I guess my friend finally admitted his feelings to himself and to you."

"He did."

"And you obviously feel the same way. I couldn't be happier."

Michael looked back. "What's going on between you two?" he said, feigning irritation. "Remember, my friend, you're celibate and, in case you hadn't guessed, Emma's mine."

"That's what the old Michael would say," Emma teased.

"You're right. How about, Steven, get your hands off the woman I love?"

"Works for me," Steven said, smiling. "Let me know when, and I'll fly home and do the wedding myself, in conjunction with your Episcopal priest, of course. That is unless Saint Peter's, San Clemente, and Bernini make you want to convert."

"You never know what could happen," Emma said, "but as I told Michael, we're getting ahead of ourselves."

"What she means is she's not taking catechism classes just yet, and we don't have a definite date in mind. We'll keep you posted."

As they relaxed, James and Steven took turns talking about what had happened since they last met. Their new jobs were working out, and they were enjoying their duties. Both reported the healing had begun. Monsignor Tomai had been buried quietly. Though not a usual practice, Masella had been cremated, his ashes scattered so he couldn't become a martyr to the liberal cause. Gusto and Enrico would stand trial and receive Vatican justice. As far as they knew, there were no plans to indict Lucio. Though his decisions were unwise, he'd committed no criminal acts.

Emma hated to say good-bye. She and Michael promised to return to Rome, to see them, and to continue clicking off the sights on her next-time-I'm-in-Rome list. "You have my e-mail address," Steven said. "If you need any help keeping this guy in line, let me know."

"I'll do that." Emma hugged Steven and James. Tears welled up in her eyes as the men hugged and again when Giro dropped them at the airport the next morning.

"Ms. Roberts," the familiar flight attendant said as Emma boarded the plane. "It's good to see you again."

Emma smiled. "It's good to see you too, Wendy, and it's okay to call me Ms. Bradford, or better yet, Emma."

"And I'm Michael Kelsey." Michael grinned as he extended his hand. "I'm sure you'll find this new and improved passenger more to your liking."

"No doubt," Wendy said, smiling as her obviously happy passengers headed to their seats and settled in for the trip home.